# B. A. PARIS
# CLARE MACKINTOSH
# HOLLY BROWN
# SOPHIE HANNAH

# The Understudy

HODDER

First published in Great Britain in 2019 by Hodder & Stoughton
An Hachette UK company

1

A CIP catalogue record for this title is available from the British Library

Paperback ISBN 9781529303926
eBook ISBN 9781529303933

Typeset in Plantin Light by Hewer Text UK Ltd, Edinburgh
Printed and bound in Great Britain by Clays Ltd, Elcograf S.p.A.

Hodder & Stoughton policy is to use papers that are natural, renewable
and recyclable products and made from wood grown in sustainable
forests. The logging and manufacturing processes are expected to
conform to the environmental regulations of the country of origin.

Hodder & Stoughton Ltd
Carmelite House
50 Victoria Embankment
London EC4Y 0DZ

www.hodder.co.uk

# I

# The Music Box

*B.A. Paris, Clare Mackintosh, Holly Brown and Sophie Hannah*

## KENDALL – Ruby's mum

For a second, all you see is beauty. That's because the eye goes where it wants, where it's drawn: to the flawless face, golden hair caught up in a bun, arm extended gracefully, lithe dancer's body possibly about to take flight. Only she's spinning slowly, toward you, and then you realize . . . her sky-blue leotard is splashed with blood. One arm is missing and the opposing leg is grotesquely twisted in a way that spells violence. A ballerina who really did break a leg, but it certainly wasn't her good luck.

*I know a place where no one's lost . . . I know a place where no one cries . . .*

The voice is haunting and exquisite. Of course it is; it's Jess Mordue's. She's incredibly talented, perhaps just as talented as my daughter Ruby, only far more beautiful. I'd never say that to Ruby, but she could hardly miss it. Jess is stunning.

Right now, we're all stunned into silence here in the head-master's office, all four of us mothers. I feel Carolyn, Jess's mom, staring daggers at me. I don't want to look at her, and I don't want to look at the demonic music box on the desk in front of us, and I don't want to look down like I'm guilty, or like Ruby is. She can't have done this. It's not Ruby at all.

The other mothers don't know the full story of who Ruby is, or who I am, or how the two fit together. They're all British, so maybe they haven't tried to imagine how hard it is to move from LA to London, leaving your husband behind, being solely responsible for the day-to-day rearing of someone as tempestuous as Ruby.

Her dream is to enter a world—a business—where beauty is revered, where Jess is likely to get breaks Ruby never will. Sometimes her insecurities take over. Sometimes it all gets out of control, and then she's truly sorry, I know she is.

As the music box winds down, the plinking piano notes first irregular and then ceasing, the ballerina's movement becomes jerkier until, mercifully, she's still. Adam Racki whispers, as much to himself as any of us, 'Unnatural deeds do breed unnatural troubles.' Then, for our benefit, he attributes, '*Macbeth.*'

Carolyn shakes her head in utter contempt for the headmaster. 'You realize what that song is, don't you?' she demands. She's physically imposing, as tall as Jess but solid rather than willowy, not one to soften her features with makeup. She leans forward in her chair, jabbing her finger toward the music box—and toward Mr. Racki—but I feel like her aggression is aimed squarely at me, two seats to her left. 'It's "Castle on a Cloud." It's Jess singing "Castle on a Cloud" Her audition song. You all get what this means.'

'None of us know yet what it means,' Mr. Racki says in that sonorous voice of his. He's not handsome but he has an undeniable presence, which makes sense given his past success on the West End. His walls display photos of him in full makeup onstage beside such luminaries as . . . well, I don't know the British theater greats, but I know they're represented. And I like his habit of quoting from plays, though sometimes the Latin is a bit much. 'We don't know who left this in Jess's locker.'

I'm not about to suggest that it was one of the other girls in the group of friends, though it is worth noting that their mothers, Bronnie and Elise, were also called into this meeting. Bronnie is sitting as a buffer between Carolyn and me, and Elise is on the other side of Carolyn. Our four girls are all studying musical theater at the Orla Flynn Academy. All us 'mums' would do anything to protect them, which sometimes puts us at odds with each other. Alliances can form and dissolve in the blink of an eye. Sometimes, I'm sad to say, we aren't so different from a bunch of sixteen- and seventeen-year-olds ourselves.

Even though Ruby took full responsibility for last year's *events*, she has been welcomed back into the fold by the girls, (thank God!) but Carolyn has never forgiven her. She's probably not forgiven me either. The whole business offended her sense of justice. She is a law professor, after all. She didn't think Ruby paid a high enough price.

Not that that excuses Ruby's behavior last year, but the notion of bullies and victims is too reductive and simplistic to fit all situations.

I glance at Bronnie and feel her silent support. Of the group of mothers, she's the most tenderhearted, though she's not the type to speak up this early. Her daughter Annabel is sweet and kind and avoids taking sides, too.

There's no point in looking to Elise, who's emanating waves of impatience. She taps her foot audibly, her impeccable fox-red bob swinging in time like an exasperated metronome. She'd prefer to be off making her millions. She's a pragmatist and a workhorse, just like her daughter Sadie.

Could it really be that just last year, we were a gang of four, like our daughters? We're all so different, but I relied on them. I miss them.

'Ruby did this,' Carolyn says with certainty.

What happened to innocent until proven guilty? Is that only in America?

'We at the Academy take this type of threat very seriously,' Mr. Racki says. 'The safety of our students is paramount. But with no witnesses and no confession, we must proceed with caution.'

Carolyn lets out an angry laugh. Then she stands up and begins to pace behind the other mums' chairs. It unnerves me, though I won't show it.

'I'm very sorry for Jess's experience . . .' Mr. Racki trails off when Carolyn halts to glare at him. He decides to appeal to the larger room, his gaze encompassing all the mothers. 'The reason I brought all four of you in today is because we need to focus on creating an environment of nurturance and empathy so that whoever did this will realize—'

'*Empathy*?!!!!' Carolyn explodes. 'Someone is threatening to mangle my daughter!'

'I've interviewed all the girls. Ruby denied any involvement, and no one saw anything.' His eyes scuttle away from Carolyn. I'm still amazed that he didn't cave to her pressure to expel Ruby last year, which must have been substantial.

The fact is, Ruby's still here. And so am I. I sit up a little straighter. Carolyn's not the only one willing to fight for her daughter. I just happen to have different weapons. I lean in and address Mr. Racki—Adam—with my voice soft in a deliberate contrast with Carolyn's bleating. For a second, I wish I still had my long blond hair to toss, wish I still dressed with a hint (or more) of cleavage, but post-chemo and post-lumpectomy, my hair's grown back at a glacial pace and it's only to my shoulders, the same chestnut brown as Ruby's. 'Ruby has no reason to threaten Jess,' I tell him.

Carolyn comes to loom over me. 'It's an encore performance!' she nearly bellows into my face. I try not to flinch. Don't show fear.

'Carolyn, sit down, please,' Mr. Racki says in the authoritative voice he must use with the girls in his charge.

Seeing that Mr. Racki won't continue until she complies, Carolyn sits down with a loud huff. I reward him with a smile.

'I'll certainly make further inquiries and tighten security measures, but everyone in this room must play their part. All the world's a stage, after all, and we need to set an example for the girls. It's just a few weeks into the term. We don't want a repeat of last year, now do we?'

Bronnie is nodding, all furrowed brow, but Elise's foot has accelerated. 'Sadie had nothing to do with last year's nonsense, and she's got nothing to do with this music box. I set a fine example for my daughter.'

'What went on last year affected their entire group, and threatened to infect the entire school,' Mr. Racki says. 'With teenage girls, it's all about dynamics. Everyone plays a role.'

'No,' Carolyn says, 'this is about Ruby. She should have been expelled already, but I'll settle for right now.'

'It wasn't Ruby,' I tell Mr. Racki. Lately, Ruby's been so much more grounded; she won't let anything distract her from her true purpose, which she's had since she was four years old. She's going to be a star.

I do worry that some of what's happened is my fault. My cancer was so tough on Ruby, and she'd acted out, which multiple therapists in LA said was not unusual. I wish I'd responded differently at the time, but I can't erase the past. London was supposed to be our fresh start, an ocean away.

But this wasn't Ruby. She promised.

'At heart, Ruby's a lovely girl,' Bronnie says. Thank goodness for Bronnie.

'*Lovely?*' Carolyn turns to Bronnie, but can't turn *on* Bronnie. Even Carolyn can't behead Bambi. 'Adam, this has Ruby written all over it.' Her use of his first name is as challenging as her stare.

7

He averts his eyes. Well, I'm Ruby's mother, dammit. 'This isn't Ruby's MO at all.'

Carolyn clearly relishes my choice of words. 'So she has an MO, like a criminal, does she?'

I ignore her. Mr. Racki's my target. 'When Ruby's confronted,' I say, 'she admits what she's done and she's remorseful.'

'You mean she cries,' Carolyn says. 'That's not the same as feeling remorse. She's an actress, after all.'

'They all are,' Bronnie says. I don't know if she means just our four daughters, or all teenagers in general. Secrecy and lying go with the territory.

'She told the headmaster she didn't do it, and I believe her.' My tone is firm. I might have a little actress in me, too. Because while most of me believes Ruby, there's a part that wonders. But I can't let on, can't let Carolyn smell blood in the water.

The truth is, I'm afraid. I'm the only one here who knows just how wrong it can all go when Ruby gets out of control.

'She manipulates you,' Carolyn says flatly. 'And now she's upping her game. Doesn't anyone else see how dangerous this is?'

Elise suddenly stands up. 'Sure, it's all very upsetting, I'm sorry for Jess, and I have no idea if Ruby did it, but it doesn't have anything to do with Sadie or me.' She heads toward the door and then asks, over her shoulder, 'Bronnie, are you coming? This has nothing to do with you or Bel, either.' Bronnie looks torn. She hesitates just a beat too long for Elise's taste, so Elise yanks open the door, says, 'I'll catch you all later,' and walks out.

Mr. Racki seems to be losing control of this meeting. He is largely ineffectual, which worked to Ruby's and my advantage when she was admitted with very few questions asked. I'm sure it didn't hurt that Nick endowed positions for two underprivileged students. Carolyn probably anticipates that I'm not above playing the cancer card or the damsel-in-distress-far-from-home card. Maybe that's why she's fit to be tied right now. She can't stand to lose, and the prospect of being bested by an inferior intellect like mine once again—well, it must be too much to bear.

Or she just loves her daughter and doesn't want to see her tormented again. I can understand that. If a music box like this showed up in Ruby's locker . . . well, I don't even like to think about that.

'This is bullshit!' Carolyn bursts out. 'Find me another suspect. I fucking dare you!'

I look to Mr. Racki imploringly, pleading my case. 'This obsession Carolyn has with Ruby—'

'I'd say it's the other way around! Ruby is obsessed with Jess! And I've fucking had it!'

'Does the person who cusses the most get their way?' I ask.

Mr. Racki is looking a bit hapless, perhaps searching for a unifying theater quote. Then he clasps his hands together and smiles around at all of us. I've seen this before, we all have, when he suddenly decides that what the world needs now is love, sweet love. Yes, he can be corny, but his heart is in the right place, and again, that frequently works to Ruby's advantage. It means he's always ready to see the best in her and give her another chance. I look at him with wide, curious, accepting eyes, while I can feel that Carolyn is tensing up, on the verge of another explosion. Maybe I shouldn't take pleasure in her reaction, not at a moment like this, but cancer taught me that you need to live life to the fullest at all times, because you just never know.

'An opportunity has presented itself,' he says. 'A new student has just started at OFA this morning. Her name is Imogen Curwood, and she doesn't know anything about the girls, or their history. She doesn't know anything about any

9

music boxes. And introducing a new person can often shift dynamics significantly, which might be just what the girls need.'

'Are you for real?' Carolyn asks.

'Very real.' His tone is jolly. He obviously believes he's stumbled upon the perfect solution. 'Imogen's arrival can be a fresh start for everyone.' A fresh start—one of my favorite phrases. This couldn't be going any better. 'Here's a chance for the girls to resolve any differences they have by welcoming a new friend, and as adults, we can give them the proper encouragement.'

I smile at him, like it's a delightful idea, and it is, because it means that Ruby isn't going to be expelled. It means Carolyn has been thwarted once again.

Bronnie smiles, too. He's her boss, after all, so she doesn't have much choice. It's a fine line to walk, being both an employee and the mother of a student.

Without a word, Carolyn storms out.

Some people are just never happy. Who doesn't love a fresh start?

## CAROLYN – Jess's mum

I slam the car door shut and sit in the driver's seat with my eyes closed, counting.

*One, two, three . . .*

Why do people count when they're agitated? Are numbers inherently calming? Let's see.

*Four, five, six . . .*

No, they're not. It's all bullshit: meditate, count to ten, paint your bedroom walls white and spray lavender mist on your pillow. You can do all of that and the real world is still out there.

*Seven, eight, fuck Ruby Donovan. Please let her get squashed to a splatter on the pavement by an obese hippo falling from a fourteenth-floor balcony.*

The real world is still out there, and you're not going to get any sleep tonight because a sly-as-fuck teenage malignancy is still persecuting your daughter.

The passenger door closes with a solid but soft *p-thunk.* I'm certain Jess isn't trying to score points by demonstrating that her approach to door-closing-in-times-of-stress is more mature than mine, but it feels as if she is.

*Nine, fuck Ruby Donovan, ten, and fuck the shitty Orla Flynn Academy.*

I should have insisted on a one-to-one meeting with Adam Racki. Why did he summon us all? There was no need for

Bronnie and Elise to be there, unless he thought Bel or Sadie might have put that monstrosity in Jess's locker, and no one thinks that. We all know Ruby did it—even Kendall knows, deep down.

I can guess why he wanted all four of us there, the sneaky worm. He wanted to dilute the Carolyn effect. ('Who can blame him?' every member of my immediate family would say. They'd expect me to find it funny, too.)

Predictably, neither Bronnie nor Elise spoke up: Bronnie because she's about as much use as a spokeless umbrella and Elise because she doesn't give a damn one way or the other. Which was convenient for Racki.

I wanted to see Kendall, so I agreed to a group meeting. There's a streak of naïve optimism in me that will not die. I hoped this time might be different, that Kendall might finally take responsibility for her despicable daughter instead of making excuses. If this music box horror show isn't enough to make her say, 'I am *so* sorry, and I'm going to come down on Ruby like a ton of bricks,' then what will?

'Mum?' Jess's voice cuts through my thoughts. 'Please tell me you didn't steam in there this morning accusing Ruby and trying to get her expelled.'

I say nothing.

'You did, didn't you? Without talking to me first. Mum!'

Jess might sound strict and bossy, but I know what's beneath that: anxiety. Fear. My daughter doesn't like to show any weakness—a trait she gets from her mother. When Ruby's antics got to be too much for her last year, she didn't cry or complain. Instead, she disappeared: from home and from school. Thanks to some cryptic pictures she posted on Instagram, we found her three days later, in Manchester. She'd been sleeping on a bench for two nights. When Dan and I found her, her face was covered with a film of grime. She grinned at us and said, 'Don't I look like a proper homeless person?' When we asked her why she'd done what she'd done, she said, 'I needed some time away from Ruby. And before you say I never have to go near her again if I don't want to . . . no. I'm not letting her drive me out of my school. I can survive any shit that Ruby's got lined up for me now.'

Adam Racki seemed sufficiently panicked by the whole thing, though whether for Jess's safety or his school's reputation, who can say, but even then he didn't properly discipline Ruby. He seemed to decide Jess's little foray into being a vagrant in Manchester was some kind of method acting exercise. And I couldn't force Jess to change schools when she was determined to prove how tough she was by staying.

'Mum! For fuck's sake!'

*Other mothers would say,* Don't swear at me. *Other mothers would take their daughters out of harm's way in spite of their protests.*

I hear Adam's voice in my head: *Here's a chance for the girls to resolve any differences they have by welcoming a new friend.* It was a pathetic, primary-school-level attempt at manipulation. You can tell a group of five-year-olds who's going to be their new friend, but you can't do it with teenagers. Was it designed to be a redemption opportunity for Ruby, after last year?

Jess was Ruby's new friend once. Evil loves to make new friends. It rubs its hands together and says, *Ooh, nice. Another victim.*

'It wasn't Ruby, Mum.'

'What?' This shocks me into opening my eyes. Jess and I don't always agree, but we have about Ruby, so far.

'The music box. She was with me all morning. She was even with me when I found it, and was as shocked as I was. She started crying. I was just, like, "What the fuck?"'

'Makes sense. Seeing it through *your* eyes gave her a few seconds of insight into her own warped mind. I'm not surprised she cried. She spent most of last year crying and apologizing, but it didn't stop her persecuting you.'

'Interesting,' says Jess lightly, twisting the rearview mirror round so that she can check her makeup. 'I thought you were going to go with the more obvious "She had to pretend to be upset in order to look innocent."'

'I'd hate to be predictable,' I mutter.

'Nothing I say about the way Ruby's mind works—'

'It works like a chemical weapon in teenage girl form.'

'—is going to convince you, even though this is so *not* her style. I keep telling you, though you never listen—we're good now, me and Ruby. My disappearing act last year freaked her out, I think. She knew everyone'd blame her if I was found dead in a ditch.'

There's no point asking her not to joke about something so horrible. She'd only say I'm just as outrageously blunt when it suits me, and she'd be right.

'So if Ruby didn't do it, who could have?' I ask. 'Bel? Sadie?'

'No and no. As if either of them would!'

I agree. 'I don't think they did. For a school to contain more than one psycho capable of nastiness at that level—let's call it the Ruby Donovan level—I don't buy it.' I pause to think. 'Who knows the code for your locker?'

'Ruby, Bel, Sadie. But . . . there's a master code that opens all the lockers. Students are in and out of the office all day—any of them could have opened a drawer and found it. What? You might as well say it. I can hear it even if you don't.'

*I don't care if Ruby was glued to your side all day. She did this. Somehow.*

'How come you're not more upset?' I ask.

'Aha! Great question.'

'Thank you.' I start the car, suddenly desperate to get the hell out of here.

'Weirdly, it's thanks to Ruby that I'm not totally trauma-tized,' says Jess. 'She's been really, like, looking after me. So have Bel and Sadie. Last year, it all got so awful, and our group nearly broke up completely, and now . . . I don't know. It feels like we're solid again. She actually said, "You of all people don't deserve this, after what I put you through last year. *I* deserve it."'

'Good point. Soon as we get home I'm going to make a music box with a maimed Ruby doll twisting around in it.'

'No you're not. Please just don't do or say *anything*. Anything involving my friends. Let *me* sort it out. Mum? I swear to God, if you say the word "prospectus" . . .'

I smile. Now that we're out of the Academy car park and on our way home, I feel better. Is it possible to be allergic to one's child's school? Am I the first parent ever to ask herself this question? In my best compromise voice, I say, 'I'm not going to send off for other schools' prospectuses *today*. But I'm also not leaving you in a place where sickos put carefully crafted threatening objects in your locker. I think my position is . . . not unreasonable.'

'It wasn't a threat, Mum. It was a bad joke. And you *are* leaving me there, because I want to stay there.'

Something strikes me for the first time: Jess is more reluctant to leave her best friends, even the one who psychologically tortured her for a year, than she is to leave the best performing arts school in London. She's brilliantly talented, but musical theater doesn't feature in her dreams the way it features in mine. If all her friends moved to a normal sixth form college, she'd probably opt to go with them.

'As long as nothing else happens,' I say evenly. I'm not conceding defeat forever. Only for now. If I push her any further, Jess will start to sound as if she's taking Ruby's side against me, and I can't cope with that. Not today.

'Hey, Dad!' She waves at Dan's bike shop as we drive along the Archway Road. 'I don't think he's there. It looked closed.'

'He'll be at home. He took Lottie to the orthodontist at lunchtime.' *And decided it wasn't worth going back to the shop mid-afternoon for only a couple of hours.* I must try not to think this thought later tonight, when I'm chucking coffee down my neck at one a.m., trying to stay awake long enough to make a dent in my Urgent Work list.

A more useful thing for me to think about is: Who made and planted that music box? If not Ruby, who was with Jess all morning, then who? She must have roped in Bel, Sadie, or both. Or even someone from outside their group of four.

I can't just let this stand, let Ruby's twisted shit escalate. If no one else is going to do something about it—and Racki clearly isn't—then I will. Tonight, when everyone else is asleep, I'm going to think this through properly and make a plan, while neglecting my work. Normally I neglect it in favor of something more fun: the musical I'm secretly writing. At the moment, I'm stuck on a song. I love what I've written so far, but I can't think of what should come next. I'm trying to tell myself this must also happen to the Great Musical Theater Librettists of our time: Sir Tim Rice, Tim Minchin . . .

*Yeah, right. It definitely doesn't happen more often to pretend-librettists who, in reality, are bored law professors.*

Maybe it'd help if I changed my name to Tim.

As I drive, I hum the song as I've written it so far. A tune came to me while I was writing the words and, though I know nothing about music, I think it's pretty good. Silently, in my head, I sing the lyrics, too.

> *Gave you a leading role (I wrote the play),*
> *Gave you a hero's soul, and lines to say,*
> *Gave you emotion, gave you strength as well*
> *But that all vanished when the curtain fell*

*So perhaps I should have said this from the start:*
*Please think about the one who wrote your part.*
*After tonight's performance, if you can,*
*Don't just go back to being the same old man.*
*Give me your word*
*That without a costume or a stage*
*Give me your word*
*That without a script's highlighted page*
*You can come up with a decent line.*
*Give me your word.*
*I've given you enough of mine.*

'What's that tune?' Jess asks. My heart leaps.

'Why, do you like it?' Someone might like my work; the first person who's ever heard any of it. That would be encouraging.

'I dunno. Stop humming, it's annoying.'

I bet that never happens to Sir Tim Rice or Tim Minchin. I wonder what they'd do about Ruby Donovan.

Of course it was her. A long summer holiday's a feasible amount of time for a spiteful, clever girl to refine her tactics. The music box is Ruby's big, bold, start-of-term statement, announcing her new MO that's far less likely to get her into trouble: She arranges for things to happen to Jess that she couldn't possibly have been responsible for. Then she cries, sympathizes, and gets to enjoy the thrill of secret knowledge while despising Jess for her credulity.

Most teenage girls, even the most treacherous and bitchy variety, wouldn't think, *Oh, I know what would be cool: a music box with a maimed replica of my victim inside it that will terrify and distress her.* Most teenage girls—most *people*—wouldn't go that far, however jealous they felt.

I have no doubt in my mind that Ruby Donovan would go much, much further. As someone who is prepared to go to great lengths myself when I really want something, I instantly recognize the go-too-far people I meet, and Ruby's definitely one of them. I can see it in her eyes. I wonder if she sees it in mine.

## BRONNIE – Bel's mum

I stand well back as the girls rush into the dressing room, their cheeks flushed with exertion, then hover as they take off their dresses, ready to hang them up. I'm glad to see that the girls are acting on Adam's request to include the new girl—Imogen—in their group. She's standing with the four of them, her back to Bel, who is unzipping her dress for her. I study her for a moment, wondering if she's going to be a good fit for their group. In my experience, odd numbers are harder work than even numbers, and the dynamics are obviously going to change. She seems nice enough—long, blond, almost white hair; wide, slightly protruding blue eyes; not as tall as Jess or Sadie but taller than Bel and Ruby. Their chatter is all about whether Adam is going to choose *West Side Story*, which they've just been rehearsing, over *My Fair Lady* for the end-of-term show. Today it was Jess's turn to play Maria and she was so good I think she'll get the part. Much as I would love her to, I don't think Bel will, although physically, with her long dark hair, she's the most suited to be Maria. And she does have a lovely voice.

To be honest, if it hadn't been for her drama teacher at school, Bel wouldn't be here. She loved playing in all the school productions but she never had any ambition to be on stage. And although she often had the starring role—she was wonderful as Matilda—it never occurred to me and Carl that

19

she might have a future as an actress. When Mrs. Carter took us aside and suggested that Bel audition for theater school, we were so surprised.

Carl wasn't keen on Bel auditioning. He's a traditionalist, and thinks she should study accountancy. He says it's a nice job for a girl and that she'll always find work. I wasn't sure at first, either. I don't necessarily think Bel should study accountancy, but the acting profession is a hard one, with its uncertainty and disappointments and no regular timetable, eating at goodness knows what time of the day and staying up all hours. I imagine you have to be quite thick-skinned to survive, and I'm not sure that Bel is. But she wanted to audition so we agreed, telling ourselves she probably wouldn't get in. That's when we learned the term *stage presence*. Apparently, Bel has got it.

I stoop to retrieve the dress Ruby was wearing from where she left it on the floor, wondering if she does the same at home. I look over to where she's standing with the others, trying to catch her eye and give her a little reprimand, not so much for myself but because she should have more respect for the costumes. The other girls at least manage to hang theirs on a hook and Bel, bless her, always puts hers on a hanger, trying to make less work for me. But Ruby can be a bit of a diva. She was awful to Jess last year. I didn't like that Bel seemed to be going along with it but I know she felt intimidated by Ruby.

I feel something hard in the pocket of Ruby's dress—it's a little piece of twisted pink plastic, the missing arm from the mutilated ballerina. I quietly slip it into my own pocket. I'm not sure if I should show it to Adam just yet; now might not be the most opportune moment. What if he summons everyone to his office again? I can just imagine Elise's reaction if she has to come back in.

She really put me on the spot when she tried to get me to leave with her the other day. What would Adam have thought if I'd left? You'd think Elise would understand that I'm in an awkward position, being both a parent and a member of staff. But I'm not sure Elise thinks at all, unless it's about herself and her career. I know it's stupid, but when I was offered this job I hoped that she and Carolyn might look at me with a little more respect. After all, it's quite something to go back to work after twenty-two years as a stay-at-home mum. I wouldn't even mind Carolyn referring to me as *wardrobe mistress* if I didn't think she was doing it to make my job seem less important than it is. But in my contract, it says *costume designer and seamstress*, so that's what I tell everyone I am. Sometimes I'd like to tell Carolyn how important I am to Adam in other ways. But I can't go into that, not without endangering everything I hold dear.

Yes, there is some picking clothes off the floor and a lot of mending, but I don't mind. I love my job and I'm grateful to Adam for offering it to me. It was after the end-of-term show last year, *Seven Brides for Seven Brothers*. I'd volunteered to help with the costumes because I'm quite handy with a needle and Bel told me that Eileen, who was the resident costume designer, was overwhelmed by the number of dresses that needed to be made. If there'd been three brides it would have been fine, but seven was just a few too many. In the event, I ended up making not only the girls' gingham dresses for the barn dance but also the dresses for the wedding scene at the end. When the show was over, Eileen handed in her notice—I think she was exhausted, poor thing—and Adam offered me her job.

I'm so glad he did. I'd be dying right now otherwise, what with Bel turning eighteen this year. She could be anywhere next year, off to university or touring with a theater group, depending on how the end-of-year auditions go, and there'll only be Toby left at home. And in three years' time, if he follows his two elder brothers to university, all my birds will have flown the nest. What would I do then, if I didn't have this job?

Carl couldn't understand why I wanted to spend so much time at the school. When I told him that I needed something to do now that the children were growing up, he said that I could do the books for his company and save him employing an accountant. But, as I pointed out, that would have been unpaid work, and with Lucas and Jon both at university, we could do with the extra money. And I get two afternoons off a week, Tuesdays and Thursdays, so it's perfect.

'Mum!' Bel comes running over and I quickly adjust my sweater so she doesn't see the bulge in my pocket. 'Sadie is having a sleepover on Friday, can I go?'

It's one of those moments when I don't quite know what to say. I don't like to be unkind, but I don't think much of Elise's parenting skills. She allows Sadie far too much freedom in my view. I've noticed dark circles under Sadie's eyes recently, and when I mentioned it to Bel, she mumbled something about Sadie being allowed to be up at all hours. She looked as if she might be about to tell me something else but I didn't push it. If there's something Bel's worried about, she'll tell me when she's ready.

It's not the only reason I'm hesitating about the sleepover. Even though Bel is looking at me eagerly, waiting for my answer, I know she doesn't really like staying away from home. It's not that she's clingy, just that she prefers sleeping in her own bed, as many people do.

'Why don't you suggest having it at ours?' I say. 'I could make lasagna.'

Bel shakes her head. 'I can't, Mum. Sadie has already offered.'

'Then of course you can go,' I tell her, feeling a little pang, because on Friday evenings she and I usually watch a film together while Carl takes Toby to karate. I make a mental note to bring some of the costumes that need mending home with me, to fill in the time.

Bel reaches up and kisses me on the cheek. 'Thanks, Mum, you're the best.' I watch her fondly as she runs back to her friends. 'Mum says it's fine for the sleepover at yours,' she says to Sadie.

'There's a sleepover?' Imogen looks at Sadie expectantly. 'Great, when?'

There's a bit of a pause and when I catch Ruby and Jess exchanging glances, I realize that Sadie hadn't intended to invite Imogen. I can see her struggling with herself, because she has a kind heart and doesn't like to upset anyone. Just when the pause is stretching out a little too long and I'm wondering if I'm going to have to intervene diplomatically, she shrugs.

'Friday,' she says.

Imogen throws her arms around her, unsettling her, if the look on Sadie's face is anything to go by.

'Maybe you'll all be able to give me a few tips,' Imogen goes on, looking around at the rest of them. 'Ruby, you dance so well and Bel, you've got such a lovely voice.'

Her effusiveness doesn't quite ring true, and when I catch Jess frowning, I know she doesn't think Imogen was being sincere, either.

'Can I take your costume for you, Imogen?' I ask, wanting to break up what is fast becoming an awkward situation.

She takes her costume from the peg and drops it into my outstretched hand, giving me a hard look to let me know she's aware I interrupted her on purpose. That look gives me chills.

Adam's suggestion that the girls include her in their group did throw me a bit. I would have preferred for him to have spoken to me before he sprang it on us. If he had, I would have tried to dissuade him. He usually listens to me on this

23

kind of matter, though during the episode with Ruby and Jess last year, I must say he was a bit remote. Another person coming along to potentially overshadow Bel is a complication that I don't need right now. Maybe I'm stressing about nothing; it's not going to be easy for the girls to accept Imogen into their group when it's always been just the four of them.

It used to be the four of us mums, too. But Kendall and Carolyn weren't even speaking by the end of the spring term. My mind turns to the music box. I don't think Carolyn should have come straight out and accused Ruby, not without proof. Maybe I should have tried to intervene, smooth things over a little. It's true that Ruby is jealous of Jess, I know that from Bel. And she desperately wants to be an actress, more so than any of the others. I hate to think what will happen if Jess gets the starring role in the end-of-term production and Ruby is her understudy. I doubt Bel will be in the running. Not that she'll mind; sometimes I think that if she was told she couldn't be an actress, she'd just shrug and say that it didn't matter. She's not that ambitious and neither am I, not like some of the pushy mothers we have at the Academy. Kendall and Carolyn definitely fall into that category, but I prefer to work behind the scenes to help Bel achieve her dreams.

The bell rings for their next class and the girls leave, Ruby and Jess with their arms linked together, as if Monday (and last term) never happened. It would be nice if Kendall and Carolyn could take a leaf out of their daughters' book and do the same. Maybe I should invite everyone for tea next week. I must remember to use mugs this time. Last time they came to tea, way back in April, I served it in pretty teacups, complete with saucers, and got raised eyebrows and a 'how quaint!' from Carolyn. It didn't stop her from eating my scones, although I kind of wished she'd choke on one. I don't know why she has to be so disparaging. Why can't she just be nice?

I pull out the little plastic arm and look at it again. Maybe I should go and see Adam, after all. I turn to leave the dressing room, slip it back into my pocket, and get the shock of my life because Imogen is standing there, staring straight at me.

'Imogen!' My right hand is still in my pocket, so it's my left hand that flies to my chest. 'You gave me a fright!' She doesn't say anything, just stands there looking at me with her unblinking blue eyes and my heartbeat, already crazily out of control, goes up a couple of notches. I wait for her to speak—but she doesn't, and as the silence stretches out between us, I try to work out how long she's been there and if she saw what I had in my hand.

'Did you want something?' I ask.

A small smile plays at the corner of her mouth. 'No, not anymore.'

I'm about to ask her what she means, then change my mind. 'Haven't you got a class to go to?' I say, the arm of the ballerina digging into my sweating palm.

'You're right, I have.' She turns away. 'Goodbye, Mrs. Richardson.'

I withdraw my hand from my pocket and take a shaky breath. This area backstage—the dressing rooms and the wings—is my little kingdom, where I rule. But the exchange with Imogen has left me with the weirdest of feelings; it was almost as if there was some kind of power struggle going on between us.

## ELISE – Sadie's mum

I frown at the shoes in the hall, sliding back the cupboard door and exchanging my heels for a pair of Mahabis slippers. I wriggle my toes, cramped from Louboutins that were never designed for hospital corridors.

'Yuliya?' I find the housekeeper in the kitchen. 'There are several shoes by the front door.'

'Yes, Mrs. Bond.' She disappears and I pour myself a large glass of Chablis. Field days—as research and development insist on calling them, as though we're sixth formers on an orienteering trip—are rewarding and frustrating in equal measures. Rewarding to see the life-saving equipment my team designed, frustrating because a day away from my desk means two catching up.

'All tidy, Mrs. Bond. I collect your dress from dry cleaner—they mend the zip.' Yuliya unties her apron, putting it in the drawer next to the oven. The polished concrete work surfaces are spotless.

'Thank you, Yuliya.'

'There is chicken stew in the oven, and I make pizza for the girls.'

'Girls?'

Yuliya looks uncertain. 'Sadie's friends? She said you said okay?'

With a sinking feeling, I half-remember Sadie asking if she

could have a sleepover. I'd been busy; yes was easier to say than no. 'That will be all, thank you, Yuliya.'

She changes her indoor shoes for a pair of ugly brown boots, but as she's about to leave she turns, her face creased with anxiety.

I sigh. 'What have you broken, Yuliya?'

'No, I—' She wrings her hands, apparently wrestling with whatever it is she wants to say. I hope she isn't going to hand in her notice. Yuliya runs our family like clockwork on wages that are—frankly—meager. Oh God, is that why she's leaving?

'Is this about money? Because—'

'Money? No, is about the new girl.' Her voice is low and urgent, and she comes toward me, gripping my upper arms.

'What new girl? What are you talking about?'

'Watch her with your family.' The whisper becomes a hiss as Yuliya leans closer to my face. My heart is a drum in my too-tight chest. 'She has the devil inside her.' With that, she releases her grip and buttons her coat. 'I see you tomorrow, Mrs. Bond.'

Shaken, I take a gulp of wine. Yuliya is prone to superstition. She knocks on wood to ward off the evil eye, and crosses herself if she spills salt. But this is a new one. I hope she isn't having some kind of breakdown—she's only halfway through the pantry audit.

Upstairs, I knock on Sadie's door.

'God, in my house people just barge in whenever they feel like it.' Jess's strident voice filters through the door.

'Come in!'

The sofa bed has been pulled out, and the single air bed squeezed between Sadie's king-size bed and the wall. Every surface is strewn with clothes.

'Sleepover?'

Sadie sighs. 'We talked about it earlier this week?'

27

'If it's not in the calendar . . .' I tap my phone and she rolls her eyes. Honestly—she knows everyone's social engagements have to go in the shared diary, otherwise how can any family function?

'Hi, Mrs. Bond.' It takes me a moment to place the blond girl sitting on the single air bed, a pair of hair straighteners in one hand.

*The new girl . . .*

'Imogen,' I remember. 'Call me Elise—everyone does.' Imogen smiles, rather sweetly. I wonder if Yuliya's been at my drinks cabinet.

'Your house is amazing.'

'Thank you.' Imogen is a seventeen-year-old drama student, not a *Beautiful Homes* journalist, but I'm still flattered. This house represents everything I've worked for. I remember standing on the road with the architectural plans in my hands, watching the bulldozers take down the grotty bungalow that had been there, and thinking, *This is it—this is what it's all for.*

'I've got work to do,' I tell the girls as my phone pings, 'but Yuliya's made pizza, and there's cider in the fridge.'

'Thanks, Elise,' Sadie says.

'Cider!' Imogen bounces on her air bed. Ruby and Jess exchange excited glances.

'I'm not allowed to drink,' I hear Bel say as I close the door. *Quelle surprise.* Bronnie Richardson's apron strings are tied tighter than a ship in a storm. Personally, I think a few pints of cider would loosen them *both* up, but I have more important things to worry about than Sadie's friends. BONDical, Limited is *this* close to securing a contract with one of the country's leading private medical firms, and although I've got a dedicated team working on the bid, I'm sure they won't mind my double-checking the application.

I'm engrossed in my work when there's a tentative knock, followed by silence. I wait; sometimes Sadie will go away if I'm busy. I squint at the screen, my eyes gritty. The numbers are right, but the bid needs more impact . . .

Another knock. I sigh. 'Yes?'

'Imogen won't stop crying.' A charcoal mask is smeared across Sadie's face.

'About what?'

The mask wrinkles as Sadie screws up her face. 'She won't say.'

My fingers twitch on the keyboard. 'I'll come in a minute.' *Ensuring a high-quality, viable service* . . . I tut, trying to find the perfect phrase . . .

'Mum.'

*Mum?* I stand up.

Imogen's head is buried beneath pulled-up knees. Muffled sobs come from beneath her arms, wrapped around her as though she's trying to be as small as possible. Ruby, Bel, and Jess are on Sadie's bed, watching *Breaking Bad*. Jess very deliberately turns up the volume. Sadie hovers between Imogen and her friends.

I could do without teenage histrionics tonight. Occasionally someone will tell Nick and me that we're lucky to have such a level-headed daughter, who doesn't act up, doesn't have mood swings. I'm scathing in my response. You don't tell someone with a well-behaved dog that they're 'lucky' they sit on command, do you?

'What's the matter?' I crouch and put an awkward hand on Imogen's shoulder. Like the others, she's in pajamas, although hers are covered in cartoons—the sort of thing Sadie wore when she was fourteen. The sobbing intensifies. 'What's wrong, Imogen?'

Slowly, she emerges, her face red and blotchy, like she's been rubbing it. I'm struck by the bags beneath her eyes.

Imogen looks more exhausted than any seventeen-year-old ever should—a sharp contrast to the fresh faces of Sadie and her friends, who value their looks too much to miss out on sleep.

She lets out a loud, choking sob. 'N-n-nothing.'

'Unless you tell me, I can't help.'

Ruby twirls a finger around her ear. 'Cray cray . . .' she says, *sotto voce*. I glare at her.

Imogen's bottom lip trembles. 'I don't want to sleep on the air bed.'

'Then swap with one of the girls on the sofa bed,' I say, but Imogen shakes her head. She pulls her pajama sleeve down— but not before I glimpse the plaster around her left wrist. Was she trying to hide it?

'I can't sleep there, either.' She scrambles to her feet, fists clenched, her back tight against the wall. Her voice is shrill, like she's ten years younger than the others, and the contrast with her otherwise mature appearance is oddly unsettling.

*She has the devil inside her . . .*

I push Yuliya's words away. 'Why not?'

She widens her eyes, her words breathy and frightened. 'There are things under the bed. Monsters.'

Ruby screams.

Jess hits her. 'You idiot—you made me jump.'

'It wasn't me.' Ruby raises both arms, fingers clawed. 'It was . . . A MONSTER!' They collapse into giggles.

When I look back at Imogen, she's staring at Ruby and Jess with undisguised fury. A shiver runs across my neck.

Imogen draws herself up and smiles politely, all trace of the frightened little girl gone. 'May I go in the big bed, Mrs. Bond, between Sadie and Ruby?' She's talking like an adult, now, and it's eerie, coming from a teenager in cartoon pajamas.

There's a sharp exclamation from one of the girls. Ruby, probably, or maybe Jess. Privately, I don't blame them.

'I won't sleep a wink otherwise.'

*Sleep a wink.* Again, that curiously grown-up turn of phrase. *Grown-up?* I think, before I can stop myself, *or otherworldly?*

*She has the devil inside her.*

Bloody Yuliya, putting stupid ideas in my head. I'm a scientist. Imogen is practically a *child*. So what if she still freaks out over monsters?

'Fine—sleep in Sadie's bed, then.'

'But that's not—' Jess stares at me, open-mouthed.

'Oh my *God*!' Ruby whirls around, looking to Sadie for backup. 'Sadie, tell her!'

Sadie knows better than to try to change a decision I've made. 'Oh okay, then. Imogen, sleep between me and Rubes.'

'What the fuck, Sades?' I've never heard Ruby this angry. Is she jealous? Worried about her position in the group now there's a new girl to contend with?

'Language, Ruby,' I say, although I couldn't give a monkey's how someone else's child speaks. 'That's sorted, then.'

'Yay!' Imogen bounds up, jumping onto the bed and sitting cross-legged, cuddling a pillow. She's all smiles, like the last half hour never happened; like a puppy who loses a ball and then finds another. I stand, wanting to get back to work, but as I pass Sadie's en suite, I see my Crème de la Mer, tossed onto a pile of cheap toiletries. I don't mind Sadie using my things—you can't invest too early in good skin—but I'm blowed if her friends are going to slather themselves in my four-hundred-pound face cream.

The counter is a mess of masks and spot treatments, liners and lip glosses. Four wash bags spill their contents into the soup of cosmetics. Ruby's will be the pink one with *Selfie Kit* in white letters on one side, which means the rose-gold bag filled with Mac and Benefit will be Jess's, and the half empty

Cath Kidston one with a flannel and some Body Shop shampoo, Bel's. Which only leaves . . .

I glance behind me, but the girls are whispering animatedly to each other, oblivious to my presence. Imogen's bag is black, with *Ted Baker* along the top. I step into the bathroom and, slowly, I unzip the bag. You can tell a lot about someone from their wash bag. Cleanse, tone, and moisturize? Or a pack of baby wipes and hope for the best? Dental floss, or a splayed out toothbrush that's seen better days?

There isn't much. A toothbrush, some makeup, and a razor. I think of how Imogen yanked down her sleeve. Self-harming? Attention-seeking? Thank God Sadie's too level-headed to be swayed by emo trends.

My hand closes around a small packet of pills. I pull it out, expecting paracetamol, but instead I see the familiar label of a prescription-issued drug. I peer at the label, too reliant nowadays on my reading glasses, and see a familiar word. *Olanzapine.*

I might not be a doctor, but there isn't much I don't know about medical equipment and drugs: What the hell is a seventeen-year-old doing with antipsychotics? I read the label—*10 mg alprazolam once a day*—then stop short.

The patient name printed on the label isn't Imogen Curwood. It's Lisa something, Lisa D . . . Dais-something. I rub at the smudges of makeup obscuring the name. Are they stolen?

I don't know what makes me look up. I only know that when I do, it's all I can do not to cry out. The eyes that meet mine in the bathroom mirror belong in the face of someone far older than Imogen Curwood.

Someone far more dangerous.

'I think you'll find that belongs to me.'

I freeze, as though I'm the child, and Imogen the adult who has caught me out. I shove the pill packet back in the wash bag and drop it onto the counter.

'Just clearing up a bit!' I say, more confidently than I feel. If it had been one of the others—Ruby or Jess or Bel—I'd ask what they were doing with drugs, where they got them from. But Imogen's eyes burn into me. My mouth is dry; a hard ball of fear settles in my chest.

A cruel smile creeps across Imogen's face. 'You should be careful,' she says softly. 'Did you know more accidents happen in the home than anywhere else?' She holds my gaze, and although I know she's just a kid, and there's no such thing as a devil inside her, I feel the blood drain from my face.

Only when I am once again in the safety of my study am I able to breathe again. Ruby is spot on: Imogen Curwood is utterly cray cray.

'Then why is she in our house?' Nick says. His laptop is tilted away from him, so my Skype view is less husband and more hotel headboard. I push my glass of wine out of view before he comments on it.

'Because Sadie didn't want her to feel left out.'

His face softens. 'That's my girl. Did you know that actors have higher levels of empathy than anyone else? I read a study about it.'

'Great, she can add it to her CV,' I say drily. 'It'll compensate for the lack of A-levels.' Nick's sitting on his hotel bed; I'm already under my covers. It's almost midnight here, and coming up to seven p.m. in Connecticut, where Nick will be till next week.

He gives me The Look. 'We've been over this a million times. Sadie loves OFA.'

Sadie had gotten straight As on her GCSEs. Her form teacher almost wept when she heard her star pupil wouldn't be staying on. So did I.

'She's happy there. Happier than she was at her old school.'

'Because there's less work—'

33

'Because there's less *pressure*,' Nick cuts in.

We'll never agree. Why pursue something in which you're so unlikely to succeed?

'I'd better go—I've got a breakfast meeting with WellFort in the morning.'

'Hope it goes well. Love you,' he says.

'Love you, too.'

Nick's face freezes for a second before he disappears and I'm left looking at my own face. My eyes are gritty and bloodshot. I push the laptop to the empty side of my bed, so I can reach it if I wake. I gave up battling insomnia years ago, seeing it instead as an opportunity to get more work done. I knock back the rest of my wine, treating myself to a little something to help me sleep.

When I wake, it's to a scream that sends me bolt upright, my heart racing. Was I having a nightmare? But no, there are running feet and shouting and crying and *what the hell is going on*? I run, groggy from lack of sleep, blinking as I emerge onto the landing into bright lights.

At the top of the stairs Sadie, Jess, and Bel are clutching each other, staring in horror at something I can't see. Bel is crying, and Jess has both hands clamped to her mouth, as though she might scream, or be sick.

'Mum!'

'What's happened?' I have the oddest feeling that something evil has entered our lives; that something in the very *air* has changed tonight.

*Lack of sleep*, I tell myself. *Lack of sleep and teenage dramatics.*

Sadie is so pale her skin is almost translucent. She extends a trembling hand, pointing down the stairs. Bel wails afresh, and clings harder to Jess.

An uneasy prickle makes its way down my back. I take another three steps until I can look over the glass balustrade down to the hall.

My hands creep to my mouth, panic forming in my throat. Ruby looks up at me from the bottom of the stairs, a mixture of fear and defiance written across her face.

But it isn't Ruby I'm staring at. It's Imogen, lying motionless at Ruby's feet, hair spread out like a halo and limbs twisted into shapes that make me wince. Every inch like the broken ballerina Jess found in her locker.

# 2

# Let the Show Begin

*B. A. Paris*

# SNAPCHAT: THE FAB FOUR

**Ruby:** Hey
**Sadie:** You ok?
**Ruby:** Sorry I left the sleepover. Had fun?
**Bel:** Not the same without you.
**Ruby:** (heart)
**Jess:** Why the freak-out, Rubes?
**Ruby:** Thought she was dead
**Jess:** Not with that friggin noise
**Sadie:** OTT?
**Jess:** Def!
**Ruby:** Wish we didn't have to hang round with her
**Jess:** Let's tell her to piss off
**Bel:** Can't, not after what Racki said
**Jess:** Fuck Racki
**Ruby:** No thanks!
**Bel:** We should give her a chance
**Sadie:** She's weird tho, right?
**Jess:** One crazy bitch!

# SNAPCHAT: JESS, BEL, SADIE

**Jess:** Hey, what was all that crazy stuff with Ruby last night? She really lost her shit

**Bel:** Just freaked out by Imo's fall, I guess

**Jess:** Nah, more to it than that

**Sadie:** Like what?

**Jess:** Dunno—think she pushed her?

**Bel:** She was in kitchen

**Jess:** Said she was

**Sadie:** TBF so did Imo

**Bel:** Weird tho

**Jess:** Both friggin weird IMHO

# BRONNIE

I can't quite believe I've managed to get the four of us together. After what happened last week with the music box, I expected Carolyn to say that if Kendall was going to be here today she wouldn't be coming, and vice versa. But they both seemed really pleased when I phoned to suggest meeting up.

Elise said she wouldn't be able to come unless we met at a hotel near her house, as she's on a tight schedule. And it had to be today, Friday, not any other day, which is perfect for me as I work on Friday afternoons and can go straight to the Academy once we've finished. On the other hand, if I didn't have to work this afternoon, I could stay right here and order one coffee after another just for the pleasure of being in such luxurious surroundings. I've never been in such a beautiful hotel before, with its pink marble floors and plush velvet sofas grouped around gold-and-glass tables. And the chandeliers! There's an enormous one sparkling right above our heads and my first thought, when I glanced up and saw it hanging there, was that if it came loose we'd almost certainly be killed, not just from the weight of it but from the glittering cut-glass beads that would do as much damage as a thousand sharpened knives. That's the problem with something that falls from above: You just don't see it coming.

'Don't the cakes look delicious?' I say, wanting to bring our discussion about whether Adam is going to choose *West*

*Side Story* or *My Fair Lady* for the end-of-term musical to an end.

Kendall smiles across at me. 'They do, but they probably don't taste as good as yours.'

I look longingly at my red velvet cupcake. 'There's only one way to find out.'

'Go ahead, Bronnie, tuck in.' Carolyn pauses a moment and I wait for the sting. 'Don't let us stop you.'

I can't help the flush that rises to my cheeks. I hate to think what her reaction would have been if I'd gone for a slice of the heavenly-looking chocolate cake that first caught my eye. I only chose the cupcake because it seemed less greedy. When you're carrying an extra few pounds, as I am, you're aware of these things.

I don't know why I let Carolyn get to me so much. Carl thinks that, deep down, she's jealous of me. I didn't believe him at first; I thought he was just trying to make me feel better about myself, like he always does. But Carl wouldn't have said it if he didn't think there was some truth in it. In retaliation, I give Carolyn's jeans and baggy T-shirt a meaningful look, wishing I had the guts to make a cutting comment about the way she's dressed, considering we're in a five-star hotel. Instead, I smooth down the flowered skirt of my beautiful silk dress, glad that Carl will never know how much I paid for it. It's just as well I insisted on opening my own bank account when I started working at the Academy, because at least he can't see what's going out of it. Or going in. Worry jabs at me and I push it firmly to the back of my mind, knowing that it won't be long before it comes back to haunt me. But for now, I refuse to let anything intrude on this lovely coffee morning.

'When I was going through my cancer treatment . . .' Kendall says, and I reach for my plate, grateful to be able to zone out for a few minutes. I'm not being mean; I'm always willing to lend an ear to a friend. But I spent a lot of time with Kendall last year listening to her cancer stories, and after a while I wanted my ear back so that I could listen to something else for a while. I really like Kendall, though. She's the only one I feel I have something in common with. I don't agree with the way Carolyn belittles everyone, and although Elise is awesome, with her glamorous life and wonderful job, the phrase *chalk and cheese* could have been invented for the two of us. We're so poles apart that we wouldn't be able to meet halfway even if we wanted to. I nearly fell off my chair earlier when she ordered a glass of champagne along with her coffee. I mean, it's ten thirty in the morning! Even the fact that none of us wanted to join in didn't deter her—she just went ahead, all on her own.

Uh-oh, Carolyn has mentioned the music box, time to tune back in. If she's chosen to touch on such a sticky subject, it can only be that she's desperate to bring Kendall's 'journey' to an end.

'Ridiculous,' she says, tossing her too-long, too-blond hair back. 'Even I can see now that it's not something Ruby would do.'

Kendall gives her a grateful smile. 'It's good of you to say so.'

'Ruby would never be so overt,' Carolyn goes on, which—to me—is another way of saying that what Ruby does is more underhand. It's something else that Carolyn does, damning with praise.

'Then who was it?' I ask. 'And why? Why would someone sabotage a music box and put it in Jess's locker?'

'I have no idea,' Kendall says. 'But, of course, the main suspect had to be Ruby.'

'Don't worry, Adam will get to the bottom of it,' I say, wanting to reassure her.

'Huh!' Carolyn shakes her head in disgust. 'Adam is about

43

as effectual as a priest in a whorehouse.' Kendall laughs, happy to have Carolyn on her side for once. Elise smiles and I wince because—well, it's a little vulgar. 'How is foisting Imogen on the girls going to help?'

'I think he's done the right thing in asking them to be responsible for Imogen,' I say. 'Maybe having someone new in their group will help dilute any tensions. It doesn't mean that he's not working behind the scenes to find out who's behind the music box.'

'Maybe it was Imogen.' We all turn and look at Elise. She gives a little shrug of her yoga-toned shoulders. 'I'm just pointing out that it happened the day she arrived.'

'But why would she target Jess?' Carolyn asks.

'Pure chance,' Kendall says, grabbing at the idea of another possible suspect.

'It couldn't have been. Remember, whoever it was went to the trouble of downloading Jess's song and engineering it so that it would play when the box was opened. No, it was definitely meant for Jess.'

'What happened at the sleepover, Elise?' I ask, both in an effort to change the subject and to try to find out what really happened, because all I got from Bel was that Imogen fell down the stairs.

'Imogen fell down the stairs,' Elise says. She looks so unperturbed as she downs the rest of her champagne that I want to shake her.

'Did you call a doctor?' I know she didn't, but I want her to see that she should have.

'No, she said she was fine.'

'But did she hit her head?'

Elise gives another of her little shrugs, infuriating me with her lack of concern. 'I don't think so. She didn't say she had.'

'What happened, exactly?' Carolyn says. 'I didn't get much from Jess because she was asleep at the time.'

44

Elise stretches her long legs, clad in beautifully tailored black trousers, in front of her and crosses them at the ankles. 'The first I knew of it was when Sadie came into the bedroom and woke me up to tell me Imogen had fallen down the stairs. Apparently, Imogen and Ruby had gone downstairs to make a cup of hot chocolate and Imogen slipped on one of the steps and fell.'

Carolyn looks like a cat who's spied a mouse. 'Where was Ruby when Imogen fell?'

It's exactly what I want to know, except that I wouldn't have asked because I wouldn't want Kendall to look at me the way she just looked at Carolyn. Put it this way—if looks could kill, Carolyn would be dead on the floor.

'In the kitchen,' Elise says. 'Imogen said Ruby had gone on ahead. By the time I got downstairs, Imogen was sitting on the floor crying and rubbing her shins. Bel was with her—the fuss Imogen was making had woken her and Jess and Sadie up. She was making a lot of noise about nothing, if you ask me.'

'If she was crying, she must have hurt herself,' I point out.

'That's just it, I had the feeling they were crocodile tears.'

'But she did have bruises. She showed them to Bel the next morning.'

Elise gives shrug number three. 'She told me she was fine. She didn't even want the ice pack Bel made for her.' It doesn't occur to her that Bel did more for Imogen than she herself did. 'I was more concerned about Ruby—she was hysterical.'

Carolyn's ears prick up. 'Ruby?'

Kendall flushes. 'She was upset, that's all. She went running back to the hall as soon as she heard Imogen cry out and when she saw her lying on the floor—well, she feared the worst. Anyone would have,' she adds defensively, reaching for her coffee.

'It was impossible to calm her,' Elise goes on, talking

45

directly to Carolyn now. 'She insisted on going home. I had to phone Kendall to come and fetch her.'

'Really?' The word drips with hidden meaning. I'm not sure what Carolyn is getting at, but Kendall isn't happy. She bangs her cup down on the saucer, making me, and everyone else in the vicinity, jump.

'Maybe she thought she'd be blamed for Imogen's fall, even though she was in the kitchen at the time,' Kendall snaps. 'She usually gets blamed for everything, whether it's her or not.'

'Getting back to Imogen,' Elise says diplomatically. 'She's a bit of a funny one. Did you hear about the fuss she made over the beds?'

'If you ask me, it's a power thing.' Carolyn has an opinion on everything. 'She wanted her own way, and she got it.' She reaches for her plate and stabs her lemon tart with her fork. 'She's trouble, I just know it. We'd do well to keep an eye on her.'

I've been watching the fascinating sight of Kendall trying to calm herself—eyes closed, a couple of deep breaths, thumb and index finger pressed surreptitiously together—but Carolyn's words remind me of something.

'Speaking of keeping an eye on things,' I say. 'Did you all see Adam's email? About drugs at the Academy?'

'If you mean the one asking parents to become vigilantes,' Carolyn drawls, 'in a word—pathetic.'

'That's not what he said,' I protest. 'He asked us to be vigilant when dropping off and picking up our children from school, that's all. And he's right, we need to be. It would be foolish to think that none of our students are taking drugs.'

'Yes, but he didn't say what measures *he* was going to take, did he?'

No, he didn't, which was something that annoyed me,

considering that last term two students were found using drugs on the premises. Because they were in their final year and about to leave, everything was hushed up. But that doesn't mean there aren't other students concerned, which is why I asked Adam to think about measures we could take to avoid a potential drug problem at the Academy. I had to really push him to send out an email to raise parents' awareness, and I was as frustrated as Carolyn by the content of his message. But I'm not about to tell her that.

Elise, seemingly bored by the conversation, lifts her wrist to check the time on her Apple watch. Worried that she might run off before I've had a chance to mention the fundraiser we need to have, to repair the school roof, I look for a way of bringing it into the conversation without the others stifling a sigh in a here-we-go-again kind of way.

'I'm going to organize a fundraiser,' I say. There's a collective, stifled, here-we-go-again sigh.

'What for this time?' Kendall asks resignedly.

'Drugs?' Carolyn quips.

'The roof. Adam asked Carl to take a look at it over the summer and he found a lot of loose tiles, a result of the storm we had last year. The Academy can fund most of the cost of the repairs but not all. So I told Adam I'd organize a fundraiser.'

'And you want us to participate.'

'I want everyone to participate,' I say firmly. 'Loose tiles are a safety risk and need to be addressed as soon as possible.'

'I'm happy to make a donation,' Elise says, which I was expecting, because she never participates, just arranges a transfer. As her donation usually surpasses anything we make from the fundraiser, I'm not about to complain.

'I'll bake some American goodies,' Kendall offers. 'And I can do anything else you want as long as it's not something creative.'

'Can you sing?'

'Yes, I've got quite a good voice.'

'Good.' I delve into my bag and take a theater program from it. 'On Saturday, we took Bel and Toby to see *Mamma Mia* at the local theater. I thought we could put on a show, with an admission fee. Sing a few ABBA songs, that kind of thing.'

Elise reaches over and takes the program from my hands, and I hope she's going to say that it's a great idea. A frown crosses her brow.

'Why have you got theater tickets stapled to the cover?'

'Oh.' I'm already blushing because I know it's going to sound stupid. 'I always save the programs from the shows we go to. I have since the children were small.'

'Wow,' Carolyn says. The *wow* is loaded, but not with admiration.

'Why, don't you keep yours?' Kendall asks, coming to my rescue. 'I always keep mine. Programs cost such a lot that it's a shame to throw them in the bin.'

'Even the tickets?' Carolyn just can't keep the amused tone from her voice.

'Sometimes.'

'Shall I make the transfer now?' Elise asks, handing the theater program back to me.

'No, not yet. Maybe you could help out on the cake stall at the fundraiser, Elise. I'm sure Sadie would love to see you there. I'll let you know the date in plenty of time so that you can get it in your diary.'

'Why not?' she says, giving me one of her rare smiles—not that she's a miserable person, but she's usually too busy to smile. 'You're right, it'll be nice for Sadie.'

I feel a little less deflated—for once, Sadie will have her mum there. But I'm still upset that nobody seems interested in my idea of a show. I shove the program back in my bag. It serves me right. The one thing I can do really well is sing—I was good at acting, too—and if I'm honest, I was hoping to impress the others with my voice. Everybody raves about how beautiful Bel's voice is, but they never think to ask if she got it from me or Carl. I'd love the others to know I've got a good voice, but it's not as if I can just stand up one day and burst into song. They'd think I was mad. *Madder*, Carolyn's voice whispers, and I'm glad she can't see the huge wooden chest I've got at home, stashed full of theater programs from every show I've ever seen.

'Let me know what you can do to help, Carolyn,' I say pointedly, because she hasn't offered anything. 'I'm sure you'll want to do as much as you can for the Academy, especially if Lottie attends next year—providing she gets in, of course.'

She gives me a sharp look, as if it's just crossed her mind that I might have some say over who gets in and who doesn't. Then, once she's worked out that I haven't, she gives me one of her superior smiles. I hate the way she underestimates me. It's true that I don't have that sort of power, but if I wanted to influence an audition, I'm sure I could find a way.

Elise checks her watch again and reaches for her Hermès bag.

'Time to go,' she says, getting to her feet.

'Me too,' I say, grabbing my Marks & Spencer tote from where I shoved it under the table.

'Already?' Kendall looks at me in surprise. 'I thought you only started at one o'clock.'

'Usually, yes, but I have to be in early today.' I know I'm blushing, I always do if I lie. But I've had enough. Anyway, without me and Elise around, it'll give her and Carolyn time to bond. Or kill each other. For once, I don't care which.

*    *    *

It takes me the whole of the journey to the Academy to relax. I don't regret meeting up with the others, but I hate how they make me feel. I know they think I'm boring, the way I'm always banging on about fundraisers, and I probably am. But someone has to organize them. And fixing the roof is important, although they'd only see that if something were to happen, and then they'd be like, *The school roof should have been a priority.* They also think I'm not capable of much, which makes me determined to prove them wrong.

I head to my workroom, which is backstage, just off the dressing room. The corridor is deserted; the students are still on lunch break in the inner courtyard and the only sound comes from my sandals as they clack along the tiled floor. A sudden movement catches my eye, a flash of blond hair disappearing into the toilet block ahead of me. I come to a stop, trying to puzzle it out, because I was the only one in the corridor, and there's no door for anyone to have come through. I give a little shrug; it must have been a trick of the light. I set off down the corridor again, but I haven't got very far when an eerie wail reaches my ears. A shiver goes down my spine and although my instinct is to flee, the sound pulls me onward, toward the toilet block, until I'm pushing the door open, my heart pounding in my chest, half-afraid of what I'm going to find. After the brightly lit corridor, it takes a moment for my eyes to adjust to the gloomy interior, and when they do I realize that the sound is coming from Imogen.

'Imogen, whatever's the matter?' I cry, dropping my bag and hurrying over to where she is sitting against the back wall, weeping copiously into her hands.

'I—I can't tell you,' she stutters, and I have to stop myself from reaching out and prying her hands from her face because it all sounds a bit—well—theatrical.

'Well, if you don't tell me, I won't be able to help you.'

Her sobs begin to subside and eventually come to a stop with a couple of hiccups. She lowers her hands, digs in one of her sleeves for a tissue, and fishes it out. As she wipes her eyes and blows her nose, I feel guilty for doubting that her tears were genuine, because it's obvious that something terrible has happened.

'I don't want to get anyone into trouble,' she says, her voice wobbling all over the place. 'It's why I haven't said anything.' She raises red-rimmed eyes and looks desperately at me. 'But I'm not sure I can keep it to myself any longer.'

'Why don't you tell me?' I suggest. She doesn't say anything, just carries on staring at me, and I'm struck at how pale her eyes are, almost devoid of color. 'It won't go any further if you don't want it to,' I go on, wondering if that's what she's waiting for.

'Promise?'

'Promise,' I say firmly.

She takes a shaky breath. 'Did Bel tell you I fell down the stairs during the sleepover at Sadie's?'

I nod. 'Yes.'

'Well, it was Ruby.'

'Ruby who found you? Yes, she was very upset, apparently.'

'She pushed me.' She says it so quietly I think I've misheard her.

'Sorry?'

'Ruby pushed me,' she repeats.

'But—' I feel horribly confused. 'Are you sure?'

'Of course I'm sure!' Her voice is so shrill I flinch. 'I'm sorry,' she says, noticing. She scrunches her tissue backward and forward in her hand. 'I knew nobody would believe me.' She sounds so miserable that my heart goes out to her.

'It's not that I don't believe you,' I explain, shifting into a more comfortable position, because I'm still crouched in front of her. 'It's just that everyone said Ruby was in the kitchen when it happened. Even you did, I think.'

'I know, but I hurt my head when I fell and my leg was really sore and I was crying and I went along with what she was saying because I felt really scared about what she'd done. I thought she might have bumped me accidentally—she was behind me on the stairs at the time. But then I remembered her stepping over me as I lay on the floor and running to the kitchen, and at first I thought she'd gone to get some ice or something but then she came back and started crying hysterically, saying, "Oh my God, Imogen, what happened, did you fall?" and then Bel and Sadie and Jess were there and she was telling them how she was in the kitchen when it happened and I didn't know what to say.' She pauses for breath. 'I mean, they're her friends and I'm only the new girl, and I knew it would look bad if I started accusing her, especially after the music box thing, because I know some people think it was her. But now I'm scared.' Her voice trembles. 'If she'd pushed me from higher up I could have been badly injured. Maybe that's why she waited until I was nearer the bottom, maybe it was meant to be a warning or something.' She looks at me in confusion. 'I don't understand why she did it. I haven't done anything to her. Unless it was because I wanted to sleep in the bed with her and Sadie. Maybe I shouldn't have made such a fuss, but I felt left out on the floor.'

In her agitation, she begins shredding the tissue to bits and I have to drag my eyes away from her fingernails, which are black with dirt, or maybe nail polish. 'We're going to have to tell the headmaster,' I say, my heart already sinking because if she's right in what she's told me, it's going to be awful.

'No, you can't, you promised! It will cause too much trouble, and I can't deal with anything else right now.' Tears well in her eyes. 'It's my dad. He's ill, really ill.'

'Imogen, I'm so sorry,' I say. 'What's the matter with him?'

'He's in a hospice.'

I stare at her. 'Hospice?'

'Yes.' Her voice breaks. 'He only has a few weeks to live. That's why I came here, to this school, so that I could be near him.'

'But—' I say, momentarily puzzled, because this is something that Adam should have told the members of staff. Unless—'Does Mr. Racki know?'

'No.' She shakes her head and tears cascade onto her cheeks. 'I don't want anyone to know because I don't want them feeling sorry for me. It's why I left my last school. I hated everyone knowing about Dad. They were only trying to be kind but it made me feel sad the whole time. I don't want that happening here.'

'I can understand that,' I say gently. 'All the same, I think Mr. Racki needs to know about your dad.'

'Please don't tell him. Maybe—you know—nearer the time. But not yet.'

It's difficult with her looking imploringly at me. When I think of all she has to deal with, I don't want to add to her distress by not giving her my word.

'All right. I won't say anything for the moment. But if your dad is in a hospice, where are you living? Your mother doesn't live around here, does she?'

She shakes her head. 'I'm staying with my grandparents. They live near the hospice, so it means I can see Dad every day.'

'It's good that you have your grandparents. But it must be difficult for them, too.'

'It is, especially as they're not in the best of health themselves.'

'Do you have someone to help you?'

'No, my grandparents don't want anyone except me.'

53

'Is there anything I can do to help?'

'No, thank you. At least, not at the moment. Maybe later.'

I can't imagine what it must be like for her to have to cope with elderly grandparents as well as a desperately ill father. But if she won't let me help, there's not a lot I can do except keep a vigilant eye on her.

'Well, if there's ever anything, promise you'll let me know?' She nods. 'And will you let me know how your dad is doing?'

'Yes. Thank you, Mrs. Richardson. I feel a lot better now that I've been able to tell someone.' She looks at me worriedly. 'But you won't say anything, will you? You won't tell anyone about Ruby pushing me down the stairs?' She senses my hesitation. 'You promised,' she reminds me.

'All right,' I say. But it seems like a promise too far, and I hate that I'm going to have to break it. There's no danger in me not speaking up about her father being ill, except to my peace of mind. But to keep silent about Ruby pushing her down the stairs—how can I keep that to myself? What if there's another incident?

Her eyes slide toward me. 'It might not have been *totally* Ruby's fault that I fell down the stairs.'

'What do you mean?' I ask, frowning. Either Ruby pushed her or she didn't.

'Well, we'd all had quite a bit of alcohol to drink.'

'Alcohol?' Even I can hear my voice rising dangerously high. But ever since Lucas got drunk at a friend's house when he was only fifteen and almost got run over by a police car on his way home, underage drinking has been a huge issue in our family. The memory of him being held up on the doorstep by two burly policemen is still fresh in my mind, six years after it happened.

'Yes, Sadie's mum gave us cider and maybe Ruby drank more than the rest of us. We were allowed to have as much as we liked,' she adds, banging a nail into the coffin I've mentally constructed in my head for Elise.

'Well, that explains it,' I say, relieved to have found a reason for what happened at the sleepover. 'It was obviously an accident.'

'What was?'

'Your fall. If Ruby *did* drink a lot of cider, maybe she was unsteady on her feet, and as she went down the stairs behind you, she lost her footing and bumped you.'

'Then why didn't she say that's what happened? Why run to the kitchen and pretend she was already there when I fell?'

She has a point. 'Maybe she panicked,' I suggest.

'No.' Imogen shakes her head vehemently. 'There was nothing accidental about the shove in my back. You have to believe me, Mrs. Richardson.' Her voice rises an octave. 'I could have been killed!'

'I'm sure it wouldn't have come to that,' I soothe. 'But I don't see what I can do if you won't let me tell anyone.' She waits, wanting more, but I'm beginning to feel exhausted by her constant mood swings. I know she's upset, but it's hard to keep up. One minute she's accusing Ruby, the next she's making excuses for her.

She has a plaster on her wrist and, noticing that it's as grubby as her fingernails, I take hold of her hand, hoping a little TLC will do the trick. 'Why don't I go and get a clean plaster for this?' I offer.

'No!' She snatches her hand back as if I've burnt her. 'I don't want anyone touching it!'

'It's okay,' I say mildly. I wonder about telling her to go and give her nails a good scrub, but decide against it. I check my watch and get to my feet, my knees stiff from squatting for so long. 'You've got twenty minutes before your next class. Do you want to stay here or would you like to come and sit with me for a while?'

'I'd rather sit here for a bit.' She looks up at me, her eyes bright with gratitude. 'Thank you for being so kind. There's no one else I feel I can confide in, and who I can trust not to say anything.'

The rush of pleasure I feel at the first part of her sentence is quickly canceled out by her mention of trust. Despite what she said about Ruby maybe being under the influence of alcohol, I'm going to have to speak to Adam.

'If you ever need to chat, just come and find me,' I tell her.

'Do you think—' She stops, seeming unsure if she should go on.

'What?'

'I know Ruby was awful to Jess last year. What if it's my turn this year? What if she's going to start coming after me?' There's a real panic in her voice. 'I'm scared, Mrs. Richardson, really scared.'

Deep in thought, I make my way to Adam's office. This could be a good time to show him the broken ballerina arm. If I tell him that I found it in the pocket of Ruby's dress after the rehearsal last week, and mention what Imogen just told me, he'll have to take some kind of action against Ruby. Poor Kendall. I wish I could spare her. Unfortunately, I can't.

'I'm not sure what this actually proves,' Adam says, holding the twisted piece of pink plastic between his thumb and forefinger and inspecting it as if it's some kind of weird insect. He's wearing an orange paisley scarf today, draped over his usual black turtleneck sweater. His scarves tend to match his mood—orange is good, yellow is better, gray is bad—and when he doesn't wear a scarf at all, it's best to keep out of his way. So maybe it's me bringing up the music box that's put a frown on his face. 'Where did you say you found it?'

'In the pocket of the dress Ruby was wearing during the

rehearsal last week,' I repeat. 'She left it on the floor so I picked it up to put on a hanger and as I was smoothing it down, I felt something in the pocket.'

'So this could have already been on the floor. And somehow got into the pocket of Ruby's dress.'

This isn't going to be as easy as I thought. I want to tell him that of course it couldn't have 'somehow' got from the floor and into the pocket of Ruby's dress all by itself, but I need to tread carefully. He's not just the headmaster, he's also my employer.

'Well, yes, I suppose so,' I say, wondering why he's unwilling to accept what I just told him. 'There's something else, though.'

I'm getting good at recognizing the sounds of a sigh being stifled. 'Yes?'

'I just found Imogen in the toilets in tears. I don't know if you're aware, but last Friday, the girls had a sleepover at Sadie's house and Imogen fell down the stairs. At the time, she said it was an accident; now she's saying that Ruby pushed her.' I pause, giving him time to process this latest piece of information. 'She asked me not to tell anyone, but it's not something I felt I should keep to myself.'

Another frown. 'Was Imogen hurt? I don't remember being informed that she'd had an accident.'

'No, she wasn't hurt, apart from a few bruises. But that's not the point, surely? The point is that she could have been hurt.'

'You're right, of course. But if Imogen doesn't want anyone to know—including me—there's not a lot I can do. Maybe she's decided to just suck it up.' He runs his hand through his thick black hair and I know I'm in for a quote. 'The web of our life is of a mingled yarn, good and ill together.'

'That's as may be,' I say tartly. 'But pushing someone down the stairs is quite a bit of ill.' He gives me a look, because

I don't usually question him, or his quotes, but I can't believe he's not taking it more seriously. 'Don't you think you should speak to the police?'

'Absolutely not.' Adam slaps his hand down on the desk, making me jump. 'Imogen didn't fall on school property or during school hours. When it comes down to it, it's got nothing to do with me, or with the school.'

'But what if this is only the beginning?' I persist. 'What if it escalates? First the music box, then the push down the stairs.'

'Bronnie.' He gets up from behind his desk, walks over to where I'm standing, and lays a hand on my arm. 'Do you really want the police coming to the school?' Heat rises to my cheeks at his touch. 'You wouldn't want them to find out about us, would you?' he asks, his voice low.

I shake my head quickly. 'Leave it with me, Bronnie,' he goes on. 'I'll speak to everyone concerned and once I have, if there's any action that I deem necessary, I'll let you know.'

He gives my arm a little squeeze, goes back to his desk, opens the drawer, and drops the plastic arm inside. Sitting down, he pulls his keyboard toward him, his way of telling me that the conversation is over. I don't like the way he does that, dismissing me as if I'm one of his students, when we both know I'm much more than that. It makes my blood boil.

'Oh, Bronnie?' he says when I'm halfway to the door. I turn, thinking he's going to ask me to go and fetch Ruby. 'I know I can rely on you to be discreet about what you've just told me. Especially as Imogen asked you not to tell anyone,' he adds pointedly.

It takes a lot not to slam the door behind me. Did he just reprimand me for breaking my promise to a student? I've always defended him to Carolyn, but now I understand something of her frustration. How can he be so unconcerned about what I've just told him? What's it going to take to make him realize how out of control things could get?

'Is everything all right, Mrs. Richardson?' Looking up, I see Jess lounging against the wall, an amused look on her face.

'Yes, thank you, Jess, everything's fine.'

'It's just that your hair is all mussed up.'

Before I can stop myself, I've raised a hand to my head and am smoothing my hair down. It feels fine to me, and I have a horrible suspicion that Jess is winding me up, trying to make me feel more uncomfortable than I already do. *Like mother, like daughter*, I think crossly, wishing I could swipe the smirk from her face.

'Did you want something?' I ask, without any of my usual warmth. Of Bel's friends, Jess is my least favorite, probably because I see too much of Carolyn in her, especially in the too-sharp tongue area.

She holds up a folder. 'I need to give this to Adam.' She's the only one of our students who would dare use his first name to a member of staff—but maybe, like Carolyn, she only considers me the wardrobe mistress. 'Except I didn't want to disturb you,' she adds, and I wonder how she can load so much meaning into so few words.

I move away from the door. 'Go on, then.'

She peels herself from the wall. 'Which scarf is he wearing today?' Her question could be innocent; students often ask me what color he's wearing before they go in to see him. They all pray for yellow, especially if they're about to be disciplined. But there's a snide insinuation in her tone that I don't like one little bit.

'I don't know, I didn't notice,' I say, walking away before I do something I'll regret.

★   ★   ★

There's still fifteen minutes left of the lunchtime break, so with Imogen heavy on my mind, I head for the inner courtyard. I spy Bel sitting on the stone bench with Ruby and Sadie and when she sees me, she jumps up and comes running over, her long dark hair flying behind her.

'Hi, Mum,' she says, planting a kiss on my cheek. 'What's up?'

'I've just seen Imogen and she looks a bit down. Maybe you could invite her to Costa for a milkshake after class to cheer her up.'

'What—today?'

'Yes.'

She pulls a face. 'Aw, Mum, do I have to?'

'No, you don't have to. It would be a nice thing to do, though. I can pick you up at five thirty, so it would only be for an hour.'

She thinks for a moment. 'Can I invite the others along? I don't mind if they're there. It's just that I don't really know Imogen.'

'Then it'll give you a chance to get to know her better. Adam did say that he wanted you to include her in your group,' I remind her.

'We try, but it's not easy. She's a bit weird, Mum.'

Anyone would be weird if their father was dying, but I can't tell Bel that. 'It must be difficult joining a new school in the final year of your studies,' I say instead.

'True.'

'Is that a yes, then?'

'If the others can come. I'll go and ask them now.'

'Thanks, Bel,' I say gratefully. 'You do know you're the best daughter in the world, don't you?'

'And you're the best mother!' she shouts, already on the way back to her friends. I can't help smiling. People are often amazed when I tell them that there are never any arguments between us and the children, but that's because they never ask us anything they know we won't agree to. And if we need them to do something, as with Bel just now, we always present it in a way that makes them think they have a choice about whether to do it or not. When actually, they don't.

I stand for a moment, watching the students milling around the courtyard, thinking about Lucas and Jon, Bel's elder brothers, who are both at university. I know they're not angels when they're away from home. I'm sure they've got drunk on quite a few occasions and I've found lighters in their pockets when I'm doing their washing, so I know they smoke. The point is, they respect us enough not to do it at home. They don't even ask if they can smoke in the house, because they wouldn't want to put us in the position where we'd have to say no. The one thing I hope is that they're not doing drugs, that the conversations Carl and I have had with them about the dangers of addiction have been enough to deter them. Communication is key in our family; we talk about everything, and despite what Carolyn thinks, I'm not a prude. When Lucas and Jon bring their girlfriends home for the weekend, I don't make them sleep in separate rooms, as she once asked me if I did. As long as the boys have genuine feelings for the girls they're with, and vice versa, I'm fine with them sleeping together under our roof. And when the time comes, it'll be the same for Bel.

The courtyard doesn't get a lot of sun at this time of year, and since I feel a little chilly, I move over to where it's warming the walls in the far corner, enjoying the calls of 'Hello, Mrs. Richardson!' as I pass by. It's easy to feel invisible when you work in the background, as I do, so it's nice to be acknowledged. I know more about each student than they would probably like, not because I have access to private information about them, but from observing them in the dressing room before and after rehearsals, when they're being their normal selves. I overhear a lot of things too, which the students trust me not to repeat and I never would, not unless it was a matter of life or death. *Life or death.* Now I'm back to worrying about Ruby, wondering if she really did push Imogen down the stairs. And what was Elise thinking, serving them alcohol? I'm surprised Bel didn't tell me; she usually tells me everything. Although she has been a bit cagey lately. Like the other day, when she was telling me that she and Sadie had been paired up to sing a duet together.

'Is Sadie all right?' I asked, remembering the dark circles I'd seen under her eyes. 'She's looking tired lately.'

'Yes, she's fine,' Bel said quickly—a little too quickly. I waited, because I could see her debating whether or not to share something further with me. 'I think she's feeling a bit under pressure.'

'In what way?' I asked. Bel seemed reluctant to say any more. 'Is she studying too hard?'

She seized on this. 'Probably.'

I knew then that she wasn't going to say more, not at that moment in time. But I didn't push it. If Bel wants to tell me, she will. Or maybe she wants to tell me but has been sworn to secrecy by Sadie, just as I've been by Imogen.

It could be that Bel didn't tell me about the alcohol at the sleepover because she was worried I wouldn't let her stay over at Sadie's again. I wonder if she actually drank any, if she succumbed to peer pressure or if she hung on to what we've told her about underage drinking. Wait until I tell Carl that Elise introduced our daughter to alcohol. I can't imagine what he'll say!

And suddenly, I know exactly what he'll say. *Bronnie, it was cider, not tequila. Maybe Bel drank some, maybe she didn't. Don't make this more than it is. Have a word with Elise if you like, but that's all.*

I immediately feel better. That's what I'll do. I'll pop round to Elise's on Monday, have a word without being too critical. Yes, that's definitely the way forward.

I've moved away from the sunny spot by the wall, ready to leave the courtyard, when I see Imogen coming out of the building. She looks around for a moment and then runs over to the bench where the three girls are sitting and throws her arms around them. Sadie pulls away, so Imogen lets go of Bel but keeps her arms around Ruby. After what she just told me, her behavior seems a bit extreme. Or maybe she's just keeping her enemy closer. Then Jess-with-the-poison-tongue arrives and the five of them chat together for a while, occasionally bumping each other with their shoulders as they mess around. Suddenly, Imogen is no longer next to Ruby, she's now standing opposite her, next to Sadie, although I'm not sure how she got there. I was watching the whole time, and didn't see her move. Weird. I fix her with my eyes, daring her to suddenly appear next to someone else. But after a moment, she whispers something to Sadie and the two of them move away and stand huddled in conversation together. What is that all about, I wonder? Is Imogen telling Sadie what she just told me, about Ruby pushing her down the stairs? She can't be, not when she told me not to tell anyone.

The bell rings for the start of the afternoon classes and, feeling strangely unsettled, I make my way to the dressing room, where I spend a couple of hours sorting through the costumes for the next big rehearsal. Carolyn is the only one hoping Adam will choose *My Fair Lady* for the end-of-term show at Christmas, and that's because she's confident Jess will get the starring role. And with just two main characters, only her daughter will get to shine. The majority of students will have to content themselves with a role backstage, which isn't necessarily a bad thing. It's important they realize that being a star isn't the be-all and end-all of musical theater, that they can still be a part of that world if they don't make it as an actor. Sadie, for example, is so wonderfully calm and organized that she'd make a brilliant director. Jess *will* be a star, I'm convinced of it, which is a shame, as she'll be doing it more for her mother than for herself. Ruby will more often than not be the understudy, allowed to shine from time to time but not quite good enough to always carry the principal role. As for Bel, she could be a star, and if that's what she wants, I'm going to do everything in my power to help her get there.

Once I've checked the costumes and sorted out the ones that need mending, I head to the stockroom to check on paint supplies. It's not really my job but Bob, the stage manager, doesn't keep tabs as well as he should, and the students often run out of one color or another when they're painting the backdrops, which causes all sorts of delays. It's just as well I decided to take a look, because it seems we'll soon be out of black. I make a note to pass on discreetly to one of the stage crew lads. It wouldn't do to give it to Bob directly; we get on well but I wouldn't like him to know I was rummaging around in the storage cupboard.

Mindful of not imposing on Bel's goodwill for too long, I walk quickly to Costa and get there fifteen minutes early. The girls are deep in conversation and don't see me come in. Not wanting to break the mood, I slide into a bench behind them and take a book from my bag to read while I wait. It's not my intention to listen to what they're saying, and I wouldn't be able to hear anything if Imogen wasn't talking so loudly. But it's clear she's enjoying being the center of attention, and I can't help feeling pleased that my plan to cheer her up has worked.

'Dad's taking me to see *Hamilton* soon,' she says, and my ears prick up because after what she told me about him being seriously ill, I know it can't be true.

64

'Wow, that's so cool,' Bel says. 'I'd love to go but tickets are like gold dust. Your dad must have got them ages ago. When are you going?'

'I'm not sure, sometime next month,' Imogen says vaguely, and then I understand. She isn't going to see *Hamilton*—her dad hasn't got tickets, she just needs to be able to pretend, if only for a while, that her life is the same as everyone else's.

'I saw it last year; it was BRI—LI—ANT!' Jess says.

'We went to see *Mamma Mia* at the weekend. It was really good.' Bel again.

'Not as good as *Hamilton*, though.' Jess pauses, just like Carolyn does before she's going to say something cutting. 'Is it true that your mum keeps tickets and programs from every performance you go to?'

'That's right,' Bel says cheerfully.

'But it's not like you're ever going to look at them again.'

'We might, when Mum and Dad get really old or if they get Alzheimer's or something. I'd hate for them to forget all the lovely times we had, so I'd use the programs to jog their memories.'

'Okay, you win,' Jess says. 'But only because you're a really nice person.' She actually sounds as if she means it.

'You're lucky,' Sadie says. 'If my mum gets Alzheimer's, I wouldn't have anything to jog her memory with. Except maybe a balance sheet.' She sounds so sad I want to give her a hug.

I wait for Ruby to chip in, because she's been silent up to now. But there's only the sound of slurping, so I ease out of the bench and walk around to where they're sitting as if I've only just arrived.

Bel looks up. 'Hi, Mum.'

'Hello, girls.' I look around the table. 'Where's Ruby?' I say, noticing that she's missing.

Bel and Sadie shift uncomfortably on their seats.

'Not here,' Jess drawls, sounding bored. It's breathtaking how much like her mother she is.

'Bel?'

'We left a bit before her,' she admits.

'How long before?'

'About half an hour.'

'If you left at four thirty, she must have left at five. So why isn't she here?'

'Oh dear, she must still be waiting for us,' Jess smirks, which makes me want to smack her, especially when Imogen starts smirking along with her.

'Where?' I ask.

'On the bench in the inner courtyard.' Sadie looks at me, a faint flush on her cheeks, and once again, I'm aware of the dark circles under her eyes. 'I guess we thought she'd know to come here.'

'Right, up everyone,' I say firmly. 'You're coming with me.'

'Where?' Jess asks.

'To find Ruby.'

'What!'

'That's right.' I ignore the daggers Imogen is throwing me and look sternly at the four of them. 'What you did isn't right. You can't leave Ruby out like that.'

'Why not? She left me out enough last year,' Jess says petulantly.

'I know, and that was wrong, too. But two wrongs don't make a right. Come on, get your stuff together.'

'I haven't finished my milkshake.' Jess scowls.

I look pointedly at her empty glass and she leans back against the seat and crosses her arms in front of her in an I'm-staying-here gesture.

'I'm staying here,' Imogen says, cottoning on quickly.

'Fine. But Jess, Bel, and Sadie, are coming with me.' Jess opens her mouth to protest but I hold her gaze, daring her to

66

defy me. As I head to the counter to pay for their drinks, I hear her and Imogen muttering and feel a pang of pity for Bel.

'Thank you for treating us,' Sadie says, when I come back.

'Yes, thank you,' chorus Imogen and Jess, who seem to have had a change of heart and are on their feet.

Bel has to run to keep up with me as I head back to the Academy, but I hate the thought of Ruby waiting in vain for the others turn up. I feel bad for Kendall, too; if she finds out that Ruby was left out on purpose, she'll feel awful. I know Ruby did the same to Jess last year, and that Imogen has accused Ruby of pushing her down the stairs, but I hate bullying of any kind, regardless of at whom it's directed.

'So how come Ruby got left out?' I ask Bel, cross about the whole thing.

'It was Imogen. She didn't want her there; she said that if Ruby came to Costa, she wouldn't, and that we needed to choose between the two of them. Jess chose Imogen, and you said I had to be nice to Imogen so I chose her, too. And Sadie did, because she didn't have much choice.' She hesitates a moment. 'I did feel bad for Ruby, but none of us really know what to think anymore. It's really hard for me and Sadie being stuck in the middle of it all. We don't want to take sides but sometimes—well, we have to.'

We've arrived in front of the courtyard so I slow my pace to give the others a chance to catch up. It's the ideal moment, I realize, to try to find out what's going on with Sadie.

'I know it must be difficult,' I say sympathetically. 'Is that what's troubling Sadie?'

'What do you mean?'

'She just seems a little listless at the moment, not her usual bright self.'

'Maybe she's not getting enough sleep,' Bel says vaguely.

'You know what her parents are like. They never check what time she goes to bed, so she's probably up all night watching series.'

'That's not good,' I frown. I'm about to ask her if she thinks I should have a word with Elise when the sound of loud sobbing reaches our ears.

'Who's that?' Bel asks, a look of alarm on her face.

'What the fuck?' Jess says, coming up behind me.

I peer into the courtyard and see a forlorn figure standing by the bench in floods of tears. 'Oh dear,' I mutter. 'Come on, you lot.'

We hurry over to Ruby and I put my arm round her shaking shoulders. 'It's just a misunderstanding,' I tell her.

'Yes, we looked for you and couldn't find you,' Bel says. 'Did you go to the toilet or something?' Ruby shakes her head violently. 'Well, we couldn't find you,' Bel repeats, 'so we went to Costa thinking that you'd gone on ahead. And then we kept expecting you to turn up.'

Ruby can't stop shaking her head, so I try to make her sit down on the bench. But she twists away as if I've asked her to sit on a bed of red ants.

'L-look,' she says, pointing with a finger that's shaking as much as her head.

So I look. And there, artfully sprayed onto the bench in black metallic paint, are the words *Here lies Ruby Donovan*.

There's a gasp from Bel and Sadie and a breathless *Fuck!* from Jess. I turn my head toward Imogen and see a look that I can only describe as pure malevolence on her face. Sensing my gaze on her, her eyes quickly become round with shock. A hand raised in front of her mouth, her dirty fingernails in full view, completes the look of surprise she's engineered for my benefit. Something jolts in my brain; I look again at the graffiti on the bench, then again at Imogen's fingernails, then back to the bench.

I offload Ruby, still sobbing with distress, into Bel's arms, because I need to think. They crowd around her—*It's okay, Rubes, we're going to find out who did this*. Is it possible that Imogen—? I cut myself off in mid-question—no, of course it isn't possible, not unless she's capable of being in two places at once, because if anyone were to ask, I'd have to tell them that the graffiti definitely wasn't on the bench when I came through the courtyard on my way to Costa. I glance over at Imogen and she meets my gaze full-on, her pale eyes never wavering. I don't know what it is, but there's definitely something weird about Imogen. Weird people get blamed for all sorts of things, whether they're guilty or not.

I remember how I suddenly found her standing in front of me backstage the other day, and the way she materialized ahead of me earlier, slipping into the toilets from an empty corridor—and then appeared next to Sadie without seeming to move—and an icy shiver creeps its way down my spine.

# 3

# On the Trail for Truth

*Clare Mackintosh*

# ELISE

It's cold but dry, already a hint of autumn in the air. I move from downward dog to dolphin pose, my forearms flat on my yoga mat, and my bottom high in the air. *Ten, eleven, twelve . . .* I tighten my core and feel the muscles in my calves tighten. *Fourteen, fifteen, sixteen . . .* We had the garden landscaped immediately after the house was built, but every scraggy cat in the neighborhood used it as a toilet, so six months later I made them take everything out again. *Twenty-five, twenty-six, twenty-seven . . .* Now we have a neat row of plastic topiary, a square of seating around a gas firepit, and this strip of artificial grass. *Thirty.* It's so much better for you to do yoga surrounded by nature, instead of in a stuffy hall.

I'm in noose pose when the doorbell rings. I ignore it—*six, seven, eight*—then remember that Yuliya refuses to work Saturdays now, and Sadie will still be in bed, dead to the world. I release my hands and stand up.

'Oh—hi, Elise.' Bronnie looks flustered, as though *I'm* the one who's just dropped in unannounced. She takes in my outfit. 'Sorry, did I interrupt your workout?' Bronnie's wearing leggings and a shapeless blue linen dress with big pockets. Unpainted toenails poke through open-toed sandals.

'No problem, I'll finish it later.' I take her through to the kitchen. The bifold doors are open to the garden, letting in a light breeze. 'Unless you'd like to join me?' Bronnie's face is a picture, like I just suggested she fly a plane, and I grin. 'Just coffee, then?'

'That would be lovely.'

We sit at the island with mugs of freshly brewed coffee from the shiny machine Nick and I had imported from the States. Bronnie would produce cake now, I think, as I look in the cupboard for biscuits. I feel the faint tug of insecurity so familiar from early motherhood, when everyone else was baking cookies and making playdough like it was easy—like they had a gene I just didn't have. My company was in its infancy then, with a tiny team that relied on me and me alone, so I found a nanny with the playdough gene, and went back to work when Sadie was a few weeks old. I clung on to the postnatal group for a while, joining in with the emails and occasionally meeting for coffee, until it became clear we had nothing in common except our babies.

I go to the cupboard for a bar of 99% Lindt chocolate. 'So much better for you than all that refined sugar,' I say, although the thought of one of Bronnie's Victoria sponges is making my stomach rumble. Before I close the cupboard I open the jar that lives on the top shelf, and knock a tablet into my cupped hand. 'Wellness supplements,' I say. 'Gwyneth Paltrow swears by them.' I swallow it dry, then sit back down.

'So . . . to what do I owe this unexpected pleasure?' I say when Bronnie's mouth works but nothing comes out. It's clear there's something on her mind.

'I'm just so worried!' It bursts out of her like water from a dam.

'What about?' A hundred possibilities flash through my mind. Is Bronnie ill? Is her marriage in trouble? Are they in debt? My heart softens. If our daughters weren't friends, I doubt Bronnie and I would cross paths, but she's a sweet woman, and with a couple glasses of wine inside her she can be quite good value on a night out. God, I hope it's not cancer . . .

Bronnie looks at me, her brows knitted in confusion. 'About the girls, of course.' There's a beat. 'Aren't you worried?'

Relief that it's nothing serious is tempered by bewilderment at Bronnie's overreaction.

'The revue, you mean?' Personally I think Adam's decision to use the forthcoming revue as an audition for the annual show is not only an efficient use of time, but a much needed injection of pressure. If these kids are serious about a career in performing arts, they're going to have to raise their game.

'No, the music box, of course!'

'Oh—that!' I can't imagine why Bronnie's so concerned— no one's pointing the finger at Bel, as far as I can see. Perhaps her job at the school means she's more involved than the rest of us parents. I break off a square of chocolate and let it melt on my tongue.

'That twisted, broken leg . . . I can't stop thinking about it.' Bronnie is close to tears. 'And that awful thing someone wrote on the bench at school yesterday.'

'What awful thing?'

'Didn't Sadie tell you?'

I cast my mind back over the last twelve hours. Sadie had cello practice, and I was working late. Yuliya made some South American concoction with way too much heat—I must speak to her about her fondness for chilies . . . 'I don't remember her saying anything about a bench.'

'Oh.' Bronnie looks mystified. 'Don't you talk to Sadie about her day?'

'Of course we talk!' I snap. 'Not all families live in each other's pockets, you know.'

There's a painful silence. I should apologize, but I'd be the first to admit that's not exactly my strong point. Besides, I'm not taking parenting lessons from a woman who still does the laundry for boys away at university all term.

'I found the missing ballerina arm in Ruby's costume,' Bronnie says. It's news to me but I hide my surprise—no doubt I should have interrogated Sadie about that, too . . . It's an interesting development, though, and more proof—if proof were needed—that Ruby planted the music box in Jess's locker.

'And now Imogen's saying Ruby pushed her down the stairs—'

'Ruby pushed her?' I cut in. 'No. Sadie's adamant that didn't happen. Imogen fell. Or she threw herself down.' I shrug. 'It wouldn't surprise me—there's something decidedly off about that girl. She unsettles me.'

Bronnie opens her mouth like she's about to defend Imogen, but something passes across her face and it's clear she's thought better of it. 'She's just a child, Elise.'

I remember the way Imogen appeared in the bathroom mirror, the stare that met mine older than her years. *More accidents happen in the home than anywhere else* . . . An involuntary shiver runs down my spine. Alprazolam produces a spaced-out, drowsy feeling—could it have caused Imogen to fall? Perhaps she was taking some other drug, too? I remember a news article years ago, about a boy on acid, convinced he could fly, who stepped off the balcony in his high-rise flat . . .

'Imogen's dad's dying,' Bronnie says. 'She needs support, not criticism.'

I picture Imogen's glassy blue eyes. Depressed or drugged up? Sad or crazy? Whatever it is, I'm not having her in my house again. 'Nothing's happened to Bel, though, has it?' I wonder why Bronnie's being so intense—so *obsessive*—about this.

'Not yet, but what if she's next?' Bronnie's voice rises a notch. I've never seen her this worked up about something.

She's normally so docile, so . . . vanilla. 'First Jess, with the music box, then Imogen falling down the stairs, and the graffiti on the bench—it said *Here lies Ruby Donovan.*' She's speaking faster and faster, gripping her coffee mug so hard I expect it to shatter. 'Who's going to be next?' It's so loud, and so shrill, it echoes.

I speak deliberately slowly, hoping my tone will prove calming for Bronnie. 'I think we need to keep things in proportion.' Bronnie's hands are shaking, her knuckles white around her mug. I reach for it. 'Shall I take that?' It's Villeroy & Boch, and they've discontinued the design—I'd hate to lose one. 'Like you say,' I continue, soothingly, 'they're just kids.' I wonder if Bronnie is having some kind of nervous breakdown.

'Exactly!' Bronnie thumps a fist on the worktop, and I breathe a sigh of relief that the Villeroy & Boch is safely out of reach. 'Children! Vulnerable children who need protection, and you don't even care!'

I sigh. How can I explain that this is just one of a million things I care about? Like Brexit, and Donald Trump, and my cholesterol, and what kind of job Sadie's going to get once she's got this musical theater stuff out of her system. 'Of course I care.' I try to see things from Bronnie's perspective. She's a housewife who makes costumes for pocket money. She doesn't employ a hundred people, chair board meetings, negotiate deals, fire-fight fallouts from other people's decisions. She's way out of her comfort zone and looking for guidance.

'They rely on us for protection, and we let them down!' She's shouting now, shaking like she's scaring herself with the force of her words. Poor woman. It's sad, really. I reach out a hand to touch her arm, but she snatches it away, jabbing a finger at my chest. '*You* let them down!'

*I what?* Any shred of sympathy I had for Bronnie Richardson vanishes in a heartbeat. I regard her coolly. 'I beg your pardon? I was asleep when Imogen fell, I could hardly have—'

'You plied them with *alcohol*!' Bronnie sounds every syllable, her mouth working like the word itself tastes bad.

I give a bark of laughter. 'A can of cider is hardly hard liquor.'

'They're underage.'

'By less than a year!' I'm shouting too, now—if you can't beat 'em, join 'em—and we glare at each other, Bronnie puce with barely contained rage. She opens her mouth to spill more crap, but before she can say anything there's a noise behind us. We both whip round, to see Sadie standing in the doorway, rubbing her eyes and yawning.

'What's all the shouting about?'

'Hello, sweetie, how are you?' Bronnie's sudden reversion to her usual cloying, condescending 'mum voice' takes me by surprise. She smiles at Sadie. Gone is the harsh, angry tone, the white knuckles, the tremor of emotion in her cheeks— gone so swiftly that I'm left with the unnerving feeling I might have imagined the whole thing.

'Yeah, all right.' Sadie looks between us.

'Bronnie just popped in to see if you're okay with everything happening at school.' I sigh, then parrot my own words. 'So . . . are you okay with everything happening at school?'

Sadie shrugs. 'I guess.'

'Excellent!' I move so abruptly I knock against the chrome stool by the breakfast bar, and it rocks on the glossy tiles. 'Sorry you had a wasted trip, Bronnie.' I begin walking toward the hall, so she has no choice but to follow me. Barely contained fury boils inside me. How *dare* Bronnie Richardson come to my door and lay blame at my feet! Whether Imogen Curwood fell or was pushed, my only involvement is owning the house she did it in. I realize we're crossing the exact spot where she lay, prone, and the image of her flashes across my mind. I remember the clutch of fear as I looked over the banister at her unmoving body, hoping for the best, but fearing the worst.

I open the door and usher Bronnie out, even as she's trying to speak. 'Elise, I really think that—'

'They're teenagers, Bronnie. I'm sure we were just as fucked up at that age.' I say a cheery goodbye and close the front door, leaving her wide-eyed.

'You're so mean.' Sadie comes out of the kitchen, eating a piece of toast. 'You know she hates swearing.'

'I couldn't resist it. Her face. Please use a plate, Sadie—poor Yuliya has enough to do already. I'll be in the office if you need me.' I walk toward my study, then turn back. 'You won't need me, will you?'

'No, I'm going shopping in town—can I borrow twenty quid?'

'Take fifty. Have lunch, too.' Perfect. An entire Saturday to work in peace.

By midday I've achieved nothing aside from clearing my inbox. I'm trying to make notes on a report from my R&D manager about the ultrasound needle we're developing, but I'm so derailed by Bronnie's visit I have to read every paragraph three times.

*You plied them with* alcohol*!* . . .

What if she goes to the police? It's precisely the sort of thing someone like Bronnie would do. I see her trotting down to the local station; picture the bored desk sergeant scribbling in his notebook, perking up as the story unfolds.

'Drunk, you say? Pushed down the stairs?'

'I hate to stir up trouble,' I imagine Bronnie saying, 'but they're just *children.*'

Could I be done for neglect? For serving alcohol to minors? If Ruby really did push Imogen down the stairs, does that make me some sort of accessory?

'Oh for heaven's sake, Elise,' I say out loud, as much to chase away the mental pictures as to snap me out of this ridiculous spiral of anxiety. This is all bloody Bronnie's fault. If she hadn't come over this morning I'd be none the wiser, and this report would be annotated and back on the desk of my R&D manager. Ultrasound needles already exist, but the imaging system BONDical is developing is of a quality far higher than anything on the market, and—more importantly—designed to be used by specially trained GPs. Imagine walking into your local surgery worrying over a breast lump, and having peace of mind—or a treatment plan—within an hour. This is going to change the world. The headlines have scrolled through my mind for the last ten years. *Experts predict the BONDical smart needle will save a million lives by 2120 ... Ultrasound, ultrasmart: BONDical's CEO is more than a pretty face ... Elise Bond sells BONDical for an undisclosed sum one source called 'mindblowing.'*

And then, before I can stop it: *Teenager injured after head of medical research organization plied her with alcohol.*

I run my fingers through my hair. *For fuck's sake, Elise, get a grip.*

But it's no good. All I can think about is BONDical's reputation. *My* reputation. However good our products, what hospital trust will touch us if I'm dragged over the coals?

I take a beta-blocker and call Nick. We're good at snapping each other out of a funk—it's one of the reasons we work so well together. That, and the fact we're both so driven. It's six a.m. in Kansas City, and when Nick answers the phone his voice is thick with sleep.

'Everything okay?'

I tell him about Bronnie's visit. The graffiti, the bullying, the veiled threat about my casual approach to drinking.

'It's only cider—don't sweat it.' In the background, there's a muffled sound. Someone turning over in bed, perhaps, or reaching for a glass of water. I close my eyes and hold the phone a little farther from my ear.

You don't *decide* to have an open marriage. At least, we didn't. Rather, it was something that evolved when it became clear that—while Nick and I loved each other—we were too independent, too selfish, to be monogamous. So we put in some rules. Only while out of town, never on home turf. Only one-night-stands—more than once becomes an affair. No photos, no personal details, no follow-ups.

I have another rule, too. I switch off my phone if I'm with someone else. Nick, on the other hand ... There's a soft cough in the background and I hear the bed creak as Nick gets up and walks across his hotel room. A slight echo to his words tells me he's moved to the bathroom.

'All kids get bullied a bit. Christ, when I was at boarding school it was all floggings and buggery, and we still turned out all right. In fact, two of the boys from my house are MPs now.'

'She implied I was a crap parent.'

'You're different to her, that's all. We've never babied Sadie, and as a result she's more mature than her peers—that's their problem, not ours. Jesus, she's been having wine with dinner since she was what—fourteen?'

'Fifteen,' I say, because fourteen suddenly feels so young, and I'm wondering what we were thinking, giving her alcohol at all. I'm wondering if we really have done this so right.

'If you ban kids from something they treat it like forbidden fruit,' Nick says. 'Then, come eighteen, they go nuts. Bel'll be a crack whore by her nineteenth birthday, you'll see.'

I laugh, which is what he intended, and the ball of anxiety in my chest eases a little. 'Thank you.'

'No worries. I'll call you later. Love you.'

'Love you, too.'

He hangs up, and I press the phone against my lips, not

thinking about Nick padding back to bed, not thinking about the warm body pressed against his, not thinking about who she is, and what she does to him. I let the phone fall onto the desk and stand up, shutting my laptop. No point in trying to work when I can't concentrate.

I wander aimlessly around the house, trying to find something to do. Yuliya has left supper in the fridge for tonight, and a bowl of crudités for Sadie to snack on, even though she'll fill up on McDonald's in town today. The laundry is ironed and put away. In the sitting room, every cushion is plumped, every strand of fringe on the rug smoothed out. The magazines, all aspirational glossies, are fanned out on the glass coffee table. I think about picking one to read in the garden, but there's something untouchable about them, so instead I put on my trainers and go for a run. I think about what Bronnie said, about my not talking to Sadie—not asking her about what's going on at school. I think about the conversations I've had with Sadie, about grades and parts and auditions, and much as I hate to admit it, I start to think that Bronnie has a point. When did I last talk to my daughter about her friends? About growing up? About *feelings*? I'm ashamed to admit that I honestly don't know.

Sadie doesn't come back from town till late, and when she does she brings a friend and they squirrel themselves away in her room, venturing out only for snacks. The second time I hear them, I leave my office to make myself a coffee I don't want, feeling a sudden urge to have some kind of interaction with my daughter. Sadie stands in front of the open fridge; her friend—a petite brunette I recognize but cannot name— shifts awkwardly by her side, as though they've been caught out.

'Having fun?'

Sadie makes a vague sound of agreement.

'Yes, thank you,' the friend says. Amina? Adriana? Something beginning with *A*, I'm sure of it. Sadie closes the fridge. Her arms are piled with snacks. Plastic-wrapped pots of stuffed olives from M&S, mini chorizo bites, parma ham, cheese.

'Tapas?' I say brightly. I imagine Bel having a friend over; imagine Bronnie calling the pair of them down to supper. *Tea*, she'd call it. Homemade soup, perhaps, or thick-cut chips she spent all afternoon peeling. I feel again that stab of inferiority, and remind myself I've spent the best part of *my* afternoon working on research that will save lives.

'Is that okay?'

'Of course, darling! Are you watching a film?' I feel as though I'm reading a script, playing a part I didn't cast for.

'*Hostel*,' the friend says, with a gleeful expression. 'It's really scary.'

'Isn't that an eighteen?' I trawl the recesses of my mind and come up with a series of snapshots involving torture. 'Are you sure that's appropriate?' I glance at the friend. 'Maybe A—' Dammit, what *is* her name? 'Your friend's parents might not approve.'

Sadie rolls her eyes. '*Alyssa*'s parents'—the emphasis is for my benefit—'are totally cool.'

I give them both a hundred-watt smile. Far be it from me to be the uncool mother. Only just as they're leaving, I spot the cans of cider in Sadie's laden arms.

*You plied them with* alcohol! . . .

'No cider.' I snatch it so abruptly, so clumsily, that half of what Sadie's holding falls onto the floor.

'What? But you always—'

'No underage drinking.' My voice is shrill, like Bronnie's was this morning. I'm reading the script again, channeling someone I'm not. Someone afraid.

83

*Teenager injured after head of medical research organization plied her with alcohol.*

Sadie stares at me for a moment, her face a mix of confusion and embarrassment. She stoops and picks up the snacks. 'Come on,' she says to Alyssa. 'Sorry about her,' I hear, as they reach the stairs. 'She's not usually that mad.'

I go back to my office. Tell myself I'll speak to her tomorrow; take her out for lunch, maybe. We can have a girls' day, before Nick gets back on Monday. But late Saturday night I find an inconsistency in the R&D report, and I spend Sunday figuring it out.

'What have you got on today?' I say on Monday morning. I don't usually eat breakfast, but I got up especially to get croissants from the bakery on the corner. Sadie dips hers in milky coffee, and I pick at the flaky pastry on mine.

'School?' she says with a question mark that might as well be a 'duh!'

'Voice coaching? Choreography?' I rack my brains to think of the subjects listed in the glossy brochure I last saw two years ago, when Sadie announced she wanted to leave academic studies behind and pursue a career in musical theater.

'What about your A-levels? Don't you want to go to university?' I was incredulous. I blame *Britain's Got Talent*, making every kid think they can be the next Ed Sheeran. 'Your maths teacher thinks you're Oxbridge material.'

Sadie wouldn't be swayed, not even when I gently pointed out that *I just don't think you're good enough, darling . . .*

'We're working on the showcase,' Sadie says now. 'It'll be the auditions for the end-of-year musical, and Adam's invited top talent scouts—everyone's bricking it. Parents are invited. You will come, won't you?'

'If I can,' I say, as I always do. After all, it's impossible to

84

*commit*, isn't it? How can I know what might come up in the meantime?

'The new girl's got Ruby twitching.' Sadie takes another bite of coffee-soaked croissant and carries on talking. 'It's only ever been her and Jess up for the leads, but now Imogen's here and Adam bangs on about her like she's Liza Minnelli—Ruby hates it.' She looks at the clock. 'Shit, I'm late.'

*Ruby hates it* . . . Enough to push the competition down the stairs?

'I'll drive you,' I say suddenly.

Sadie looks at me in surprise. 'Shouldn't you be going to work?'

'So I'll be late.' I pick up my car keys, ignoring my daughter's open mouth. It's not as though I *never* take her to school, for heaven's sake. There was that time she had to take her cello, and the Tubes were on strike and . . . actually, did I get her an Uber? Well, anyway, I've definitely done it.

As soon as Sadie disappears through the Orla Flynn Academy doors, I get out of the car and make for the headmaster's office. If Ruby pushed Imogen down my stairs, then Imogen didn't fall. And if she didn't fall, no one will say it was because she was drunk, and if they don't say she was drunk, they can't point the finger at me, and if they don't—

'Mrs. Bond, come through.' Adam Racki interrupts my thoughts, coming out of his office to the room where his secretary works, and where I am perched on a chair that has seen better days. In fact, now that I think about it, the whole academy has seen better days. The new roof Bronnie keeps banging on about is long overdue, and although the auditorium and dance studios are state of the art, backstage is shabby and old-fashioned. 'What can I do for you?'

'I'd like you to expel Ruby Donovan.' No point in beating about the bush.

'That seems a little extreme.' Adam rests his elbows on the arms of his chair and steeples long, thin fingers. His desk is in chaos, half-drunk coffee cups hiding between precarious piles of scripts. A dozen Post-it notes of varying colors decorate his desk phone with reminders to CALL THE OLD VIC and SUBMIT GRANT APP. A heart-shaped sticky note with GRACE2504 curls at the edges, and the handset itself bears a lurid green note wondering if there might be a CHEAPER QUOTE FOR ROOF? Adam Racki has clearly never heard of Marie Kondo.

'So is pushing another girl down the stairs,' I say, refocusing on the matter at hand.

Adam closes his eyes for a moment, as though he's grounding himself. As though this isn't the first conversation he's had about Imogen Curwood. 'I've spoken to the girls about what happened at your house.' Am I imagining the extra emphasis at the end of that sentence? Or has Bronnie been filling Adam's head with notions of my negligence? 'And Imogen is quite clear that she simply tripped. No one was anywhere near her at the time.'

'She told Bronnie Richardson that Ruby pushed her.'

'"Upon my soul, a lie, a wicked lie,"' Adam says, half under his breath. He smiles, and gives a little nod, like he's taking a curtain. '*Othello*.' He holds up both hands, palms uppermost, like he's asking for divine inspiration. Or giving it, which is perhaps more his style. 'Who knows what goes on in a teenage girl's mind?'

I make speech marks in the air. '"The price of admission to being in the room with me is I get to tell you you're full of shit if you're full of shit."'

Adam looks uncertain. '*Blood Brothers*?'

'Steve Jobs. Now look here, Adam, we all know what a bitch Ruby Donovan can be—to be quite honest, I wouldn't put it past her to have pushed Imogen. Expel Ruby, and you cut off the problem at the source.'

'Believe me, I was most insistent Imogen tell me the truth, and given the tears—trust me, it wasn't a comfortable conversation—I'm confident I got it. No one pushed Imogen Curwood. Least of all Ruby.'

'Ruby Donovan is a bully.' I have no intention of letting her off the hook that easily. 'She made Jess's life a misery last year—'

'That was all sorted out long before the summer,' Adam interrupts.

'Except that it clearly hasn't been, because poor Jess had that terribly distressing music box in her locker.' I accept I'm being a little disingenuous. *Poor* Jess is more than capable of holding her own—like mother, like daughter—and the music box was a joke at best, ghoulish at worst.

'There's no evidence that Ruby planted the music box.' Adam sits heavily in his chair, meaning I have to sit too. 'I don't know if Sadie mentioned it, but Ruby was the subject of an unpleasant piece of graffiti on school property last week.'

I shrug. 'So someone's giving her a taste of her own medicine—or trying to throw us off the scent. Either way, remove Ruby Donovan, and you remove the problem from school.' *And from me*, I add silently.

'And if it was Jess who did the graffiti?'

I let out a sharp *tsk* of annoyance. Music boxes, graffiti . . . it's all so petty. All I'm interested in is putting the blame firmly on those responsible, so that no one casts aspersions on an innocent parent who *in good faith* let five *almost legal* teenagers have *a few cans* of *very low-alcohol* cider. 'Expel her too, then,' I tell him, exasperated. Why does everything have to be so complicated?

There's a beat. Adam leans forward. 'Perhaps I should expel everyone?'

I narrow my eyes. 'Is that supposed to be funny?'

'Not remotely, Mrs. Bond.' Adam holds my gaze. 'I can assure you—this is no laughing matter.'

I don't make it into the office till ten thirty, and I leave again at four.

'Is everything all right, Elise?' My PA, a bright Swedish girl studying for a PhD in the evenings, is used to my arriving at eight and leaving twelve hours later. She never leaves before me, and I wonder now what time she'll go home today.

'I thought I'd pick my daughter up from school for a change.'

'Oh! I didn't know you had children.'

Maja has worked at BONDical for the best part of a year. Something twists inside me, and as I drive back to OFA I'm not thinking about Imogen Curwood or Ruby Donovan or the possibility of my reputation being tarnished by underage drinking accusations. I'm thinking about Sadie, and me and Nick, and whether our insistence on raising an independent, free-thinking child might not have gone as well as we thought.

'What are you doing here?' Outside OFA, Sadie leans through the open window of the Merc and eyes me suspiciously.

'I thought it would be nice to pick you up.'

'You dropped me off.' She slides into the passenger seat and waves goodbye to Ruby, Jess, and Bel, who walked out of school with her. She spins round to face me, her eyes wide. 'God, Elise, you haven't—you haven't been *sacked*, have you?'

'Sadie, it's my company. I *am* BONDical.'

She relaxes, but as I pull into traffic, I see her tense again. This time she's less sure of herself, less willing to hear the answer. 'Are you and Dad getting divorced?'

*Dad.* Sadie calling us *Mum* and *Dad* is a surefire sign she's not happy.

'No!' I reach out a hand to find hers, my eyes flicking

between the road and my daughter. 'Sweetheart, no. It's nothing like that. I just . . .' I trail off, unable to put into words everything I'm thinking. 'I just thought it would be nice.'

We drive in silence for a while, traffic making the journey longer than Sadie's usual Tube commute would have been.

'So,' I try after a while, 'who did you hang out with today?'

'The usual crowd. Ruby, Bel, Jess.'

'Did you eat lunch together?' Christ, this is boring. Is this really what other mothers do? Do they *really* enjoy it? I channel Bronnie again. 'How are you feeling today?'

Sadie gives me a side-eye. 'You are being *so* weird.'

I abandon my attempts at parenting small talk and get down to business. 'Speaking of weird, what's the latest on Imogen Curwood?' I check my mirrors and change lanes, cutting ahead of a bus hell-bent on overtaking me. *Ha! Beat you.*

'She's still cray cray, if that's what you mean. She lost her shit today because someone moved her stuff and she couldn't find her hairbrush, and Ruby said she'd used it to clean the loo only obviously it was just a joke but you'd never know it because Imogen was like *screaming* at her. It was hilarious.'

The start of a headache nags at my temples. 'Bronnie Richardson thinks Ruby pushed Imogen down the stairs.'

'She wouldn't do that.' Sadie starts to untangle a coil of headphones in her lap. The lights in front of us change to red, and I stop the car and turn to Sadie.

'Tell me honestly, do you think Ruby Donovan is dangerous?'

'She's one of my best friends!'

The two things, I think, are not mutually exclusive. I repeat my question, and this time Sadie sighs. She twists the head-phone cable around her fingers.

'Ruby can be a bit full-on. Bitchy, sometimes. But she's

really nice to me.' Behind us, a car toots impatiently; the light is now green. 'Most of the time,' Sadie adds.

I pull away. *Most of the time.* Okay, so Ruby Donovan is a two-faced bitch. But does that make her dangerous?

'She thinks she's better than the rest of us.'

'And is she?' *Bronnie wouldn't ask that,* I think with a wry smile. Bronnie would jump in with a *She most certainly isn't!* and a *Sweetheart, you're the best in that school and don't let anyone tell you otherwise.* Bless her.

Sadie considers the question. 'She's better than me,' she says slowly, 'but she isn't better than Jess. And even though some people don't rate Bel, I think she's the best in our year.'

'But Ruby still thinks she's the star?'

'She had offers from all the best stage schools in the States before she came to OFA.' She picks at a knot in the headphone cable, and carefully unwinds it. I'm confused. Kendall and Ruby are from California, for heaven's sake! They're a stone's throw from Hollywood! I don't know much about *the industry,* but surely if you want to be an actress, living in America is a pretty good place to start?

'Why would you come to London when you could go to New York?' I ask Sadie. 'Broadway's bigger than the West End, right? Brighter lights, better audiences?'

'Maybe they just liked the Orla Flynn Academy more,' Sadie shrugs. 'Life isn't always about searching for the absolute *best* of everything, you know. Sometimes people just want to be happy.'

*Life isn't about searching for the best?* If I hadn't been there at the Portland Hospital when Sadie was born, I might question whether she was even my daughter. I turn to look at her, but she's staring out the window, the headphones finally untangled, and her earbuds in. So much for mother-daughter time.

By the time we're home, the germ of a doubt that started

in the car has grown to fully-fledged suspicion. There's something not quite right about Ruby Donovan's story. I send a text to Kendall.

*Just between the two of us, all this business has made me wonder if OFA is really such a great school. Thinking of looking elsewhere for Sadie—any schools in the States you'd recommend?*

Bait laid, line cast. And now I wait.

It doesn't take long.

I spend the evening in my office, catching up on all the work I missed today, and wondering how on earth anyone is able to work part-time. Sadie and I cross paths briefly in the kitchen—her dropping off an empty plate of food prepared by Yuliya, me picking up a full one—but otherwise I'm alone. I'm eating quinoa one-handed when my mobile buzzes. I smile as I see the opening words; I knew Kendall wouldn't be able to resist the chance to show off . . .

*Ruby had offers from all the top schools in America, but we turned them down for OFA—I hope we made the right decision! Auditions back home are fiercely competitive, so Sadie might feel more comfortable in the UK. xxx*

I register the burn. I might be pragmatic about Sadie's lack of potential in theater, but that doesn't mean I want other people pointing it out.

The apple doesn't fall far from the tree, does it? I wonder how much of Kendall's passive-aggressive bitchiness Ruby has inherited, and whether Sadie and the other girls cope with it as well as they seem to.

I read the text again, and smell bullshit so strongly there could be a herd of cows in my kitchen. *You're a liar, Kendall Donovan*, I think. *I just don't know what you're lying about . . .*

Two hours later I'm still at my desk, staring at my screen. Another evening, another spreadsheet . . . Only *this* spreadsheet isn't filled with year-end profits or with margins and predicted buy-ins. *This* spreadsheet is a comprehensive list of stage schools in the US, complete with addresses, phone numbers, and the last recorded principal. At the top of the final column, a question: *Did Ruby Donovan audition for a place at your academy?*

I get lucky with my first call: a sloppy assistant who doesn't think, or doesn't care, about data protection.

'Let me just . . .' There's a tapping of keys. 'Nope, no one of that name recorded.'

I type the letter N into the last column of the first line, then pick up the phone again.

'I'm sorry, we don't keep records of auditions.'

'I can't release that information, ma'am.'

'Can I ask why you want to know?'

I hang up. This isn't going to work. For every school secretary happy to check their records for a Ruby Donovan, there are six more who won't—or can't—tell me if they've met her.

'What school did you audition for, Ruby?' I say out loud. I sit up, tutting at my ineptitude. I'm looking at this the wrong way round: not what school did she audition *for*, but which school did she audition *from*? If what Ruby did was bad enough to get her blackballed, someone at her old school will know about it.

I drum my fingers on the desk for a second, then bring up the website for the Orla Flynn Academy.

I never planned to go into medical research. I didn't go to medical school, or have designs on being a doctor. It was the technology I loved. I built my first computer back when they were the size of fridges, and had an email address when they were all strings of numbers. I grew up on forums, even met Nick on a Yahoo chat thread. People are unreliable, inconsistent; you know where you are with computers.

I scan the screen, but there's no login area, no *staff only* button. Deftly, I move the cursor to end of the URL and type */admin*.

*Username:* _____

*Password:* _____

I type in *adamracki@ofa.co.uk*, then tab to the password field. Birthdays. It's always birthdays, isn't it? I search my WhatsApp messages for the thread Bronnie started a few months ago. *A certain headmaster is going to be the big FIVE OH soon—I've started a collection so we can show our appreciation of everything he does.* I grudgingly handed over a tenner and signed the card Bronnie had made, using old photos of Adam in his acting heyday.

*Last chance!* the message read, further down the thread. *The big day is tomorrow!*

Perfect. I type *140569* into the password field.

*Password not recognised.*

Crap. I try *14051969* but get the same result.

Does Adam have any pets, I wonder? Bronnie would know. But just as I'm wondering how I can subtly text Bronnie to find out, I remember the heart-shaped Post-it note. *GRACE2504.*

*Welcome back, Adam Racki,* flashes my screen. I take a triumphant swig of wine. Who needs hackers when people are still stupid enough to write down their passwords? I hum happily to myself as I find my way through the system to the student records.

It's disappointing. A list of grades (I note that Jess didn't score the distinction Carolyn made sure we all knew about last year, and file the knowledge away for the future) and a record of fees paid, but little else. No free text reports, or mention of detentions or sanctions, and—most frustratingly—no mention of which school each student attended before arriving at OFA.

I click back to the list of students and scan the page, hoping for inspiration. Ruby, Jess, Sadie, Bel . . .

I stop. Read the list again.

Where is Imogen?

I read the list three times. It changes nothing. Imogen Curwood isn't there. She doesn't exist. I shiver, remembering the way she appeared so suddenly behind me in the bathroom. *Like a ghost*, I think before I can stop myself. *A ghost student.*

'That's enough,' I say out loud. I have work to do. There must be another way to find out where Ruby went to school. I shut down the school website, resisting the temptation to change Sadie's grades, and flex my fingers at the keyboard. *Ruby Donovan: Who are you* really?

The first few Google search pages all relate to the Orla Flynn Academy. *Ruby Donovan gave an assured performance as Priscilla . . . Residents of the Memory Lane Retirement Home were treated to Christmas carols sung by students of the Orla Flynn Academy.* I scroll down and down, clicking through the pages, clicking on dead links, on useless links, on links for Ruby Donovans in Ireland, in Canada, on foreign exchange programs in Russia. I find a good, clear photo of Ruby, and drag it to my desktop, then upload it to Google for a reverse image search. I search and I search and I search . . .

I don't even bother looking for Ruby on Facebook. She might have a profile, but she certainly won't use it, and if she's on Twitter, it'll be to retweet pithy observations about Jeremy Corbyn and to fangirl Ruthie Henshall. No, I know where today's kids hang out. If Ruby's anywhere—if she's *been* anywhere—it'll be Tumblr.

It wasn't even called 'blogging' when I was doing it. They were just diary entries, on a clunky platform that later morphed into LiveJournal, with comments from other people geeky enough to know how it worked. In today's high-tech society, the world and his wife have blogs, and everyone's grandma's on Twitter. I keep my life to myself nowadays, but that doesn't mean I'm not *au fait* with what platforms are hot.

It takes me half an hour.

There, buried in a page of one-word comments—*Sick!, Lol, FML*—is Ruby Donovan. *Cool,* her comment reads. Such a wordsmith . . .

The post prompting all these erudite comments is a photograph of a gymnasium, benches lining one long side. In the center, on a floor covered with blue crash mats, is a group of ponytailed girls in red-and-white cheerleader outfits. Eight of them lie on their stomachs, beaming at the camera, while another eight stand in a circle behind them, looking up at their final number, who is flying high above them, legs scissored either side like they've been dislocated. The photo is a riot of pompoms and shiny white teeth.

*Cool.*

Clicking on Ruby's name doesn't give me much. She has a Tumblr account, but doesn't post. I go back to the cheerleading photo and scan the girls' costumes, but there's no school logo, no team name . . . *They should really sort out their branding*, I think idly, and I'm conscious that I'm wasting time now, that all I've found is a photo of a cheerleading team—there's nothing to suggest that Ruby has any connection to them, beyond finding the photo online.

But wait . . .

There's a woman in a fire service uniform. She's sitting on the benches—clearly spectating, not on duty—and I imagine her leaving work early to watch her daughter perform. I wonder if any of *her* colleagues said, *I didn't know you had children.* I look at her for a moment, at her face shining with pride, then I snap myself out of it. I zoom in on the picture. Her badge says *LA City Fire Department.* Los Angeles. This is Ruby's old school, I just know it.

There are signs above the benches—support and sponsorship from businesses. We do the same from time to time at BONDical, if the PR opportunities are good, or the cause convincing. I scan them for something local. Not a chain, nothing generic . . .

I find it.

The Draycott. *Relaxed dining in Pacific Palisades*.

I hit Google again—*Schools in Pacific Palisades*—then search *Ruby Donovan Palisades High*, when I get a result.

And there she is: Ruby Donovan, Palisades High School, 2016. Bingo. I pick up the phone. I've been doing my research back to front. Why call a hundred possible outcomes, when you can call the control? Hear it straight from the horse's mouth.

'Oh hello, may I speak with the school counselor please?' My accent, already polished, morphs to somewhere between Emma Watson and the Queen.

'Please hold.'

I'm through. 'I'm calling from the Orla Flynn Academy in London—I'm head of student care here.' *Nice touch, Elise,* I think. Maybe I should be the one on stage . . . 'I'm concerned about one of our pupils and I wondered if, as her former counselor, you might be able to give me some guidance.'

'I'll certainly try!' The counselor is warm and reassuring.

'Her name is Ruby Donovan.' I hear a sharp intake of breath. 'You remember her?'

'Of course. She . . . I . . .' The woman stops, but I don't speak. Leave an uncomfortable silence, and someone will fill it. They always do. 'I guess I shouldn't be surprised you're having problems,' she says eventually, but her voice is lower, quieter, like she's frightened of being overheard.

'She's an excellent actress,' I say, 'but her behavior is a little . . . erratic.'

The counselor gives a humorless laugh. 'That's one way of putting it. To be frank, I'm astounded you guys took her.'

My pulse picks up. I see Nick's number flash up on my mobile and I reach out and cancel the call. This is too important. 'Ah yes, she had some problems with you, didn't she?' I try to keep it casual, but I can feel the tension crackle down the line, and when the counselor speaks again, she's cautious. She knows I'm fishing.

'Perhaps if you email through a request, I can speak to the principal and—'

'Or you could just tell me—'

'I have to go now.'

'Please!'

'Look.' There's a pause, and I know she's wrestling with her conscience. 'I'm not putting my job on the line for Ruby Donovan. You want information, you'll have to go through the proper channels. All I'm saying is I'm surprised you took her. No one in America would touch her after what she did.'

There's a click, and the line goes dead. I pick up my mobile and find Kendall's text again. *Ruby had offers from all the top schools in America, but we turned them all down for OFA.*

Kendall Donovan is a liar.

'What do you think she did?' Nick got back an hour ago, with a Chinese takeaway. We've both been so busy it's been ages since we've spent an evening together, so now we're in the living room, picking at leftover spring rolls we're too stuffed to eat, and watching a film we've wanted to see ever since it came out.

'I can't think what could be so bad she'd be blackballed from an entire country.' I'm catching up on emails on my phone, and I double-check what I've written before pressing send.

'Gossip travels fast in a closed industry.' Nick looks up from the report he's reading. 'I'd imagine the networks in theater are pretty tight. Maybe she stole something. We should ask Yuliya to keep an eye on her, next time she comes over.'

I picture Ruby. A bit bitchy, sure. A bit too full of herself. But also funny and sparky, and a good friend to Sadie ... I'm struggling to reconcile the two halves of the same girl. On the TV screen, Ethan Hawke delivers a sermon to a wary congregation, and I realize I have absolutely no idea what's going on.

'When's your San Fran trip?' Nick says. 'I can't find it in the diary.' He's looking at his phone, and on a reflex I do the same, pulling up the family Google calendar.

'Wednesday.' It's there, he just hasn't looked properly. 'We should find a date for Rupert and Jolie to come over—they had us for supper at New Year, do you remember?' We scroll through the calendar on our respective phones, and eventually find a Saturday in March next year. 'I'll ping them an email—put a placeholder in for now.'

Diaries sorted, we watch the rest of the film, and I finish my emails and clear away the Chinese. I go to bed with a promise from Nick that he'll be up shortly, and I give him the sort of lingering kiss that carries an invitation for more. An hour later he still isn't up, and as I'm drifting off to sleep I wonder if it would be too much to schedule *that* into the Google calendar as well.

I spend two nights in San Francisco and two in Silicon Valley, speaking to investors half my age taking home twice my salary. As I pick up my phone to check in for my flight home, I have an idea.

I couldn't.

Could I?

I email Maja. *Change my flight and book me a hire car—I need to extend my trip.* She replies within minutes. *No problem. Where are you going?*

I smile. *Pacific Palisades*, I write.

It's time to find out what Ruby Donovan did.

Kendall's rented apartment in London is nice, but this is something else. House envy isn't something I experience very often, but as I pull up in front of her Californian home I feel a twinge of jealousy. It's still twenty degrees here, I remind myself, compared to the rainy twelve back home: Everything looks better in the sunshine.

The house is set back from the road, behind a curved drive with electric gates. The drive slopes upward, with the house at the top, so that although the building is only three stories it towers over me. There are balconies on the top two floors. What garden I can see isn't big, but it's immaculately maintained.

It wasn't hard to find the address.

'Let me guess—you've written a blockbuster,' the man in the store said, when I told him I was looking for Greg Donovan, the TV network vice president. He leaned forward conspiratorially. 'He gets a lot of those.'

'Do you know where he lives?'

'Do you know, I think it's slipped my mind . . .'

I slip a folded twenty in his top pocket, and he grins.

'Well, look at that—I've just remembered it.'

He writes down the address and waves me off with a cheery 'Good luck, Spielberg!'

I press the buzzer. Behind the gates, a black Mercedes Cabriolet sits in front of a triple garage. I wonder if Kendall's car is inside; I wonder what she drives, when she isn't being too freaked out by roundabouts to rely on cabs.

'Hello?'

I feel a frisson of nerves. I pretend I'm here to see a client, to broker a deal. I pretend this is business. 'Hi, my name's Elise Bond—I'm a friend of Kendall's from London.' There's a pause, and I hold my breath. But then the electric gates roll silently to one side, and I'm walking up the drive, and I think I better make up a plan—fast.

The front door opens before I get to it, and a man with damp tousled hair leans in the doorway. He's late forties, tall and well built, with a well-practiced smile and perfect teeth. He's barefoot, with sweatpants rolled up at the ankle, and a dark gray T-shirt that clings to a well-formed chest. *Well hello, Greg . . .*

'I hope you don't mind my dropping in.' I take the lead, offering my hand and shaking firmly. 'I had a meeting in Santa Monica, and I suddenly thought, doesn't Kendall come from round here, and . . .' I hold out both hands. *Ta da!* 'We mums are all such good friends back home, and I thought, poor Greg, all on his own here . . .' I pout. Yes, really. Who knew I had it in me? Turns out I'm quite the actress.

'Well, it's good to meet you! Come on in!' If Greg's enthusiasm isn't genuine, it's impossible to tell, and within seconds I'm sitting on a vast U-shaped sofa, upholstered in soft blue velvet. The living room is on the first floor, at the back of the house, with double doors on the balcony thrown open to make the most of the view. The walls are painted the exact color of the ocean, and I grudgingly admit that Kendall has great taste. Or perhaps her designer does. One wall is lined with bookshelves, and I tilt my head to make out some of the titles. *Living Your Best Life. How to Talk to Your Kids So They Talk Back. What You Really Want in Bed—And How to Ask for It.* I stifle a snort.

'Coffee? Or something stronger?' Greg gestures to the coffee table—a slab of rock that looks like it's been hewn from the shoreline—where an open bottle stands next to a half glass of wine. Traces of fine white powder linger in the texture of the table; a solitary credit card giving the game away.

*While the cat's away, eh, Greg?* I like him already. 'Maybe just a small one.'

He brings me a glass and we toast *to the kids*, and make small talk about the weather here and in London, and the exorbitant fees we pay so that our children can fulfill their dreams of being on stage.

'It's all Ruby ever wanted to do,' Greg says. 'When she was little she'd put on shows for us all the time. I even took her to the studios once, and got the guys to do the lights, camera, action—you know, the full nine yards.'

Well, that explains Ruby's sense of entitlement . . .

'Sadie was the same. She was so good academically, but she lived for Saturdays, when she had drama school. She just used to . . . light up.' The memory makes me smile. Sadie would come back fizzing with excitement, showing off new dance steps and racing upstairs to learn her lines.

'She's competent,' I said to Nick once, 'but she's not gifted—not like she is in maths.'

'But she's happy.' He's soft, that's Nick's problem. Indulgent of anything his baby wants to do.

'You must miss them both,' I say to Greg now.

'They came back for the summer, but Kendall wants to stay put for the rest of the year—she says there'll be auditions, and . . .' He reaches for the bottle and I let him top up my wine, not wanting to interrupt the flow. I can always get a cab back to the hotel Maja's booked for me in Santa Monica. 'I guess it'll be turkey for one this Thanksgiving!' He laughs, but it's short-lived, and he stares into his wine glass.

I go in for the kill. 'It must be tough, especially after all that business at Palisades High.'

Greg looks up sharply, and I rearrange my features into something I hope approximates *supportive and sympathetic*.

'You know about that?'

I make a noncommittal sound that could just as easily mean *Yes, your wife told me* as *Yes, I stalked your daughter online and impersonated a teacher to extract information from her school.*

Greg gives a deep, shuddering sigh. 'It was awful.' I can hear the blood singing in my ears. *This is it. He's going to tell me.* I edge a little closer to him on the sofa, my face still oozing sympathy. He's wearing aftershave—something musky and woody—and this time the shiver that runs up my spine has nothing to do with nerves. Greg Donovan is a very attractive man.

'It put a strain on us all,' Greg's saying. 'Me and Kendall, Kendall and Ruby, Ruby and me . . . none of us quite knew how to deal with it. Kendall wanted us to have therapy, but—' He breaks off with a bark of laughter. 'How do you talk to a therapist about something like that?'

'Absolutely,' I say soothingly. *Get to the point, Greg.* I pour us both more wine, desperately trying to think of something I could say to prompt a more useful explanation. I think of Nick's guess that Ruby might have stolen something. 'Were the police involved?' It's a bold question, but it pays off.

'They were here before the paramedics.' He stares out at the ocean, reliving a scene I still can't see for myself. *Paramedics? What the hell did Ruby do?* 'There was an investigation, of course—Vee's parents saw to that—but ultimately Ruby was cleared.' *Vee? Who's Vee? Another girl, presumably—a friend of Ruby's?*

'You poor things, it must have been dreadful.' I slide along the sofa again, so close to Greg I can feel the warmth of his thigh against mine. He barely registers me.

'It's a relief to talk about it, to be honest. For nearly two years it's been this terrible shadow hanging over us. Kendall went to pieces, and I wasn't much better.' He looks at me. 'Pathetic, huh?'

'Anyone would have been the same,' I soothe. I try another tack. 'Vee's parents must have been beside themselves.'

'They were distraught,' Greg says. 'She was their only child.'

*Was.*

I only just stop the gasp that rushes up from inside me. *Was.* Vee—whoever she was—is *dead*.

'We'd had problems for years—called into the principal's office to sort out whatever spat the girls were having that week.' He pauses. 'Ruby bullied Vee. That's the ugly truth. It hurt to admit it then, and it hurts now.'

I have uncovered Kendall's lies! I am triumphant! I am Sherlock Holmes, Columbo, Miss Marple! My detective powers know no bounds! I drain my wine in celebration, and put a hand on Greg's knee in commiseration. *What else can I persuade you to tell me, Greg Donovan?*

'You're so brave to say it. So many parents are blind to their children's faults.'

'It nearly broke our marriage.'

'How awful.' My voice has become breathy, reassuring. I think about Kendall and Ruby, keeping this gargantuan secret, lying to us all for more than a year.

'Ruby's my daughter, I love her, but I look at her and I think: Maybe she did do it . . . of course Kendall won't entertain the idea that Ruby pushed Vee deliberately—'

'Pushed her?' I interrupt before I remember that I'm supposed to know what's happened, but we're a bottle of wine down, and Greg's too wrapped up in memories to notice the slip.

'Down the stairs.'

This time I can't stop the 'Oh!' that escapes through rounded lips before I clap a hand over my mouth. Ruby Donovan pushed a girl down the stairs.

*Just like she did with Imogen Curwood.*

103

I need to know *everything*, and there's only one way I'm going to get it.

I slide my mobile out of my pocket and look at the missed calls on the screen. Then I hold my finger firmly over the power button, and turn it off.

Looks like I won't be needing my room in Santa Monica tonight.

***

*You know what actors are?*

*Liars.*

*Think about it: they spend their whole lives pretending to be someone they're not, convincing an audience that what they see is the truth. Hiding behind costumes, wigs, makeup. Changing their voice, stooping, limping, shouting. Lying.*

*But then, everyone tells lies, don't they? Big ones, small ones, white ones . . .* That dress looks great; I won't be late; it's not you, it's me . . . *We lie to protect ourselves, to protect each other, so as not to hurt feelings. We lie without thinking, and we lie for reasons seemingly small and insignificant, when it barely matters if we're unmasked.*

*Only sometimes, it does matter.*

*Sometimes, no one can ever know the truth.*

# 4

# The Performance

*Holly Brown*

# KENDALL

Ruby hasn't left her room all day, not even to eat, and the revue show (which is doubling as an audition) is in less than two hours. I've asked to come in; I've asked her to come out. She won't, and she doesn't want to talk, either. It's been days since the sleepover but she must still be having flashbacks to Imogen at the bottom of the stairs.

I'm sympathetic, of course. If I'd been there, it would have jarred me, too. But Ruby completely lost it, drawing the kind of attention neither of us needs, and while she tells me she didn't say anything to the other girls to give us away, her behavior . . . well, I'm sure they dissected it plenty after she left. That's why I always tell her: Make sure you're around even if you don't want to be; don't give people an opening to talk behind your back. Everyone's so quick to cast aspersions on other people rather than looking at themselves.

I knock on the door again. This time, I don't say anything. She knows. We're going to be late if she doesn't take a shower and start putting on her makeup. Artful concealment of acne takes time, and hers has been horrible over the past weeks, ever since the music box.

As far as I know, no one—not even Carolyn—is blaming Ruby for it anymore. She wouldn't have been invited to the sleepover if they did. I wouldn't have been invited to tea. Carolyn isn't really the apologizing type, but at least now she's down on Imogen instead of Ruby. That's the last I heard, anyway.

I can't afford to get paranoid, and I can't let Ruby, either. That's when impulse takes over. The fact is, the simplest explanation is generally true. In this case, Imogen fell down some stairs because Elise served them alcohol. Elise is always trying to appear perfectly self-confident and immune to other people's opinions, but she wants to be the cool mom. She's never asked what any of us think about her liquoring up the girls. In the same way Carolyn isn't one for apologies, Elise isn't one to ask permission.

I actually think Elise and I have more in common than she'd ever want to admit. I know what it's like to put on a false front when, underneath, you're drowning in insecurity. That was me, pre-cancer. I suspect that Elise brandishes her success, her travel, her open marriage, and her laissez-faire parenting so we'll all envy her, when meanwhile, she doesn't ever feel good enough. Early on, I tried to connect with her about it, but she's not a person who has true connections. Despite this Jess and Ruby situation, Carolyn and I have been real friends before, and someday maybe we will again.

It's apparent that I've been let back into their circle on a provisional basis. There was the tea, but the only text exchange any of them initiated since was when Elise asked about performing arts schools in the States for Sadie, and I had to be honest about how competitive they are because I would hate to see Sadie's heart broken. Sure, I left out some personal details, but she couldn't be bothered to respond. Even Bronnie's texts have been infrequent and perfunctory.

It's like I'm on probation as a friend, which is depressing since I was the one who worked so hard to form the mums group last year. What they're telling me is that I have to keep Ruby in line, somehow. Any more missteps from her, and I'm out, too.

The problem is, Ruby's got an iron will. If she really doesn't want me to know something, there's no way I'm going to get it out of her, and if she means to do something, I can't really stop her. That's why I feel on edge these days, like the rug can be pulled out from under me at any time. The mums group has meant more to me than to any of the others because they all have their husbands, their families. My world in London is small, and I don't want it any smaller.

I'm not only thinking of myself; I'm thinking of Ruby. I imagine that she's on thin ice with the girls. She's been vindicated where the music box is concerned, but that doesn't mean they fully trust her (and I don't imagine that her histrionics and leaving the sleepover early helped with that). I'm not sure I trust her right now either.

Since the music box, it seems like I'm always banging on her closed door—if not literally, then figuratively. In California, we were so close. She left things out, sometimes even big things, but all teenagers do, right? When we talked, I had some influence. Or at least, I had some warning. I knew when things were likely to explode.

Ruby's saved me before, and now I have to save her. That's all there is to it. I have to save her from herself.

Our two-bedroom flat is small, just a thousand square feet, which might not be small by London standards but our house in Pacific Palisades was five times that. It still is. Greg's been living there alone for the past year. He's visited us in London twice during that time and showed no interest at all in meeting Ruby's friends or mine. Best to leave it all behind, and focus on our fresh start.

The other night, when I picked Ruby up in a taxi (I hate driving in London so much I never got a car), tears were streaming down her face. She threw herself in my arms like she was a little girl again, and all she would say is, 'Someone knows.'

Deep down, I'm afraid, too. But I don't want to give in to that. Imogen fell down the stairs, that's all. The girl is strange, all the mums have agreed on that.

I sit down in the living room on the aquamarine couch, determined not to pace. I can't let Ruby's mood infect me. Have to stay positive.

I decorated for maximum serenity, pale rose and lilac now that I don't have to accommodate Greg and bookshelves full of Thich Nhat Hanh and Deepak Chopra and my collection of *O* magazines, along with the latest nonfiction on self-compassion, assertiveness, and parenting. The last book I read said that teenagers have the acceleration system of a Porsche and the brakes of a 1952 Chevy. Basically, it's amazing that any of them ever get out of adolescence alive, but I hope that means that Ruby's difficulties with self-control are developmental, that she can outgrow all this.

We're going to be late. I just need to barge in, that's all. Take charge, in a loving manner.

I stride over to her door, knocking forcefully. 'Ruby, you should probably get in the shower.' There's no answer, though she must have heard me. I repeat myself, louder.

'No.' Her voice is muffled, so it's hard to pick up the emotion attached.

'You don't want to miss the revue.'

'Wrong.' It's not the acoustics, I realize. It's that her voice is devoid of expression, like she's retreated into herself. Given up.

I take a deep breath. 'Open the door, please, honey. We have a little time to talk. Maybe I can help.'

'You can't.'

There it is, that resignation. No one likes to hear their child hopeless, but with Ruby, it feels especially dangerous. I try to turn the knob, but it's locked. That's new, I think. Or maybe I just haven't tried before. 'Let me in, okay?'

Silence.

'Let me in,' I say, more of a command, with love behind it. Tough love, that's what it was called when I was growing up, though my parents didn't have to get tough much. I was too eager to please. Sure, I'd lie to them, but only because I wanted their approval, and sometimes that meant abandoning the truth.

Ruby's different. She'll let me think badly of her; it's other people who matter to her. But the books say that's because she feels safe with me. She knows she's not going to lose my love. It's a privilege when your kids shit all over you. It means you have a strong bond.

Parenting books can be so contradictory, though. Sometimes you're left standing in the hall with no idea what to say or do next. Should I insist she get ready this instant? Insist she talk to me? Let her make her own decision, miss the revue, and deal with the consequences?

I know Ruby. The consequence might be too much for her to handle. She hates to be left out more than anything, and if she doesn't go to the revue she doesn't get to sing, which is part of the audition process, and then she won't be cast in the show.

If she doesn't go tonight, she'll regret it. I know that for certain.

'Whatever you're feeling in this moment,' I say, 'it's not worth missing out on your chance to be in the musical. You've got a real shot at being the lead.'

Nothing.

'I'm just saying that this isn't forever. It's a blip—'

Ruby yanks the door open. I'm startled by her appearance. Her eyes are slits, as if she's been crying all day, and my pep talk has obviously enraged her, because she's yelling. 'Here lies Ruby Donovan! Is that a blip, Mom? Does that sound like a fucking blip to you? Bel's mother didn't think so!' Her chest is heaving.

'What are you talking about?' She hasn't screamed and cursed at me like this since ... And Bronnie's involved somehow?

'It was written on the bench, Mom.'

'You're saying someone wrote "Here lies Ruby Donovan," like on a tombstone?'

'I told you.' She sounds triumphantly hysterical. 'I told you someone knows. They know about our lies, and they want me dead.'

'No, it could mean something else.' But I can't think of another solitary thing.

Imogen at the bottom of the stairs, and now this.

Before I can formulate a proper response, Ruby's slammed the door in my face. I don't blame her. This is partially—mostly?—my fault.

It's a little after three a.m. in California. Well, Greg can catch up on his beauty sleep some other time.

I try his cell first. Then it's the home phone, which never rings, but when it does, it's from the nightstand on what used to be my side of the bed. Impossible for him to sleep through.

In all the time we've been in London, I've never called him in the middle of the night, but I still brace myself for his irritation. He often thinks I'm making too much of the drama between the girls, that I'm getting too involved. 'You and your "mums,"' he once said, with a disdain worthy of Elise. But when he picks up, he sounds flustered instead. 'Kendall? What is it? What's happened?'

'Get the laptop,' I say. 'We should at least look into each other's faces for this.'

'Okay.' He's so pliant. I should call him in the middle of the night more often.

When his bleary-eyed, handsome, wrinkleless (i.e. Botoxed) face appears on my screen, he's visibly nervous. 'Kendall,' he says, his voice suffused with a syrupy love that I haven't heard in I don't know how long. 'It's so good to see you.'

'You, too,' I say quickly. 'Do you know why I'm calling?' I have the sudden thought that his unusual anxiety is because Ruby's already told him, that they're now the ones with a secret and I'm losing control completely.

'No, I have no idea.' But he's not entirely convincing.

'Do you know about the bench?' I demand.

'Bench?' His confusion, however, is persuasive, and his relief is obvious.

'Someone wrote "Here lies Ruby Donovan" on a bench. It's obviously a threat.'

'Or a prank.'

When I don't bite, I can see his wheels turning. He's trying to find the right thing to say, calculating how to best placate and soothe me. Maybe that's what all husbands would do in this situation, but it bothers me. It's just so immediate. Doesn't he have any actual concern for his daughter? Is he so conditioned to assume that I'm being irrational?

For the past year, I've been a single parent. I've kept him abreast of what's happening, but he hasn't been asked to do anything. He and Ruby have their weekly chats, and he and I text most days and talk once a week, on average, and that's it. That's all the effort he has to put into this family.

But he'd say that's my doing. He never wanted us to leave.

Greg's not a bad man. By LA standards, he's actually pretty good. It's just that my standards have changed.

'She doesn't want to go to the revue tonight. She's too upset.' Maybe I should just let her stay home where she'll be safe. But that's like giving in to whoever wrote it, letting them win, and Ruby loses out on what she cares about most. Besides, no one can get to her when she's surrounded by people.

'Tell her she has no choice. It's for her own good.'

Doesn't he know Ruby at all? Ruby always has choices. 'The door is locked.'

'Get a screwdriver and take it off the hinges if you have to. This is why you're in London, right? So she can take advantage of every opportunity. Tell her that if she's not going to do what she needs to do, then she doesn't need to be there.'

'You mean threaten to take her back to LA?' The parenting books say that you should never threaten a punishment that's too painful for you to follow through on. I don't want to go back. I can't.

'Maybe London isn't working out. And then there's you and me and the distance . . .' We never talk about it directly, what the distance is doing to us. Seeing my reaction, he backs away, to a safer subject: 'All this teen drama, and then how you and your friends get involved. I don't think it helps to keep hashing it out. It makes it all seem more important than it is. It makes it real.'

What Ruby said comes back and slaps me in the face: *Bel's mother didn't think it was a blip*. Bronnie was there, but she never told me what happened. She might have assumed Ruby did, but a true friend would ask how Ruby was bearing up, and how I was. I feel a surge of anger. I'd thought we were the closest of all the mums; I'd thought she was a good person, but perhaps in this group, there are no good people.

'I'm sorry,' Greg says. 'I can tell you think I'm overstepping. That's why usually I don't say much.' I hadn't realized that was why; I'd thought it was because our dramas weren't nearly as interesting to him as the ones he produced. 'But I'm not there, so what can I do, really?'

He can be so passive-aggressive. He thought that my whisking Ruby away to London was no good for her and he's not above occasionally sticking a knife in and giving it a little twist.

If I confided just how afraid I actually am, Greg would probably remind me that this is all about teen-girl dramatics, and just look at social media, so many threats, such rare follow-through. And if he said that like a supportive husband who loves me, it might have the desired effect. I'd feel like I had someone to hold me up. A good marriage is scaffolding, or so the books say.

Did we ever have that? It's hard to say. When the cancer hit me, I hate to even admit this, I cried the most about losing my hair, my *look*. I needed Greg to tell me that what made me special and beautiful had nothing to do with my hair. But all he'd done was the equivalent of patting me on the back and saying, 'There, there.'

That's when my heart began to harden toward him. He took me to all my medical appointments and whenever the doctors or nurses were around, he was attentive as could be. He asked all the right questions. He held my hand. But when they left, he dropped it. He checked out and excused himself to make work calls, or if he stayed in the room, he'd scroll around on his phone. He was doing just enough to keep up appearances. And how did I know that? Because I'd lived my entire life that way. It was why we'd gravitated toward one another, and now we can be summed up in four words: I've changed; he hasn't. Or two words: Irreconcilable differences.

I know he loves me, to an extent. I know he didn't want me to die. I also know that it would be easy enough for him to replace me with a younger model—literally, a model who's younger.

I took time off from my job in real estate to focus on my health, and that's when I became addicted to self-help books. There was this whole world of personal reflection and responsibility, an industry full of it, and I'd never even known about it before. I'd never known me.

Once I was in remission, I realized I didn't want to go back to the person I'd been, the one who'd been a natural at tapping into other people's insecurities and activating their desire to buy the house at the very top of their price range, rather than the one they could actually see themselves living in. So I quit. But what do I do next?

It has to be right, because a part of me still can't help caring what other people think. Old habits really do die hard; even cancer can only put them into a coma for a little while, and then they wake up.

It's like how none of the other mums know that I'm dissatisfied with Greg. I want them to believe I have a husband wonderful enough to put me up in a flat in London so Ruby can go to the most prestigious performing arts academy. I let them think that being here is only about Ruby, and while it is, primarily, it's also a reinvention for me, an escape.

Our house in Pacific Palisades was so well appointed and so well kept that it could have been photographed at any time, and I actually used to have architecture and design magazines fanned out on the coffee table, waiting for guests. Here in the London flat, we live in a deliberately different manner. I force myself to toss my jacket over the back of a chair; I don't put every dish immediately in the dishwasher; I let laundry pile up sometimes, just because. It's like training. I'm trying to show Ruby we can live for ourselves and not for company. Ruby wants to be on the stage but the flat shouldn't look staged. Honestly, though, the few times a mum has come by, I've scrubbed the place down and had to fight the urge to fan out magazines.

I try hard not to react too strongly to the goings-on among the girls, but Ruby feels it all so deeply, and people misjudge her so much. All she wants is to be liked, to be valued, and people can turn that into something awful, like she's some kind of villain, when she's just human. She's just a girl. My little girl.

That's when my fear is overtaken by rage. 'They're fucking doing it again!' I say. 'They're ganging up on her!'

'You think it's the whole group?'

'I don't know! But whoever it is, they're not getting away with it.'

Cancer taught me to value the warrior inside of me. She showed up when everything happened with Vee. She's always made Greg a little uneasy, and I see it in his face. He's trying to figure out how to tamp me down.

'You're going to tell me not to worry? It'll all be okay?' I'm taunting him. Daring him.

He averts his eyes. He's never liked a fight, and mostly, I don't either. But sometimes they're necessary.

'I do think it'll be okay,' he says quietly. 'But maybe what's needed is to just come home. Put our family back together.'

Pull Ruby out of school when she's on the verge of getting a lead? That could be just what she—or they—want. 'You don't know what we need.'

He sighs. 'Maybe I don't.'

Neither of us says *I love you*, though it's our customary sign-off, whether we feel it or not. I disconnect.

I see a flash of something in my peripheral vision, and it's Ruby. She's in the doorway of her room. It's not a big flat. What did she hear?

She's still in her grubby T-shirt and shorts. She comes over to me and hugs me from behind. 'I'm going to take my shower now so we won't be late.' I'm grateful for her change of heart but concerned about what she just heard between her dad and me, especially that last part where he talked about moving home. He's mentioned it before, and fortunately, she never heard.

Could it be that what she really wants—what she needs, as Greg said—is for us to go back? That she is behind at least some of what's happened lately within the girls' group, that it's a cry for help or—more characteristically of Ruby—a push?

I force a smile. 'It's going to be a great night.'

She assumes a worried expression. 'You do believe me, don't you?'

'Believe you about what?'

'That someone knows. That someone's after us.'

Us? 'What do you think we should do?' I keep my voice level. *Please, don't say go back to LA. Please, I can't go back to the scene of the crime.*

She shrugs. As in, I'm the parent; I'm the one who's supposed to know what to do.

So she's not trying to force my hand and send us back to Greg. Not consciously, anyway. But Ruby's subconscious is powerful. On sleepless nights, it's occasionally crossed my mind that one of these times, if I'm not her ally, I could be her target.

Her anxiety intensifies, her face naked as a small child's. 'You'll always be with me, right? No matter what?'

As in, no matter what terrible thing she's done now? But I have to tell her the truth: 'Always. No matter what.'

The first person I see in the OFA foyer is Elise. Well, she's not the first, there are some other parents milling around, but she always stands out, with that red hair of hers and her bearing, like she thinks she owns the place. It's a bit of schadenfreude that her daughter is the least talented. It's no accident that I poke at that fact, all straight-faced and innocent, and sometimes it has the intended effect. When she's rankled, she breaks character. She's almost human.

I don't see the other mums. Elise has been chatting with the dance teacher, and when she spots me, she makes a beeline. It's like she's been waiting for me, which is unique in our relationship.

'Are you on your way to the auditorium?' she asks, a stupid question since that's where the revue will be held and it's fifteen minutes till showtime. It was no small feat to get Ruby out of the taxi and backstage where she belongs. 'Let's walk together.'

'Sure.' I try not to give her an odd look as she twines her arm through mine. 'How are you, Elise?'

'Exhausted. Jet-lagged. The usual.' She waves her free hand. 'But I wanted to thank you.'

'For what?'

'For not being territorial about your husband. It was lovely to meet him in LA. Traveling can be lonely, and I so enjoyed getting to have a drink with a new friend.'

We're almost to the auditorium, and I'm reeling from what she's obviously dying to tell me: that she spent time with Greg. A drink. *A new friend.*

'He enjoyed meeting you, too,' I say.

Elise gives me a look like she doesn't quite believe that—doesn't believe I knew? Doesn't believe he enjoyed meeting her?—and then I see that it's more smug than that. The cat that ate the canary. My canary.

Elise loves to flaunt her open marriage so she can prove how unconventional she is compared to the rest of us. Needless to say, Greg and I have no such arrangement. I think of how strangely he behaved on the call earlier, the way he greeted me at first, nervous and too loving. He thought I was waking him up to confront him about Elise.

Of all the people he could have slept with, he had to pick my frenemy?

He wouldn't have gone looking. She picked him so she could humiliate me. That's what she's trying to do right now, and I can't give her the satisfaction.

Still, Greg's sex life is the least of my concerns right now. Elise said they had a drink, and Greg has always been a total lightweight when it comes to holding his alcohol. A loose-lipped lightweight.

Imogen falls; then *Here lies Ruby Donovan*; and finally, Elise and Greg. What did Greg tell Elise? And what did she tell the other women?

Because Elise and I are in the auditorium now, beside the row where someone easily could have saved me a seat, only they didn't. Carolyn is there with her husband, and Elise's husband has a jacket across her seat, and then there's another seat saved by Bronnie's husband, since she's working backstage, and then there are all of Bel's siblings.

'Sorry,' Carolyn says, sans remorse. 'There just wasn't room.'

'Yes,' Elise says, 'we needed all the seats for ours.' As in, they all have people, and I've got no one, especially since Elise helped herself to my husband.

'I like to be in the front row anyway,' I tell them, and I'm sure they don't believe me—they're exchanging glances, but I just need to make my escape. 'I'll see you all later.'

I flee to the front row, thoughts racing. *Someone knows,* Ruby said. *They're after us.*

It sure feels like it right now, like it's not just Ruby. I'm not ancillary, or beside the point. Elise was waiting for me. Targeting me and my marriage. Targeting Ruby and my secrets.

I shouldn't be shocked that Elise would do this. It's not like I ever really believed we were friends. Just friendly. No, cordial. No, not even that, because Elise doesn't traffic in social niceties. This is all my fault, and now Ruby will suffer right along with me. I never should have made those digs about Sadie not being talented. When Elise mentioned her company being in the *Times* or the *Guardian,* when I would play dumb and say, *I haven't seen it, does anyone read newspapers anymore?,* when I tried to puncture her ego, I never thought . . .

I've been so stupid. Someone like Bronnie could get away with that, someone who's truly innocent, but not me. When I poked Elise, I was poking a bear.

Someone knows. But what, exactly, do they know? Even if Elise thought the best way to get information from a man was pillow talk—and I just need to push the image of those two in my bed aside for right now—Greg isn't much of a source. He doesn't know what really happened with Vee.

Though the curtain is down, I can hear the backstage hubbub with the sound checks and vocal warm-up exercises. Jess pushes back the side of the curtain impishly to peek out at the audience, and I can see her, Bel, and Sadie giggling. Ruby's not with them, but Imogen doesn't seem to be either.

Ruby has the kind of clarion voice that cuts through din, and so does Jess. I can make out Jess talking about famous agents and West End producers who they hope will be in the audience, and then the excited laughter of all three girls.

I don't know if Ruby is isolating herself or they're ostracizing her. Has there been a game of telephone with the mums that's trickled down to the girls, and one of them—all of them?—wrote *Here lies Ruby Donovan*?

Whatever the other mums think they know, they're not making it easy for me to find out. When I turn around and try to catch their eyes, they're not having it. They're too busy laughing and talking with each other and their husbands, and I can't help feeling like they're performing their gay old time just like their daughters are backstage, so that Ruby and I can both feel what we're missing.

They're not going to get away with this shit. Not the mums, and not their daughters.

My anger bubbles up, and I marinate in it for a few minutes before walking up the four steps to the stage and through the side of the curtain, just where the three girls were a few minutes before. I survey the backstage. It's the usual: girls powdering themselves at the long vanity, or vying for one of the few full-length mirrors near Bronnie's wardrobe area (where is Bronnie?), chattering in various stages of undress, some more brazen, some more modest, the energy levels high with excitement and anxiety. But I don't see Ruby, and I don't see who I'm looking for.

Then I notice that Jess and Sadie are half-hidden behind the vanity, speaking with intensity. That's not surprising from Jess, who has some of her mother's rectitude and bombast, but Sadie is matching her. I'm glad that I wear flats now instead of heels so I can inch closer. Not too close, the last thing I need is to be branded a creeper, but I can hear snippets. Jess is telling Sadie she needs to 'come clean.'

Sadie's always been the diplomat. She's never been cruel to Ruby that I know of. Well, not to her face.

But I can't linger. I don't belong backstage, and I'm drawing stares from a few other girls nearby. I step away from the vanity and ask another girl if she's seen the headmaster. The girl shakes her head, visibly annoyed. 'He was here,' she says, 'and he needs to get back quick. He better not delay the show.'

Like he's her servant. These kids are so entitled. Is that how Ruby talks, too, when I'm not there to hear her?

I'm thinking where to go next when I see Imogen. She's alone at the barre, stretching out one leg in a languorous, sensual fashion. She gives me a heavy-lidded smile. It's like she's flirting, or like she's drugged, or both.

I smile back, but I'm disconcerted. Some instinct sends me deeper into the backstage bowels, toward the darkness where the rigging and the pulleys are, sets that are only half-painted. That's where I find Mr. Racki.

And Bronnie.

She's up against the wall and his back is to me. He's whispering in her ear. It's not sweet nothings, that's apparent from her pained facial expression. Though they're not touching, the moment has an intimate feel. I'm embarrassed to have come upon them and since they haven't yet seen me, I could just withdraw as if I haven't seen them. But it occurs to me that it's much smarter to let them know I have. I might need an advantage in the conversation that's about to commence with the headmaster, or in the ones that are yet to happen with Bronnie and the mums.

'Mr. Racki,' I say, 'I need a word with you.'

Both are startled, though Mr. Racki spins around and recovers quickly, gracing me with a pleasant expression, no shame in evidence. Bronnie, however, is not quite as practiced in the art of being caught in a seemingly compromised position. She scurries away, avoiding eye contact. It could be because she's guilty; it could be because she thinks I am. Whatever rumor has spread through the mums group must have reached her, too.

Fuck every last one of them.

'What can I do for you, darling?' Mr. Racki asks in a way that's so very him that I think my eyes might have deceived me. Perhaps he and Bronnie had just been talking about costumes or some other school business and wanted to do it in private.

'Maybe we should talk somewhere else. Out of the shadows.' I mean it archly, but he just nods mildly in response.

Could it actually be? The headmaster and *Bronnie*, having an affair?

It's nearly unfathomable. If it is true, though, it means Bronnie isn't who I thought she was. None of us are.

'Follow me, please,' Mr. Racki says, 'and watch your step.' He leads me through a dimly lit labyrinth with wiring and cables along the floor and then we step out into the blinding fluorescence of the hallway. I guess I should have thought of this before, that OFA is a very old building and there could be little-used passages, allowing for unseen ingress and egress. Not a comforting thought, given the perilous situation Ruby and I are in.

Mr. Racki's office is way at the front of the building, so he takes me into an unoccupied rehearsal space instead. It must have been recently vacated by the orchestra, as all the music stands are still set up, some with sheet music splayed open.

'I've been meaning to call,' he says apologetically. 'With the preparation for the revue, time got away from me. The play's the thing, as Hamlet said.'

I get it now, how the quoting infuriates Carolyn. This isn't a play, it's my daughter's life. 'If you'd called, what would you have said?'

'The sleepover wasn't on school property so it's not really my domain, but with the unusual events of late, I'm having unusual conversations. May I ask what Ruby said happened at the sleepover?'

'Imogen fell.'

'I don't want to speak out of turn.' He's obviously uncomfortable and would like to extricate himself from this conversation. Is it because of what I just witnessed between him and Bronnie? Or could they possibly have been talking about Ruby and me, with Bronnie sharing Elise's choice tidbits?

'Imogen fell,' I repeat, though my voice is a little shaky.

'I'm worried about Ruby. There's tension again among the girls. Not as bad as last year, thankfully, but still. "We're through with lies and liars in this house. Lock the door."' I stare at him, perplexed. What lies—and what liar—is he talking about? *Cat on a Hot Tin Roof.*'

'I've got a quote for you: "Here lies Ruby Donovan."' That bench is on school grounds, and he didn't call me to say anything about it. But now he's talking about a sleepover that happened off-campus and distracting me with theatrical allusions. He's doing damage control, that's what this is. Britain is less litigious than the US, but a negligent headmaster can still get in a whole lot of trouble.

I'm not about to let him wriggle out of his responsibility. He needs to protect my daughter. That's what I came to tell him, and he's doing a good job of deflecting. But I'm not going to let him get away with it.

'We've cleaned the bench,' he says, 'and we're looking into who might have done that. In the meantime, perhaps we could schedule another hand-holding vigil.'

I can't believe I'm actually empathizing with Carolyn right now. This is so aggravating. There's a real issue here. 'Whoever wrote that on the bench could be the same person who left the music box. It could be someone engaging in a reign of terror.'

'And I thought I was the one prone to dramatics! Lovey, I assure you, I'm handling this. I just can't handle it right this instant. The revue's going to start late, as it is.'

The hell with the revue. He's not going anywhere. 'You said you meant to call me, and I want to hear what you have to say. What you're going to do to protect Ruby.'

'It's my job to protect all the girls at the Academy.' He hesitates. 'There's been a suggestion that Imogen didn't fall down the stairs. That she was pushed.'

*'Pushed?'* I gape at him. The picture is coming into terrible focus. Ruby was back in with the girls before the sleepover, and she's out again now. Elise visited Greg. *Here lies Ruby Donovan.* 'Are people saying Ruby did it?'

He doesn't want to answer.

So yes, someone's said it. But if they knew about Vee, couldn't someone else have pushed Imogen to make it look like it was Ruby? To frame her?

His eyes skitter toward the door. 'I'm truly sorry to have upset you. I just thought that you might be able to shed light on what's been happening, and I wanted to make sure Ruby was okay.'

Make sure she's okay. As in, make sure she's not deranged. As in, not placing threatening music boxes in lockers or pushing girls down flights of stairs. Not going back to her old ways. Or finding new ways.

Then it hits me: Elise didn't go to the States until after the sleepover. The only person at Elise's house that night who knew about Vee was Ruby.

All the vigilante mom in me dissipates. I'm thinking of what Ruby whispered to me in the taxi when she'd been too distraught to stay the night: 'Someone knows.' I'd assumed she was talking about the past, but she could have been talking about what she'd just done. She was afraid someone saw her push Imogen down the stairs.

I never asked her directly if she did it. I didn't think I needed to. We were supposed to be aligned, agreed that we never wanted to go back there again. This was our fresh start. This was our bond.

'I really do need to go,' Mr. Racki says. He pauses in the doorway. It must be because I look upset, and despite my earlier irritation with him, I know he's truly a good man, and good men don't like to cause women to be on the verge of tears and then slip away.

Only he's telling me Ruby's not a good girl, and he has no idea what kind of woman I am.

'The show must go on, right?' I say flatly.

I can feel him debating whether to say anything further. It's like his conscience wins out. 'I've known a lot of teenage girls at the Academy, and Ruby is quite complicated.' He sounds sympathetic, like he's trying to let me know that I shouldn't blame myself too much for how she's turned out. 'The most complicated are those whose desires appear the simplest, when they want just one thing.'

'To be the best.'

'To be *loved*. She'll do anything for it.' He sounds sad now, as if he knows her fate already. He's already seen how her story ends in other girls who've passed through the Academy. In that same subdued voice, he says, 'Dashed hopes, and good intentions. "Good, better, best, bested." *Who's Afraid of Virginia Woolf?*' He just can't resist educating me, can he? 'Ruby's lost, and the stage is a terrible place to try to find yourself, because you're always playing someone else.'

There's a knock on the door, and a girl's voice says, 'Headmaster, we need you!'

'I'm so sorry,' he tells me, and I don't know if he's referencing leaving me in this condition, or if he means he's sorry about Ruby—the way she is, how it's all going to turn out.

I basically stagger into a chair. Ruby doesn't feel loved, is that what he's saying? If that's true, then I've failed at the most important task of motherhood. Mr. Racki didn't say he knew for sure that she was guilty, but I got the sense he believes it. That it's the kind of thing a complicated girl like Ruby might do.

What I don't understand is the ambiguity. Did Imogen say she fell, or did she say she was pushed? Was she too frightened of what Ruby would do next to say that she was pushed? Or did another girl claim to be a witness but doesn't want to go on record?

Ruby's not some thug. She doesn't go around threatening and intimidating people. That's not her style at all.

But she can be impulsive. I don't know what Imogen said to Ruby at the sleepover. Maybe she goaded her, and Ruby snapped. I'm sure she would have been sorry afterward. Tormented. That's why she's been acting the way she has. And then Imogen struck back with *Here lies Ruby Donovan*.

Yes, that makes sense.

No, it doesn't. Ruby was trying so hard this year. It was going so well.

If Ruby had pushed Imogen, she would have told me. She knows she can trust me. I wouldn't just turn on her, no matter what she did. We've already proven that to one another.

No matter what. Isn't that what she said earlier tonight? This is all my fault.

I need to get back to the auditorium for the revue. Sick as I feel, I have to be there for Ruby's performance. Otherwise, she could feel even more unloved, and then who knows what she'd be capable of.

No. I know my child.

I remember how when I was ill, she would curl up against my side, thirteen years old going on four. Sometimes I even caught her sucking her thumb. There's no way that was an act, though she is an actress.

I return to my seat in a stupor. I'm not turning around anymore. I don't want to see the other mums who are so sure of themselves, and of their children.

The theater dims, and the house lights go up. The first student begins to sing. It's warbling, really. She's nowhere near Ruby's league, and I shouldn't note that, but it's just automatic. She's the competition. I want Ruby to finally get the lead so she can stop trying to be good enough; she can just know that she is. I've been trying for so long to help her lose out gracefully, and look where we are. So I have to hope for a win. And I have to hope that Mr. Racki is just jaded. He's mistaking Ruby for some other girl.

There's an empty seat next to me, and someone slips into it. I glance over, assuming it'll be a parent, hoping for Bronnie ready to explain, but it's Imogen. She's got flowers woven into her hair, and looks lovely and demure. I think of the vibe she gave off while she was stretching, the seduction in it. It's almost like she's a different person. She whispers so she won't disturb the show. 'You're Ruby's mum, right?'

'I am. And you're Imogen.'

She nods joyfully, and I can't help thinking that she doesn't seem like someone who's recently been thrown down some steps. Plus, she's approaching the mother of the supposed perpetrator. Mr. Racki must have heard wrong, or the girls are playing a prank on him. What was Jess saying to Sadie backstage? They need to come clean. Maybe they need to tell Mr. Racki—and their mums—the truth.

Imogen is giving me the creeps. Her gaze is fixed on me, and her manner too childlike. I'm not buying it. I wish she'd go away so I could think clearly. 'Don't you have to get ready?' I ask. She must be performing tonight.

'I don't like to over-rehearse. I keep it natural, if you know what I mean.'

I want to ask why she sought me out, what happened at the sleepover, what her deal is. But I can't, not here, and there's something about her . . . I wouldn't believe anything that came out of her mouth anyway.

I give her a smile that's meant to say this conversation is over, and then I turn back toward the stage so I can pretend to listen.

But my eye keeps returning to Imogen. The way she's leaning slightly toward me, it's like she's begging me to ask. Here lies Ruby, and here sits Imogen. I lean over to her and whisper, 'Are you enjoying the school so far?'

'Oh, yes! Very much!' she trills. A few parents give her reproving looks. She peeps at me coquettishly, like we're being mischievous together. Then she lowers her voice. 'Everyone's been so welcoming.'

'You mean the gang of four?'

She laughs. 'Is that what they used to call themselves?'

'Sometimes. Not often.'

'Well, I guess it's still a gang of four.' She's watching the performance but I get her meaning: She's replaced Ruby.

'Yes, it still is,' I say tightly. 'Ruby, Jess, Sadie, and Bel.'

She gives me a sidelong glance. 'It's not my fault, you know. I've got no qualms about a gang of five.'

As in, she's not elbowing Ruby out of the way, it's the other girls. But is it all of them, or just one? Jess would be the most likely culprit, a little payback for last year. 'Do you know why Ruby's been left out?' I hate that I'm soliciting her insight into the group, but that's what it's come to. She's seeking me out when no one else seems to want to talk to me.

'I've no idea,' she says airily.

'But you're saying it's not coming from you?'

She gives me an innocent look. 'The other girls are the ones who have a history with Ruby.'

It's true, but I have no reason to trust her. The fact that she's throwing suspicion on the others could make her all the more likely to be guilty. 'Which girl in particular seems to have a problem with Ruby?'

She turns back to the stage, my question hanging in the air.

It's like she's toying with me, and on some level, I welcome it. That's because Imogen being a sociopath is vastly preferable to Ruby being one. Of course, a sociopath-free school would be best for everyone, but you can't always get what you want.

'What really happened at the sleepover, Imogen?'

'Just girl stuff.' I have the distinct impression that she enjoys needling me. I can certainly understand the temptation to throw her down the stairs.

Not that I'm condoning it, if it happened. But it wouldn't have to be Ruby. Imogen seems like the kind of person who enjoys getting under people's skin, and she could have taken aim at any of the girls that night.

Imogen didn't sit next to me by accident. There's something she wants me to know, and it could be that one of the other girls pushed her and it's being pinned on Ruby. Imogen could be Ruby's guardian angel. Stranger things have happened.

I sneak a glance back at Carolyn and Elise. Am I imagining it, or do they not seem to like my talking to Imogen?

'How did you end up at the bottom of the stairs?' I ask. Who knows, Imogen could appreciate directness.

She looks apprehensive for the first time since sitting down, her eyes darting. Who's she looking for? Who's she afraid of? Or who does she want me to think she's afraid of?

It's so hard to know what's real, when these girls are all actresses.

They're also just teenagers. Impetuous and occasionally cruel, but they're not criminal masterminds.

'I fell,' Imogen says, like she's desperate for me to believe her.

'You'd been drinking alcohol, right?' I say. See, this is about Elise's bad parenting, not mine. Elise is the one who seduces other people's husbands, not me. Elise is the one who can't be trusted, and her daughter is the one who has to come clean, not mine.

Imogen doesn't answer my question. Instead, she says brightly, 'So how's Ruby doing?'

'She's backstage—you could always go and ask her.' Then I feel a chill. I didn't see Ruby when I went looking for Mr. Racki. I can't check on her now, not without drawing suspicion.

'I don't think Ruby likes me much,' Imogen says.

'What gives you that impression?' I'm fast losing the stomach for sleuthing. I don't want to keep talking to this girl; I want to find *my* girl.

'I excel at theater because I'm good at reading people. I'm also a great mimic. I'm always learning from the people around me.' Imogen stares at me, unblinking, and my already-chilled blood goes icy. She's saying that turnabout is fair play. Ruby attacked her first, and now Imogen is attacking back.

'Why are you here, Imogen?' What's her game? Why did she come to OFA?

'No one else was sitting next to you. I thought you might want some company.'

By now, the second girl is finishing her song. I haven't heard a note. I'm too focused on Imogen, and whether she's a danger to my daughter or it's the other way around. My radar says something is very wrong, but then, my radar is pretty self-serving at the moment. I want her to be the villain, not Ruby. Anyone but Ruby.

'Where's Ruby's dad? Why isn't he here?'

'He's back in the States.'

'In Los Angeles, right? Isn't that the performing arts epicenter?'

I bristle. 'Not for musical theater.'

'Why not try for schools in New York to be close to Broadway?'

I can feel her studying me closely. They say sociopaths are good at mimicking normal behavior. That could be what she was telling me a few minutes ago. She's trying to learn to act like a person through observation.

It wasn't even a week ago that Elise was asking questions about schools in the States, and less than that when she was buddying up to my husband. Now Imogen is talking about Greg and about schools. Coincidence?

'Why didn't Ruby want to stay in the States, Kendall?' Imogen says.

'That's none of your business,' I snap, 'and don't call me Kendall.'

'That's your name, isn't it?'

'I'm Mrs. Donovan to you.' I've always let Ruby's friends call me Kendall, but Imogen is definitely not Ruby's friend, or mine.

Everything about my body language says she should stop talking. But Imogen is relentless. 'Being so far from your husband must be really hard on your marriage. You know, I don't think I'd move to a whole different continent unless there was something I really needed to get away from.' Imogen shifts her pose, so it's therapist-style. I can imagine that she's seen some therapists in her time, and now she's imitating them, perfectly. I saw one myself for a while after the cancer diagnosis, and Ruby tried a few. She didn't like talking to them; she said she preferred to talk to me.

I have a truly nauseating thought: Just because Imogen's a sociopath doesn't mean Ruby's in the clear. It doesn't have to be one or the other. It could be both. They sniffed out their own kind, and they don't like the smell. It's a battle for dominance and at the moment, Imogen is on top.

I sound like a lunatic. Ruby didn't push Imogen. I know my daughter.

'I bet Ruby wishes her dad was here,' Imogen says.

'And where's your family?' It's a jab. Intellectually, I get that she's a seventeen-year-old girl, but it just doesn't feel that way. And I don't feel like myself. I feel like Carolyn. For once, someone can think whatever they like about me. I don't have the patience for image management anymore.

She shifts back toward the stage. 'I don't have a mother and my dad's ill.' She says it in a monotone that is eerily similar to the way Ruby spoke through the door earlier today. 'He's dying.'

'I'm sorry,' I say, but I can't access any true sympathy, not now.

'Are you, now?' That stare again. 'Say it like you mean it, Kendall.'

The impudence. I can't get over it, coming from a young girl. But then, she said herself she doesn't have any parenting. A dead mother, an ill father. She's practically feral.

I'm willing her to go away, but she doesn't. She must be feeding on the tension, like it's sustenance. I tell myself that Ruby is fine, she'll transform as soon as she's under the lights. She lives to perform.

The next girl sings, and then another after that. This is intolerable. I want to crawl out of my skin. I wonder if I can ask Mr. Racki to shuffle the order and have Ruby perform sooner. Let him know I'm not feeling well after our talk earlier. He's susceptible to that sort of thing. Then I'll have an excuse for being backstage, and I'll confirm that Ruby is okay.

Mr. Racki doesn't think Ruby is okay at all. He thinks she pushed Imogen. I want it to be impossible but unfortunately, it's not.

In my head, I'm replaying my talks with Ruby, and my conversation with Mr. Racki, and now, with Imogen. Not to mention what Greg didn't say earlier, and what Elise did. It's all too much. I don't know what—or who—to believe.

Sadie takes the stage and she's well-rehearsed, technically proficient, and perfectly competent but, as always, there's no magic in it. I know that she'll be relegated to the chorus as per usual. I look back at the row of mums, wanting to gloat. But Elise and her husband (I've never even met him and can't recall his name) are watching, and I'm surprised to see that her head is on his shoulder, how connected to one another and proud they look. I feel like crying. Then I feel like screaming, asking him if he knows who his wife really is, what she did during her jaunt to Los Angeles. Do they know that their little angel up on that stage needs to come clean?

I'm gripped with hatred. Elise was with Greg in some shape or form, and she must know that marriages break up over infidelity all the time; she's trying to destroy Ruby and me, trying to tear my family apart, and why? Unlike Carolyn, who's at least ostensibly protecting Jess, Elise has made it clear that this is all beneath her, she won't be swept up in teenage nonsense, so it has to be for another reason. It must be because I see through her, right down to her inadequate soul, and for that, she wants me to pay, and she'll use my daughter to do it.

I'm seething as Annabel steps into the spotlight. From the first note, Bel owns the stage, she owns the room. I turn to see if Elise is registering the contrast between Bel and Sadie, and notice that Imogen is studying her nails, visibly bored. It's like she's not even concerned about the talent level of the other girls; she's just that self-assured, or she really doesn't care about getting cast at all. If my mother was dead and my father was dying, I might not care either.

Maybe Imogen is going crazy, but it's temporary. It could be grief. She might be furious that she's losing her other parent and she's taking it out on Ruby. Or she's not doing anything to Ruby, and she's just a socially awkward girl, and I've misread this entire interaction.

Bel is finishing her song. Carl and their brood are on their feet, applauding. No one else has given their children a standing ovation, it's actually frowned upon, because we're trying to treat everyone equally, but no one can hold it against the Richardsons. They're just spontaneously overcome with their love. It's impulse-driven, but in the best way. They're driven by love, while Ruby is driven by . . . it's not hate, I don't think. She doesn't hate Jess, who's one of her best friends. But Imogen's a different story altogether.

Does Carl know that Bronnie was recently in a huddle with the headmaster?

It's Jess's turn to walk to the center of the stage. As usual, she's spellbinding before she's even opened her mouth. But then the music starts.

It's 'Castle on a Cloud,' the song from the music box. I look back at Carolyn in disbelief. Her husband is listening, completely unaware that anything's amiss. He might not even have known that was Jess's audition song, or that it was the one from the music box. OFA is really Carolyn's domain. But then, what isn't Carolyn's domain?

Carolyn doesn't turn in my direction, in anyone's direction, really. She keeps her eyes on the stage. Elise seems equally unfazed, and I wonder if she knew it was coming, if she and Carolyn planned it together, giddy with their own cleverness.

Jess is a strong girl who doesn't like backing down, but this had to be engineered by Carolyn. It's to show that Jess will not be cowed, that she'll reclaim her audition song, but it also says that the music box hasn't been forgotten.

It's a message to Ruby. No, a message to me. I'm the one sitting by myself, after all.

Here lies Ruby. Here lies Kendall, pretending to be a good mom.

The first verse is ending, and my stomach tightens. I don't want to hear those lines—*I know a place where no one's lost / I know a place where no one cries*—because I'm already picturing that broken ballerina spinning and spinning, one arm missing, one leg mangled. I notice that Carolyn isn't smiling anymore. She might have just realized that she isn't fully in control, and that her daughter is taunting her persecutor. When Jess gets to those lines, none of us know what's going to happen, if the music box was not merely a threat but a prophecy.

Just then, there's a bloodcurdling scream from backstage.

I know that voice. I'm running, and Imogen is matching me step for step. It's like she was waiting for it, she's so quick off the block. But she's been next to me for the past fifteen minutes. She's in the clear.

I'm backstage before any of the other parents from the audience since I was in the front row. I push through the throngs of girls so that I can get to Ruby, who's shaking all over.

Bronnie's already there, appearing distraught, but she hasn't approached Ruby. Everyone's formed a circle, a boundary, as if my little girl is some sort of leper.

I take Ruby in my arms, murmuring that it'll be okay, I'm here for her, always. No matter what.

I look back at all the parents who've pushed through, and I light on Carolyn and Elise. Carolyn's as cold as I've ever seen her. Elise is somewhere between mildly curious and bemused.

Bronnie asks, almost in a daze, 'Who would do something like that?'

Carolyn says, 'Just some psycho,' and I notice that her eyes are on Ruby and me.

But Imogen—she's right next to us. She's inside the circle, and she strokes Ruby's back. There are tears in Imogen's eyes, and if you didn't know better, you'd think she really was full of compassion.

I don't know anything anymore.

Then I see it, what must have prompted Ruby to scream like that. Along the wall, there's a row of hooks where the costumes hang, pre-performance. They're all empty now, save for Ruby's. Suspended from her assigned hook like a deadly necklace—a threat and a suggestion—is a noose.

# 5

# Truth Crash

*Sophie Hannah*

## SNAPCHAT: MINGES & WHINGES

**Sadie:** Ruby bubba you ok? WTF??

**Bel:** That thing was so fuckin creepy. Whys everyone calling it a noos?

**Jess:** Noose: with an e. That's what it was.

**Bel:** What even is that?

**Ruby:** Am okay thanks Sadie ♥

**Imogen:** Are you rly Ruby? Ngl, I so wouldnt be ok if some-one had put noose round neck of my costume. Its such a hateful thing to do

**Jess:** Srsly Bel you don't know what a noose is? It's what was hanging round Ruby's costume. It's what you hang someone with or use to hang yourself.

**Imogen:** Lol rip 💀

**Ruby:** Sorry guys can we not talk about it 💔 💔

**Sadie:** 'Lol rip'? Srsly, Imogen?

**Jess:** Sensitive much (Bel do you know what that means?)

**Imogen:** Trying to cheer Ruby up and lighten the mood! 😊 😊

**Bel:** F off lol not my fault I never heard of noose before. Sadie u okay?

**Imogen:** Why wouldnt Sadie be okay?

**Sadie:** Fine bel thanks.

**Jess:** Sadie WTF? Whys she asking that? You got a secret you two?

**Sadie:** No secret 😊

**Ruby:** It had a long blond hair kinda wound round it

**Jess:** The noose?

**Ruby:** Yeah

**Jess:** What kinda blond? Like my kind or your kind?

**Bel:** Lol Jess your hairs not blond its brown

**Jess:** It's fucking golden blond, and fuck off 😊 😊 😊

**Bel:** Lol just messing with you i wish I had your hair honest to god Im the one with boring brown hair

**Ruby:** It was same blond as Imogens

**Bel:** maybe it was meant for Imogen

**Imogen:** Stop it your creeping me out!!

**Jess:** or Imo put it there

**Imogen:** What just cos Ruby said a strand of hair was same colour as mine? No one even saw this hair or can prove it was there.

**Ruby:** I saw it

**Imogen:** Ruby jesus christ are you saying you think I did the noose?

**Sadie:** Guys can we all think before we say shit. No one knows who did it and Ruby's had a horrible experience lets not make it worse.

**Imogen:** Whoever did noose messed up your song Jess. Big drama, right in the middle of your song. Why would I wanna do that?

**Ruby:** Aaand . . . you're saying I would. Nice try, pin the blame on the victim

**Jess:** I don't think you did it Rubes, or music box. Ngl, my mum does tho. Imogen, STFU.

**Imogen:** We only have Ruby's word for it that hair was there and was my colour

[Notification: **Ruby** has left the chat]

**Sadie:** She's gone.

**Jess:** Fucks sake, Imogen

**Imogen:** OMG i do not understand why is it okay for her to accuse me but I get shit for saying it wasnt me? Jess you know what she put you through last year

**Jess:** Yeh and you don't so back the f off. You been at OFA like 3 minutes WTF do you know

**Imogen:** music box made you think she was starting trouble again right?

**Jess:** She. Did. Not. Do. That.

**Imogen:** so you say

[**Jess** has left the chat]

# CAROLYN

I feel a strange mixture of excitement and dread as the four of us—me, Elise, Bronnie, and Kendall—slide into our booth. We've come to one of my favorite restaurants: Gymkhana, on Albemarle Street. It's a haven of elegance with a serious, almost secretive atmosphere: all dark woods, muted colors, and hushed voices—perfect for whatever revelation Elise is about to hit us with. I'm trying to convince myself that I don't mind not knowing in advance, that I'm fine with finding out at the same time as Bronnie and Kendall.

The more contact I have with Elise, the less sure I am about her. Do I like her? Does she like me? Why do I even care?

It was her idea that the four of us should meet for lunch. She assigned the task of arranging it to me. Her text message read: *We need to talk urgently: you, me, K & B. I've got wall-to-wall meetings today—can you arrange? Lunch tomorrow, or dinner. Can't really wait longer than that. Sushi'd be great, or Italian. You are NOT GOING TO BELIEVE what I found out while in America.*

*Tell me!!* I texted back.

*Not by text. This needs face-to-face meeting*, came her reply.

Did she know what she was doing, I wondered, and was it deliberate: confiding at the same time as not really confiding, singling me out for special treatment, then pushing me away?

Or was I creating drama in my mind that simply didn't exist in Elise's?

I resented the implication that I was less busy than she was, but I did as instructed nonetheless and made the arrangements. My one act of rebellion was the choice of restaurant: upmarket Indian instead of sushi or Italian.

*Fine by me, but you might want to manage expectations (Bronnie's) re cost as it looks pricey*, Elise texted back.

I wrinkled my nose, and gave myself permission to think less of her for using the phrase *manage expectations* unironically. It's such a manipulative idea. I've always found it baffling that people say it without embarrassment. 'I wanted to manage her expectations' is a more polite way of saying, 'I wanted to control her thoughts.' It's repellent. Much better to tell everyone the truth, and let them be in charge of how they respond to the plain facts.

'Don't worry, lunch is my treat,' I texted back on an impulse, through gritted teeth. 'Pathetic, Carolyn,' I muttered to myself. Elise was throwing her weight around (or was she? Perhaps she was just trying to get something sorted while in a hurry) and I'd let myself get riled into doing the same. Now I was going to have to buy an expensive lunch for three women who weren't even my friends.

As it turns out, it's Kendall who says, 'Wow, look at the prices,' as she turns the pages of her menu.

'Carolyn's picking up the tab,' says Elise.

'Are you sure, Carolyn?' Bronnie asks me. 'I'm happy to split the bill.'

'I'm sure,' I say, thinking that she's changed her tune. It wasn't too long ago that she was tutting and sighing over the cost of a latte in Caffè Nero, and claiming that she couldn't afford a taxi and would run to the Tube station in the rain instead. Maybe she's taking the opportunity to look generous because she knows there's no danger of me taking her up on her offer.

'Well, next time it's my treat,' she says with a smile. She's sitting directly opposite me, and it makes our booth feel unbalanced, tilted. There's palpably less tension on our side of the table. Kendall and Elise, opposite one another next to the wall, aren't smiling. Kendall looks nervous. She must be wondering why she's been included again, after we all steered clear of her on Noose Night. I wish that name wasn't so temptingly alliterative—then I could maybe stop thinking of it as Noose Night.

Elise says, 'Today's lunch isn't going to be any sort of treat, I'm afraid.'

'It is for me,' I quip. 'I'm going to be having my usual: minced goat meat with a side dish of goat brains.'

'Ugh, that's disgusting,' says Bronnie. 'Are you serious?'

'Yup. It's divine. I have it whenever I come here.'

'I've got some pretty serious things to say, and not everybody's going to like hearing them,' Elise presses on.

'What things?' asks Kendall. 'Why don't you say whatever you have to say instead of dropping hints? You're talking about me, aren't you? *I'm* the one who won't like it, whatever it is.'

'Shall we order first?' I suggest. 'I'm starving.'

'Me too,' says Bronnie.

I wave at a waiter, who nods at me from across the room.

'You've told us quite a few lies, haven't you, Kendall?' says Elise. 'You and Ruby, you've both lied in a pretty significant way. Would you like a chance to set the record straight now, before I tell everyone what I've found out?'

Kendall says nothing at first. Then she says—she almost hisses—'You're so sure, aren't you?'

'Sure of what I found out while I was in America? Yes, I am. I wouldn't have arranged this lunch if I was in any doubt.'

'So sure you're better than me. So superior.'

'What's going on?' Bronnie looks at me, then at Elise, then back at me.

A different waiter, not the one I waved at, appears at our table. 'Good morning, ladies. Oh—I apologize. It is good afternoon already. Have you dined with us before?'

Nobody has apart from me, and it takes them a frustratingly long time to order. Kendall asks for a Diet Coke, nothing else.

Once the waiter has moved away, Elise says matter-of-factly, 'I don't think I'm superior to anyone. It's going to be a lot easier to sort this out if we keep accusations and personal attacks out of it and concentrate on the facts. Kendall . . . are you going to tell them or shall I? Maybe it'll be easier for you if I do the talking, which I'm happy to do, but . . . you need to understand, there's no way of avoiding this now.'

'Someone tell me what's going on,' I say.

Kendall looks down at the table.

'Well, first of all, Ruby wasn't offered places by all the best US stage schools,' says Elise. 'In fact, she wasn't offered a place by any. She was blacklisted by all of them. That's why she applied to the Academy and came to London. The only way she could find a decent place to take her was to leave the country.'

Bronnie turns to Kendall. 'Is that true?'

'It's true,' says Elise firmly. 'The problem is, even Adam Racki all the way over here in England wouldn't have let Ruby in if he hadn't been sent fake references—by you, Kendall.'

'How did you find all of this out?' Kendall whispers.

'Wait—you mean it's *true*?' I say.

'I just told you it's true,' Elise says briskly. Obviously it hasn't occurred to her that I might not believe her without question. 'And you're not going to bother denying it, are you, Kendall? I hope not.'

'You patronizing bitch!' Kendall spits at her.

Elise holds up her hands. 'I'm sorry if it sounded patronizing, but let's not deflect here. You faked good references—glowing references—for Ruby to get her into the Academy. In doing so, you deprived Adam Racki of the ability to protect his other students. Didn't you?'

'Protect?' says Bronnie anxiously. 'From . . . from *Ruby*?'

A waitress appears with a tray. One by one, she places our drinks on the table. I'm sure she takes less than ten years to do so, though it doesn't feel that way. I wonder if she can detect the tension between us.

Once she's gone, Kendall says, 'You have no idea—no idea at all. What was I supposed to do, just let everyone assume the worst about my daughter, who I *knew* was innocent?'

'Innocent of what?' I ask. The room tips. I'm aware that my breathing has speeded up. What are we about to hear? I've always thought that there was something seriously wrong with Ruby Donovan—much more than the usual bitchy teenage girl stuff. Am I about to be proved right?

'Ruby bullied a girl in America—much like she bullied Jess last year,' says Elise, keeping her eyes on Kendall. 'And then one day, this girl—Vee, her name was—was at Ruby's house, Kendall's house, and she died. Fell down the stairs to the cellar.'

Wow. Did Ruby kill someone? Without any evidence in either direction, I'm sure she did. I'm certain Ruby Donovan is a murderer.

'No!' Kendall wails, tears streaming down her face. 'Ruby *did not* bully Vee—that's a lie. It's a fucking lie.'

Suddenly, the restaurant has gone from quiet to silent. Heads turn, then awkwardly turn back to concentrate on the food on the tables in front of them. Everyone is now ostentatiously minding their own business.

Kendall lowers her voice. 'The relationship between Ruby

and Vee . . . it was completely different from . . . They weren't *friends*. Ruby and Jess are friends, and yes, Ruby was jealous of Jess and behaved badly, but Vee? Ruby would never have been envious of her. She was weird and creepy and . . . physically unattractive.'

'Unattractive? Oh, heaven forbid,' I blurt out. *Your daughter's a fucking killer.*

'Carolyn,' says Elise sharply, as if she's my mother.

'Vee latched on to Ruby and wouldn't accept that Ruby didn't want to hang out with her.' Kendall looks only at Elise as she speaks. 'Vee's parents decided to define that as bullying—as if Ruby had a duty to socialize with a girl she barely knew and didn't really like, a girl who had an unhealthy obsession with her. It was pure bullshit.'

'Go back to the "she died" part,' I say to Elise. I can't bring myself to speak to Kendall, though I know I ought not to believe it's necessarily the mother's fault if the daughter's evil. I can't stop thinking: It could have been Jess. Ruby could have killed Jess. She still could, if we don't do something. She's clever enough—puts a noose where Ruby's costume should be, does the graffiti against herself, makes it look as if she's the target, so that when she attacks the true target—Jess—no one suspects her. Was the music box, in retrospect, a little too obvious? Did she think twice after that and change tack?

'The official version of the story is that Vee fell down the stairs,' says Elise.

'She *did* fall,' Kendall insists.

'No one at Vee and Ruby's school thought so, though,' says Elise. 'Everyone believed Ruby had pushed Vee, and killed her deliberately. Just like everyone at the school believed Vee's version of the bullying story, not yours or Ruby's. That's why Ruby couldn't get a reference, and why no US stage school would take her.'

'What would you do if that happened to Sadie?' Kendall

asks her. 'If you *knew* she wasn't the monster everyone seemed to think she was, and you wanted her to have a new start, a second chance? You'd do what I did!'

'Fake some great references and lie my way into a school far enough away for my plan to work?' Elise shakes her head. 'No, I wouldn't. I have principles.'

Kendall tries to stand, then falls back into a sitting position. There isn't enough room to stand in the booth. The table is fixed to the floor, the banquettes' seat cushions extending to just beneath it.

Her face contorted with rage, or perhaps pain, Kendall spits at Elise, 'Ruby didn't bully Vee, she didn't so much as *touch* her that day, and she certainly didn't kill her. You know *nothing*.'

Bronnie puts her head in her hands. 'This is so horrible,' she says. 'I can't believe we're having this conversation.'

'We need to be having it with Adam Racki,' I say.

'Yes, as soon as possible,' Elise agrees. 'This is serious. Threatening incidents have been happening, and we've had no proper response from Adam. Now we know Ruby was blacklisted in America because everyone apart from her mother thinks she killed a girl, he has to act fast. It's a safeguarding issue, even apart from the fraudulent references.'

'Elise, please don't tell Racki.' Kendall grabs her hand across the table.

'I have to, Kendall. You must realize that. I'm not proposing to go behind your back. I think we should all talk to him together, actually. I'm going to ring him and arrange a meeting as soon as possible.'

'And you expect me to just . . . dance to your tune?'

'Does it matter if she's at the meeting or not?' I ask Elise. 'I mean, Adam's going to be expelling Ruby, right? There's no other possible outcome, not now. I can understand why Kendall doesn't want to face the consequences of her dishonesty and endangering of our daughters in front of us. Why does she need to be there?'

'Do you really think Ruby will be expelled?' asks Bronnie.

'Of course,' I say as decisively as I can, as if my saying it firmly enough can make it a reality. The truth is, I fear it might not happen, even now.

'I think she can't be allowed to stay,' says Elise, sounding all regretful and reluctant about it.

'If she is, I'll contact the *Mail* or the *Sun* and tell them about Vee's suspicious death,' I say. 'That sort of negative media attention would soon persuade Adam to get rid of her.'

'Fuck you, Carolyn,' Kendall says in a low voice. 'Just . . . fuck you. Excuse me, Bronnie. I'm not sitting here . . .'

'Kendall, stay where you are,' orders Elise. 'Carolyn, you're not helping: needlessly antagonizing Kendall, threatening to manipulate Adam . . .'

'All right, I'll shut up.' Not helping? I'm not trying to help. Elise might be able to operate strategically and manage outcomes at all times, but I can't, and I don't want to. I'm a human being, not a multinational corporation's marketing department. Ever since I found out that Ruby is probably a murderer, there's been a flow of burning rage inside me that wants only to crush her—her and her mother.

Elise is already on the phone. 'Hi, it's Elise. Elise Bond, Sadie's mum. That's right. I'd like to arrange a meeting with Adam Racki, please—it's extremely urgent. What? I'm afraid I'm not going to go into detail until I'm in the room with him. No, I'm not going to do that. Sorry, but this is highly sensitive. Carolyn Mordue, Bronnie Richardson, and Kendall Donovan will also be at the meeting—if you tell Adam that, I'm sure he'll be able to work out what it's concerning.'

'Bronnie . . . move!' Kendall snaps at her. 'I'm not going to your meeting and I'm not sitting here ... Let me leave, please.'

Bronnie looks at Elise for direction. God, she's so pathetic. Hasn't she got any ideas of her own? Elise nods as she's saying, 'Tomorrow at four? Is that the soonest? ... All right, tomorrow at four, then.'

Bronnie shuffles out of the booth. As soon as she's moved aside, Kendall's on her way—grabbing her bag, hurrying to the door. 'Kendall, please be at the meeting tomorrow,' Elise calls after her. 'There's no point running away from this.'

Kendall's gone. Good. I don't want to have lunch with her any more than she wants to have lunch with me.

'No tabloids, Carolyn.' Elise raises her eyebrows at me. 'It's not necessary. Adam won't be able to let Ruby stay, not after this, and once the gutter press gets hold of it, they're uncontrollable. You think they wouldn't turn on you? They would. You don't want them pointing the finger at Jess, do you?'

'What do you mean?'

'Once they find out that Ruby spent the best part of a year making Jess's life a living hell, who do you think they'll figure might go after Ruby with nooses and malicious graffiti?' Elise smiles as if she's trying to help. Managing expectations. 'Ruby's main victim: Jess. Or her mother: you, Carolyn.'

*No, that can't be right*, I want to say. Surely no one would suspect Jess and me of anything. Does Elise suspect one of us? Both of us?

A waiter arrives at our table with a tray of food. I was starving a few minutes ago. Now I'm wondering if I'll be able to eat a single mouthful, or ever come here again.

The next morning, after making myself some late breakfast and then throwing it away uneaten, I decide to work on my musical and ignore the mountain of university work that I ought to tackle, that I ought to have tackled weeks ago. It's becoming almost second nature to pretend that the work I don't want to do simply isn't there, which is a bit scary. I remind myself for the four hundredth time that we cannot afford for me to lose my job. Today, for the first time, I notice that, despite this being as true as it's ever been, there's a part of me that's arguing with the official line, saying, *You know what? We'd be fine. We'd be absolutely fine if I handed in my notice and never went back to the law faculty.*

*No, there isn't,* I tell myself firmly. *There is absolutely no part of me that's saying that or even thinking it.*

I hate to admit it, but I can almost understand how Kendall Donovan ended up so deep in denial. Did she convince herself that the references she faked for Ruby were real, because only she, as her mother, knew Ruby's true inner goodness? I can imagine her kidding herself in that way.

*Which is not what I'm doing with Jess. It's not the same at all. I know Jess wasn't responsible for the noose—it's beyond doubt.*

I push these thoughts out of my mind and turn my attention to an unfinished song from my musical that's needed a last verse for a while. I wrote the first two verses in the summer, and I've tried writing the final verse at least a dozen times, and always ended up deleting it. None of my draft final verses so far have escalated and advanced the song sufficiently, and I really want some significant ramping up of scale and bite at the end.

It's not a key song in the musical; it's sung by a group of minor characters and is part of the subplot rather than the main plot, but I love it and want to keep it if I can only think of a way to wrap it up properly. It's the song that will cause controversy if the show ever reaches a stage or an audience— maybe that's why I love it so much, troublemaker that I am. It's called 'Can We Drug You?' A group of horrible teachers sings it to a rebellious (but good and slightly heroic) pupil

153

who has done nothing wrong apart from having ideas and opinions the teachers don't like. They're explaining that the only way they'll let him out of the Detention Unit is if he agrees to be drugged into silent obedience. People will no doubt think it's a comment on the ADHD phenomenon and Ritalin, but it's not. It's about how those in power hate and fear original thinkers.

*People? What people? Face facts: No one's ever going to see your musical or hear the song.*

I tell the discouraging voice in my head to fuck off and stare at my screen—at the two verses I've already written. Suddenly, I have an idea: Teenagers, traditionally, don't need to be persuaded by their teachers to take drugs. It's something they do for fun.

I start to type . . .

*Can we drug you?*
*With a staff member's sign-off, it's all aboveboard.*
*Please don't shrug! You*
*know cool teenagers take drugs of their own accord.*
*As you glug, you*
*feel your mind calming down, all stress melting away.*
*Hate to bug you,*
*but this term has been tough. Let's improve it today.*
*With an 'Oh, what the heck!' chuck this muck down your neck.*
*Can we drug, can we drug, can we drug you?*

Yes. I like this. I really like it. It needs something more at the end, though. A final flourish . . .

*Catatonia's a breeze!*
*Just say, 'Thanks, Miss—yes, please.'*
*Can we drug, can we drug, can we drug you?*

I hear footsteps on the stairs outside my room and slam my MacBook shut.

The door opens. It's Jess, with her phone in her right hand as it almost always is these days when she's not on stage. 'I need to talk to you about Ruby.' She frowns. 'What are you doing?'

'Working.' And I should have been. I feel terrible, suddenly—as if reality has just strolled into the room and woken me up. If we lost my salary, Dan would have to close his shop and go out and earn proper money. Much as I've wished he would spontaneously decide that's what he wants to do, I don't want him to be forced into it.

Once you get to where I am professionally, it's almost impossible for them to sack you, but if I keep neglecting to do the work they pay me for . . .

*Professor of Law at the University of Cambridge. Remember that description, because that's what you are. You're not Lin-Manuel Miranda. Lots of people would give anything to have your job.*

'If you're working, then why's your laptop shut?' Jess asks impatiently, as if exposing her mother's lies is only item one on her tediously long to-do list.

I need to start being more careful. Her antennae are super-alert; she misses nothing. 'I . . . because I heard you coming.'

'I might have had one quick question and been gone by now. Why would you close down your computer?'

'I didn't close it *down*, I just closed it. I can open it in a second, it's not a big deal. Why are you interrogating me?'

Jess narrows her eyes. She wants me to know I'm under suspicion. 'Are you having an affair?'

I laugh. 'No.'

'Then what? The way you said "no," like, "No, it's not *that*"—'

'Huh? I said "no." Just a normal "no."'

'Mum, every time I come in here, you slam your laptop shut like you're some kind of spy. *Are* you a spy?' Her phone buzzes. She glances at it, murmurs, 'Fuck off, Bel,' then turns back to me. 'That girl's so thick, I swear to God. Ugh, I don't even care—lie if you want. Everyone else does.'

'What do you mean?'

'Bel and Sadie have obviously got a secret they're desperate to shove in the rest of our faces. They've been doing that stupid "Let's talk later, when no one's around, about *that thing only we know*" and then denying there's anything they're keeping from us. I don't care, I'm so over it. Point is . . .' Jess sighs. 'You never listen to me, and you *reeeally* need to. I know you think Ruby put the music box in my locker, and did all the other shit, but she didn't. The noose thing—'

'You mean the noose that coincidentally ruined your song *and* turned Ruby into a sympathy-deserving victim who therefore couldn't be the perpetrator?'

Jess shakes her head. 'Listen to yourself. You hate her so much, you can't even talk about her in a normal way. You start ranting like a maniac. Your voice has, like, actual key changes.'

*Ruby killed someone. Did you know that? Does that change your view of things at all?* I don't say that, because I agreed with Bronnie and Elise that we wouldn't tell the girls until after we'd spoken to Adam Racki. Maybe Jess will never need to know that she was targeted for persecution not merely by a teenage bitch but by a cold-hearted psychopathic killer. With any luck, Ruby Donovan will be on a plane back to America this time tomorrow and we'll never need to worry about her again.

I haven't even told Dan about what Elise found out in America. I'm so used to thinking of myself as the problem-solver in our family, I can't bear to present him with an as-yet-unsolved problem. Or maybe I don't want to discuss it because I might blurt out all my fears, fears I'm ashamed of having: that even now, Adam Racki will take Ruby's side as he did last year. He'd say he didn't—that he was impartial, and simply trying to find a peaceful resolution—but that's a lie. He could and should have expelled Ruby for what she did to Jess, and he didn't. In my book, that's taking her side.

'What do you want me to say, Jess? Yes, I think it was all Ruby. All the things: the music box, the graffiti, the noose. Don't you, really? I mean . . . who do we *know* is a nasty piece of work? Ruby. Who's demonstrated that she likes making you miserable? Ruby. She went too far with the music box, and everyone was shocked. Suddenly, something had happened—she'd *done something*—that wasn't passive-aggressive but was straight-up blatant aggressive, and every-one was all "Poor Jess," people you don't even know that well hugging you in the corridor and telling you they think you're great—and not only students. Teachers too. Isn't it likely that Ruby, who's been so jealous in the past that she's spent months trying to make you feel like shit, might be jealous again, might think, "What can I do to make people feel sorry for me instead of Jess?" Hence the graffiti, the noose . . .'

'No! Mum, you don't know Ruby like I do. Yeah, she can be a bitch, but she's not insane. And this noose thing is prop-erly crazy. And so is . . .' Jess stops.

'What? What else is crazy?'

'It's not a thing. It's a person.'

'Who?'

'Imogen Curwood. She's insane, Mum.'

'Why?'

'I don't know. Nature or nurture, take your pick.'

'No, I mean—'

'No one else can see it, but you'd have to be blind not to. I think it's her. All of it. The music box happened the day she joined the school. The same *day*.'

'But . . . Imogen didn't know you when you found the music box. Had you even met her?'

Jess shakes her head.

'Then why would she want to do that to you? How would she know that "Castle on a Cloud" was your song?'

'I've no idea. But there's something not right about her, Mum. She's sneaky and creepy and . . . kind of . . . what's the word. Ghoulish. There's something ghoulish about her. She makes me shiver, just thinking about her.' Jess stops. She seems to be weighing up whether or not to tell me something. 'Ruby says there was a blond hair wrapped around the noose,' she says eventually. 'Same blond as Imogen's hair.'

'Even if that's true, a hair can come from anywhere. And that's if it's *true*. Given the source . . .'

Jess rolls her eyes. 'There's no point talking to you about it. You're convinced Ruby has to be the villain of everything. Mum, her finding that noose didn't only mess up my song, it meant she didn't get to sing hers. She didn't even make it onto the stage. I *know* Ruby. You don't. You only hear about her secondhand from me.'

*And now from Elise.* I try to look open-minded.

'Ruby knew the audience was full of theater agents and producers,' Jess says. 'There's no *way* she'd sabotage herself like that. I mean, *I* was excited about singing for that audience, and I'm not desperate to be a musical theater star the way Ruby is.'

*Then why the hell are we paying a fortune for you to train to be one?*

Is it my fault? I might be the one earning nearly all of the money these days, but am I also the one to blame for wasting it? Have I pushed Jess towards musical theater because it's the world I want to live in and can't?

'You don't need to be desperate to be a star,' I say. 'You *do* need to realize that you're the most talented student in your year, and you owe it to your talent and to the world to—'

'Ugh, not this speech again. I'm trying to persuade you, the most stubborn woman in the world, that you're wrong about Ruby. With the music box and the graffiti, okay, I wouldn't swear on my life, but the noose *was not her*. Apart from anything else, the psychology's all wrong.'

Having made her point, Jess looks down at her phone and starts to text, moving her thumbs as quickly and deftly as if texting were her first language.

'What psychology?' I ask.

'Hang on, I just need to reply to Bel.'

More thumb-jabbing. Then Jess looks up. 'Ruby. She's all about status. That's her *thing*. She fears more than anything that her status will take a dive—that she'll fall totally off the grid. Don't ask what the grid is. It's not a real thing. I can't explain it. Point is: Ruby's so insecure, she can't handle it if she's not seen as the most powerful and popular person in any group. That's why she spent months trying to undermine my confidence. I seemed more powerful to her, only because I don't really give a toss about status or what anyone thinks of me. Or, I *did* seem like that, until she started her shit, and then I seemed unhappy and unconfident for a while, which is what she wanted. She knows that if someone's a victim of *any* kind of bullying, that lowers their status. Didn't some kids get bullied at your school?'

I nod.

'Right. And weren't they the lowest status kids? The least powerful, the least attractive friendship options?'

It's a good point. I remember trying to be as kind as I could to Debbie Lynam, who'd been ostracized by most of the girls in our class, at the same time as hoping that no one would see me talking to her in case her social untouchability rubbed off on me.

'Most girls at the Academy are popular or very popular,' says Jess. 'Ruby'd rather die than arrange to make herself look like the most hated girl there—the only one getting a noose left where her costume should be, and fucked-up graffiti about her scrawled on walls. It's so humiliating. She'd never do that to herself. Pity's not what she wants. It never has been. She wants . . . social capital. Or she did. I'm not sure what she wants now—probably just to find out what sick fuck is doing all this shit to her.'

'And she suspects it's Imogen?'

'Yeah, she does. And I *know* it's Imogen. It has to be.' Jess looks down at her phone. 'And here it is,' she declares triumphantly. 'The proof! The noose wasn't Ruby. See? I knew it.'

'What proof?' I ask.

Jess's thumbs are flying again: ninety words a minute with only two digits. It's impressive.

Having sent her message, she shoves her phone in her pocket and says, 'Bel's just texted saying her mum was in the costume room all evening until the noose was found, apart from about ten minutes—and during that time, Ruby was in her line of sight the whole time. I've asked her to find out where Imogen was during those ten minutes. Unless Bronnie says the same about her—that she could literally see her, which I highly doubt she will, then . . .' Jess shrugs.

I finish her sentence for her: 'Then Ruby has an alibi, and Imogen doesn't.'

'I'll be interested to hear from Bronnie whether that's true or not, about the crucial ten minutes and her being able to see Ruby all that time,' says Elise a few hours later. We're in her car, driving to the meeting with Adam Racki. She rang me at lunchtime and offered to pick me up on her way in, even though I live nowhere near her. 'There's something I want to tell you, before we meet the others,' she said.

So far, she hasn't told me and I haven't asked. I don't want to give her the satisfaction. Last time, like an overeager idiot, I said, 'Tell me!!' I've resolved not to do that again.

'Bronnie could have made a mistake,' I say. 'She could be remembering incorrectly. I mean ... this is Bronnie Richardson we're talking about.'

I want Ruby to be responsible for every bad thing that's happened. I need someone to find proof that she killed this Vee girl, and I need to hear, in a few months' time, that she's in prison in America.

'True,' says Elise. 'What's also true is that Jess is absolutely right: Imogen Curwood *is* creepy. I've had the girl at my house overnight, remember? That whole night was deeply weird—and that was Imogen's doing. Sadie agrees.'

'So you're with Jess on this?' I ask her. 'It's all Imogen, all the dodgy, scary stuff? Imogen and not Ruby, the probable murderer of Vee?'

Elise seems to be thinking about it. Then she says, 'No. I still say it's Ruby. There are two problems with the theory that it's Imogen. One: Exactly like American Vee, Imogen happened to fall down some stairs when Ruby was right there with her.'

'Exactly,' I say. This is the kind of reasoning I like.

'There's an undeniable link there,' says Elise. 'Two girls, on two separate occasions, end up at the bottom of flights of stairs, and there's Ruby Donovan at the scene of the so-called accident, both times, in two different countries. Part of me thinks that can't be a coincidence.'

'And number two?'

'Hm?' Elise frowns.

'You said there were two problems with the theory that Imogen's behind it all.'

'Oh. Yes. The second problem is that Imogen Curwood doesn't exist.'

The traffic ahead has slowed to a standstill. Elise swears under her breath as she brakes.

'*What?*' I say.

'This is why I'm driving you in,' says Elise. 'I wanted to tell you before we went into the meeting with Adam—I've found something out that I might want to use as leverage if I have to, if Adam won't give Ruby Donovan her marching orders. You're a law expert. I want your legal opinion about how much trouble I might be in if I reveal what I've found out.'

'You mean . . . in America? The Vee story?'

'No. That, I'm going to reveal. Why do you think I demanded a meeting this afternoon? I was told the Vee story, and about the blacklisting and the fake references, by Ruby's dad. I didn't have to break any laws to get that information.'

'By Ruby's *dad*? Kendall's husband?' Who is this woman? What else is she capable of? If she's tracked down and spoken to Ruby Donovan's father . . .

'Uh-huh,' says Elise. The cars in front of us are moving again, and we start to pick up speed. 'He didn't admit it in words, but it's clear he thinks Ruby pushed Vee to her death. When I told him that was what he believed, he didn't deny it. Just looked hellishly miserable, poor sod.'

'So . . .' I'm thinking furiously, trying to catch up, to shake off the feeling that I'm being manipulated. 'What do you need legal advice about? My specialty is international environmental law, by the way.' *Yes, that is as dull as it sounds.* 'I'm not sure I'll be able to help you.'

'Probably not, but you might have a better idea than I do.'

'I'll do my best,' I say.

'Okay, so: The Academy keeps records like all educational establishments, right? One of the things it records on its various databases is student details, obviously—names, addresses, everything you'd expect.'

'Right,' I say.

'What would you say if I told you I'd gained access to those records?' Elise sounds proud. 'Secretly and illicitly.'

'How?' I ask.

Elise smiles enigmatically.

'What did you find?' I ask, silently cursing myself for breaking my resolution.

'It's more a question of what I didn't find. I didn't find—couldn't find—any record at all of Imogen Curwood being a student at the Orla Flynn Academy.'

'What? That's . . . but she *is* a student there. We know she is. She's with our girls every day.'

'Yeah, and maybe she shouldn't be. Officially, there's no Imogen Curwood at the school.'

'Are you sure you . . .'

'Didn't make a mistake, didn't misread the records, checked the right year group? Yes. I'm sure. There are forty-six students in our daughters' year. Imogen Curwood isn't one of them. Has it occurred to you that they might both be bad news—Imogen *and* Ruby?'

I open my mouth to protest, to say that no, that would be implausible and too much of a coincidence, when an idea, a new possibility, smacks into me at full speed, pushing my breath to the back of my throat, making me dizzy.

*Both of them . . .*

'I screwed him, you know.'

'What?' I manage to say.

'Kendall's husband. Greg.'

'You had sex with Ruby's dad?'

'Uh-huh. He's hot. Doesn't look anything like Ruby—that might have put me off. Do you disapprove?'

'No.' I don't care who Elise sleeps with. Why would I? It strikes me as a slightly strange thing to do, but that's probably because I've never had enough spare emotional energy even to consider cheating on Dan. All my secret-life escape activity has gone into my musical, and fantasizing about having a show on Broadway or at the West End. I'd fuck Cameron Mackintosh in a heartbeat if I thought it would help my cause, but he's gay.

'Actually, I did Kendall a favor,' says Elise. 'He was thinking of divorcing her. More than thinking. He was going to do it, soon as he plucked up the courage to tell her. I persuaded him out of it. Worked the old Elise Bond magic and saved Kendall's marriage.'

She's probably waiting for me to ask her why and how she did this, but I can't be bothered. Maybe a night of passion with Magic Elise was all Greg Donovan needed to get him back on the straight and narrow. Who cares? I'm not remotely interested in the Elise-Greg-Kendall love triangle. All I want to think about right now is my new theory. The more I consider it, the more likely it seems.

'You disapprove,' says Elise. 'That's fine—I don't mind. It's okay for people to be wrong about me.'

'Elise, do you think it's possible that . . .'

'Wait, watch . . . what the . . .'

I look up to see what she's sounding so panicked about. Elise screams. I open my mouth to ask what's wrong, but I don't hear my own words, only a terrible, metallic crash-crunch sound, then more screaming.

*If Elise is screaming, she must be okay. She's alive.*

The car spins to the side at what feels like a hundred miles an hour. My arms are flailing around for something solid to grab hold of.

I don't know how much time passes before we stop moving. I don't trust it at first: the stillness. Elise lets out a strange, high-pitched laugh. Then she says, 'Run away, you coward piece of shit!'

'Who?' I ask. We're on the pavement, still in the car, still upright. I don't think I'm injured, though my heart's hammering so hard, it feels like a pulsing wound trapped in my chest. The impact must have pushed us up here.

'Whoever just drove into us. Didn't you see? A car made a beeline straight for us—boy racer, probably. He accelerated for no reason and rammed straight into us from behind. Then drove away.'

'Did you see him? His face, I mean.'

'Didn't see anything.' Elise exhales slowly. 'Tinted windows.'

'So it might not have been a "he."'

'That tire squeal as he drove away was classic boy racer. Fucking dick! That's it for my car—no way this isn't a write-off.'

A police car, its siren blaring, pulls up across the road. An overpowering tiredness sweeps over me. Soon we're going to be caught up in official accident reports. I wish we could skip that part. I look at the clock on the dashboard. It's 3:46. Our meeting with Adam Racki is at 4:30. Can we make it in time? How long will this police interrogation take?

There's a snag in my brain, something I nearly noticed . . . Nearly but not quite. What was it? I try to go back in my mind, retrace my thoughts. That's it: the clock on Elise's dashboard, and the time. 3:46. Specifically, the '46' part . . .

'You said there were forty-six students in our girls' year,' I say quietly as a police officer gets out of his car and starts walking toward us.

'Excluding Imogen, yes,' says Elise.

'That's not right. Without Imogen, there are thirty-seven in the year. With her included, thirty-eight.'

Elise sighs. 'Look, I'm the one who's been nosing around in the records. I'm telling you: there are forty-six.'

'But there *aren't*. There just aren't. Did you recognize every name?'

'I mean . . . no,' she admits after a short pause. 'I don't

know anyone by name apart from Jess, Ruby, Bel—Sadie's friends. That's it.'

How can she be so uninterested? We've been to so many school events where the other students are there with their families. Then I realize: Generally, Elise hasn't been there—she's usually away on a work trip, or too busy at the office to turn up.

'What makes you so sure there are only thirty-seven?' she asks me.

There's no way I'm ever going to tell her or anyone the shameful truth: that I know the name of every student in Jess's year at OFA, and exactly how many of them there are, because in my stupid deluded head, her classmates make up the imaginary cast of my pretty much imaginary musical. Many times over the past few months, I've typed up a cast list on my laptop, then deleted it, then started again, moving this or that person from ensemble to minor part to lead role and back again as I alter my assessment of their various talents and develop my idea of the show.

'I just know,' I say. 'Thirty-seven. Thirty-eight with Imogen.'

The police officer taps on the roof of the car and Elise lowers her window. Another man's voice coming from somewhere nearby, not the policeman's, says, 'The other car was out of control. It was speeding along way too fast and crashed right into them.'

'We're both fine, thanks,' Elise tells the small crowd that has gathered. 'Shocked, but in one piece.'

I let her do the talking while I puzzle over why there are records in OFA's system for nine students who aren't there. And no records for Imogen. *The ghoul.* Where is she now? In a class, sitting next to Jess, maybe? The thought makes me shiver. I don't believe in ghosts, but they're well known for being in two places at once. Could it have been Imogen, driving the car that . . .

No. That's crazy. She can't possibly know that Elise has just told me there's no trace of her in the Academy's records. There's no reason for her to think we're suspicious of her.

*She can't know ... unless ...*

No. It's ridiculous. *Ghoulish* is just an adjective. Imogen Curwood is not a fucking ghost.

'Is it true, Kendall?' Adam Racki asks.

It's five thirty, an hour later than planned—thanks to the car accident—and we're all in his office. I was surprised at first when Elise and I arrived and found Kendall here, but really, how could she stay away? However much she'd rather never see me or Elise again, she'll feel it's her duty to speak up for Ruby.

'It's not true that Ruby killed Vee,' she says quietly, as if on cue. 'Not deliberately and not accidentally. She didn't do it, no matter what anyone says. I know the whole world suspects her, but they're wrong. It's only because Vee's parents told everyone at the school a twisted version—'

'What about the rest?' Adam cuts her off. 'Ruby's stellar references, the US performing arts schools that were all desperate to have her?'

'All lies,' I tell him.

He ignores me, keeps his eyes on Kendall.

She nods. 'Everything else Elise has said is true—all apart from the bit about Ruby pushing Vee down the stairs. I wrote those references myself. They weren't real. They were a lie. It was all a lie. I wanted Ruby to have a chance. I didn't think of it as wrong, really, didn't think I was harming anyone. All I cared about was my daughter and how I could make things right for her.'

'This is very serious,' says Adam.

'I think you're going to have to ask Ruby to leave the Academy immediately,' says Elise.

167

He turns away. God, he's useless. What's he waiting for? Will he ever realize that he's in charge here, and do something decisive? At this rate, I might have to go to the *Sun* or the *Mail* after all. I'm not scared of any questions they might ask. I can't believe I ever was. How did I let Elise plant that fear in my mind?

For the first time I wonder if perhaps Elise herself is scared of that kind of attention. If she'll break into school records and sleep with someone else's husband, what else might she be willing to do that she wouldn't want to come to light?

'Why?' Kendall asks her. 'Why will Ruby have to leave the Academy immediately?' She's not full of rage and fear, as she was at Gymkhana; today she's dry-eyed and calm. 'Because I got her in here under false pretenses, or because of the strange things that have been happening?'

'Both, I would have thought.' Elise looks at Racki. He's decided to act like we're not here, staring out the window as if he's alone in the room.

'I wouldn't,' says Kendall. 'Now that Adam's seen how brilliant Ruby is with his own eyes, what does it matter that I faked her references? She's easily talented enough to be here.'

'Kendall, it's not about talent,' Elise says. 'No one's denying that Ruby's a gifted actor and singer. It's about character, and the safety of the other students.'

'The noose and everything that's happened lately, that's not Ruby,' says Kendall. 'Someone else did those things. Bronnie, tell them—tell them how you know Ruby *can't* have put the noose there herself.'

'I don't think she can have done it, Adam,' says Bronnie, after a brief hesitation. 'I was in the costume room all evening apart from a few minutes—and I could see Ruby that whole time. But . . .'

'But what?' I ask.

'I'm so sorry to have to say this, Kendall, but . . . Imogen told me that Ruby pushed her down the stairs. At Elise's house, on the night of the sleepover.'

'What?' Elise frowns. 'She told me the opposite: that no one pushed her. She made a big point of it. Actually, I remember thinking there was something double-edged about the way she said it. It was odd. She could have just said, "I fell down the stairs," but it felt more like she was making a point of saying that she fell and, honest, guv, no one pushed her.'

'You mean she insisted no one pushed her in a way that made it seem as if someone did?' I say. I can imagine exactly how that would have sounded.

Elise nods. 'She seemed to be protesting too much, now that I come to think of it—she could have been covering up for Ruby.'

Finally, Adam makes a contribution. 'Why would she protect Ruby if Ruby had just pushed her down the stairs?' he asks.

I shrug. 'I've no idea. Perhaps she was trying to hint that Ruby had attacked her but was too scared to say it out loud. Maybe Ruby said, "Tell anyone and you're dead."'

Kendall's on autopilot, shaking her head.

Elise says, 'Once someone's pushing you down the stairs, you're in physical danger—I'd have thought that'd be scary enough. You'd speak up, surely.'

'And she did, eventually,' says Bronnie. 'She told me. Maybe in the moment, at Elise's house, she wasn't sure what to do. Then she thought about it afterward and realized she needed to tell someone. But then . . . why would she beg me not to tell anyone?'

'You're all missing something obvious,' I say. Taking a deep breath, I get ready to share my theory and risk being called crazy. How can I be wrong? I can't be. There's no other explanation that makes sense.

Elise gives me a sharp look. I've promised that I won't mention anything about her little hacking adventure. 'I think Imogen's not who she's claiming to be,' I say.

'What on earth do you mean?' asks Adam.

'I think Imogen Curwood probably isn't her real name. I think her English accent, however convincing, is fake. She's likely to be American—like Vee, the girl who died. There has to be a link: First Vee falls down the stairs and dies, then Imogen falls down the stairs and blames Ruby . . . What if Imogen's a member of Vee's family or . . . sent by them, somehow? Maybe they didn't like the idea of Ruby getting away with what they saw as the murder of their loved one and coming to England to start a new life, get a second chance.'

Everyone stares at me.

'Think about it,' I say. 'Jess swears blind that Ruby can't have put the music box in her locker because they were together all morning. So who did? That music box appeared the day Imogen started here—the very same day. Imogen didn't know Jess at that point. She had no motive to attack her. So what if Jess wasn't her intended victim? What if her aim was to make *Ruby* look guilty, maybe get her expelled? That didn't work—for some reason you don't expel bullies, Adam—so she adapted her plan and turned on Ruby directly: the graffiti appeared, then the noose. And if Ruby was the one she came here to target, what was her motive? If she's who she claims to be—Imogen Curwood, new to the school—she doesn't yet know Ruby well enough to want to harm her. She certainly didn't on her first day, which is when the music box happened. Her being here, everything she's done, *must* be linked to wanting payback for Vee—it's the only story that makes sense. First chance she gets, the sleepover at Elise's, she trots down the stairs, lies at the bottom of them, starts screaming, and makes out that Ruby pushed her—first by hinting, then by telling Bronnie and swearing her to secrecy.'

'I think we need to hear from both girls,' says Adam. 'Ruby and Imogen. Wait here, all of you.'

A few minutes later, the door opens. Adam walks in, with Ruby and Imogen trailing behind him. Ruby is crying and shaking a little. Imogen is staring straight ahead, eyes wide and clear, as if she's staring at someone on the opposite side of the room, someone who isn't there.

*Creepy. Ghoulish.*

'Thanks for coming to talk to us, girls,' says Adam, as if they had a choice. 'We'd like you to tell us about what happened at Sadie's house, when you all stayed there recently. Imogen, you told Mrs. Richardson that Ruby pushed you down the stairs?'

Imogen looks shocked. 'No, I didn't. No one pushed me.' She turns to Elise. 'Mrs. Bond, I told you at the time, don't you remember? I fell. It was an accident.'

'Imogen, that's not what you said to me,' Bronnie protests. 'Adam, I promise you, she *did* tell me Ruby pushed her.'

'I didn't push anyone,' Ruby weeps. 'I didn't touch her.'

'She really didn't,' Imogen says. She walks over to Ruby, puts her arms round her, and gives her a hug. 'It's okay, Rubes. *We* know you didn't do anything, even if they don't believe us.' Ruby pulls away from her.

I've had enough of this freak show. I'm on my feet before I can stop myself. 'Get them out of here, now,' I hear myself snarl. 'Fuck off, the pair of you.'

'Carolyn,' says Elise in a warning tone.

Adam looks at her, as if for guidance. When she doesn't

respond, he says, 'Um . . . all right, thank you, girls. That'll be all for now.'

Once they've gone, I say to Adam, 'If you're waiting for me to apologize, don't bother. I want them gone, permanently. You've got grounds to expel both of them. Bloody well do it or I'll . . .'

'I've no grounds to expel Imogen,' says Adam. 'There's no evidence that she's done anything wrong.'

'Are you crazy?' I snap. 'She's done *everything*. It's all been her.'

'She lied, Adam,' says Bronnie. 'About what she told me.'

Adam sighs. 'I think I need to bring her father in. It's not right that you're all here, participating in this conversation, while Derek Curwood knows nothing about it.'

'He can't come in,' says Kendall. 'He's dying.'

'What?' Adam looks puzzled. 'No, he isn't. I saw him the other day. He dropped Imogen off. Waved at me before he drove away. He seemed fine.'

'Imogen told me he was in a hospice, about to die,' says Bronnie slowly.

'More lies!' I say.

'I'm going to bring Mr. Curwood in,' says Adam, sounding decisive at last. 'I also need to speak to the board of governors before I do anything.'

'In the meantime, can you . . . I mean, can you send Imogen home?' asks Kendall. 'Can you suspend her? I'm pretty sure my daughter's at serious risk of harm—assuming you're not going to expel her immediately either. How would you feel if it was *your* child who'd had the noose treatment?' As soon as the words are out, Kendall covers her mouth with her hand. 'Oh, my goodness, I didn't think . . . I'm so sorry.'

'It's okay,' says Adam, though his face has lost some of its color. 'I'm never sure how widely known . . . Some of you don't know this about me, as I don't mention it very often. I

lost a child to AML many years ago—acute myeloid leuke-
mia. That's why I would never be cavalier about the problems
we're dealing with here. Rest assured, I'm taking all of this
very seriously. I'm going to speak to the governors about
everything that's happened. I also need to take legal advice
on behalf of the school. There are things you don't know
about Imogen. I probably shouldn't tell you this, but . . . well,
she has a history of self-harming.'

'The dressing on her wrist.' Elise looks at me.

'I don't care,' I say. I'm on my feet, heading for the door.
For the time being, it seems, Ruby and Imogen are being
allowed to stay in the building, and I can't stand to look at
Adam Racki's face for one more second.

'Where are you going?' Elise calls after me.

Nowhere. I just have to escape, before I lash out with more
than rude words. I leave the room, slam the door behind me,
and lean against it, closing my eyes.

When I open them a few seconds later, she's there. Imogen.
Standing on the other side of the corridor, looking straight at
me with a peculiar expression on her face, arms hanging
unnaturally by her sides. I make an undignified noise and try
to back away, then realize I can't; there's a door behind me.

'It's okay, Carolyn,' she says. 'I'm not going to hurt you.
I'm just an ordinary girl. Like Jess.'

***

*I enjoyed making up my 'dying father' story. The strange thing is,
so much of it's true. Almost all of it, apart from the dying father
part. What do details matter, though? Emotional truth is far more
important than boring old facts. Can I make myself cry in five
seconds by thinking about losing someone I love? Yes. I don't need
a terminally ill father in order to imagine how it would feel to
have one. I know all about loss, and, when you boil it down—
that's what an audience wants: the bare-bones, elemental experience. The archetypal suffering. If they get that accompanied by a*

173

*description of a yellow-painted room in a hospice that doesn't exist, who cares? I haven't even told anyone the room is yellow yet. Maybe I never will. Still, it's important to know all the details of your story, even the ones you might never need to tell. You've got to have it all straight in your head. The details matter. And the facts matter, of course, but one fact matters far more than all the others: No one understands the agony of loss until they've experienced it for themselves. And that's what I'm here to help with. I'll make the most oblivious among them understand, before too long.*

# 6

# Revelations

*B. A. Paris*

## SNAPCHAT: BEL, SADIE, JESS

**Bel:** Hey anyone know why Rubes has deleted her account?

**Sadie:** Instagram too

**Jess:** Guilt

**Bel:** Think she really did push Imo down the stairs?

**Jess:** Yep!

**Bel:** What about you, Sades?

**Sadie:** Dunno. Don't want to think Rubes would do something like that

**Jess:** Would loved to have been in Adam's office earlier. Your mum say anything, Bel?

**Bel:** No, just that we shouldn't judge

**Jess:** Sounds about right

**Bel:** Bog off. What about your mum? She was there too

**Jess:** Polite version—Rubes is a big fat liar.

**Sadie:** What about Imo? You trust her?

**Jess:** About as far as I can fart

# BRONNIE

My head is pounding by the time Bel and I get home. Normally we chatter away during the journey, but she seems as preoccupied as I am. Although I can't wait to talk through everything with Carl, I'm glad he's not back yet because I need some downtime. That meeting in Adam's office was the most upsetting of my life, and not just because he told us about his daughter. I stick my head around the door of the sitting room, where Toby is watching television, and have a quick chat with him about his day. Normally I'd tell him to make a start on his homework but tonight, I'm happy to leave him where he is.

'Cup of tea?' I ask Bel, slipping off my shoes.

'No thanks, Mum, I've got stuff to do.'

I look at her in surprise, because we always have a cup of tea together when we come in. But she's already turned away. Remembering how silent she was on the way home, I'm about to ask her if everything is all right, then decide I don't want to know the answer—not yet, anyway. I don't think I could cope with anything else just now; I'm still reeling from what Carolyn told us at lunch yesterday, about the real reason Kendall and Ruby left the US.

I fill the kettle and while I'm waiting for it to boil, my indignation rises. I can't believe Kendall lied to us all like that. What I can't get my head round is, if Vee's death really was an accident, why didn't Kendall just tell us about it? Anyone would understand that she needed to get away after something so terrible happening in her home. Imagine having to live in a house where someone has died! If I were Kendall, or Ruby for that matter, I'd never be able to go down to the basement again, never be able to look at those stairs without seeing poor Vee lying at the bottom of them. I'm surprised they haven't decided to sell the house.

I felt awful when Carolyn insinuated that Ruby might have had something to do with Vee's fall because I couldn't get what Imogen had told me out of my mind, about Ruby pushing her down the stairs at the sleepover. I'd never told Carolyn and Elise, and although part of me wanted to, I didn't want to add fuel to the fire. But then, when Adam hauled Imogen and Ruby into his office, Imogen ended up telling everyone herself. I could barely look at her; I couldn't believe that she'd lie to me about something as serious as her dad being ill. I felt so stupid—thank God the other mums didn't make a big thing of it. Carolyn missed a golden opportunity there but fortunately, Vee's death trumped my naïvete. I'm furious with Imogen. What sort of person lies about their father being seriously ill? Isn't she worried about tempting fate? Her poor father; how would he feel if he knew what his daughter's been saying about him? As with Kendall, I don't understand why Imogen lied. Maybe it was to gain my sympathy, so that I'd be more inclined to believe what she'd told me about Ruby. Well, I don't care what Adam said about her self-harming, she's not getting any more sympathy from me!

I'm so grateful that Bel has never caused Carl and me a moment's worry. I can't imagine what it must be like to be Kendall, knowing her daughter's a bully, or Carolyn, knowing that someone hates her daughter. If it were me, I wouldn't be able to sleep at night. And there's definitely something wrong with Sadie, although I'm probably losing more sleep over it than Elise is. In fact, I doubt Elise has even noticed.

I make tea, putting a teabag straight into the cup and adding hot water. I usually use a pot but desperate times call for desperate measures. I carry my unbrewed tea over to the table and sit down, thinking about the meeting. It didn't feel right that there was only a small pause in hostilities after Adam told us about his daughter—but that's Carolyn for you. She's like a dog with a bone when she thinks she's onto something.

'Mum?' I look up and see Bel standing in front of me. 'Can I talk to you for a moment?'

She looks as if she has the weight of the world on her shoulders, and I immediately feel guilty. I knew she was preoccupied with something; I should have asked instead of putting my own needs first. 'Of course,' I say, pulling out the chair next to me.

She sits down. 'It's about Sadie.'

'That's funny, I was just thinking about her.'

'I'm so worried about her!' It bursts out of her like water from a dam, and when her eyes fill with tears, I know it has to be more than Sadie watching too many series late at night. *Please don't let her be pregnant,* I think, putting my arm around Bel and drawing her close.

'Why don't you just tell me?' I say gently. 'Whatever it is, I'm sure we can sort it out.'

'I think she's taking drugs, Mum.' It takes a while for the words to sink in and when they do, I realize it's one of those days that's just going to keep on smacking me in the face. She can't hold her worry in any longer; tears spring from her eyes and I can feel her body shuddering against mine.

'Drugs?' I can hardly get the word out. 'Bel, are you sure?'

'As sure as I can be.' She reaches behind herself, grabs the roll of kitchen towel from the side, tears off a piece, and blows her nose. 'You've noticed, haven't you? You've noticed how awful she looks. And she hardly eats anymore and when I asked her what was wrong, she said she didn't want to talk about it.'

'But that doesn't mean she's taking drugs,' I say. 'You said yourself that she's allowed to stay up all hours. Maybe her body clock is out of sync or something.'

Bel shakes her head violently, sending her dark hair tumbling over her shoulders. 'Today, at lunchtime, she went off without me—she said she needed to be on her own. I was really worried so I waited at the gate for her to come back. She had her head down, reading something, and as soon as she saw me, she stuffed it quickly into her bag as if she didn't want me to see it. So when she wasn't looking, I took it out to see what it was.' She digs in her pocket and brings out a shiny pamphlet, the sort you find in health centers, folded in half. 'Look,' she says, unfolding it.

So I look. There's a picture of a bottle of pills, a syringe, and the words *The first step is admitting you have a problem* on the front.

'This is awful, Bel,' I say, taking it from her. For a moment I feel completely out of my depth. I might have been able to believe that Jess was taking drugs, or Ruby—but Sadie? She's even more level-headed than Bel. 'I just can't believe it. I mean, why? And how?'

'The how's easy, Mum. Drugs are easy to come by at the Academy, as long as you have money, which Sadie does. Her mum's always flinging twenty-pound notes at her, sometimes fifties. Guilt money, Sadie calls it. The why is more difficult.'

'You said she felt under pressure. Could that be why?'

'Yes, but she's not under pressure academically. And lately, she doesn't seem that interested in performing. I've Googled it—being moody, withdrawn, not being able to eat or sleep are all classic signs of drug addiction.' She looks at me in anguish, her huge brown eyes still bright with tears. 'What are we going to do, Mum?'

'I'm going to have to tell Elise,' I say, my heart sinking.

Bel nods. 'You won't tell Mr. Racki, will you? She might be expelled, like those students last year, and I don't want that to happen.'

'No, don't worry. Sadie needs help, not to be expelled.'

'When will you speak to her mum?'

'As soon as possible.' I think for a moment. 'I'd rather tell her face-to-face than over the phone. I'll text her now, ask if I can see her before she starts work tomorrow. I can always go in late.'

Bel leans over and gives me a kiss. 'Thanks, Mum. Thank you for always being there for me. That's Sadie's problem, I think. She doesn't really have anyone there for her.'

I make her a cup of tea, because I want to make sure she's all right. By the time she leaves to go and do her homework, she's in a much better frame of mind. I check on Toby, who can't believe his luck at being allowed to watch even more television, and take my mobile from my bag.

*Elise, could I come over and see you tomorrow morning, at whatever time suits you?* I add *It's urgent*, in case she thinks it's about the fundraiser.

I have to wait until almost ten o'clock before I get a reply.

*If it's about the fundraiser, I'll get my assistant to make a transfer tomorrow.*

*No, it isn't about the fundraiser!* I reply indignantly. I don't want to say that I need to talk to her about Sadie in case she starts demanding why and it's not something I want to talk about by text. *It's about something much more serious.*

*How about Monday next week?*

*How about tomorrow morning?* I retort.

*Busy all morning, I can be at the house at 12. Will need to leave by 12.30. Will that do?*

I want to tell her that I'll make sure to talk quickly but she'd probably reply *Good*.

*Yes. Thanks, Elise*, I write instead.

I don't feel like going to work the next morning, which is a first for me. I thought it would help if I wore my lovely silk dress, because it usually makes me feel a million dollars, and I need to feel confident today if I'm to tell Elise about Sadie. Not that it matters what I wear, because as soon as I set eyes on super-glamorous Elise, I'll feel like a shitty five-cent piece.

I need to speak to Adam but I'm dreading him bringing up what went on in his office yesterday. I also don't know if I should say something about his daughter; if I don't acknowledge what he said, it might seem as if I don't care. As I walk down the corridor, I see him disappearing into his office and catch a glimpse of yellow. I slow my pace, trying to reconcile myself to the fact that he's wearing a yellow scarf. It seems wrong, somehow.

'Ah, Bronnie!' he says cheerfully when he sees me hovering uncertainly in the doorway. 'Just the person I was looking for. Come in!'

'Good morning, Adam,' I say stiffly, unable to match his jaunty tone.

'I'll be putting the list up this afternoon,' he says, beaming. Seeing my bewildered expression, he laughs. 'The cast list for the end-of-term musical! I've decided to go with *West Side Story* but,' he taps the side of his nose, 'don't tell anyone.'

'I won't,' I say. The musical is the last thing on my mind. 'Adam, I need to take an early lunch today. I hope that's all right.'

'Take as much time as you want, Bronnie. The Academy will still be here when you get back.'

I manage a watery smile. 'I hope so. Thank you, Adam.'

'No, thank *you*, Bronnie. I wouldn't be able to manage without you.'

Catching his meaning, I flush to the roots of my hair. 'Adam, I—' But he cuts me off.

'I meant the Academy wouldn't be able to manage without you,' he says smoothly. 'And you wouldn't be able to manage without the Academy, would you, Bronnie?' I stare mutely back at him. 'That's a lovely dress you're wearing,' he goes on. 'Is it silk?'

'Just like your many scarves, Adam,' I snap, and am rewarded by the smile disappearing from his face.

*I can't do this anymore*, I think as I walk away from Adam's office. It's not worth the risk. I stand to lose everything; Carl will never forgive me if he finds out and I'm not sure I can count on Adam to stand by me. I was stupid to have become involved; I knew it was wrong but I was too weak, and Adam too persuasive. But really, I only have myself to blame. When did I decide that what I had before wasn't enough?

The bell rings for the start of lessons and I make my way to the staff room, safe in the knowledge that it'll be empty. I drink a cup of coffee that I don't really want, wondering how I'm going to fill the time before going to Elise's. There's always a costume that needs to be mended and I'm able to sew without thinking too much about what I'm doing, so I tip what's left of my coffee down the sink and leave the room. The students should already be in class at this time of the day—no one has free periods first thing in the morning—so when I see someone leaving surreptitiously through a side door my suspicions are immediately aroused.

'Well, I'll be blowed,' I murmur, realizing that it's Imogen. 'Where the hell does she think she's going?' I march after her, intending to ask her if she's going to visit her sick father, just to see her squirm. Adam said he's an optician in town but I doubt she's going there, not at this time of day. *So where does she live?* I wonder as I hurry after her. *With her father or with her grandparents? Does she even have grandparents, or was that another of her lies?*

I follow her across the inner courtyard, trying to time my footfalls with hers so that she won't hear my steps echoing behind her. She goes through the front gate and onto the street, then runs across the road, narrowly avoiding being run over by a bus. With a blast on its horn, the bus rushes past and as it pulls into a nearby bus stop, I get ready to cross over. But Imogen has gone. I look around in bemusement, pulling my cardigan closed, because there's a chill in the air. How does she do that, being there one minute and not the next? She was right in front of me a few moments ago. There aren't many people around so she should be easy to spot— yet I can't see her. And then, just as the bus is about to move off, I see her long blond hair swinging behind her as she walks along the top deck. Without thinking about what I'm doing, I dash across the road and leap onto the bus, nearly being smashed between the doors as they close.

'That was close!' the driver says cheerfully.

'Sorry,' I say breathlessly, fumbling in my bag for my card. 'Where is this bus going? I just want to make sure I'm on the right one.'

'Brixton.'

Brixton? Oh God. I make my way to the back of the bus, stepping over outstretched legs and bags of shopping. Carl would be horrified if he knew I was on my way to Brixton— it's one of the roughest areas in London. I cram myself reluctantly next to a man three times my size. I don't want to miss Imogen getting off and it's the only seat that has a good view of the stairs. I can't believe I'm actually following her. For a start, it must be illegal, and secondly, what am I going to do if she sees me? None of the other mums would have such

185

qualms, I realize. I realize something else too—that the only reason I'm sort of okay with what I'm doing is that, when I tell them, they might be impressed with me for once. If only I didn't crave their admiration, my life would be a whole lot easier. But whatever I'm doing, even if it's something as simple as baking a cake, I'm continually referencing the other mums. What would they think of this cake I'm about to bake? What would they think of this dress I'm about to buy? What would they think of this book I'm about to read? To use one of Bel's expressions, it's toxic.

I'm so wrapped up in the scene unfurling in my mind, the one where Carolyn tells me I'm amazing to have done what I did, that it's a while before I realize that I have no idea where I am. The bus pulls into a stop and I'm tempted to get off while I still have a chance of finding my way back to the Academy. A pair of denim-clad legs appears on the stairs and I start to get to my feet, breathing a sigh of relief. But to my dismay, they don't belong to Imogen. The legs and other passengers get off and the bus continues on its way. I peer through the window. What is this area, with its boarded-up shops and groups of young men huddled on street corners? I wouldn't dare get off the bus now unless there was a taxi ready and waiting to take me straight back to the Academy. But there don't seem to be any taxis at all around here.

The bus slows to a stop. I turn from the window just in time to see Imogen stepping off. I leap to my feet.

'Excuse me, excuse me,' I say breathlessly, pushing my way down the aisle. Imogen was the only passenger to get out, so the doors have already closed again. I feel a surge of panic. 'The doors, please! I need to get off!'

Fearing that I'm about to vomit on them, the passengers grouped near the exit move back and begin shouting at the driver.

'Open the doors!'

'There's a woman here that needs to get off!'

'Open the fucking doors, mate!'

The doors thankfully reopen and before I know it, I'm standing on the pavement, not quite sure how I got there but relieved not to be going all the way to Brixton. And then I look around, and if a bus had been coming the other way, I'd have run straight across the road and jumped on it, because I've never felt so out of place in my life. Apart from Imogen walking twenty yards or so ahead of me, oblivious to the cold in her tiny crop top, there are only men around. And the way they're looking at me as I hurry after her makes my skin crawl. *Don't be silly, Bronnie,* I tell myself sharply, *they're only men, not murderers.*

'Not so fast.' A man steps out of a doorway and stands in front of me, tall, threatening, and reeking of alcohol. Instinctively, I clasp my bag to my chest. 'Where are you going in such a hurry?'

'My daughter.' My voice comes out in a squeak. 'That's her up ahead. I need to catch her up.'

He leers into my face. 'Don't you want to spend a bit of time with me first?'

'No, not really.'

'Did you hear that, Kyle?' He turns to someone standing in the doorway. 'Not very polite, was it?'

'Excuse me.' I try to step round him but he moves with me, blocking my path. My heart starts beating faster. I don't want to antagonize him, but Imogen is getting farther away. What should I do? *Carolyn. Think Carolyn.*

I draw myself up to my full height. 'Get out of my frigging way!'

His eyes narrow. 'What did you just say?'

'I said—get out of my frigging way!'

He reaches into his back pocket and steps right up to my face. The smell of him turns my stomach.

'Don't waste your time, Daz,' his sidekick drawls from the doorway. 'She's old, and ugly as sin.'

Incensed, I turn on him. 'And you can fuck right off!'

I'm almost as shocked as they are. I have no idea where that came from. It's as if I've been possessed by Carolyn. Luckily, 'Daz' finds it hilarious and when he doubles over, laughing like a hyena, I push my way past him, anger making me stride rather than run. And maybe it's because of the way I'm walking, in a don't-mess-with-me kind of way, that nobody comes near me as I hurry after Imogen.

I manage to close the gap between us just before she takes a sharp left into a narrow side street. I follow her cautiously; both sides of the road are lined with run-down terraced houses and Imogen is crossing over to one of the nearest ones. I dart back around the corner, my heart thumping in my chest. I haven't come this far and been scared out of my wits to have Imogen see me now. I feel terrible for doubting her. From the glimpse I had of the street, it's entirely possible that her grandparents live somewhere like this. They could have moved here when they were first married and lived here ever since. The little terraced house would have been their pride and joy until age and ill health made it difficult for them to cope. I peer carefully into the road, already wondering how I can help, from baking a cake for Imogen to take to them to offering Carl's services in repairing the front of the house, and see Imogen waiting patiently on the doorstep.

A man opens the door. Not her grandfather; he looks too young. It must be her father—no, it can't be, not dressed like that in scruffy jeans and a dirty sleeveless T-shirt, not with tattoos running the length of his arms. My senses are immediately on alert; something feels wrong. All I can think is that Imogen has come to the wrong place, or has been lured here and is about to walk into a trap of some kind. I take a step forward but before I can do anything, she leans in and kisses the man full on the lips. I blink rapidly, wondering if I'm seeing things. I take another look and see the man cupping her backside with both hands, pulling her further toward him until she disappears into the house. An eerie silence descends on the road, broken only by the resounding slam of the front door.

A man pushes past me, bumping my shoulder. I whip round, thinking I'm about to be mugged, but he doesn't appear to notice I'm there. I catch a glimpse of glassy eyes and ribs protruding beneath the thin T-shirt he's wearing, despite the cold. His bare arm is scored with needle marks. My stomach churns. I'm so far out of my comfort zone that all I want is to get back to the Academy. As I move back out onto the main street, I take a last look behind me and see the man disappearing into the house where Imogen is. I feel sick and afraid at the same time—there's no way I can leave now, I'm too worried for Imogen. I need to get her out of there.

Without giving it too much thought, I cross the street, march up to the front door, and knock loudly. It's opened almost straightaway by the man who pulled Imogen into the house. He looks even worse close up, with his pockmarked skin and sunken eyes.

'What do you want?' he says rudely.

'Imogen,' I say, shivering from cold, or maybe something else.

'Imogen?'

'That's right.'

'Never heard of it.' He starts to close the door. 'You won't find it here.'

I put my hand out, stopping the door from closing. 'I'm not leaving without Imogen,' I say with more assurance than I feel.

'I just told you, I don't sell it. Try some other doss house.'

'I know she's here.'

'Who?'

'Imogen.'

'You're fucking nuts, lady. If you don't want what I'm selling, piss off.'

The door slams in my face and, furious, I raise my arm to knock again, ready to tell him that he's the one who's nuts because Imogen isn't an it, she's a she. And then a light bulb comes on in my brain. Realizing what our conversation was really about—as far as he was concerned—I turn around and run down the path, along the street and back out onto the main road, my heart pounding so hard I can hardly breathe. There's no way I'm getting a bus back—I look around and see a taxi on the other side of the road. I run over, almost getting hit by a cyclist in the process, and yank open the back door. A giant of a man crouches there and a small scream escapes me before I understand that he's only trying to get out. I move aside to let him by, then hurl myself onto the back seat before the driver can move off.

'Are you free?' I ask, my voice all over the place.

'Looks like it,' the driver says grimly. 'Where to?'

I'm about to ask him to take me back to the school when I realize that I may as well go straight to Elise's. I find her address on my phone and check the time. It's only ten fifty, so I'll be there too early. It doesn't matter; I can always find a café.

It's a while before my heart rate is back to normal, but worry gnaws away at me. Maybe I should have tried harder to see Imogen. But once I guessed that the man was a drug dealer, all I wanted was to get away. How can he possibly be her boyfriend? He must be at least thirty. What if he has her hooked on drugs? What if he's using Imogen as his way into the Academy? What had Bel said only last night? *Drugs are easy to come by at the Academy.* Is it possible that it was Imogen who introduced Sadie to drugs? Remembering how I saw them huddled together a couple weeks back, I know I need to speak to Elise fast. And Adam, because he should be told about Imogen.

The traffic is so bad that I'm only twenty minutes early at Elise's, so I walk around the neighborhood, practicing what I'm going to say and how I'm going to say it. The houses are amazing—huge, double-fronted, four-story, white-painted palaces—and I wonder how Elise feels about having one of the smallest houses on the street. It's still impressive, though. I see her click-clacking down the road in her heels and go to meet her.

'I hope you haven't been waiting long,' she says, a frown on her face. 'I told you I wouldn't be here until twelve.'

'Just a few minutes,' I say, wondering why she always has to sound so impatient.

I follow her in. I never feel comfortable in Elise's house. It's like being in a show house, and I'm so scared of breaking something, or leaving a fingerprint on a glossy surface, that I turn into a nervous wreck. I especially dislike her kitchen, where we're heading now. She waves me over to one of the ridiculously high bar stools.

'Tea?' she offers as I clamber up.

'Please.'

'Turmeric or fennel?'

'Actually, could I have a coffee?'

As she walks around the kitchen, preparing my coffee, her reflection is mirrored over and over again in the chrome surfaces.

'I don't suppose we could go through to the sitting room, could we?' I ask. Her eyes widen in surprise, as if I'm a trades-man asking to use the main entrance, and something snaps inside me. 'These bar stools may be the latest design but they're bloody uncomfortable! And you might like seeing yourself reflected a hundred times over but I don't!'

A frown creases her brow. 'Are the stools really uncomfortable?'

'Yes! It's like being perched on a bloody pole. And before you ask, your kitchen is so clinical it's like being in a hospital!'

'Oh.' She takes a bottle of water from the fridge, pours herself a glass, then fetches my coffee from the machine. 'Well, if that's how you feel, come on through.'

I slide off the bar stool and follow her through to her enormous sitting room. There are four large sofas to choose from, and I imagine their family evenings—Elise, Nick, and Sadie sitting miles apart, each on their own chair—if they have family evenings.

'So what's this about?' Elise says, sitting down on one of the sofas.

'Sadie,' I say, wondering if I should sit next to her, or in the nearest armchair. But it's so far away I'd have to shout to make myself heard.

'Sadie?'

'Yes,' I say, sitting down next to her.

She gives an exaggerated sigh. 'This isn't about her having a bit of alcohol from time to time, is it?' she says, sounding bored.

During all the pacing I'd been doing while I waited for her, I'd been trying to work out how to break it to her gently. But her attitude rips my kid gloves off.

'No, it's about her taking drugs!' I say furiously.

She looks at me in bewilderment. 'Drugs?'

'Yes. Surely you must have noticed how dreadful she's been looking?'

Elise shakes her head. 'I—'

'You can't have missed those huge circles under her eyes,' I persist, digging the knife of bad parenting in a little deeper. 'Bel said she's barely eating and sleeping.'

'Sadie can't be taking drugs,' she says, smoothing her skirt down several times, a sign that she's lost some of her composure. 'She's too—sensible.' She falters on the word.

'I'm sorry, Elise, but all the signs are there. The good thing is that she's aware that she has a problem and seems to want to do something about it.'

'Why, have you spoken to her?'

'No, but Bel found this in her bag.' I pull out the leaflet and hold it out to her. She accepts it slowly and looks at it for a minute, taking in the photo and the title: *The first step is admitting you have a problem.* The blood drains from her face. She reaches for her glass and takes a long drink, buying herself some time.

'She—she wanted to speak to me about something last night, she said she had something to show me. But then she couldn't find it and I told her it didn't matter, that I was busy anyway and she started crying. I asked her what the matter was but she just shook her head and went upstairs.'

'Did you go after her, ask her what was troubling her?' The blood rushes back to her face, turning her skin crimson. She gives her head a small shake and I sit there in silent disapproval.

'It's not Sadie,' Elise croaks. 'It isn't Sadie.'

'No, I know Sadie isn't supplying drugs,' I soothe. 'Although I think I know who is,' I add grimly.

'No.' Elise shakes her head so violently that one of her earrings nearly hits her eye. 'It isn't Sadie who has a problem—it's me!' She looks up at me, agony in her mascaraed eyes. 'I didn't think she'd noticed, but she's not stupid. She got that leaflet for me, Bronnie.'

I stare at her. 'Oh, Elise,' I say, my heart sinking.

She searches for a tissue and when she can't find one, I fish one from my bag.

'It's clean,' I say. 'A bit crumpled, but clean.'

'Thank you.' She wipes her eyes, blows her nose, almost in control again. 'I know you must be judging me, Bronnie, but I couldn't do the job I do, work as hard as I work, if I didn't have some kind of vice. It's just not sustainable.'

'Then is it really worth it? You're addicted to alcohol, Elise!'

She flinches. 'Not addicted,' she says fiercely.

'Well, I wouldn't know much about it,' I say tartly. 'But neat vodka at midday sounds like an addiction to me, especially as I'm guessing it isn't your first. You've got to get help, Elise. I know you love your job, but you love your daughter more.'

I'm sure I only imagined a slight hesitation. 'You're right, of course I do. Poor Sadie, she must be so worried.'

'Will you speak to her tonight?'

She nods. 'I'll come and pick her up from school.'

'Will you be able to get away in time?'

'I won't go back to work this afternoon.' She gives a small laugh. 'I think I need to sort out my own problems before I tackle anyone else's.'

'That's a very good start. I know this might sound a bit strange, but I'm glad it's you who has a problem and not Sadie. Bel will be too.' I pause. 'Do you mind if I tell her? It's just that Sadie might need someone to talk to, and she and Bel are really close.'

'No, of course you can tell her as long as she keeps it to herself. Please thank her for looking out for Sadie.' She reaches over and gives me a hug, slightly awkward, but a proper hug. 'You've helped me.'

'That must be a first,' I say.

'Don't keep putting yourself down, Bronnie. We all envy you, you know.' I look at her in surprise. 'It's true. You've got the most important thing in the world right: motherhood. I've always been shit at it.'

'But you're going to be less shit at it from now on,' I say, making her laugh. 'I better go, Elise. I've been away from school all morning.' I suddenly remember that I haven't told her about Imogen—but maybe it's not the right moment.

I'm so lost in thought as I return to the Academy that I miss my Tube stop and have to walk back. I'm almost there when I see Kendall ahead of me in the street.

'Kendall!' I call.

She turns. 'Oh hi, Bronnie,' she says unenthusiastically.

I'm glad to see she can't meet my eye. 'Shall we have a coffee?'

'Shouldn't you be at work?'

'No.'

We head to the nearest café, which—luckily—has a spare table near the window. We have to squash past pushchairs and step over dogs to get to it.

'So, how are you?' I ask once we've ordered our coffees.

'All right, I suppose.'

'Why didn't you just tell us the truth?' I ask, plunging right in.

'Because I knew you'd all think the worst.'

'We're only thinking the worst because you've made it seem as if you had something to hide.'

'Look, I'm sorry. I wish I'd done things differently. But right now, I've got more important things to think about. Imogen, for a start.'

I take a breath. 'Speaking of Imogen, I saw her leaving the Academy this morning when she was meant to be in lessons. So I followed her.'

'Where to? The shop that sells rope?' she says bitterly.

'No, to somewhere out Brixton way.' It's not that her sarcasm is lost on me, but I'm in a hurry to tell my story.

Kendall gives me a reckoning look. 'Isn't that kinda breaking the law—you know, following a pupil?'

'Probably. But it's just as well I did. You'll never guess, Kendall—she went to this grotty area, full of druggies—I was nearly attacked, but I just thought of Carolyn and swore at them—and she went to this house and this awful man opened the door and Imogen kissed him!'

Kendall shrugs. 'So she's got a boyfriend. But I agree, she shouldn't be sneaking off to see him during school hours.'

'You're missing the point! For a start, he's much older than she is; he must be at least thirty. And . . .' I take a quick look around me and lower my voice. 'I think he's dealing drugs.'

'Dealing drugs?'

It's not the first time I wish someone had taught Kendall how to whisper.

'Yes. But keep your voice down.'

'Why do you think he's a drug dealer?' she hisses.

'Because he looks like one! And then this dodgy-looking guy came along, he was definitely on drugs, and he went into the house. It was awful, Kendall. I knew I couldn't leave without speaking to Imogen so I went and knocked on the door. Her boyfriend opened it and it was really strange—when I asked to speak to Imogen, he thought I was asking to buy drugs. He actually thought Imogen was the name of a drug!'

'He was having you on,' Kendall says, looking amused.

'No, that's just it, he wasn't. It was as if he'd never heard the word "Imogen" before.'

Kendall is silent for a moment and I give her time to come up with an explanation.

'Did Elise say anything to you about her trip to the States?' she says.

I stare at her. 'Kendall, did you hear a word I said? I think Imogen's boyfriend might be using her as a way of getting drugs into the Academy!'

196

'Then you need to speak to Adam about it.'

'I'm going to. I just wanted to see what you thought first.'

'Me?' She gives me a tight smile. 'Oh, I don't know anything anymore. I have no idea what anyone is up to.'

I open my mouth to tell her that she should be taking what I've told her more seriously, and realize how unhappy she looks. 'Is something the matter?' I ask.

She toys with her coffee cup. 'I just wish Elise hadn't looked Greg up.'

'Because everyone knows about Vee now?'

'No. Because I don't know what went on between them.'

I can feel myself frowning. 'Are you suggesting what I think you're suggesting?'

'You know that Elise and Nick have an open marriage, right?'

'But even so!' She stares mutely at her coffee. 'Have you asked Greg?'

'He says they had a drink together.'

'And you don't believe him?'

'I don't know what to believe.'

*Neither do we, Kendall,* I think. *Neither do we.*

I don't stay long with Kendall because she's more preoccupied by the possibility that Elise slept with her husband than the possibility of drugs at the Academy. I can't blame her; if it were Carl I'd feel exactly the same. Not that Carl would ever look at Elise—although, if he ever finds out what I've been up to, he might end up looking elsewhere. My only comfort is that Carl isn't sophisticated enough for Elise, so there's no danger there.

Danger is everywhere else, though. On impulse, I take out my phone and call Carolyn.

'Hi, Bronnie,' she says cheerfully.

'I'm not disturbing you, am I?'

'No, it's fine. What's up?'

'I was just wondering if the police have made any progress in finding who ran you off the road yesterday.'

'Well, they've managed to trace the vehicle, but it was a hire car, so they don't have a name yet. But what they do have is a photo taken by a speed camera just after. It was a woman.'

'A woman?'

'Yes. The image is too grainy to see her face clearly but guess what—she has long blond hair!' She sounds triumphant.

'Well, at least that's something to go on,' I say.

'Bronnie, you're not getting it. Long blond hair—who do we know who has long blond hair?'

'Um—'

'Imogen!'

'What—you think it was *Imogen* who tried to run you off the road?'

'Why not? We've already established that she's crazy.'

'But why? And anyway, can she even drive?'

'She's seventeen, isn't she? I don't know who's worse, Ruby or Imogen. They're both bloody dangerous, if you ask me.'

'Have you told Adam?'

'Not yet, the police only just phoned Elise so I'm going to wait until they have a name for the person who hired the car. Without it, Asshole Adam will only say I'm jumping to conclusions, that I have it in for Imogen, blah, blah. But I'm going to get that little bitch, Bronnie, one way or another.'

By the time I get to the Academy, it's gone three. I head straight for Adam's office, hoping he's not going to bawl me out for being absent most of the day.

He's not there so I go to look for him. As I walk toward the staff room, my eye is caught by a large notice pinned to the board in the central hall announcing: *And the winner is …* WEST SIDE STORY*!!!*

I hurry over, my heart racing. If Jess has the lead role, it won't matter that Adam didn't choose *My Fair Lady*. Carolyn will still be horribly smug. *Please don't let Jess be Maria*, I pray. I look at the cast list, and my mouth drops open. It's Bel! Bel has got the part of Maria! I feel a rush of happiness, followed by a surge of triumph that all the hard work has paid off. I'm dying to phone Carl, but it's Bel's news to tell, not mine.

I look quickly down the list and see that Sadie is Bel's understudy, not Jess or Ruby. In fact, neither Jess nor Ruby has a major role, as the role of Anita has been given to Imogen. I frown, wondering at Adam's motivation. Is he using the fact that Jess's song at the revue was cut short, and Ruby didn't get to sing at all, as an excuse to exclude them? I hate what's going through my mind. It feels disloyal to Bel. But what if she only got the role of Maria because Ruby and Jess were out of the running? I know the awarding of roles isn't dependent on how the students performed at the revue, but I can imagine certain people seeing it that way. Or— even worse—what if Adam has given Bel the role as a thank you to me?

'No need to look so glum, Bronnie!' Adam's voice comes cheerily down the corridor, and I can't work out whether it's better that he's in a good mood, considering what I've got to tell him about Imogen. 'Anybody would think you weren't pleased that Bel will be playing Maria.'

'Of course I'm pleased, it's wonderful!' I wait until he's standing close to me, then plunge straight in. 'It's just that I wouldn't like her to have got the role because of—well, you know,' I say, my voice low.

'That's absolutely not the case,' he says firmly. 'You know as well as I do that Bel will be outstanding as Maria.'

'But as Jess and Ruby didn't get to audition properly, maybe they should audition again.'

'That's not going to happen.' He lays a heavy hand on my shoulder. 'You worry too much, Bronnie. I know Jess and Ruby will be disappointed, and I imagine Jess's mum is going to have something to say about it. But I awarded the roles to the students who I know will do them justice—and who should be rewarded for their good behavior.'

Now I'm wondering if he left Ruby out as punishment for her bullying and left Jess out to punish Carolyn for hers. I feel the beginnings of a headache and wish I could postpone speaking to him about Imogen.

'Actually, Bronnie, there's something I want to talk to you about. Do you have a minute?'

'Of course,' I say, my heart starting to beat faster.

I follow him to his office, steeling myself. He waits until I'm sitting on the other side of his desk.

'Unfortunately, I haven't been able to get to the bottom of that nasty business with the noose,' he says, and I breathe a silent sigh of relief that it's only that he wants to talk to me about. 'Now, I know I've already asked you, but are you *quite* sure you didn't see anyone in the dressing room during the revue?'

'I'm positive,' I say, realizing that my life would be a whole lot easier if I could point my finger at someone.

'You know the students better than I do,' Adam goes on. 'Do you think Ruby could have put it there herself?'

'I suppose,' I say reluctantly.

He strokes his chin. 'What about the graffiti on the bench? If I remember rightly, you said you left the school around five o'clock. Did you see anyone hanging around the inner courtyard?'

'No.'

'And you didn't see any graffiti on the bench?'

'No.'

'So it's possible that Ruby sprayed the bench herself?'

'Why would she do that?'

'We know she's a little disturbed, because of her behavior last year. It wouldn't have been difficult for her to take a can of spray paint from the store cupboard and graffiti the bench. As you just confirmed, there was no one hanging around the inner courtyard at five o'clock because school finished at four thirty. Theoretically, Ruby could have sprayed the words on the bench herself—there was no one around to see her do it—and then screamed blue murder when you and Bel turned up.'

'Except that she was already hysterical when we arrived,' I say, wondering why he's so desperate for Ruby to be the culprit.

'Exactly!' he says triumphantly.

'I don't understand.'

'Ruby said that the graffiti was on the bench when she arrived at five o'clock.'

'That's right.'

'And she was still crying about it thirty minutes later? It doesn't add up. Why sit there crying for thirty minutes instead of going to tell someone about it? I was in my office, she could have come to me.'

What Adam needs, I think grimly, are a couple of children. Then he might understand how it's possible for a teenage girl to cry solidly for thirty minutes over a bullying incident and not tell her headmaster about it, a headmaster who she knows considers her a troublemaker. Then I remember that he *did* have a child, and hate myself for forgetting.

'What about Imogen?' I ask.

He frowns. 'Imogen?'

'Yes.'

'What do you mean?'

'Well, as Jess's mum pointed out, all these things started happening the day she arrived.' I look at him meaningfully. 'How much do we really know about her?'

'As much as we know about any other student.' He looks down at a letter on his desk in an I'm-not-talking-about-this-anymore kind of way.

'We don't, not really. There's something you should know, Adam. I saw Imogen leaving school today, so I followed her.'

His head snaps up. 'What do you mean, you followed her? Where to?'

'To what I presumed was her grandmother's house. She told me she was living with them and that they were in ill health, so I thought there must be an emergency for her to leave school without authorization.' I expect him to pounce and tell me that he authorized her absence, but he doesn't. 'Except that a man answered the door, a man too young to be her grandfather—or her father, for that matter.' He waits for me to go on. 'It was obvious from the way they were behaving that he was her boyfriend.'

'So Imogen has a boyfriend,' he says, shrugging. 'I'm sure lots of our students do.'

'Yes, but he's a good ten years older than her, maybe more. It's not just that, though. I think he's a drug dealer.'

'You think?'

'I know.'

'How?'

'Because when I went to the door and asked to speak to Imogen, he didn't seem to know what I was talking about and said that if I didn't want what he was selling, I should piss off.'

'That doesn't mean he was selling drugs. It could have been televisions, mobiles—anything.'

'No.' I shake my head. 'He's a drug dealer, I know it.' I look him straight in the eye. 'Why are you so reluctant to believe it? Imogen could be in danger!'

His face darkens and I'm glad that I've finally got through to him. 'I could have you sanctioned for this, Bronnie.'

My mouth drops open. 'For being concerned about the welfare of a student? If you'd seen the man she was kissing on the doorstep, I think you'd have been worried too!'

I don't know who's more surprised at my tone, me or him.

'Nevertheless, it could be seen as stalking.'

'Not if I only followed her once.' He looks at me, daring me to go on answering him back, and for a moment, I hold his gaze. But then I drop my eyes.

'I thought I should mention it, that's all.'

'And now you have.' He gives me a quick smile to take the sting from his words. 'Leave it with me, Bronnie, I'll take care of it. And don't forget to see if you can find any claimants for the lost property,' he adds, reminding me of my place. 'Some of the students are on a break now. Why don't you take the basket round?'

I leave Adam's office, worry stabbing away at me. It was stupid of me to antagonize him like that. If he wanted to, he could make my life very difficult.

I find the lost property basket and make my way to the inner courtyard. A couple of boys pick out sweatshirts and another takes a pair of filthy trainers that I'm glad to see the back of.

'My leggings!' Ruby says in delight, dragging a pair from the basket.

Jess peers in. 'My bra!' She waves it around in triumph and I wonder how, at the time, she hadn't noticed she hadn't put it on, given the size of her breasts.

'What about you, Imogen, anything in here that belongs to you?' I say, trying to keep my voice even because I'm finding it hard to look at her, given what I've learned about her. She stares back at me with her unblinking blue eyes, as if she's weighing me up, making me wonder if her boyfriend told her about the woman who called looking for 'Imogen' and she's put two and two together. 'Hurry up,' I say, shaking the basket at her. 'I haven't got all day.'

She takes her time rifling through the stuff and eventually finds a leg warmer. I'm about to move on to the next group of students when she quickly takes a hairbrush that's now lying at the top of the basket and hides it under the leg warmer, as if she doesn't want anyone to see it. But I'm past wondering about her bizarre behavior. I'm more worried about her drug-dealing boyfriend.

The bell rings, putting an end to my effort to get rid of the lost property. I dump the basket in the staff room, deciding it will be more effective to stand at the gates later on and catch the students as they're leaving. Desperate for some peace and quiet, I hurry to my workroom. I'm almost there when I hear the sound of raised voices coming from the dressing room next door.

'Do you really think I would have jeopardized my own audition, you stupid fucktard?' Ruby is yelling. 'Bel, tell them! Your mum was backstage, she would have seen me if I'd put the noose there myself, right?'

'Who are you calling a fucktard?' Jess's voice rings out.

'Her!' Ruby's voice trembles with rage. 'That fucking weirdo over there! Come on, admit it, bitch from hell! You're the one doing everything, not me!'

There's the sound of scuffling, followed by a cry of pain from Imogen. I burst into the dressing room and see a tangle of arms and legs, some of which belong to Bel.

'Oh my goodness!' I cry. 'Girls! GIRLS!'

Bel turns and to my relief I see that she and Sadie aren't fighting but trying to pull an out-of-control Ruby off Imogen, who is cowering on one of the benches, sobbing in great gulps. I rush toward them. 'What on earth is going on?' I say, wedging myself between them. 'Ruby, that's enough! RUBY!'

Ruby looks at me, her face white with anger. 'She's a lying bitch! She's trying to make out that I'm responsible for the noose and for pushing her down the stairs!'

'You did push me down the stairs!'

Ruby bursts into tears. 'I hate her! She's been sending me notes—' She's crying so much she can't go on.

'What notes?' I ask, trying to make her sit down.

'Why don't you ask her?' she rages. 'She's crazy!'

'Pot kettle black,' Jess murmurs.

'See!' Imogen says triumphantly. 'Even your friends think you're mad!'

Ruby whips round but none of her friends will meet her eye, not even Bel.

'Fucking bitch! Fucking lying bitch!' Ruby breaks free of me and lunges at Imogen. 'What about you, what about the lies you've told, about your father dying when all along he's alive and well! And you self-harm, do you? Well'—Ruby is beside herself with rage—'I DON'T BELIEVE A WORD OF IT!' Before I can grab hold of her, she reaches out and rips the plaster from Imogen's arm.

'Ruby!' I say. But I'm staring not at a wound but at the tattoo that was hidden by the plaster—*Sky above me, earth below me, fire within me.*

'Ow!' Imogen shrieks, covering it quickly with her hand as the others rush over. But Jess pulls her hand away, and, with a cry of rage, Imogen shoves her aside and runs from the dressing room.

'See?' Jess says triumphantly. 'Mum was right. She said Imogen self-harming was a load of bullshit.'

'Language,' I say distractedly, my mind on the tattoo. I've seen it somewhere before.

'But why pretend that she self-harms?' Bel asks, puzzled.

'To get attention. She's *crazy*.' Jess points her finger at her head, miming madness. 'Did you see the way she was crying when Ruby barely touched her?'

'It's a really pretty tattoo, though,' Sadie says. 'I wouldn't mind getting one like that.'

I look around. 'Where's Ruby?'

'Don't know,' Jess shrugs. 'Shall I go and look for her?'

'No, I'll go. And keep quiet about what just happened, please. We wouldn't like Adam to hear about it, would we?' I add severely.

I leave them whispering among themselves, wondering what else is going to happen before the day is out. I'd give anything for a cup of tea, but finding Ruby is my priority. She was so upset. It's not that I condone her behavior—no one should resort to physical violence, no matter what the provocation— but I can't help feeling sorry for her. She must be feeling so alone, completely abandoned by everyone.

I check the three toilet blocks but there's no sign of Ruby. I head for the courtyard, my mind on Imogen's tattoo, wishing I could remember where I saw it. It was some years back. Maybe at a party I went to, or while I was having my hair done. Hairdressers often have tattoos, don't they? Wherever it was, it had made a huge impression on me. I loved the image the words conjured up, of a free spirit walking the earth, answerable to nothing and no one, and I remember thinking that if I ever decided to get a tattoo, it would be that one. Not that I've ever been a free spirit. Nor will I ever be one, which is quite sad because sometimes, just sometimes, I'd love to tell everyone—Adam, the other mums, even Carl and the children—to sod right off.

I get to the inner courtyard and see Ruby sitting on the bench where someone sprayed *Here lies Ruby Donovan*. The words are gone now, helped on their way by some solvent and steel wool, with Bob supplying the elbow grease.

Even at a distance I can see the tear streaks on Ruby's face. My heart goes out to her and I hurry over, ready to give her a hug.

'There's someone on the roof!' Imogen's voice rings around the courtyard and I might have thought it was another of her lies if it wasn't for the urgency behind it. Looking up, I see a slate heading straight for the bench where Ruby is sitting.

'Ruby!' I cry.

At the sound of my voice, she raises her head. But because she doesn't understand the urgency, she doesn't move. The slate hurtles towards her and, using every fiber in my body, I throw myself at the bench.

# 7
# All the Players

*Holly Brown*

# TEXT MESSAGES: KENDALL AND GREG

**Kendall:** Something's happened to Ruby.

**Greg:** More bullying?

**Kendall:** It's not just bullying. When will you get it?

**Greg:** How can I get it? You won't talk to me.

**Kendall:** This isn't about us, it's about Ruby. There's been an accident. I don't know the details, headmaster was cagey on the phone. I'm going to the school now.

**Greg:** Is she hurt?

**Kendall:** He said it's not serious, but she's upset.

**Greg:** Let me know if you need me.

**Kendall:** Was that sarcastic?

**Greg:** God, Kendall, what do you think of me?

**Kendall:** I'll text you later when I know what's going on.

**Greg:** Why text now, with no solid info? To stress me out? To punish me?

**Kendall:** Because you're still her father.

**Greg:** And I'm still your husband. Stop avoiding me. Stop ignoring me.

**Kendall:** You're the one who's avoiding. I asked what you did with Elise, and you didn't answer.

**Greg:** I'm sure I did.

**Kendall:** No, you turned it back on me. Blamed me for moving away. For moving Ruby away. Like it's my fault you fucked my friend.

**Greg:** I didn't fuck your friend!

**Kendall:** You fucked my frenemy. Whatever, I'll text you later about Ruby.

# KENDALL

It's nowhere close to rush hour, but even so, the taxi's crawling along like a tortoise. I should have taken the Tube. You should always take the Tube. What you shouldn't do is text your philandering husband in a panic. It never ends well.

Why couldn't Adam Racki have just told me over the phone what happened to Ruby, and what kind of shape she's in now? He basically hung up on me, which tells me he's scared.

As he should be. The bench graffiti happened at his school, and he's done nothing about Imogen, and now Ruby's had an 'accident.' He's not going to get away with it. And whoever's terrorizing Ruby isn't going to get away with it, either. There are no accidents.

We start to go at a decent clip in one of the designated taxi lanes. That lasts about ten seconds before a bike gets in our way. I feel like screaming. There should be a police escort. I need to get to my baby. She might be injured, she's definitely upset, and she needs me. I don't want anyone else with her in that place. It's not safe. Who knows what she might say?

'Are you going as fast as you can?' I ask the driver. 'I'm in a hurry.'

'Yes, ma'am.' He's an older gentleman and his tone is studiously patient. It says that everyone's in a hurry, all the time.

'No, I mean, it's an emergency. Something's happened to my daughter.'

'How old is she?' He sounds more engaged now, though I hadn't intended it as a conversational overture.

'Sixteen.'

'And what's happened?'

'I don't exactly know.'

He gives me an odd look in the rearview mirror. *How can you not know?* his eyebrows say.

I want to tell him to sod off, as the Brits say. I used to be charmed by all their slang, and the accents, and high tea, and manicured gardens, and brick landmark buildings everywhere. When I first arrived, I'd say things like, 'The problem with LA is that it has no history.' But now all I see is the gray and all I feel is the damp. My daughter's at school surrounded by maniacs and I'm stuck in bloody traffic.

'I'm sure she's fine,' he tells me, and I nod so he'll shut up.

But part of me agrees with that look he gave me, the one tinged with judgment. It's my business to know. She's my child, and she's nowhere near fine, and it's my fault. I should have pulled her out of the school already, like Carolyn always threatens to do with Jess. I should have taken her back to the States. No, I should never have brought her to London at all. Greg isn't right about much, but he may have been right about that. There was no talking to me at the time, though. I'd been high on my post-cancer wisdom, sure that a fresh start would cure all ills. A new environment was supposed to mean a whole new Ruby. It was a place to try out the whole new me.

For a while after the move, I'd felt vindicated. She'd hooked up with the other girls to form the gang of four, and she seemed so happy. I'd hooked up with the other mums. But then, within months, Ruby was back to her old tricks, targeting Jess, and now she's being targeted herself.

The mums can be so self-righteous, taking the slivers of what they think they know about Vee and creating a narrative about Ruby. Of course I had to maintain that Vee's fall was an accident. I can't trust them with the truth. I have to hope Ruby realizes the same rule applies to their daughters.

Ruby took it so much easier on Jess than she had on Vee. That was part of why I leapt to Ruby's defense with Mr. Racki last year. Because as bad as it looked to him and the other mums, especially Carolyn, I knew that it actually represented an improvement. Ruby had been less manipulative and had exercised greater self-control than with Vee. She'd also picked a much stronger victim this time. Jess can more than hold her own.

Maybe that's what this is. Jess is striking back now, and she's not playing around. This time, Ruby's the one in danger.

The cab pulls up in front of OFA and I thrust way too many bills at the driver before taking the steps two at a time to get inside the building. Racing down the hall and into the office, I stop short when I see who's at the front desk. What's Bronnie doing at the computer? Is she just that desperate to be around Adam Racki? I flash to when I came upon them backstage at the revue, and remember thinking that the two of them had been about to go in for a clinch or had just exited one.

Bronnie looks awful. Her hair is a mess (from Adam's hands running through it?), her face pink and blotchy (from the press of his stubble against it?). The best description of her expression is a cross between rattled and guilty. When she opens her mouth to speak, nothing comes out.

'What are you doing here?' I say, harsher than I intended. Or perhaps just as harshly, I don't know anymore.

'I'm just, you know . . .' She looks around like she's hoping someone (her lover?) will intervene. 'Doing some data entry.'

So that's what they're calling it these days?

Mr. Racki emerges from the inner sanctum of his office and Bronnie hurries out immediately. He's usually impeccably groomed but now his hair is slightly askew, just like his tweedy scarf. When he clasps my hand, his feels clammy and insubstantial. I get it: He hasn't got the strength for this job. Hasn't got the stomach. Carolyn's known that all along.

Last year, it was her daughter being bullied, and now it's mine. Coincidence?

There are no coincidences, and there are no accidents, much as I wish there were.

'Mrs. Donovan,' he says, and I note his formality. No *lovey* or *darling* today. 'I'll take you to Ruby, but I wanted to tell you about the accident first.'

'Could you be brief, please?' Best to start out polite. If I have to get vicious later, so be it. Kill them with kindness first.

'The school's been planning to get some roof work done. We'll obviously move that up and it'll start right away.'

So Ruby fell off the roof, is that what he's saying?

'A slate became dislodged.' I have the sense that he's chosen the word 'dislodged' with some care. 'We're all grateful that Bronnie was there, and she was able to get Ruby to safety. Without Bronnie, it could have been much worse. She's the kind of brave, quick-thinking employee that we're so lucky to have here at the Academy.'

Yes, *he's* lucky to have her, all right.

In light of this information, Bronnie's behavior seems additionally odd. Why would she have hurried off without any sort of acknowledgment about what had happened to Ruby when she'd actually been there? She sure hadn't acted like a hero; she'd seemed like a woman with something to hide. It was as if she didn't even know me, or wished she didn't.

And now Adam Racki is using her to try to cover his ass, pretending that Ruby hadn't been endangered by the school—no, it was quite the contrary! She'd been protected by the headmaster's most cherished employee.

Meanwhile, Ruby must have been terrified. A slate had nearly crushed her. She could have died, is what Mr. Racki is telling me.

'How could you have let this happen?' I say.

He starts to reach out a hand to me, then thinks better of it and drops it to his side. 'I am truly sorry. But I can assure you, nothing like this—'

'I need to see my daughter.'

'Yes, of course.' Only he doesn't move. 'I just really feel—'

'I don't give a shit how you feel. I need to see my daughter.'

'What I mean is,' he says quietly, 'I understand what you're feeling. More than you know. We'll talk more later. My door is always open to you, Mrs. Donovan, and to Ruby.'

He leads me up the hall and knocks on a door. The nurse opens it in her absurdly starched uniform, right out of central casting, and I can see beyond her to where Ruby is sitting on a cot, feet flat on the floor, back ramrod straight, immobile. From this angle, in profile, I can't tell if she's eerily composed or catatonic. Whatever it is, it's unnatural, not Ruby at all.

'It's your mother,' the nurse says, and Ruby reanimates. She runs into my arms, sobbing, as the nurse departs. Tears rush into my eyes, too. They're not just sympathetic, because her feelings are running right through me. Her every fear, her heartbreak, they've always been mine, too, in one closed circuit, an unbreakable bond.

I'm so relieved that she's alive and safe, and she lets me hold her tighter than she has in I don't know how long. Then she retracts her head and I see her face. I gasp involuntarily at the sizable bandage on her right cheek. Mr. Racki had said she wasn't 'seriously' injured. This isn't serious? She's an actress!

'When the slate crashed,' he explains, 'it shattered. There were some shards. The paramedics have already been here and I made sure they knew what sort of school this is. They were very careful in stitching her up.'

'Stitches?' Done by paramedics, not by a plastic surgeon? I'm filled with horror. The cut must be at least four inches long, based on the size of the gauze, and I can't estimate how wide, and it's obviously deep enough to require suturing.

My baby will be scarred.

Her career. Her life. For a split second, I'm watching them both go up in smoke.

Then I notice that Ruby's watching me, and I know I have to compose myself. I need to be strong for her. 'I'm so thankful the slate didn't land on you, and that none of the shards went into your eye. All the damage will be superficial.'

She laughs with sudden harshness. 'Who looks beyond the surface, Mom?' She moves away from me, taking a seat on the nurse's cot. Her back is concave, like she wants to curl into herself. She wants to disappear.

I finally take in the whole of her. She must have bled a fair amount—the top of her light blue leotard is mottled red.

Oh my God, it's just like the music box. How had I not picked that up sooner? Light blue is Ruby's color, not Jess's. That ballerina wasn't meant to be Jess; all along, it was Ruby. Whatever's gone on today, it was set in motion weeks ago. Months, maybe.

What teenager could have done this kind of planning? None that I know, not even Ruby herself.

But Imogen has never seemed like a teenager. She always seems younger, or older. And there's something almost ... otherworldly about her. She's not precisely there when things are happening; she has alibis (like sitting out in the audience next to me), and yet she's always nearby, just outside the frame.

'I'll leave you two alone,' I hear Mr. Racki say from what seems like very far away but I know is only a few feet behind us. He shuts the door behind him.

She's started crying again, noiselessly, soaking the gauze with her tears. Her chestnut hair has broken free of the bun at the nape of neck and it looks wild. She's hurting so badly, and I wish I knew what to say, how to take it away.

My heart aches. I know that Ruby's worries about her appearance aren't only based on her profession, they're deep-seated insecurities. She's always cared immensely about beauty and her perceived lack of it. She'd push the prettiest little girls off the slide or out of the sandbox. In third grade, Ruby wrote a fairy tale about an ugly little girl with a beautiful mom that ended with the little girl drowning in the sea. Her teacher recommended therapy, but Ruby insisted it hadn't been about her and me, and I believed her. Even then, she was a great actress.

She's been fighting so hard this year not to feel inferior to Jess and to make sure that even if she did have those feelings, she didn't act on them. I know Ruby. Even if the scar is small, she'll fixate. Her blue eyes, so much like mine, will go right to it, seeking it out, the way she's always lasered in on her imperfections.

'I'm ruined,' she chokes out.

'No, you're not.' I take the seat beside her on the cot, wanting to hold her again, but something in her posture tells me not to try.

'Don't pretend, Mom. You know it, too. You were disgusted when you first looked at me.'

Why hadn't Mr. Racki at least warned me about the location of the supposedly minor injury? Then I would have prepared my face; I would have prepared my words. Ruby's so sensitive, and now she's saddled with the image of my initial reaction.

I wasn't horrified by her; I was terrified of what this could mean. But I can't tell her that, because we don't yet know what it means. We don't know how bad any of this will be.

'I was angry with the school for letting this happen, that's all,' I say. 'I could never, ever be disgusted by you.'

She doesn't answer. She doesn't believe me.

'It must be hard to think clearly when you're still in shock from the accident.'

'It wasn't an accident. Someone was on the roof just before the slate crashed down where I was sitting on the bench.'

I'd thought the situation was suspicious, that it was more than an accident, but somehow, I hadn't imagined this. If a person had deliberately pushed the slate, knowing Ruby was directly below . . .

Someone had tried to kill her.

'Who was it?' I ask.

'Imogen couldn't tell. It all happened so fast.'

'Imogen was there?' As in, she was the witness, not the suspect?

'She called out that someone was up on the roof, and then Mrs. Richardson pushed me out of the way. Imogen saved my life.' I wish she didn't sound so gloomy about that fact.

But we can handle that later. She'll sleep in my bed, we'll watch movies and eat her favorite junk food, I'll paint her nails. For now, I need the details. 'Did anyone else see the person up on the roof?'

'Only Imogen. Headmaster Racki started to call the police and Imogen took it back. She said it had just been a flash of something in her peripheral vision, not an actual person.'

So Imogen didn't want the police called. I wouldn't put it past her to have a juvenile record. This is a girl who enjoys telling people her perfectly healthy father is dying. But she's also the girl who saved Ruby's life. You don't always get to pick your heroes.

'It doesn't matter, though. I might as well be dead.' Ruby gestures toward her cheek.

'Don't say that! Your life is about a lot more than how you look.'

'What casting agent will consider me now?'

'There might not even be a scar. If there is, we'll see the best plastic surgeon back in LA. They can fix it with lasers. We'll figure it out, I promise you.' Here I go again, leading her right back into the land of the superficial. 'You're talented and a hard worker. You're a loving person. That's what matters.'

She gives me a contemptuous sideways glance.

'I'm so sorry if I've given you the impression that . . .' I don't know how to continue. Have I given the impression that her only value is if she's likable and pretty and talented and successful? I know I never said it, but she could have seen it in me, because I used to think that's the only value I had, too. 'I love you, Ruby, more than anything. All I care about is that you're next to me.'

'I saw your face,' she says.

'I just knew that you would be upset, that's all.'

'Stop lying!' she snaps. 'I was ugly already, and now I'm going to be monstrous.'

'That couldn't be further from the truth. Even if there's a slight scar, you're going to learn that in life that's what adds character. The hard times shape us. We learn from our scars.'

'I don't want to be a character actress! I want the lead. I wasn't getting cast anyway, and now it'll never happen. Since they all think I'm a monster, why not just look like one?'

'No one thinks that.'

'They asked me about Vee.'

'Who did?'

'Jess and Sadie and Bel. They don't know what happened with Vee, or at least, they're saying they don't, but they'll find out soon enough. They were already looking at me like a . . . like a . . .'

She dissolves into tears again, and I squeeze her shoulders. She shrugs me off.

'They hate me,' she says, 'and they're right to hate me.'

'No, they don't.'

'Then where are they?' She makes a demonstration of looking around. 'No one's come to check on me.'

'Maybe they don't know what happened. Mr. Racki's protecting your privacy.' Even I know how lame that sounds, so I try again. 'Maybe they think you were taken to the hospital.'

'They don't care if I live or die. Or if they have a preference, it's for dead.'

'No one wants you dead,' I say, but after today, with the slate, it's a ridiculous contention. Someone was up on the roof. Someone tried to kill my daughter.

What should I do? No parenting book has covered this scenario, I'm sure. Do I call the police? Mr. Racki didn't think there was any point, since no one saw anything, really. Except Imogen, and she's already recanted. But then, Mr. Racki has a reason not to want the police involved. Then all the parents—even the ones whose kids tell them nothing— would hear about it, and so would the media. He has a lot to protect. I think of what he said to me at the revue. When he labeled Ruby as 'complicated,' I heard 'dangerous.' He might not think a girl like Ruby is worth the risk.

I could call the police myself, but Ruby's not exactly a sympathetic victim. And in the unlikely event that the London police contact their LA counterparts, we'd be sunk.

So we're on our own.

'I just can't do it anymore,' she says. 'The lying, the covering up.'

'What's the alternative?' It comes out a little angry. We're in this together, that's our pact. There's no giving up. No giving in. No one gets to bully us into submission. 'What do you think they'd do if they knew the truth?'

It's like I can feel the energy being leeched from her body. 'Maybe I don't care. Maybe I just want to be free.'

I was in the kitchen, making tea because I didn't know what else to do with myself, because when in London, do as the Brits do, and that's when I heard it. I knew just what it was, and yet I managed to be surprised all the same.

The irony? I'd just finished texting Greg to tell him that Ruby would be fine. Yes, she had a cut on her face, but I'd be taking her to a plastic surgeon in London to follow up and make sure it was healing properly. He didn't need to know how despondent Ruby had seemed, all that talk about everyone hating her, how limp her body had been against mine. No, he needed to know what I wanted to believe: that somehow, it would all be fine. I'd make it so, through sheer force of will. I had beaten cancer, and we'd beat this, too. Never say die.

Then came the thud.

I tore through the apartment, glad for once that it was so diminutive, because it meant I got to her fast. She was on the floor of her room and she was wailing. It was a terrible animal sound, such abject pain and frustration, and the noose was still around her neck. Thankfully, it had been the one from the prop room, so it couldn't hold her weight and, instead, sent her crashing to the ground.

I knew she'd meant it—that it was no cry for help, that it was a sincere wish to die—because she ran toward the kitchen and tried to grab a knife out of the butcher block. If I hadn't chased her, hadn't tackled her, she might have . . . I can't even say it.

I will never forget that moment, the agony of having to press my full weight onto my sobbing, writhing daughter as she begged me to let her up, begged me to let her end it all, to do what her suicide note had promised:

*It's time to give the people what they want.*

That wasn't all it said. She talked about having pushed Vee down the steps, and wanting to relieve me of my burdens. She said that she couldn't live with the secrets anymore. *You win*, she wrote.

She must have been talking to her tormentors. She was ready to give up. But I won't let them win.

Ruby is in the psychiatric hospital on a locked ward now. For the night, at least, I know she's safe, and she's resting. They had to sedate her heavily because she was so upset at having lived. Judge me if you will, but I couldn't just sit there by her bed all night. I had to do something. I have to find out who my suicidally distraught daughter was addressing when she wrote those words: *You win*. Because sometime in the not-too-distant future, she'll be coming back out of that hospital, and when she does, I have to make sure she's truly, lastingly safe. That means I can't just wait, I have to act.

Something tells me to go through Ruby's room, that there are things she hasn't told me, things that could become clues. I yank open every drawer, look under the bed, toss aside all the clothes littering the floor of her closet, and there they are—three pieces of cardboard. Three anonymous notes.

I don't know the order in which they arrived, though I'd guess it's this:

*I know what you did*
*I know what you are*
*I KNOW YOU*

I lay them out, trying to see if there are clues within the clues. Whoever did this cut letters from magazines and glued them onto the cardboard. It's cartoonishly amateur yet remarkably cruel, just like a teen girl would do, and she's succeeded, hasn't she? Ruby wanted to die. If she'd used a real noose, she'd be dead already.

I don't know how these were delivered or when, if one of them was waiting for her somewhere after the slate fell and that's what drove Ruby over the edge. Could someone have been getting into our flat, leaving these in Ruby's room? Then she would never feel safe; she'd never feel free, to use her word. She'd feel hunted.

But if they were delivered to the house, they might not have been meant for Ruby. Could they have been intended for me, and by hiding them, Ruby was trying to make sure I was the one set free?

If I want the answers, I have to go find them, and I need to start with the person who has the least reason to lie. That's the person who definitely didn't do this. I can't believe it myself, but it seems that's Imogen.

I can thank her for saving Ruby and find out if maybe Imogen does know who she saw on the roof and is too afraid to tell the police, for whatever reason. I don't care about the reason, and she should know that. I just need the truth, and I'm willing to pay for it.

I can't help thinking that if situations had played out differently, Ruby could be Imogen. Ruby could be the one with no mother to speak of. She could be the one with no guidance and little to lose, preyed upon by nasty older men. Perhaps I could help Imogen in some way, at the very least let her know that I can see she has a good heart underneath that peculiar exterior. Well, *a* heart, anyway.

At OFA, rehearsals for the end-of-term show start right away, and they're only canceled for the most dire emergencies. My guess is that a slate nearly crushing Ruby wouldn't qualify. Imogen is in *West Side Story*, so that means she's probably at school.

I'm in the taxi, having once again forgotten the lesson about taking the Tube, and I have to hope fervently that I haven't missed everyone. I haven't been very lucky lately, but right then, I catch a break. The girls are streaming out of the building in pairs and trios and quartets, and I don't see Jess, Bel, and Sadie, but I do see Imogen emerging, alone. She's changed out of her school uniform into a short, skin-tight dress. Her hair is slicked back, and she's wearing a ton of makeup, including bright red lipstick. That must be what the dodgy boyfriend is into. It makes me sad for her. She's just a teenager who's lost her way, that's all.

I beckon for her to join me off in the shadows beside the large stone steps. She looks around nervously and then says, 'Let's just talk here.'

So I ascend the steps to meet her. I'll just have to use my inside voice. 'I wanted to thank you for what you did yesterday for Ruby. If you hadn't yelled, Ruby might have been seriously hurt.' She's still hurting, of course, and in the psychiatric hospital, but I'm not going to share that with Imogen, not until I know for sure that I can trust her.

'Yeah, well.' Imogen flicks some lint off her shirt, as if that's how much she cares about Ruby. Ruby's just a speck to her.

I decide to ignore the gesture and its implication. 'Thank you, from the bottom of my heart.'

She lets out a little scoff.

'I understand this act you're doing, and you don't need to.' She starts to smile. 'Oh, you do? You get me?'

'It's like how you were baiting me the night of the revue. It's all part of the way you keep people far away, so they won't know the real you. All the things that hurt you.'

'Did you get that from one of your self-help books?'

How does she know what I read? Has she been in my apartment? No, more likely it's something that Ruby mentioned, or something the girls laugh at me about. It's not cool to care about anything.

I continue doggedly. 'When you helped Ruby, you showed me what kind of person you really are.'

Her smile disappears, as if instead of a compliment, I'd just delivered a stinging blow. 'Why don't you get out of my fucking way?'

'I don't know what I've said to upset you, but that wasn't my intent.' I need her. She might be the only one who can tell me who was up on that roof, who's really behind what's been happening to Ruby. When Ruby comes home from the hospital, I want to be able to tell her that all the craziness around her is going to stop, that it'll finally be okay. Imogen could be the key. 'I was hoping that we could help each other.'

'And just how could we do that?' She thrusts out her hip. I think it's equal parts defiant and make-me-an-offer. Which is perfect.

'Maybe you could use a little extra pocket money.' I'm trying to be delicate. 'Whereas I could use some information. If you caught a glimpse of who was on the roof, that's worth a lot to me. I'm not suggesting you go to the police and tell them, if that's uncomfortable for you, but if you could tell me, I'd *really* appreciate it.' It's coming out unbearably awkward. Of course it is. I've never even tried to slip a maitre'd cash to get a good table and now I'm trying to turn a teenage girl into a paid informant. I feel like a pimp.

But she seems to be considering it. Then she looks me right in the face and says, slowly and deliberately, 'You don't know fuck-all about what I could use, *Mrs. Donovan.*'

That's what does it, the emphasis on my name, the suggestion of an insult about my station in life and my marriage, the insinuation that I'm not what I appear to be, because as she starts to walk away, I grab her arm and spin her. I've always been stronger than people expect, when I choose to exhibit it, and for the second I've got Imogen's flesh clamped in my hand, I enjoy her flash of fear.

'What's going on here?'

I look up, and at the top of the steps, there's Adam Racki. I wonder how long he's been standing there watching, deciding when to make his entrance. Once a thespian, always a thespian.

I drop Imogen's arm. She rubs it pointedly. Theatrically.

He walks down the steps and says to Imogen, in a voice that's lowered, nearly conspiratorial, 'Are you all right?'

As if I've threatened her! She's the one who was just cursing at me.

But I did manhandle her, that's true. I might have even left marks.

I feel frightened by the surge of anger that had rushed through me, that split second of being both so in control and so out of it, and the pleasure I took, and the fact that I've been seen. What if there are marks? What could Mr. Racki do with that?

Ruby almost died today. Twice. I'm not myself. Adam Racki would certainly understand that. He's always been a reasonable man.

'I'm fine,' Imogen says. 'I just want to go home.' She's using her little girl voice. Surely Mr. Racki can see through that? If he was listening in on our conversation, then he knows how she was just speaking to me. Imogen might have done the right thing earlier today when it came to Ruby, but she's still one fucked-up kid. I'm a responsible adult. He can't actually take her side over mine.

Then again . . . he can if he wants to rid himself of Ruby and me, if we've become liabilities.

He pats Imogen on the back. 'All right, darling. Go home, take a bubble bath. Pamper yourself, okay?'

She walks down the steps without a backward glance. Mr. Racki turns to me. 'Mrs. Donovan.' His voice is cold. 'I would have thought you'd be home taking care of your daughter. Does she really want to be alone, after the day she's had?'

I've played plenty of cards with him before, to good effect. Might as well try the suicide one. 'Ruby's in the hospital.'

'But I thought . . .?' He trails off, confused. He's assuming I'm referring to the slate.

'The psychiatric hospital. She tried to kill herself. She's in a locked ward right now, sedated.'

He looks like he's been slapped. But he recovers quickly and his face is nearly liquid with sympathy. No, not just sympathy. Empathy. Oh, right, he had a daughter, too.

I wait for him to tell me that he understands, or that he knows what I'm going through, or that he hopes Ruby will get the help she needs, he's in our corner . . . I don't know, just something headmaster-ish. Instead, he takes me in his arms with such extreme tenderness that I begin to cry. It's the first time I've been able to release all the stress of the past day, the past weeks, and it's not sexual in the slightest, but there is chemistry. There's a cellular awareness that he's a man and I'm a woman, and I need that. It's been so long.

'"How can I hold you close enough?"' he whispers into my hair. '*A Doll's House.*'

For a second, I think he's giving me a clue. I picture the ballerina's missing arm, so like a doll, and then I realize that it must be the name of the play he was quoting.

Somehow, that sobers me enough that the tears stop, but I don't let go.

★　　★　　★

229

After a visit to the hospital, where I plant a kiss on Ruby's head (not that she even stirs, she's so zonked out), I'm back in the taxi, following my sixth sense. It hasn't led me astray yet. And there they are, the three other mums, Elise probably into her third gin and tonic by now. She's generous buying rounds when what she really wants is for others to keep up.

Elise's favorite watering hole is—what else?—a hotel bar. She loves shiny reflective surfaces, all onyx and silver, loves looking at herself, loves controlling where everyone meets. If she'd seduce her friend's husband, it's not beyond reason to think she'd hurt that same woman's daughter.

'Hello, Kendall,' she says, drily, as if she's been expecting me all along, as if I hadn't been left off the guest list on purpose. 'So lovely to see you.'

'Kendall!' Bronnie says, a bit flustered by my sudden appearance, standing up to give me a hug. 'How's Ruby?'

She must mean how's Ruby been doing since the slate incident. They can't know about the suicide attempt, since I haven't told anyone and patient information is confidential.

Part of me wants to fully hug Bronnie back, to heap gratitude on her for risking life and limb to push Ruby out of the way since, obviously, Bronnie could have been crushed herself, had she gotten the timing just a bit off. But then I also wonder: How was her timing so spot on that she was right there, ready and willing to play the hero? Almost like there'd been some orchestration, or like she was currying Adam Racki's favor.

I choose not to answer her question about Ruby, instead saying stiffly, 'Thank you for looking out for her today.'

'I wish I could have done more.' Her eyes are limpid. 'I mean, I wish she hadn't gotten that cut on her face.'

'We all wish her a speedy recovery,' Carolyn says, as if she'd like to dispense with the whole tiresome business as quickly as possible. 'We were just talking about Imogen, how that girl is not right in the head.'

I've had it with them scapegoating Imogen. What a convenient target she's been, a way to play innocent and pretend it's not one of them, or one of their girls. I take the cardboard notes from the large bag at my feet and slam them on the table.

'For fuck's sake, Kendall!' Elise sputters. 'You've spilled my drink.'

'Buy another.' I glare all around. 'You think Imogen's behind these, too?'

They study the notes, Carolyn with the greatest degree of interest. She looks at me, her eyes bright. 'Where did you get these?'

'I found them buried in Ruby's closet.'

'Ruby didn't tell you about them herself?' Bronnie asks.

'So we don't have the same relationship as you and Bel do,' I say. 'I guess I'm not the mother you are.'

'I didn't mean that. I just meant that it must have been difficult to come across these. What did she say when you talked to her about it?'

'She didn't say anything because she's locked up in a mental hospital.' I look at each of them in turn, scrutinizing their reactions. 'She tried to kill herself today, thinking that's what all of you—and your daughters—wanted.'

Bronnie is visibly shocked, and shaken. Carolyn is reservedly surprised, while Elise is unmoved, throwing back the remnants of her G&T. 'Is she okay?' Bronnie manages.

'Of course she's not okay,' I say. How dim can a person be?

'I meant—is she okay physically? How did she . . .?'

'She tried to hang herself. Fortunately, it didn't work.'

Now Elise's eyes are bright, though it's with amusement rather than curiosity. Somehow, despite everything, I'd never

231

imagined she could be this cruel. 'Wait, let me guess. She used the prop noose? And—shocker—it failed?'

I feel like I might lunge across the table at her. 'She didn't know it would fail. She truly wanted to die, because of you and your daughters. I want to know who's been pushing her toward this with the music box and the noose and these notes.'

'Wait, the music box? That was for Jess,' Carolyn says.

'The light blue leotard,' I say. 'That's Ruby's color. Jess never wears it. When I went to pick Ruby up at school today, there was blood splattered on her. Because of the cut on her face. It's all been meant for Ruby. Everything's been designed to harm her, or to make it look like she harmed someone else. It's all about Ruby.'

'Spoken like a true narcissist's mother,' Elise says. 'Have you ever considered the very real possibility that Ruby did all those things herself? She pushed Imogen. She hung the noose to get sympathy. Then she pretended to commit suicide with that same noose, as if she'd been driven to it. She left these notes for you to find. What's the common denominator? Wherever Ruby goes, there she is.'

'The notes were hidden! She didn't want me to find them.' I look to Bronnie and Carolyn. Are they really going to stay silent in the face of Elise's hideous, immoral accusations? My daughter's in the hospital! She wanted to die. When she wakes up, she probably still will. I don't know what I can do about that, so I'm here doing this, trying to find out the truth. Trying to get some measure of justice.

'Let's face it,' Elise says. 'Ruby is obsessed with attention. She'll do anything to get it. Rather like some other people we know.' She stares at me, her meaning clear. She thinks the apple doesn't fall far from the tree.

'Let's all take a breath,' Carolyn says. 'Kendall, you are coming in hot. But I understand it. I mean, I can't understand it because Jess has never had those types of tendencies, though I can imagine how upsetting it must be. And Elise, I do get what you're saying. Ruby has been somewhat erratic in her time at OFA.'

'We just can't rule anything out, that's all.' Bronnie seems to mean it to be soothing but I feel electrified with betrayal.

'Can't rule it out? You honestly think Ruby could have done all this herself?' I nearly shout at her. People at other tables are staring. For once, I could not give a shit.

'I just think that it could have been a cry for help,' Bronnie says. 'She has trouble talking about her feelings, so she acts them out. You've told me that yourself.'

All this time, I trusted her the most. I confided in her. Now she's using my own words against me? My vision actually blurs with rage.

'What the fuck do you know anyway?' I say. 'Your head is so far up Adam Racki's ass that you wouldn't recognize the truth if it bit you on the nose. Whoever heard of a wardrobe mistress doing data entry? You'll do anything to be near him.'

'Data entry?' Elise perks up, as if that's the juicy part of what I've just said. I will never understand that woman. Not that I want to.

I've tried hard not to imagine what Greg could have possibly seen in her. Best case scenario, he was choosing my antithesis. I've also tried not to imagine where it happened—whether they first met in a hotel bar like this one, or if Elise has been in my bed.

I need to stay focused. This isn't about Greg and his disloyalty right now. It's about Bronnie's. 'You were there when the slate fell. How could you save Ruby and still doubt her?'

Bronnie won't look at me, and I'm not sure if it's because of shame or anger. I did just expose her little whatever-it-is with Adam Racki.

'You seem like you could use a drink, Kendall,' Carolyn says. 'I'll grab you a chair.'

While Carolyn's gone, Elise and Bronnie ignore me totally. As I lurk between them, my avenging angel persona is wearing off like a spell, and I'm not sure who to replace it with. The Kendall who was always hoping they'd like me, though it's looking like none of them ever did? The Kendall who was reborn after cancer? The Kendall who wanted everyone to think she had a marriage so solid that it could go global? The Kendall who's failed at mothering her poor, damaged girl?

I have so much to be guilty for, but I've held it at bay by storming around town, investigating, getting nowhere. Now it's washing over me, full force.

Carolyn returns with the chair. I perch, thinking that I haven't even told Greg the latest. He doesn't know that Ruby's in the hospital.

It's not an oversight. I've been holding off for fear that he would get right on a plane, and I just can't face him. Not after what he's likely done with Elise; not when he's likely to blame me for Ruby's situation, and he might very well be right. I can still hear those words from her suicide note. There was no accusation in them, and that's what hurts the most.

'So what we need to do now is review the evidence,' Carolyn says, 'as calmly and rationally as possible.'

Bronnie nods, while both Elise and I look at her like she's lost her marbles. At a moment like this, sounding logical might be the craziest thing of all.

'None of us want some psycho on the loose,' Carolyn explains. 'None of us want to be targeted, or to have our daughters targeted. So we need to put our heads together and puzzle this out.'

Carolyn might be right. At any rate, this gives me a chance to observe them all. I don't know if I'm keeping my friends close right now or my enemies closer. But Ruby's bedded down for the night, and I don't have anywhere to be. I have too much adrenaline to go home and sleep. Not that I'd want to sleep; I can't bear to dream.

Carolyn gives a recitation of all the events since the music box, concluding, 'Kendall is correct in that everything either points to Ruby or was aimed at her, except for when Elise and I were sideswiped by a car.'

'Which could have been random,' Elise says.

'Just because it doesn't fit the pattern doesn't make it random,' Carolyn counters. 'My best theory is this: It's Imogen, with an accomplice. We can all see that Imogen is unhinged in a way that's very different from how Ruby is unhinged. No offense, Kendall.'

There are no words.

Carolyn smacks the table. 'I've got it! Imogen's dodgy boyfriend is her accomplice.'

'And the motive?' Elise asks.

'Ruby was with Imogen's boyfriend, so Imogen was mad at Ruby, because girls are often stupid that way, thinking the other girl is to blame instead of the bloke, and because he wanted to get out of hot water, he agreed to help Imogen harass Ruby.'

'Ruby wouldn't touch some wannabe drug dealer,' I say. She's had limited interest and experience with boys; it's not where her head is right now. Even if she did change her mind, there's no way she'd be with the man Bronnie had described. 'This is pure fantasy.'

Carolyn is undeterred, and Elise seems like she could be persuaded to the theory. Their opinions of Ruby are that low. But it seems to me that Carolyn is grasping at straws, like she's trying to cast suspicion elsewhere and keep it off her and Jess, when the Mordue women have the strongest motivations of anyone. Who knows, they could have been sending Ruby those notes, hoping she'd off herself, and when it wasn't working fast enough, they rigged the slate to fall.

Though Bronnie's the one whose husband is a roofer. Maybe there really wasn't anyone on the roof. Bronnie rigged the slate to fall and then came to her senses at the last minute.

Am I actually suspecting Bronnie of trying to murder Ruby?

I feel dizzy. I don't know if I've eaten anything since breakfast, and my tenuous grasp on reality is loosening by the second.

'We're all on your side, Kendall,' Bronnie says gently. 'We all want to find out who did this.'

'How about this instead? Imogen wanted Ruby's place in the group,' Carolyn suggests, 'and Dodgy decided he'd help her get it.'

'Couldn't they just all be friends?' Bronnie says. 'Wouldn't it have been easier?'

Carolyn shakes her head like Bronnie is hopelessly naïve. 'There's not room for everyone. The Academy will never be some hippie commune, no matter how many love-ins Adam organizes.'

'But Imogen had already taken Ruby's place in the group before the noose. Why keep going?' I say.

'To make sure that Ruby wouldn't worm her way back in.' It's crazy to think Carolyn's a law professor. She seems so comfortable convicting people without sound evidence. Or perhaps she just has no qualms about redirecting suspicion from her and Jess.

Or just from Jess. It could be that Carolyn thinks her daughter had a hand in all of this, and she's already launching a preemptive cover-up just in case. Defense attorneys never ask if their clients are guilty; they don't want to know. The same could be said for mothers.

'Assuming Imogen is behind everything,' I say, 'why would she pick Ruby?'

'Imogen targeted Ruby because Ruby had targeted Jess previously—i.e. Ruby had it coming, in Imogen's mind,' Carolyn says.

'Are you forgetting that the music box had already been put in Jess's locker the day Imogen arrived?' Bronnie says. 'Imogen wasn't at the school last year, so how would she have known all of this and had time to make a music box with a Jess-shaped ballerina singing Jess's audition song?'

'Let's say the music box was someone else, maybe Ruby,' Carolyn says, 'but then Ruby saw the error of her ways, and everything after was Imogen and Dodgy, including running the car off the road.'

'In my heart,' Bronnie says, 'I just don't think it's Imogen. She's a seventeen-year-old girl who was desperate to make friends. So she told some lies along the way to garner attention or sympathy—'

'She said her father was dying!' Carolyn bursts out. It's clear that she's not about to allow any defense of Imogen to go unchecked.

To her credit, Bronnie won't be silenced. 'She told some lies, but she wasn't backstage when the noose was hung. She was sitting in the audience with Kendall. Then when the slate fell, she wasn't on the roof; she was the one calling out in order to save Ruby.'

'She must have loosened the slate earlier,' Carolyn says. 'She engineered it to fall, and she planned to call out so she could look heroic, and she could pretend that someone else had been up on the roof to cast suspicion elsewhere, but she didn't think anyone would actually be close enough to save Ruby.'

'Wait, you really believe that Imogen is a cold-blooded murderer?' Elise asks.

Carolyn nods firmly. 'I do. Well, she's a cold-blooded attempted murderer, and it's up to us to take her down. We have to protect Ruby.'

Now she's crossed over into absurdity. She's got to be covering for someone. Either she's looking after herself and Jess, or she's looking after Elise and Sadie. After all, Jess was telling Sadie backstage that she needed to come clean, and Elise hates me enough to try to seduce my husband. Those two mother-daughter pairs are the most suspicious—not that Bronnie's in the clear, but Elise and Carolyn have seemed a whole lot chummier lately.

'Let's put our cards on the table here,' I say. 'None of you really want to protect Ruby. You don't care what happens to her, or to me.'

'You can't think that,' Bronnie protests.

'Why wouldn't I think that?'

'Oh, poor Kendall,' Elise says, dripping with sarcasm. 'She and her darling daughter can take turns playing the victim.'

'You've never bothered to get to know either of us,' I say. 'So you might try shutting the fuck up.'

Elise does the opposite, of course. 'You came here tonight, guns blazing, using Ruby's hospitalization as a way to get the upper hand, demanding answers from the rest of us. But you haven't given us any real answers, have you?' I don't say anything. 'I'm talking about Vee, of course. That bullshit you fed us about how she really did just fall, and Ruby got blamed, and it was so hard on her, she became a pariah, blah blah fucking blah.' Her eyes are flashing. What did I ever do to her? Why does she hate me so much? 'Your own husband thinks Ruby's a psycho who pushes girls down flights of stairs. And how do you think she got that way?'

'Fuck you,' I say.

'Very clever.' Elise grins, like she's the one with the upper hand now.

'It is important that we cut the crap, Kendall,' Carolyn

says. 'We need to be honest with each other if we're going to keep the girls safe.'

'All your girls are safe. It's Ruby who's not. It feels like one way or another, my girl is going to die.' There, it's out. My greatest fear. I stare at the table, trying not to cry. They won't get my tears.

Bronnie reaches out and touches my arm. 'I'm so sorry for all that's happened. But I have to agree with the others. You need to tell us the truth. How else can we help?'

Ruby wanted her story out there. She said it herself, in the suicide note. And earlier in the day, too, at the nurse's office. She wants to be free. I'm only honoring her wishes.

No more delaying. It's time to start the performance.

'You're right, I haven't been completely honest, and I told Ruby to keep secrets, too. I didn't want you all to prejudge us, and I was sure that the worst was behind us. But obviously . . .' I trail off strategically, hoping to engender compassion. But even with Bronnie, it seems that I have to earn it.

'First, there are some things you need to understand about Vee,' I say. 'I'd thought there was no way that was her given name, but later, after I met her parents, I found out that it was. They were theatrical people themselves, and they'd wanted a *V* name, for some reason, and then they said, "Well, how about Vee?" They were hard people to take seriously, like their daughter was.'

I see in Elise's eyes: *Get on with it*.

'Vee and Ruby didn't like each other initially, but then they became friends. It wasn't the smoothest friendship because as freshmen at an elite private performing arts school, they were in competition. Vee and Ruby were the two best, and sometimes Vee won and sometimes Ruby won. There was a certain amount of rivalry is what I mean.'

I see it in Carolyn's eyes now: *Get on with it*.

Then it's all too much—the pain and the shame and the uncertainty of what's going to happen next, the sheer terror of tomorrow and tomorrow and tomorrow—and I burst into tears. Bronnie is instantly nurturing, and Carolyn and Elise soften a little, but they're not going to turn to mush. They're still waiting to hear the story before they decide what they think of me, and of Ruby.

'I'm sorry I lied,' I blubber, 'but I wanted Ruby to have a fresh start at OFA. That's why we were willing to move so far away from home.'

'That, and no school closer to home wanted to take her,' Elise has to interject.

'Yes, she did get turned down from other schools, but that wasn't fair. It was on the basis of rumors, not fact. Only I couldn't go in front of all the admission boards and explain it, so she got rejected, and it devastated her. Think how your girls would feel.'

'So what precisely happened?' Carolyn asks.

'Vee was over at our house like she often was, and she fell down the stairs.'

'Really, Kendall? That's your story and you're sticking to it?' Elise says, disgusted.

'That's what we told the police,' I say, genuinely tearful at the memory. It was terrible for Ruby and me. 'We said that we'd both been in the kitchen downstairs and heard Vee tumbling. We had this rug at the top and we moved it so that it looked like Vee had slipped.' Bronnie is staring at me in horror; the other two are impassive. 'I know how it sounds, but you have to think how it would have looked. Vee and Ruby had been having some issues in their friendship, and no one would have believed the truth.'

'Which was?' Elise says.

'That Vee and Ruby were arguing at the top of the stairs, and Vee was the aggressor. She was angry and she grabbed

Ruby. Ruby broke the grip like anyone would have done and somehow, Vee fell. It really was self-defense—Ruby was scared, she thought Vee might push her down the stairs—but we were afraid the police wouldn't believe that. We thought it was best to say it had been a total accident, that we were nowhere near Vee.'

'You thought the best way to go was to lie to the police?' Carolyn and that smug mug of hers. Like she wouldn't do the same. Like she wouldn't do worse.

'We did,' I say, as humbly as I can. 'In hindsight, I still don't know if it was the right call. Maybe it would have been better if the police had investigated and exonerated her, because everyone at school was so eager to let their imaginations run wild. It was a drama school, after all. So they concocted all these stories about what kind of person Ruby was, and they ran around calling her a murderer. What if the police had listened and railroaded Ruby? What if she'd wound up in prison for a crime she didn't commit? Think about what you would have done if it were one of your daughters.'

'I can see your dilemma,' Bronnie says, her face full of sympathy.

'So that's it?' Elise says. 'That's the whole truth?'

'That's the truth,' I say.

'I can see how it all could have happened,' Carolyn says, 'and I can also see how the other students could believe Ruby would have done the pushing.'

Even at her most compassionate, Carolyn can't resist the dig. I wish all the mums could have seen Ruby during those nights after Vee died, when she was sobbing and terrified. They have no idea what it's like to hold and comfort their children night after night, and then day after day, as the rumors swirled. They've never had to flee a country only to find themselves in a new pit of vipers.

241

It's so easy to sit in judgment when your daughter is the one getting the parts, not the one coveting them; when your daughter hasn't had her beloved grandfather die at the same time she watched her mother battle cancer; when their children haven't been through what Ruby has or seen what she has. And sure, they don't know everything she's done, but I don't know everything about them or their daughters, and I'm okay with that. I'm not going to paw through their garbage or fuck their husbands to find out. There are lines I won't cross, ever. Can they say the same? One of them might have tried to kill a child. My child.

I have to save Ruby. No matter what. It's what Ruby and I always say to each other, but they're not just words. We've lived it. She knows I'll always be there for her, no matter what. I've proven it. She's proven the same.

This is the story she wanted me to tell. These are the lies that will hopefully keep her alive. So why do I still feel so guilty?

It's just how moms are, I guess.

I use a cocktail napkin to blot my eye makeup. It's exhausting, crying in front of these bitches.

'Has anyone from that story shown up in London?' Elise asks, always the first to return to the business at hand. But right now, I don't mind. At least she's searching for other suspects instead of accusing Ruby again.

That means she bought what I was selling.

For the first time that night, I want to smile. But instead, I shake my head. 'Vee's parents are still in LA and, as far as I know, they believed the results of the investigation that ruled it an accident. Vee wasn't well-liked at the school. Ruby was her only friend. I can't come up with anyone who'd want to get revenge on her behalf.'

'Seems like we're back at square one,' Elise says. 'Unless we think Imogen is behind everything. Do we think that?'

Carolyn raises a hand. Bronnie and Elise look dubious. So basically, I've got nothing.

'I don't know what to do,' I say. 'When Ruby gets out of the hospital, do I bring her back to the school, the scene of the crime? Will any of your girls treat her with kindness or will they avoid her? Will they smile in her face and eviscerate her on Snapchat? Whatever happens, she'll be on the outside, because tomorrow everyone's getting their photos taken for the show's program, and she'll still be locked in a psychiatric ward—'

'That's it,' Bronnie cuts in. 'I know where I saw Imogen's tattoo.'

# 8

# Picture Perfect

*Clare Mackintosh*

# ELISE

'Holy crap, Bronnie, what the hell do you have in here?' Kendall helps Bronnie pull the large trunk from beneath the window of her kitchen, where it acts as a table between two shabby armchairs, threadbare on the arms. We drag chairs from the scrubbed pine table and sit in a circle around the trunk, and I'm reminded of being at school, of the arrival of a package from overseas parents and the reverence with which each treat would be lifted and unwrapped. Chocolate, new clothes, cans of drink ... exotic sweets with foreign names, to be passed around after lights out to salve the pangs of homesickness. We've all cancelled our plans for today, following Bronnie's revelation, which she flatly refused to act on last night.

'Carl will be asleep— he has to be up in the morning.'

God forbid Bronnie's husband doesn't get his beauty sleep ... And so here we all are, at a sodding tea party, sifting through junk in the hope of finding out where Bronnie has seen Imogen's tattoo before.

Carolyn lifts the lid. 'What *hasn't* she got in here, you mean,' she says with a low whistle. The trunk is large and battered, with tatty remnants of the leather straps that would once have been buckled tight around it. The corners are dented, and every surface is peppered with stickers, from holiday destinations and anti-fracking declarations to Disney characters and easy-peel satsuma labels. I imagine Bel or one of Bronnie's boys taking a piece of fruit from the bowl and absentmindedly scraping the sticker off, pressing it onto the trunk. I wonder if Bronnie doesn't notice or simply doesn't care. Her kitchen is large—originally two rooms, judging by the beam that runs above our heads, and filled with color. A dresser groans with china, much of it hand-fired and painted by toddlers, and every wall is covered in postcards, photographs, and framed certificates for everything from university degrees to twenty-five-meter swimming.

'It's my keepsake box,' Bronnie says. There's a defensive edge to her voice, but as she looks down, her eyes are soft. *It's a mess*, I think, but something stops me from saying it. At some point the trunk had sections—you can see the runners where boards would have been inserted to partition it into thirds—but now the contents are free to roam where they please. A pile of papers slides in among bits of plastic—toys from McDonald's Happy Meals and 3-D glasses from cinema films. Newspaper cuttings crumple against photographs, against leaflets from National Trust houses and steam train days out. Perished rubber bands poke from between tin foil packages and stack upon stack of gift tags from birthdays and Christmases past. It looks like the contents of a recycling box.

'And this is where you think you saw the tattoo?' I say, my heart sinking at the scale of the task before us. This trunk—this box of landfill—is not what I imagined when Bronnie said she knew where she'd seen Imogen Curwood's tattoo. This is not what I envisaged when, infected by Bronnie's excitement, we raced to her house, interrogating her on the way.

'I don't *know*!' she said in the end, exasperated by our questions about whether the tattoo was exactly the same or just similar; in a photograph or described; on a real person or a character or . . . 'I just know it's somewhere in the trunk in my kitchen.' I had thought the offer of tea when we arrived redundant—we surely wouldn't be here long enough to drink it—but as I look at the heap of stuff in front of us, I'm glad of the pot of Earl Grey, peeking out from its knitted cozy, and of the plate of homemade scones Bronnie produced from an old tin that once held Christmas chocolates.

'It was in a photograph, I think,' Bronnie says. She doesn't sound convinced. We're all still staring at the pile of memories, not knowing where to start. At least, three of us are. Kendall is somewhere else, her eyes haunted with everything that's happened. An unfamiliar feeling tugs at my insides. *I feel sorry for her*, I realize, in spite of the lies she's told.

I wonder what else she's kept from us. I wonder what secrets the others have—nothing would surprise me now. This room is filled with hidden truths. Carolyn knows something's up with the school records, and Kendall knows Bronnie has access to the computer system, but only I know why those two facts might be significant. Did Bronnie create records for students that don't exist? Is it down to her that Imogen Curwood hasn't been enrolled?

'It was definitely a theater show.' Bronnie hesitates. 'Or TV. Or I guess it could have been a film . . . but definitely an actress.' *An actress—you'd know all about that, wouldn't you?* Butter-wouldn't-melt-in-her-mouth Bronnie Richardson . . . could she really be a fraudster? And if so, for what purpose? Unless she gets a raise if there are more students . . . but that wouldn't make sense. I wonder if Racki knows, if they're working together, even.

'Come on.' Carolyn rolls up her sleeves.

'Is there any kind of filing system?' I say hopefully. Carolyn snorts. I sigh. 'Let's get started, then.' We dive in, each picking out items and putting on the kitchen table anything that might help us with our search. Theater programs, old copies of *The Stage*, newspaper clippings, cinema tickets stapled to their magazine reviews. Everything else, we leave on the floor. The kitchen looks like a beach after a storm, flotsam thrown up by the waves and caught by the shore. I pick up a small wooden fork. 'Why?' I ask Bronnie.

She smiles shyly. 'Whitstable, May 2005. Bel was four. It was the first time she'd seen the sea. We drank lemonade and ate fish and chips on the beach, and the kids fell over in the surf and got soaked through.'

I look at the others, expecting to see rolled eyes, but I've misjudged it.

'You can't beat chips on the beach,' Carolyn says.

'What a lovely memory.' Kendall's eyes glisten, and it's clear she's thinking of Ruby, of her own family holidays.

'She'll be okay,' Bronnie says softly. Kendall nods, and swallows hard.

The smirk on my lips dies. I imagine eating fish and chips on the beach with Nick and Sadie instead of retreating to our rooms with a plate of food Yuliya's left in the fridge. Maybe I'll suggest it when Nick gets back from Glasgow. I can almost see the confusion on his face. *Why would we do that, Elise?*

I imagine taking lemonade on a picnic, instead of gin-in-a-tin. I imagine getting a buzz from the beach, instead of from pills. Shame washes over me as I think of Sadie taking the blame, hiding the dirty secret I thought I hid so well.

'How long have you known?' I asked Sadie. Bronnie had left, and Sadie was home from school, and I knew I couldn't leave it a moment longer. I had trembled as I waited for her key in the lock, and it took all my reserves not to reach for something to counterbalance the adrenaline.

'Like . . . always, I guess.' Sadie was tearful, suddenly younger than her years. No—I stopped myself. Suddenly *the age she really is*. A teenager. Not the adult Nick and I made her be, with our laissez-faire attitude to bedtimes and TV and alcohol. Sadie *had* to be an adult, I realize now. One of us had to be.

'I'm going to stop,' I told Sadie.

And I know I can. I'll approach it like any other challenge: with timelines and objectives and project plans. Operation Clean-and-Sober Elise starts now. I haven't yet done anything with the leaflet Bronnie gave me—*the first step is admitting you have a problem*—but I will.

I pull myself back to the present and pick up a receipt. I show it to Bronnie, who thinks for a second.

'July 2015,' she concludes. 'Jon's graduation. We'd hired his gown and mortarboard but when we went to pick it up they mixed up the order and handed him a choir boy outfit instead. We only realized when we got to the college and he went to get changed.'

We all laugh, and suddenly, instead of being frustrated by the time this is taking—by the time I'm spending away from the office, and by the inadequacies of caffeine without an accompanying Xanax—I feel a surge of warmth. I'm not good at friendships—not like Sadie is. I say the wrong thing, try to be helpful but end up offending. So I don't tend to bother. I tell myself I don't need friends. I have Nick, and Sadie, and colleagues who know exactly where I'm coming from—who don't take offense when I'm blunt about their work. But this . . . this is nice. I take a bite of scone, spread with Bronnie's homemade jam.

I'm finding it hard to reconcile this woman who bakes and crafts and keeps a trunk filled with family memories with a woman who might have created records for students that don't exist. A sudden thought strikes me that Adam Racki might have forced her to do it. But I picture him in his black roll-neck sweaters, and the scarves that only just stop short of being foppish, and the idea is laughable. Adam Racki couldn't force his way out of a paper bag.

I sift through a pile of finger paintings, and put them on the floor. 'You know, you could scan most of this.' I pull out my phone. 'Look, there's an app for it.' I swipe through Sadie's nursery efforts. 'It's filed in date order, or you can use themes—nature, family, craft activities, and so on. Then there's no need to keep the originals.'

'I don't think . . .'

'It's easy, I promise. I'll send you a link.' I feel that warm glow again, in spite of everything. This is what friends do, isn't it? They help each other out. Bronnie's probably a bit daunted by the idea of digital life, but once she gets the hang of it, she won't look back.

*Friends.* Can you be friends with someone you know is lying? Here we all are, sitting like best buddies in Bronnie's cozy kitchen, all with secrets to hide. All pretending, all acting. How long before someone cracks?

'I declutter twice a year,' Kendall says as she pulls out a signed T-shirt and refolds it like she works at GAP. I peeked into her wardrobe in Pacific Palisades, when Greg went to use the bathroom. Every garment was color-coded, the rail like a graduated paint chart. At the bottom, racks of shoes slid silently out for inspection.

'I was holding on to a lot of negative energy,' she says. 'Decluttering makes me look forward, not back.' I think of the self-help books on Kendall's Californian shelves; no doubt there is a whole section devoted to *tidy house, tidy mind* . . . Thinking of Kendall's house brings a flush to my face and I root around in the trunk to hide it. I broke the rules by sleeping with Greg. *No photos, no personal details, no follow-ups. No friends' husbands.*

'How about you, Carolyn?' Kendall asks. 'Are you a hoarder?'

Every time I look at Kendall I feel an unfamiliar stab of guilt. I was on a secret mission, I remind myself. I bet James

Bond isn't troubled by remorse. But nevertheless, the memory of Greg's skin on mine lodges uncomfortably inside me, like indigestion or a splinter.

'My office is packed to the gunwales,' Carolyn says. 'But that's less about hoarding and more about just not throwing anything out.' While the rest of us have been sifting through the trunk (and, incidentally, leaving it in significantly better shape for Bronnie), Carolyn has been reading the huge array of theater programs that now litter the kitchen table. I'm not even convinced she's looking for the tattoo picture. 'I keep thinking I should have a clear-out, but there's always something more important to do. Ah! I think I saw this production of *Annie!*' She flicks through the program, then gives a bark of laughter. 'I definitely did. I remember thinking the orphans weren't exactly starving.' She points to a photograph of a fat kid leaning on a mop, a mournful expression on her chubby face. We all laugh.

'Christmas 2010,' Bronnie says. 'I wasn't working then, and Carl put all his loose change in a big pickle jar at the end of each day, so we had enough for the tickets. We didn't tell the children till we were on the way to the theater—you should have seen their faces!'

'You have such a great family,' Kendall says. Her eyes are shining and there's a tremor in her voice. She squeezes Bronnie's arm. I think of the casual way Nick and I book tickets for *La Traviata* or *Hamlet* or *Death of a Salesman*, and of the numerous times we've had to cancel because of work, and have left the tickets unused. I think of Bronnie, working part-time at the school, full-time as a mum to Bel and her brothers.

'You really do,' I say softly, and Bronnie looks up in surprise. Of all the mothers, Bronnie and I have the least in common, and because of that, I've never taken time to get to know her. But I wonder now if Bronnie might be just as driven as I am. She just happens to be headed in a different direction. I survey her for a second while I make up my mind. Do I want to do this? Do I want to risk blowing everything apart, just when we're all getting along?

'Your job at the Academy must have made things easier on the money front,' I say. I guess I'm doing it. I feel Carolyn's eyes on me, curious at my change in tone, and I see a nervousness creep over Bronnie's face.

'Y-yes.' Bronnie reaches for something—anything—from the trunk. 'I think this is from—' But I'm not letting her off that easily. 'Although I can't imagine part-time wardrobe mistress jobs are especially well paid. Unless, of course, you bolt on a few . . . extras?' I take a punt, implying I know more than I do. 'Creating student records, for example . . .'

I should be getting a surge of adrenaline from the game-playing, but something's missing. It feels like I'm acting, and my heart isn't in it. I tell myself I'm missing the edge I get from pills, but it isn't that.

It's Bronnie's face.

My instincts were right, but Bronnie isn't defensive or angry. She's hurt. And it doesn't feel like a game anymore but like a wolf rounding on a deer. It feels unfair. It feels like bullying.

I drop the pseudo-innocent tone. 'You created fake student records, didn't you?'

Bronnie crumples like she's screwed-up paper, covering her face with her hands and sobbing noisily. Kendall instantly moves to her side, rubbing Bronnie's back.

'What are you talking about? What student records?'

'Ah!' Carolyn is quick on the uptake. 'There are more students on paper than there are in the school,' she says succinctly. 'And I'm guessing our Bronnie created them.'

'What? Why?' Kendall stops rubbing Bronnie's back. We wait for Bronnie to get her choking sobs under control.

'The . . . school . . . gets . . . grants . . .' Bronnie starts. She pauses, taking a long, juddery breath before continuing, calmer now. 'Based on the number of students on the books.'

'And you pocketed the extra cash?' Carolyn said. Bronnie's head jerks upward.

'No! I would never do that!' She looks wildly around the room. 'I never took a penny. It all went to the school. You know what a terrible state the building's in, and we simply don't make enough to cover the outgoings. Adam said it wasn't hurting anyone—it was Arts Council money, being used for the arts . . . he said the school would close without it.'

'So what was in it for you?' I say.

Bronnie chews the corner of her bottom lip. 'You're right: Part-time wardrobe mistresses don't get paid a lot. I got something extra in my pay packet.' I'm about to ask another question when Bronnie lifts her head, suddenly defiant. 'We needed the money. We're not like you.' She looks at us all. 'I stayed home with the kids when they were young, Carl doesn't earn much, and we have a huge mortgage. I did what I had to do!'

Bronnie stops talking, and it's like someone let the air out of a balloon. I wonder if Carolyn and Kendall feel like I do, that this might have mattered a year ago—before Imogen, before the notes and the threats and Ruby lying in hospital— but it doesn't matter now.

Is fraud better than popping pills, or worse? Better than drinking a bottle of wine a night? Better than letting the housekeeper handle your daughter's first period? I'm hardly in the running for mother of the year myself.

'Bingo.'

We spin round to look at Carolyn, and whatever might have happened next is swept away by that single word, soft but jubilant. *Bingo*.

'What is it?'

'Have you found something?'

'What have you got?'

The three of us speak at once, and Carolyn looks at us in turn, a theater program in her hand, and a triumphant look in her eyes. The brochure is closed, Carolyn's finger marking a place, and the act is tantalizing, almost mocking. She's enjoying this, I realize. She likes knowing something we don't—the performer with a final act to go—and for a second I think she wants to keep whatever it is to herself. But she doesn't—of course she doesn't. We're all on the same side, after all. I think. Gradually, she lowers the program until it's resting in her lap. Her fingers flirt with the pages but still she doesn't open it.

'Well?' Even Kendall is starting to lose patience with Carolyn's theatrics.

'*Snow White*,' sighs Bronnie. 'Christmas 2013. The boys didn't want to come, so Bel and I went on our own, and—'

'Is it the tattoo?' I put an abrupt stop to Bronnie's jaunt down memory lane.

Carolyn looks up. She grins, and opens the program so slowly it's all I can do not to snatch it from her hands and do it myself. We crowd around her like kids about to be read a story. The brochure is cheaply made; the show itself a second-rate affair somewhere between am-dram and fringe. The page Carolyn marked is the cast list, their headshots taking up more space than the accompanying list of acting credits.

We all see it at the same time. Long hair, twisted over one shoulder. A smoldering look with the hint of a smile. Chin, cupped in one hand, the elbow resting on something unseen. And there, on her exposed wrist . . . *sky above me, earth below me, fire within me.*

*Snow White*, reads the caption above the actress's name. *Lisa Daisley.*

'Who's Lisa Daisley?' says Bronnie.

The name feels familiar—it nags at me like a child tugging at my hand. *Lisa Daisley* . . . I can't place it.

'It's the same tattoo,' Kendall whispers.

'It's the same girl.' Carolyn smooths a crease from the page, holds up the photo to the light. The hair's different, but Carolyn's right. The girl in the photo is undoubtedly Imogen Curwood.

'Maybe she uses a stage name for professional work,' Bronnie says. Carolyn raises an eyebrow, and Bronnie looks between Kendall and me for support. 'Lots of actresses do.'

'Of course they do, but this,' Carolyn brandishes the cheaply made brochure, 'is hardly Broadway!'

I catch the hurt in Bronnie's eyes. I think about her and Bel, planning their girls' night out, picking their outfits, queuing for tickets, buying ice cream at the interval as a treat they can't afford. Poring over this same program that Carolyn is so quick to dismiss, then storing it carefully away in the trunk in the kitchen. Making memories. 'Bronnie's right,' I say. 'Lisa Daisley could be a stage name.'

But just as the words leave my lips—just as Carolyn narrows her eyes at me, with a look that says, *Since when were you in Camp Bronnie?*—I have to take them back. Because suddenly I remember where I've seen that name before. 'It *could* be a stage name . . . but it isn't.' I shoot Bronnie an apologetic look. 'Lisa Daisley is the name on the prescription pills I found in Imogen's makeup bag.'

'Now you tell us!' Carolyn explodes. 'Could you not have shared that information with us before?'

Typical Carolyn—foisting the blame onto me. 'I told you I'd found pills—' I color at the mention of pills, wondering who else knows, who Bronnie has told. But when I catch her eye she gives the tiniest shake of her head. *No one. I haven't told anyone.*

257

'You didn't say they said "Lisa Daisley" on the label—'

'I didn't think it was relevant! I thought they were her grandmother's, or she'd nicked them, or bought them on the internet. And anyway,' I raise my voice before Carolyn can open her mouth again, 'I'm not the one on trial!'

There's a moment's silence, while Carolyn and I stare each other down, neither of us willing to break away first. It's Kendall who defuses things, albeit unwittingly.

'It says here that Lisa Daisley is seventeen,' she says, pointing at the actress's bio. 'Which would make her . . .' She counts off the years on her fingers. 'Twenty-one now.' Outraged, her voice rises a notch. 'I can't believe she's been *lying* to us for all this time!'

Bronnie flushes, her own shady dealings all too recently exposed. I see Carolyn's eyes widen, and her mouth twitch.

'Pots and kettles,' Carolyn says. Kendall looks blank.

'People in glass houses?' I offer, but the sarcasm is lost on her. Surprisingly, it's Bronnie who takes charge.

'I think what they're trying to point out, Kendall, is that you've been more than a little economical with the truth yourself.' It's Bronnie's turn to feel awkward—from one liar to another—and I shoot her a look of solidarity. Who'd have thought it—Bronnie Richardson and me, with something in common?

I didn't know it was possible for a person to go so red. A deep crimson flush floods from inside the collar of Kendall's shirt and makes its way to her hairline like high tide. She opens her mouth, closes it again, then repeats the motion. A fish out of water.

'Right, enough pissing about.' Carolyn slaps the theater program against her thigh, letting Kendall off the hook, and snapping us all back into action. 'Imogen Curwood—or Lisa Daisley, or whatever the fuck her name is—has been playing us all for fools for the best part of a term, and now it's time to turn the tables.' She gives a slow smile. 'And I know just how to do it.'

'How?'

But Carolyn ignores Bronnie, instead pulling out her phone and tapping furiously at the screen, cursing whenever her fingers find the wrong key. I see the familiar screen of a search engine, but as I lean across to see more, Carolyn angles the phone away from me. She winks. 'All in good time.' There she goes again: hogging the limelight . . .

Bronnie puts the kettle back on, and Kendall fills up the milk jug, and while Carolyn taps at her phone, the three of us sit around Bronnie's pine table and drink tea and eat scones. We gloss over the lies we've told, like politicians burying bad news. We talk about the school, and I grudgingly agree that yes, perhaps BONDical *could* sponsor a production to raise money for the new roof, and then we drift away from school stuff and onto clothes, and why it's so completely impossible to find shoes that are both practical *and* stylish.

'Shhhhh!' Carolyn says suddenly. The three of us look up, startled. She's pressing her phone to her ear, one finger of her other hand held up in warning, and a mischievous smile on her face. Silence falls. 'Oh hell-ooooo!' Carolyn's voice has changed. Down an octave, deep and throaty, like she smokes forty a day. 'Do I have the pleasure of speaking with Lisa Daisley's agent?'

Kendall and I exchange glances. Bronnie claps a hand to her mouth, as though if she didn't, something might escape.

'How absolutely *marvelous*, I'm so *thrilled* to get hold of you,' Carolyn purrs. 'Now, listen, I've got the most *darling* part I know Lisa will be *perfect* for, but it's horribly short notice. Musical, big budget, West End, long run, Leo Douglas directing . . .' There's a beat as she listens. 'Wonderful! Today at . . .' Carolyn checks her watch. 'Midday?'

I hold my breath.

'Really? You don't need to check with Lisa?' Carolyn's face is deadpan—I could use someone like her in the boardroom. 'That's simply *marvelous,* sweetie. Do you know the Mews Studios? Oh, she's rehearsed there before? *Wonderful!* We'll see her then.'

Carolyn puts down her phone, drops her head to her chest and holds out both arms like a leading lady anticipating her curtain call flowers. 'Boom.' She looks up. 'As I believe the kids say.'

'You didn't ...' Bronnie is in awe. Carolyn's eyes sparkle.

'I bloody did.'

'Where are the Mews Studios?' Kendall asks. The flush has disappeared, and she's leaning forward, anxious to be involved, to be included. It crosses my mind that if it weren't for Ruby being in hospital, we might not have glossed over her actions as easily. She has, after all, lied to us for an entire academic year—as has her daughter. But right now dealing with Imogen Curwood is more important than anyone else's dramas. Lucky for Kendall, I think, and for Bronnie. And, I guess, for me. I wonder idly what Carolyn's secrets are.

'It's a rehearsal space in Camden—a friend of mine owns it. It won't be a problem to borrow it for an hour or so.' She stands up. 'Well, what are you all waiting for? We've got work to do.'

The Mews Studios are housed in an unprepossessing building in the heart of Camden, which could easily be mistaken for a home for accountants rather than performers, were it not for the inspirational stickers adorning the otherwise plain front door. *If you never jump,* reads one, *how do you know if you can fly?* Carolyn enters a series of numbers into a keypad, and the door clicks open.

Unlike the Orla Flynn Academy, where leg-warmered boys leap down the hallways, and pockets of girls in low-slung yoga pants harmonize in stairwells with irritating frequency, the corridor that greets us is stark and cold. Four glazed doors are marked *Studio 1, 2, 3,* and *4* respectively, and I look through the door of number one to see a square, unfurnished room. A barre runs along one side; the opposite wall is entirely covered with mirrors.

'She sublets to teachers,' Carolyn says, leading us toward the end of the corridor. 'Ballet, tap, modern . . .' On a noticeboard to my left I see a clutch of flyers advertising classes and pointe shoes for sale, as well as a reminder that all students wishing to enter the southwest regional hip-hop contest MUST REGISTER BY FRIDAY!!! A pair of double doors stretches across the short wall at the end of the hall, flanked on either side of the corridor by two narrow doors marked *Stage left* and *Stage right.*

*Silence beyond this point!* reads a stern notice on each of the side doors, printed in bold font and underlined in red marker pen.

Carolyn pushes open the double doors, and flicks a series of lights on a panel to her left. One by one, the house lights switch on. We're in a theater. A small theater—there can't be more than a hundred and fifty seats—but a theater, nonetheless. At the back of the banked seats, bang in the center, is the lighting desk. Carolyn walks toward it and runs a hand over the switches. For a moment she's lost in thought, but then she looks round and focuses on us. 'We've got an hour. Kendall, find some paper and pens, and knock up some signs. "Auditions here," that sort of thing.' Carolyn checks off the tasks on her fingers, and Kendall nods eagerly, no doubt keen to re-ingratiate herself into the fold. 'We'll need a sheet with audition times—make up a bunch of names so she thinks we've been here all day—and something directing all auditionees to stage right. Or left—it doesn't matter. And a big sign on those double doors that says no entry.'

Kendall scurries off, and Carolyn looks at me. I lift my chin a fraction. *Go on, then,* I think. *Try bossing me around like that. See how that goes down for you* ... As though she can read my mind, a hint of a smile plays across her lips, and her shoulders relax a little.

'I think we need a dress rehearsal,' she says. 'How do you fancy playing Imogen Curwood?' She gestures to the stage.

'I'd be delighted.'

'How about me?' Bronnie says, like a kid left out at play-time. 'What do you want me to do? Should I help Kendall with the signs? I used to do a lot of arts and crafts with the kids, I could—'

'There's something much more important I need you for,' Carolyn says, cutting in, and I swear Bronnie grows an inch, right there. Carolyn gives a sly smile. 'Lisa Daisley's an actress, and actresses deserve an audience.'

'You want me to round up some people?' Bronnie's confidence wavers. I have a sudden image of her standing on Camden High Street wearing a sandwich board and carrying a giant foam arrow. *This way to the free theater show* ... I stifle a laugh and make my way to the front of the auditorium for my 'dress rehearsal.'

'Not *people*,' Carolyn says, enigmatically. 'A *person*.' She puts an arm around Bronnie and leads her out of the theater, briefing her in a low voice that disappears completely as the double doors swing shut behind them. I roll my eyes, even though there's no one here to see it. Carolyn is in her element, orchestrating this plan. Directing her minions (I'm obviously not including myself in that), drip-feeding information, keeping everyone on tenterhooks.

There are no steps at the front of the auditorium, and the stage comes to just above my waist. I pull myself up—all that yoga has done wonders for my arms—and walk to the center of the stage. A pair of black curtains covers the rear half of the stage; more curtains screening the entrances stage left and right.

I was a tree, once, in a school production of *The Wizard of Oz*, in which my sole responsibility was to turn to my left and block Dorothy's way with the branches I held in my outstretched hands. Only, as Dorothy and Toto—a vicious cairn terrier belonging to the French mistress—approached, I caught sight of my father in the audience, looking at his watch. *This had better be good,* he'd said earlier that evening. *I turned down dinner at the Groucho for this.* I froze.

Dorothy coughed. She nudged me. She cast a desperate glance stage right, to where the prompter sat with script in hand. But still I didn't move. In the end Dorothy spun me round and lifted my arm herself.

'The tree's alive!' she cried.

'Are you sure about that?' came a shout from the audience. 'Looks a bit wooden from where we're sitting!'

I fled the stage to the laughter of two hundred people tickled by my father's joke.

I jump as the double doors open and Carolyn strides in, looking pleased with herself. 'The trap is set!' she says dramatically. 'Now let's see what it'll look like for Lisa.'

'She'll see us the second she comes in.' I cross the stage, then immediately turn round, as though entering from the wings. I take in the rows of seats, flipped up like at the cinema; the lighting desk, Carolyn ... 'She'll make some kind of excuse, or just run out, or—' I break off as Carolyn flicks a switch and plunges us into darkness.

It is the sort of blackness you can *feel*; the sort of blackness that touches your skin and envelops you so tightly you daren't take a single step. I try to remember how far I am from the edge of the stage; I try to remember what direction I'm facing. My pulse races. 'Carolyn?'

Silence. Where is she? Fingertips run down my spine, and I twirl round, my hands in front of me, clutching at nothing.

And then: light. Hot, white, bright. So intense I have to hold my hand in front of my face.

'Can you see me?'

I look toward Carolyn's voice, to the middle of the auditorium, where I know the lighting desk is, where I know she is standing. There is nothing. Nothing but a bright white spotlight, trained on the center of the stage.

'I can't see anything at all,' I say. My voice sounds thin and reedy.

'Then we're ready.'

At eleven forty-five there's a commotion on the other side of the double doors. They burst open, Bronnie falling into the auditorium with a look on her face that is part panic, part relief. Behind her, keeping up an angry commentary, is Adam Racki.

'For the last time, Bronnie, will you please tell me what is going on? I've got choreography at one fifteen.' He takes in his surroundings, his brow creased in confusion, then looks between Carolyn, me, and Kendall, whose posters and signs have been carefully affixed to their relevant doors. 'Ladies,' Adam says, manners superseding his frustration. 'This is a surprise indeed! "Confusion now hath made his masterpiece."' He laughs as though he's made a joke, looking around expectantly for someone to explain, but Carolyn only smiles.

'Shall we take our seats?' she says.

Perhaps it is her quiet confidence that stops Adam asking questions, or perhaps the bubbles of anticipation that are currently fizzing and popping inside me have somehow escaped into the atmosphere. For whatever reason, Adam doesn't resist. He follows Kendall and Bronnie to the row of seats directly in front of the lighting box, where Carolyn remains standing. There's a rustle as we take our seats, and I half expect an announcement to turn off our mobile phones and be aware that there will be *no flash photography or recording devices, please.*

'Quiet . . .' Carolyn whispers. From the other side of the double doors comes a muffled noise. A door swinging closed. Footsteps. Is it her? Is it Imogen? Carolyn takes down the house lights and turns on the spotlight, creating a perfect circle in the center of the stage. There are more footsteps, a fluttering of the black drapes that hide the wings, and then Imogen Curwood steps onto the stage. Beside me, Adam makes a sound—the beginnings of an exclamation I cut off with an elbow in the ribs.

*Don't give the game away too early. Let her hang herself, first . . .*

'Center stage, please, darling,' Carolyn says. She's using the same voice she adopted for the telephone call to Lisa's agent. Imogen trots obediently across the stage and stands in the spotlight. She blinks, and even though I know she can't see us, I shrink back in my seat.

'What's your audition song?'

'"Castle on a Cloud,"' Imogen—Lisa—says. I hear a sharp intake of breath from behind me, and despite the dark I can picture the outrage on Carolyn's face. Jess's audition piece. There's a pause, then Carolyn speaks again. 'When you're ready.'

Imogen's voice is clear and strong, and for a moment I forget why we're all here. I close my eyes and let the notes fill the air. *I know a place where no one's lost, I know a place where no one cries . . .* I think about the day Imogen arrived at OFA, about the day the music box was planted in Jess's locker. I think about the day this all started.

Is this the day it all ends?

Carolyn must be thinking the same, because she cuts into Imogen's song with an abrupt 'Thank you, darling, that will be all,' swiftly followed by: 'Full name and age, please.' I hold my breath.

Imogen's gaze is steadfast. She looks directly into the light—directly at us.

*She can't see us,* I tell myself silently. But my pulse is racing so loudly I'm surprised everyone can't hear it.

'My name is Lisa Daisley, and I'm twenty-one years old.'

And then everything happens so fast. The spotlight snaps off, and the house lights on. Everyone's on their feet, Adam muttering, *What the hell's going on?* and Carolyn yelling at Imogen—at Lisa—*You lying bitch!* Bronnie imploring everyone to *Let's all just sit down and talk about this, shall we?* And in the middle of it all, Lisa Daisley, her mouth wide open.

I expect her to run off—I wonder if Carolyn expects us to chase after her, and decide she can bloody well whistle for it—but Lisa doesn't move. She's visibly shocked but, slowly, her mouth closes, and she regains some composure. She gives a bored sigh, and folds her arms across her chest, like the disgruntled teenager we all thought she was.

'I think it's about time you told us what you're playing at,' Carolyn says. '*Imogen.*'

Lisa looks at Adam, no doubt expecting him to defend her, the way he has done all term, but he's standing in stunned silence, his face white with shock. She's played him just like she's played the rest of us, I think, and I almost feel sorry for him. I hand him the theater program from Bronnie's keepsake trunk, folded open at the page with Lisa's bio.

'She's not a student,' I tell him. 'She's a professional actress.' I watch him scan the page, his mouth working but no words forming. Eventually, he looks at Lisa, and slowly he makes his way out of the row of seats and down the aisle toward the stage.

'You've got some explaining to do, young lady. Why did you lie about your age? About your name?' His voice begins measured, but gradually the volume increases until he's bellowing.

'"What's in a name?"' Imogen—Lisa—says, in a voice thick with sarcasm. '"That which we call a rose, by any other name would—"'

'How dare you!' Whether Adam is referring to Lisa's presence in his school or to her audacity at mocking his predilection for theater quotes, it's unclear, but either way, I've never seen him so angry. He's reached the stage now, and he looks to each side, perhaps hoping for steps. Not a yoga devotee, then.

'What the hell are you doing in my school?'

There's a flicker of hurt in Lisa's eyes. Her shoulders drop. 'I just wanted another shot at it,' she whispers.

'Speak up!' Carolyn calls. 'You are an *actress*, after all.' She draws out the word, catty as her daughter, as she walks towards Adam. Bronnie, Kendall, and I join her, and we stand, looking up at the stage like Lisa's a statue on a plinth.

Lisa's eyes fill with tears. 'I didn't go to stage school,' she says. 'I wanted to, but we couldn't afford the fees—Mum was on her own, and she was doing two jobs just to keep a roof over our head. So I left school at sixteen, and I worked in McDonald's, and I went to every single audition in *The Stage* until finally I got a part.'

'My heart bleeds,' Carolyn mutters.

'I got an agent, and an Equity card, and things really started to take off. It felt like my big break was just around the corner—that I'd get something long-running or high-profile, and I'd be able to take care of Mum when she got older.' Lisa's eyes are shining, and I hear a surreptitious sniff from Bronnie. 'But it didn't work out that way.' She hangs her head. 'After *Snow White* the auditions dried up, and my agent stopped calling. She said people wanted "fresh talent," and I wasn't "fresh" anymore.' She's crying properly now, great fat tears that run down her cheeks and soak into her T-shirt.

'So you lied about your age and applied for my school?' There's a note of incredulity in Adam's voice. Lisa nods.

'I've always looked younger than my age—I was playing twelve-year-olds when I was seventeen. The caliber of agents you attract to your end-of-year shows is legendary'—at this, Adam puffs up with pride—'and I thought if I could just get in front of them, they might think that *I* was fresh talent, too, and, and . . .' She gulps the words, thick with tears. 'And maybe I'd get a second chance at the only thing I've ever been good at. The thing I've dreamed of doing my whole life.' Her confession dissolves into wails.

'You put the music box in Jess's locker, to make everyone think Ruby was bullying her,' Carolyn says. It isn't a question. Lisa nods.

'I needed to be the best in the school. I needed Ad— Mr. Racki,' she corrects herself, 'to put me forward for auditions, to talk about me to agents.' She looks down at us, her eyes pleading for an understanding she won't find. Not from me, anyway. She can turn on the waterworks all she likes.

'Ruby's so good at everything,' Lisa says. 'I thought if she was worried about school, if she thought someone was after her, it would knock her confidence and . . .' She tails off.

'You. Presented. My. Daughter. With. A. Noose.' Kendall spits the words out like bullets. 'You sent all those awful notes!'

'I never meant any harm to her, you have to believe—'

'You wrote *Here lies Ruby Donovan*!' Kendall shouts, and the accusation echoes around the auditorium. Lisa's shaking, now. She cuts a pathetic figure alone on the stage, her face streaked with mascara. So much for fresh talent. 'Can you imagine how that made my little girl feel? To see her name on that bench, like it was a grave? And now she's lying in hospital, having tried to kill herself!' Now Kendall's crying, too, and Bronnie moves to put an arm around her.

'What did Ruby ever do to you?' Bronnie says.

'She was competition,' Lisa says, screwing the heels of her palms into her eyes.

Carolyn bristles. 'And Jess wasn't?'

I almost laugh. Only Carolyn could feel slighted that her daughter isn't perceived as worthy of death threats. I feel a sudden and unfamiliar urge to be with Sadie, to take my non-death-threat-worthy daughter out of this toxic environment. Lisa's actions disgust me. I might eliminate competition in business, but I play fair. This isn't playing fair.

'Your mother would be ashamed of you, young lady,' Bronnie says, prompting a new bout of tears from Lisa. 'The noose was bad enough, but what about the slate? That could have killed Ruby!'

Lisa stops crying abruptly. She casts a panicked look at Adam, and I wonder if this is it—this is the moment that's going to make him call the police, demand justice, do *something*. But he's catatonic, his eyes wide with shock, a tremor running through his body. I try to imagine what it would be like to uncover such toxicity in BONDical, just as Adam's seeing it unfold from OFA, and I decide it's possible that I too would be rooted to the spot, unable to function. You think you run a tight ship, that you know the people you work with. But how well do we ever know our colleagues? Our friends? Our children?

'I didn't push the slate onto Ruby,' Lisa says, but I'm not sure I believe her. It's too loud, too insistent.

'Liar!' Kendall says.

'Wait a minute,' Bronnie says. 'It was Imogen—' She corrects herself. 'Sorry, *Lisa*, who called out that she saw someone on the roof. Lisa didn't try to kill Ruby—she *saved* her.'

We look at each other. It doesn't make sense.

'I saw the slate slipping,' Lisa says. 'It was caught on something, but I could see it was going to fall, so I shouted that someone was up there. I thought it would scare Ruby—make her feel like someone was after her—'

'Someone *was* after her,' Kendall says. 'You.' She's not shouting now, but her voice is full of bitterness, and who can blame her?

'This is . . .' Adam casts about for a word. '*Monstrous*,' he finishes. Yes. It *is* monstrous. I look at Lisa Daisley, at her slim figure, her blond hair, her striking blue eyes. Evil comes in many forms. *This thing of darkness*, I think, remembering my classroom readings of *The Tempest*. I glance at Adam. His bloody quote thing is contagious.

The head's fists are balled by his sides, and a pulse throbs in the side of his neck. 'I should call the police.'

There's a beat. Lisa stares at Adam. Her eyes are dry now—the look in them pure hatred—and I can't help but wonder if the flurry of tears was all an act, if all of this is just one big performance.

'And let them find out you've been defrauding the Arts Council?'

Bronnie lets out a little cry. 'How do you know about that?'

'Oh, I know a lot of things.' Lisa's smile is smug, and beside me I feel a surge of rage from Kendall.

'How *dare* you stand there, smirking, like you've done something clever? My daughter could have died!' Kendall puts her hands on the stage and leaps up in one fluid moment. I wonder if she'd like details for my *Ashtanga* class. A look of alarm crosses Lisa's face as Kendall lunges across the stage with the roar of a tigress protecting her cub.

*She's going to kill her*, I think, and I jump onto the stage—not because I care about Lisa Daisley, but because I find I *do*

270

care about Kendall. And I don't trust Lisa one bit. Beside me, Carolyn scrambles onto the stage like a pregnant woman getting out of a pool, and Bronnie and Adam are up too, and all that's missing are the torches and pitchforks.

Lisa turns tail and runs, frantically scrabbling at the black curtains behind her until she finds the gap in the middle.

'After her!' Carolyn screams as Lisa disappears through the curtains. We're only seconds behind her, and the blood sings in my ears as I snatch back the curtain and pull it hard across the stage, only . . .

'Where the hell is she?' Kendall looks around in confusion.

'She was right there,' Bronnie says.

The rear of the stage is flanked by solid walls. An old piece of painted plywood leans against the back, and a coil of rope gathers dust on the floor. But otherwise the stage is empty.

Lisa Daisley has vanished.

*Ghost students*, I think, shivering. But then I hear running feet from somewhere within the bowels of the theater, and the slam of the front door echoing down the corridor.

'What the . . .' And then I see it. The magician's friend. The opening in the floor, leading to the crawl space beneath the stage, and from there to freedom.

The bench in the courtyard at OFA has been scrubbed clean, but a pale outline of the graffiti can still be seen. *Here lies Ruby Donovan.* I shiver. We all wanted to pick up our girls from school today. Needed to. Even Kendall is here, clinging to the reassurance of familiar surroundings, before she goes back to the hospital to be with Ruby. Every few seconds the silence is punctuated by Bronnie or Kendall or me, circling around questions that have no answers.

'How *could* she?'

'What possessed her?'

'Should we have realized sooner?'

Only Carolyn is silent. She stands a few steps away, still part of the group, but somehow disconnected. Her expression is dark, and every now and then her face moves like she's having conversations in her head.

'What are we going to tell the girls?' Bronnie says.

'The truth.' Kendall is firm. 'If you lie to kids, how can they learn who to trust? Besides, our kids are smart—they'll figure it out themselves if we don't tell them.'

For once, Kendall and I are on the same page. Bronnie looks anxious, but she nods slowly.

'I guess I can't wrap Bel up in cotton wool for ever.'

I glance at Carolyn, ready to exchange *who'd have thought?* glances, but she's still in a world of her own, staring at the school like she has X-ray vision. I find it odd that she's been so badly affected by Lisa's confession—after all, she was the one who found Lisa's photo, who set up the platform for her downfall. I wonder if perhaps she's thinking about the times she accused Ruby of faking the threats against herself; if she's thinking of the way Ruby bullied Jess last year, and how it could have been Jess driven to attempt suicide, not the other way around.

But then she turns to us and speaks, and it's something else entirely.

'I don't buy it.'

We stare at her.

'Why was there no school record for Imogen? The fake records served a purpose, but if Lisa applied with a fake ID for Imogen, why wasn't there a file created?'

As one, we turn to Bronnie.

'I had nothing to do with it, I swear! I didn't even know there was no file for Imogen—I mean Lisa—until you told us, Elise!'

*Methinks the lady doth protest too much . . .*

I've no time to dwell on Bronnie's claim, because Carolyn is in full flow. 'How did Lisa know Ruby was "the competition"?' She makes quotes in the air and doesn't wait for an answer, although I'm not sure any of us has one to give. I certainly don't. How *did* Lisa know?

'And why Ruby?' Carolyn says. 'Why not Bel? Let's face it, she's got more stage presence in her little finger than the rest of the school put together.'

Bronnie flushes with pride. Carolyn takes a few paces to the left, then turns and strides back—a leading lady with an audience in the palm of her hand. 'How did Lisa know that Jess's audition song was "Castle on a Cloud"?' A sharp breeze blows through the courtyard, and an empty can of Coke skitters against the concrete slabs. I pull up the collar of my coat around my neck as I try to find the answer. Could the audition pieces be listed online? Might Lisa have come to a revue last year, when the girls all performed? Carolyn is still pacing, still throwing out questions with the sharpness of a barrister.

'The music box was planted in Jess's locker the day Lisa arrived at OFA.' She wheels round, jabbing a finger toward us. Bronnie flinches. 'The *same day*. How could she possibly do that? How could she do any of it?' Carolyn waits for her words to sink in. But she hasn't finished, and there's a hard knot in my chest, because I know exactly what she's going to say.

'Unless, of course, she had help.'

The empty Coke can throws itself against the wall with a clatter. The wind circles the courtyard, the high walls producing an eerie moaning sound I've never noticed before. I glance up at the roof. *Was* it an accident? Or did Lisa really see someone up there? Someone who wanted to hurt Ruby? Someone who was helping Lisa get what she wanted . . .

'From who?' Kendall says. She looks wildly around the courtyard, as though a police line-up might suddenly appear.

273

I tap my fingers together. I'm trying to slot together the pieces of a jigsaw; I've got the corners and the edges, but the middle is missing, it's muddled and blurred. I look at Carolyn. The brooding look has disappeared, and there's a spark in her eyes. An uneasy feeling settles over me. *It's always you,* I think. *First on the scene, first to discover the clues . . .*

'Someone who knows Ruby,' Carolyn says. 'Who knows Jess. Someone who could pass that information to Lisa. Someone who didn't want to get their hands dirty.'

Bronnie gasps. 'You're not suggesting it was one of our girls?'

Another piece of the puzzle slips into place. 'No,' I say slowly, my eyes trained on our mutual friend. 'I don't think she is.' The uneasy feeling grows until it's pressing hard against my chest. 'I think Carolyn's suggesting it was one of us.'

★★★

*I gave quite a performance, don't you think? Worthy of a lead role, an encore, a solo curtain call. A Tony-winning production, with me in the star part, and the chorus nobodies scurrying about at my feet. They all think I'm one of them, singing from the same song sheet, dancing the same steps, but it's all been an act. All the while I've been following my own script. My own agenda. And it's almost time for the final act . . .*

# 9

# Finding Grace

*Sophie Hannah*

# CAROLYN

Bronnie and Kendall stare at me, slack-jawed with shock. Elise and I exchange a look, and I know she's thinking what I'm thinking: *Are they really so naïve?*

'One of us?' Bronnie says finally, her voice cracking on the last word. 'No, I don't . . . *No one* thinks that's possible.'

'I do,' I say.

Elise backs me up. 'There's no reason why it shouldn't be one of us.'

'What are you talking about? I'm not conspiring with anybody.' Kendall sounds panicked. She looks at Elise, then at me, then back at Elise. 'Are you, Elise?'

'No, but if I were, I'd hardly tell you. That's how it works.'

'What about you, Bronnie?' I ask. 'Any conspiring to declare?'

Her face crumples. 'Please don't tell the police,' she whispers.

'What?' It can't be this easy. 'You're admitting it was you? You and Lisa have been colluding all this time?'

*It can't be Bronnie Richardson, of all people. Can it?*

Bronnie looks confused. 'No, that's not . . . no. I'd never write horrible graffiti about anyone or do the noose thing.'

'Are you sure?' I ask. 'You're in charge of costumes. For shows like *Oklahoma!* and *Oliver!* in which nooses feature.'

'You think *I* put the noose . . .? I didn't. I swear, Carolyn, that wasn't me. Only a monster would do that. I thought you meant . . .'

'What?' I snap.

Elise walks toward her, slowly. 'You said, "*That* wasn't me." But something was you, wasn't it? Something apart from making records for students who don't exist, I mean. What was it that you did, Bronnie? Spit it out. You're looking guilty as hell. Did you know there was no record of Imogen in the system? Did you know she was Lisa Daisley?'

'No!' Bronnie wipes her eyes and nose. 'Carolyn, I promise you, on my life, I knew nothing about that and I never colluded with Lisa to do anything or torment anyone.'

'Of course you didn't,' says Kendall, eyeballing me furiously as if I've committed a terrible faux pas.

'I've never even had a parking ticket,' says Bronnie. 'I'm a good person—just a wife and mother, trying her best, and yes, sometimes making mistakes.'

*Christ on a fucking cracker.* I don't expect Bronnie to be Inspector Morse or anything, but has she never watched TV, or a movie? Doesn't she know it's possible for someone seemingly safe and middle class to be a deranged psychopath on the down-low?

Bronnie's just confessed to participating in a serious fraud. She might well have done worse things, ones she's not yet willing to admit to. And doesn't Kendall understand that a charismatic manipulator can appear *more* deeply shocked and innocent than all of the innocent people around her, who aren't trying quite so hard?

I almost laugh at the idea of Bronnie Richardson as charismatic. Elise, too, looks as suspicious as I feel. The bonds that seemed to exist between the four of us in Bronnie's kitchen not so long ago are splintering pretty fast.

'Of all of us, you're the one who'd find it easiest to hatch your plans with Lisa Daisley,' I say to Bronnie. 'I'm not accusing you, I'm simply stating a fact. You work at the Academy—doing admin as well as wardrobe, as you've just told us. Who knew Fake Imogen was starting at the beginning of the autumn term? I didn't. Elise and Kendall didn't, as far as I know. But you could have. Who got the lead role in the forthcoming musical? Your daughter. And why? Because, *ever-so-conveniently*, both Ruby and Jess didn't get to perform that night, thanks to the noose drama.'

'Who was best placed to put that noose where Ruby's costume should have been?' Elise joins in the interrogation. 'You told us yourself: You were in the room with Ruby's costume most of that night.'

'And you were the one who just happened to have a past connection to Lisa Daisley,' I say. 'It might have been a clever double bluff, you suddenly saying, "Wait! I know where I've seen that tattoo before," and seeming to help solve the mystery.'

'You're a grade-A bitch, Carolyn Mordue,' says Kendall breathlessly. 'A ruthless, heartless predator!'

'Kendall, your daughter's in the fucking hospital. I'm trying to find out who put her there. Think what you like about me, though—I honestly don't give a shit.'

'A *double bluff*?' Bronnie blurts out, wiping new tears away with the back of her hand. 'Are you serious? What kind of world do you live in?'

'Same one as you. One in which teenage girls are tormented so badly that some of them run away from home, and others try to kill themselves.'

'But . . . but I mean . . . if anyone was thinking of doing a double bluff, I'm not even the most obvious person!' says Bronnie. Then she actually points her finger. Not at me, which I could have understood, but at Kendall. 'What about her?'

'Kendall?' I laugh. 'What, you mean the one whose daughter tried to kill herself? I suppose her plan might have gone badly wrong, but—'

'Yes, it might have, because she took it too far.'

'Bronnie, why are you accusing me?' Kendall sounds confused.

'Last year, who was the most hated girl at OFA?' There's a wildness in Bronnie's eyes that I haven't seen before. 'Ruby, right? Word got around about how she treated Jess. Carl and I used to say to each other all the time: "Thank God she's not ours. Can you imagine having a daughter like that? You'd be so ashamed."'

Now tears are streaming down Kendall's face.

'And then, this year—new term, new start—and what happens? Fake Imogen appears—a grown adult pretending to be a teenager, an imposter posing as a legitimate student—and the most *terrible* things start to happen . . . to Ruby. And suddenly everyone feels sorry for her. Suddenly it's "Poor Ruby," and, oh, look, Imogen's been behaving *really* obviously like a proper weirdo, and all of this started the *day* she arrived at OFA.' Bronnie pauses for breath, red in the face.

'So your theory is . . .' Elise prompts her.

'Kendall could have hired Lisa Daisley and paid her a load of money to come here and be Fake Imogen and play the role of an even worse bitch than Ruby. Then all the girls could bond together, against the common enemy, and suddenly Ruby wouldn't look so awful, because there'd be a genuinely scary psycho to be the new bad guy.'

'It's possible, but it doesn't sound likely,' says Elise matter-of-factly. 'Though it has to be more likely than Bronnie and Lisa Daisley being in cahoots.'

'Why?' My money's still on Bronnie. She's beside herself with panic, can hardly keep still. I think she's the one.

'If our mystery conspirator pushed the slate off the roof, it can't have been Bronnie. She and Lisa were both in the courtyard when the slate fell and nearly killed Ruby.'

'What about *you*, Elise?' says Bronnie.

'What about me?' Elise fires back, a small smile on her face.

'You're the one who cares least about all of this. From the start, you've had this superior air—as if you're above it all, as if it doesn't affect you or Sadie.'

'Have I? I suppose that's fair. Ask yourself this, though: Would I have that "air," as you call it, if I were the guilty party? Wouldn't I try to blend in by whipping up as much hysteria as possible, like you lot constantly do?'

'What about Carolyn?' says Kendall. 'No one can deny that she probably hates Ruby enough to want to drive her to suicide.' She turns to face me. 'You and your oh-so-clever double-bluff theories!' A drop of her saliva lands on my cheek and I make a show of wiping it off. 'The cleverest double bluff of all would be to present yourself as the person really keen to investigate and get to the truth while all the time you're the one behind everything.'

'It's a good theory,' I concede. 'Unfortunately for you, I have a slate-day alibi. Cast iron. I was at Bristol University that day, examining a PhD thesis called *Agent-based Models of Law in Multi-level Trade Regulation*. It was as much fun as it sounds.'

I turn away from her, pick up my bag, and head for the door. 'This is getting us nowhere. We can swap accusations and defenses all day long and we'll achieve nothing.'

'What's your plan?' Elise calls after me.

'To take some action for a change, instead of just talking and arguing endlessly,' I tell her. 'To take some action *alone*,' I add under my breath as soon as I'm out of the room and out of earshot. There's one person who can tell me who Fake

Imogen's ally at the academy is, and who *will* tell me, even if I have to use violence to squeeze the truth out of her: the woman herself.

Lisa Daisley, here I come.

Fifteen minutes later, I'm in a dingy internet café in a basement, with a Styrofoam cup of coffee beside me, searching the hell out of Lisa Daisley. I haven't got my laptop with me and I need a bigger screen than my phone's for something as important as this. Jess would say this is a symptom of me being 'so old.'

The three other computer terminals are occupied by young men, all of whom have an unfortunate look about them. Downtrodden, Downcast, and Down-at-heel. None of them seems aware of the others, or of me, which is ideal.

Lisa's agent's website has her listed, but offers no useful information. She evidently hasn't starred in many shows, because hardly anything comes up about the real Lisa Daisley, a.k.a. the fake Imogen Curwood.

I can find only one result that's useful, on a website called mandy.com. This tells me that three years ago, Lisa played Felicia Montealegre in a play called *Len and Ezra* at Bromley Little Theater in Kent. I also learn that in 2016, she was in a show called *One Man, Two Guvnors*, in which she played a character called Rachel Crabbe.

I finish my coffee, buy another one from the blank-eyed, stringy-haired man behind the counter, and sit back down at my terminal. Unable to think of where to look next, I stay on mandy.com and try to find out more about the two shows Lisa Daisley was in.

I feel a sudden tightness in my throat as I start to read about *Len and Ezra*, which turns out to be a play about two men trying to write a musical together. *Fucking idiot, Mordue. Can't you even read the word* musical *without envy starting to spurt and flow inside you—in case the musical in question is better than yours, or more successful, or both?*

This isn't even a real musical; it's a made-up one that's the subject of a play. There's no way it can be better, or do better, than mine. Still, I can't stop myself reading the blurb of the play, to see if I can work out how good the non-existent musical in *Len and Ezra* might be if it were real.

Oh, my word. It's unbelievable, the shit some people come up with. This sounds *so bad*—which delights my competitive heart, but confirms my belief that there's no justice. A dreadful play about a dreadful, pretend musical, and yet it got staged at a real theater.

I read the plot synopsis again, to check I didn't imagine how bad it was: 'It's a long time since *West Side Story* took the world by storm, and American musical theater composer Leonard Bernstein fears that his glory days are long gone. Envious of Andrew Lloyd Webber's success with the musical *Cats*, he decides that he too must collaborate with a modernist poet in order to prove he's no has-been. He approaches Ezra Pound, whose poem "Meditatio" begins with the line "When I consider the curious habits of dogs . . ." and suggests that, together, the two of them try to repeat Lloyd Webber and T. S. Eliot's winning formula. Instead of *Cats*, their musical, based on Pound's poetry, will be called *Dogs*. There's only one problem. Pound's dubious political affiliations . . .'

I can't bear to read any more. I close the link and click on the one for Lisa Daisley's other show, *One Man, Two Guvnors*. Scrolling through the cast list, I come to an unusual name that seems familiar: Khye Munton. Where . . .?

Before I've finished asking myself the question, I have the answer. I close this link, go back to *Len and Ezra*, and click on *Cast*.

There it is: Khye Munton also played Ezra Pound. He's been in two shows with Lisa Daisley. I wonder how well he knows her. Aren't theater people supposed to drink together after the show finishes, into the early hours?

I go back to Google and type Khye Munton's name into the search box. There are quite a few results for him. He's played some starring roles, by the look of it. It doesn't take me long to find out who his agent is. Thankfully, it's not the same agent as Lisa Daisley's; it's a different one, who has no reason to be suspicious.

His name's Simon Lowings. The agency he works for is called Independent Talent. I type the number into my phone, then close down the computer, pick up my bag, and head outside.

I wait till a pair of large lorries have driven past, one after the other. Then I make the call. Simon Lowings is away from his desk, but a colleague manages to find him. By the time he states his name and asks how he can help me, I've decided to be honest. 'My name's Carolyn Mordue,' I tell him. 'I believe you're Khye Munton's agent?'

'That's right.' Lowings sounds happy about this.

'I need to talk to Mr. Munton fairly urgently, about a mutual acquaintance: Lisa Daisley.'

'I'm afraid I can't—'

'I know you can't give me his number, but I was hoping you could give him mine and ask him to please ring me? It's really important.'

'Well?'

'Please? If he doesn't want to contact me then he doesn't have to, obviously. I'm only asking you to give him the option of helping me.'

'Who are you?'

'Carolyn Mordue.' I say it slowly, so that he can write it down.

'No, I mean . . .' Lowings leaves the sentence unfinished.

'Oh, you mean, who am I in the world of showbiz? Am I someone important? No.' I resist the urge to ask Khye

Munton's agent to help me change that by agreeing to represent me and my half-finished musical. 'I'm nobody. I'm actually a law professor at Cambridge.'

'Oh.' Lowings clears his throat. 'All right, I'll give Khye a call—he should be coming out of a rehearsal any minute now. I'll pass on your number and your request.'

'Thank you so much,' I say.

Ten minutes later my phone rings. The screen says *Unknown number*. My heart starts to beat a little faster. Could this be the call I'm hoping for? Can it be this easy? Copying Simon Lowings, I answer the call and say my name instead of *hello*, something I've never done before.

'This is Khye Munton.'

'Oh . . . hi. Thank you so much for ringing.'

''S no problem. You want to talk 'bout Lisa?'

'Yes, I do.'

'She okay?'

'Yes, she's . . . I'm not ringing because something bad's happened to her or anything like that.'

'I don't care.'

'Pardon?'

'Don't really know her. Don't now and never did.'

'But you were in two shows with her, right? *Len and Ezra* and *One Man, Two Guvnors*?'

''S right.'

'So you must know her a bit?' I press on. How can an actor have such a toneless voice? Maybe he saves his expressive powers for when he's on stage.

'Hardly. Spoke to her a few times. Why d'you want to know?'

Can it do any harm to tell him the truth? I decide not. He's assuming this is going to be a boring chore call about a woman who means nothing to him; I'd like to shock him out of that assumption.

'Since September, Lisa Daisley has been lying about her age and identity. Under a false name—Imogen Curwood—she enrolled at the Orla Flynn Academy, a performing arts school in London, and pretended she was seventeen years old. She then did a whole lot of deeply sinister things, including throwing herself downstairs and pretending she was pushed, threatening other students with nooses, that kind of thing.'

'Shit.' Khye Munton breathes. 'For real?'

'Uh-huh.'

'Can't imagine the Lisa I knew doing any of that.'

I roll my eyes, glad he can't see me. 'Why not?' Why can nobody but me imagine anyone they know doing evil things, and why can I imagine it of *everybody* I know, all too easily?

'She was always . . . it sounds harsh, but she was dull. Never really chatted to the rest of us in rehearsals. Sat in a corner staring at her phone most of the time. Can't see her having the imagination to think of a false ID and all that other shit.'

'So for both shows you were in together, Lisa didn't socialize with the rest of you?'

'Not really. She was often dashing off to do various other jobs. Bar work, that sort of thing. Always harder up than the rest of us, she was. And even when she did come drinking with us, it was weird.'

'How?'

'One time she told this strange story about her friend who had killed herself—like, I was ready to feel sorry for her, but she kept going on about how angry she was, and hadn't the friend thought about what it would do to *her*, to Lisa?'

'Is there anything you can think of, any detail about her that might help me to find out more about her? Her family, her background, people who knew her well, or better than you did?'

'Sorry. I've told you all I know about her. Oh . . . well, not that this'll help you, but I know she went to the same posh boarding school as Adrianna de Miquel. Proud of that, she was. Wanted it included in her bio in the program notes for *Len and Ezra*, and threw a hissy fit when she was told there wasn't the space.'

I've never heard of Adrianna de Miquel. After thanking Khye Munton for his help, I look her up on my phone. She's one of the stars of *The Filter*—a TV drama I've heard of but never watched. And there's the name of the posh boarding school she attended: Villiers in Kent.

Who knows a person's true character, and that of their family, better than the teachers who see them day in, day out for all of their secondary school years? Lisa Daisley might not be seventeen, but she's in her early twenties. Many of her teachers will likely still be at Villiers. And it's a boarding school, so if I set off now, there should still be plenty of staff around by the time I arrive.

I might not have found out much from Khye Munton, but at least I know where I'm going next. That's good enough for now.

I cannot believe this is a school. I mean, I know it is, because of the signs on the large gates, but it certainly doesn't feel like one. If I didn't know better, I'd be convinced I was in the grounds of a large country park or some aristocrat's estate, with fields, tree-lined avenue, and the gentle slopes of hills in the distance—and all of this encircled by high, solid walls.

It's getting dark by the time I arrive. I get out of the taxi that's brought me from the station, pay the driver, and walk in through the enormous iron gates. There are several buildings in the distance, amid the greenery. I don't know which one to aim for.

I walk for several minutes along what I suppose you'd have to call the school's main road, until I come to a post which has several signs attached to it, pointing in different directions along many different paths. I read a few and am none the wiser: *Darville, Elstow, Goundry*. What the hell are they? Thankfully, one of the signs says *Main Reception*.

I follow the path indicated and arrive after a nearly ten-minute walk at a large building with a porticoed front. There's a solid oak door that looks as if it must weigh about thirty tons and require an army to pull it open. Nothing I do with its handle can persuade it to move.

I ring the bell to the right of the door and wait.

After about half a minute, the door is opened by a middle-aged woman with tortoiseshell-framed glasses on a chain around her neck and a helmet of silver hair. 'May I help you?' she asks me with a cautious smile. She's wearing a pale blue suit with a black cowl-neck jumper. There are two strings of pearls around her neck that look real. Her shoes, perfectly coordinated with the rest of her outfit, are black with blue bows on them.

My mind flies immediately to a problem I don't yet have and probably never will: What will Carolyn Mordue the musical theater librettist wear? She'll need a very different wardrobe from Carolyn Mordue the law professor, who hasn't had her unruly hair professionally done in years, who wears black trousers, scuffed black slip-on pumps, and whatever blouse happens to fall out of the wardrobe first. Professor Carolyn doesn't give a toss what she looks like, but I want to go into my new career, assuming I get to have one, looking perfect for my role, like this woman standing in front of me. I don't know who she is or what she does here, but everything about her hair, outfit, and manner tells me that she's somebody very senior at one of the most expensive and prestigious boarding schools in the country and that it would be almost impossible for her to be anything or anywhere else. What does Andrew Lloyd Webber wear most days? Maybe if I . . .

*For God's sake, focus, woman!*

'My name's Carolyn Mordue,' I say with a smile.

'Lovely to meet you. I'm Audrey McBeath, the deputy head of Villiers. Who are you here to see?'

'I'm afraid I'm here without any sort of appointment, in the hope of talking to somebody—no one in particular, just anyone who can help—about one of your former pupils.'

'Ah! Adrianna de Miquel, no doubt.'

'No. Not her.'

'Really?' Audrey McBeath raises her eyebrows. 'You're not a journalist, then?'

'Nope. Law Professor, University of Cambridge. Much duller.' My credentials worked with Simon Lowings. I can't believe the Deputy Head of Villiers would be immune to the 'Professor at Cambridge' effect.

'And which former pupil are you here about? We have quite a few famous ones, though none quite so stellar as Adrianna.'

'Lisa Daisley. Does that name ring any bells?'

'Of course,' Audrey McBeath says smoothly. 'We rarely forget our girls, particularly not those who come here on full scholarships as Lisa did. Her family were poor as the proverbial church mice, but Lisa was—is—extremely bright. I remember her well.'

'How long was she a pupil here?'

'Her whole school career.'

*And you didn't like her.*

I don't know why I'm so sure I'm right. Audrey McBeath has done and said nothing unprofessional or untoward. Still, I trust my instincts.

'So, that would be . . . what? Age eleven or twelve to sixteen? Eighteen?'

'No, our girls start in Year Nine. And most, though not all, stay to do A-levels here. Lisa did. She left after Year Thirteen.'

'So, aged eighteen?'

'That's right. What's your interest in Lisa?'

'I'm happy to tell you, but it's kind of a long story,' I say. 'Is there any chance . . .?' I nod at the cavernous flagstone-floored entrance hall behind her.

'Of course. Do come in.' She opens the door wider and stands back. 'How rude of me to keep you on the doorstep. I'm afraid my office is full of workmen's stepladders at the moment. Oh, don't ask, or I might cry.' She does the opposite and laughs. 'They were supposed to be finished two weeks ago. This way—we'll go to Deryn's office instead.'

I follow her along two wood-paneled corridors. Framed drawings and paintings line the walls, most of them about a hundred times more original and better executed than the hackneyed dross and pretentious non-art I see in the windows of, respectively, Cambridge and London art galleries. 'You evidently have talented students,' I say.

'Hm? Oh, the pictures! Yes, art is one of our strengths. Actually, we're equally strong in the sciences, but we can't put that on the walls. Ha!'

I wonder if Lisa Daisley was good at art, and if any of her paintings are on these walls. As I walk alongside Audrey McBeath, I imagine how I would feel if I turned a corner and saw a portrait in oils of Fake Imogen and Bronnie Richardson, arms linked. *Self Portrait With Evil Plot Bestie* by Lisa Daisley.

I shake my head at my own foolishness as Audrey says, 'Here we are!' There's a gold plaque on the door that says *Deryn Simmons, Head Teacher*. With the corridors being as beautiful as they are, I'm expecting great things from the room I'm about to walk into.

I'm not disappointed. There are large, mullioned bay windows with a view of the most perfect rectangular green lawn I've ever seen. Floor-to-ceiling bookshelves, many bowed in the middle, cover two whole walls. In front of these there's a semi-circle of armchairs, and, on the other side of the room, a tall gray filing cabinet, a large leather-topped desk, and a high-backed leather chair. Behind these, with hardly any space between them, are several rows of framed official Villiers school photographs, each of which looks as if it contains the entire school population, teachers and pupils, all sitting in rows. It's slightly dizzying to look at: all those tiny dot-faces.

'Is Lisa Daisley in one of those?' I ask Audrey, nodding at the pictures.

'Probably several. She was here for many years. Please, do sit down. Would you like some tea or coffee?'

'I'm fine, thank you.'

When she perches on the edge of the desk instead of sitting behind it or in one of the comfy chairs, I decide that I didn't imagine the very subtle tone of discouragement in her voice when she asked if I wanted a drink. She wanted me to say no. She's been perfectly friendly, but she wants me to leave sooner rather than later.

Why? Because she's busy, or because of my interest in Lisa Daisley?

'Tell me about Lisa,' I say.

'What do you want to know? I've already told you, she's very bright and comes from a family with no money to speak of. Why are you interested in Lisa, if you don't mind my asking? Has she . . .'

'Has she done something? Is that what you were going to say?'

My question is met with a rather desperate smile. 'I'm wondering how I can help you, that's all.'

I don't see any point in stalling. 'This might take a while,' I warn her.

She walks over and sits in the chair beside me. 'I have some time,' she says.

'There's been some trouble at my daughter's school, which started when a new girl, Imogen, arrived.' I tell her about the music box, the pill bottle with the wrong name on it, the fall downstairs, the graffiti, the noose, the slate, all the strange comments Fake Imogen made. 'The head of the school did nothing to help us,' I say bitterly. '*We*—me and three other mums—were the ones who found out that Imogen wasn't who she was pretending to be. We were the ones who sent her packing.' In case Audrey hasn't already worked it out, I add, 'She was Lisa Daisley.'

'I see,' says Audrey McBeath.

'Can you think of any reason why Lisa would do something like that?'

'No. No, I can't.'

I wait for her to say more. That better not be all she has to offer.

Eventually, seeing that I'm waiting, she says, 'I can't say I knew Lisa hugely well when she was here—and the actor you spoke to, he's right in a way. She wasn't an easy girl to get to know. Her parents . . . As my colleagues and I always say: You meet the parents and suddenly the children make perfect sense.'

'What do you mean?'

'Lisa's mother was rather brusque and critical. And her father was extremely socially awkward. They both were, really. A peculiar family. Ah, well!' She pats her lap.

It's a signal for me to leave, now that she's satisfied her curiosity.

'Is there anything else you can tell me about Lisa that might be of use to me?' I ask.

'Use for what purpose? I don't quite understand . . . You say that she joined your daughter's school under false pretenses, so . . . presumably she's now been removed and won't be causing any problems in future?'

'Is the name Ruby Donovan familiar to you?' I ask her.

'No. Not at all. Who is she?'

'Are you sure?'

'Positive.'

'How about Bel—Annabel Richardson? Or Bronnie Richardson?'

'Never heard of either of them.'

'Elise or Sadie Bond?'

'No. Sorry.'

'Someone's been helping Lisa to do all these horrible things to other girls, and I thought, if you maybe recognized any of those names as someone who had some connection to Lisa . . . but clearly you don't, so . . .' I break off with a heavy sigh. 'To be honest, I'm not sure why I'm here. I just . . . all this confusing stuff has happened and I want to try to work out what the hell's going on.'

I stand up, walk over to the window, and stare out at the grass. When I'm sure that Audrey can't see any part of my face, I introduce a tremor into my voice, to give the impression that I might be crying. 'I thought if I could find someone who had known Lisa, who maybe knew what made her tick . . .'

'I quite understand,' says Audrey, 'but I'm afraid . . .'

'Oh, it's not your fault,' I say. 'It's just that my daughter was bullied last year, and the bully *totally* got away with it, and now this: Lisa pretending to be Imogen and doing all these things, and I have no idea *why* . . .' I sniff and shudder. Turns out I quite enjoy acting.

'I've got an idea,' says Audrey McBeath, her voice gentler than it has been previously. 'Why don't you wait here while I make us a pot of nice strong tea and find some tissues? Deryn usually has some on her desk, but I can't see any.'

Unbelievable. She's a Nice Strong Tea truther. *Nuclear war devastated your home? Have a nice strong cup of tea! It'll cure everything!*

I murmur about how embarrassed I am to be making a fuss, and before too long Audrey's arm is draped around my shoulders and she's promising to tell me everything she can remember about Lisa Daisley when she comes back with the tea. Finally, after I've surely earned several Oscars, she leaves me alone in the head's office.

*Please let the filing cabinet not be locked.*

I clocked the little keyholes in the top right-hand corners of every drawer the second I stepped into the room. None of the keys are there, so if the drawers are locked . . .

They aren't. Infuriatingly, they also don't contain any files full of addresses or confidential records. In the top drawer there are some Reebok trainers and tennis balls. The second drawer is full of bottles of perfume: Shalimar, Caleche, Jo Malone's Amber and Lavender, one I've never heard of, called Subterfuge, that smells strongly of lemons even before you open the bottle.

Drawer after drawer disappoints me. That's it. There's nowhere else in the room to search—the desk doesn't have any drawers. Looks as if I'm going to be relying on Audrey McBeath's tales of the Lisa she knew, after all, hoping something in what she tells me might provide a clue.

*I have to know. Which of them has been helping her?*

I'm eager to find a way for it to have been Bronnie, despite her solid alibi for the slate incident. I fear it might have been Elise, and I don't want it to be. Hard as I try, I can't think why Elise would want to enlist Lisa Daisley to kill Ruby, or scare Jess, or do any of it.

What about Kendall? What if she secretly wants to kill her own daughter? I could hardly blame her. After all, her daughter is Ruby Donovan, Superbitch. It might have been Kendall who leaned across a table in a bar one night and whispered to Lisa, 'Okay, this is how we'll do it. First we're going to scare the living daylights out of Jess Mordue. I've got this music box . . .'

Something occurs to me that hasn't before: Whoever engaged Lisa Daisley to perform these dubious services to terror and disharmony must have actively wanted her to act like a freak. She didn't try to blend in or act normal. From the day she arrived at OFA, she behaved like a weirdo, setting off as many alarm bells as she could.

*So that everyone would believe that all the threatening incidents were her doing.*

The plan, presumably, was for us all to be absolutely sure Imogen was the bad apple. Why? So that, when Ruby was killed by the falling slate and it was clear that Imogen couldn't have done it, everyone would nevertheless suspect her? 'Somehow, it must have been her,' we'd all say. 'She must have arranged it.' Yet we'd be unable to prove it. And, meanwhile, the true culprit, the one who hired Lisa Daisley, would have got away with murder.

I curse under my breath. This theorizing is getting me nowhere. I walk over to the school photographs on the wall. Beneath each photo, inside its frame, is the date it was taken and the full list of names of all the teachers and pupils pictured.

When would Lisa have been at school? I work it out as best I can and find a photo with a date that I hope will work. Scanning the faces close up, it doesn't take me long to find Fake Imogen. Her hair's much shorter and she's slightly heavier, but it's unmistakably her. Despite being certain, I want to check. I look at the list of names of pupils on the second row. There it is: Lisa Daisley, at the center of a string of names.

I blink and take a step back. *It can't be . . .*

It's not Lisa's name that's shocked me off balance. It's the one next to it. The girl standing to Lisa's right, presumably. Yes: The caption beneath the picture says *left to right*.

I look at the girl standing beside Fake Imogen. She's not smiling. She's wearing round wire-framed glasses and has thick auburn hair in a long plait that's draped over her shoulder.

Her name, according to the list I'm staring at, is Imogen Curwood.

'I should have told you straightaway,' says Audrey as we sip our tea. 'Every time you asked me if I knew this name or that name, I was frightened you'd ask about Imogen Curwood. That name is a very significant one at Villiers, you see. And you'd said that the student Lisa pretended to be was called Imogen, though you didn't mention a surname, and then you asked about all those people I'd never heard of.'

I should have asked about Imogen Curwood, too—if Audrey recognized the name. Why hadn't I? 'Why is Imogen Curwood significant to Villiers?' I ask now, reminding myself that it's the girl with auburn hair in a long plait that I'm talking about. Not Lisa Daisley.

'Nobody at Villiers likes to talk about it, because it's a stain on our otherwise excellent reputation,' says Audrey. 'We weren't officially culpable, but we didn't do enough to stop it. If we'd been more vigorous, less naïve—'

'About what? Did Lisa Daisley harm the real Imogen Curwood in some way?' This is surreal. Am I about to hear that Lisa killed Imogen, then adopted her identity?

Audrey's expression tells me I'm way off the mark. 'No. I don't know why Lisa has been using Imogen's name. Especially . . .' She breaks off.

'What? For God's sake, spit it out.'

'Imogen Curwood was a troubled girl. Academically, she was brilliant. But she was pathologically competitive and if she thought anyone had wronged her she would take against them and . . . well, victimize them. That's the only way to describe it. So when another girl, Grace, had the audacity to outshine her, she became a target.'

'Imogen bullied her?'

'Horribly. And Grace was a sensitive girl. She went to a teacher for help, and I believe Imogen was spoken to, but it didn't stop the bullying. Imogen was clever enough to find new, subtler methods of tormenting Grace.'

*Like Ruby.*

'Grace took her own life, in the end,' says Audrey, almost in a whisper. 'It was a terrible tragedy. A girl with her whole life in front of her, a lovely, kind, talented . . .' She stops and covers her mouth with her hand.

If I'm ever diagnosed with a terminal illness, I swear to God I'll spend my last few months on earth hunting down vicious teenage bullies and shooting them dead. Ruby'll be top of my list.

'What happened to Imogen Curwood?' She'll be next on my list, unless someone's taken care of her already.

'Her family moved to America, to give her a fresh start.'

Again: so like Ruby. Crossing the Atlantic to escape a horrible, guilty past. Ruby coming this way, Imogen Curwood going that way . . .

'Her name was never in the public domain in relation to Grace Racki's death, but everyone associated with Villiers knew, and—'

'What did you say?' I leap out of my chair, sending my teacup flying across the room. 'Did you say Grace *Racki*? R-A-C-K-I?'

Audrey nods. The room spins. I make an effort to breathe. Drops of tea drip from the fingers of my right hand.

'What was Grace's father's name, do you happen to remember?' I manage, somehow, to force the question out.

'I do,' says Audrey. 'Poor man, he was utterly devastated. The whole family was, of course, but him especially. Adam, his name is. Adam Racki.'

★★★

*There are outrages and pernicious offenses all around us in this world that I would once not have believed possible. For instance: You can be the heartbroken father of a teenage girl who committed suicide and still be told that there are certain things you mustn't say about suicide because they're insensitive and will trigger people.*

*You can't say that if teenage girls are relentlessly bullied, they might hang themselves, like my darling Grace did, because then more bullied teenage girls might get ideas. Another danger of you pointing out this self-evident fact is that more bullies will think, 'Ooh, if I make her life hard enough she'll hang herself and I'll win.' In order to avoid the twin perils of encouraging bullies and encouraging suicides, a father who has lost his daughter in this appalling way cannot say, 'Bullies cause suicides.'*

*That's right: You can't say that the bully is to blame for the suicide of your beloved child. Even though you know it to be true, people will queue up to tell you it's not. And it's not only enemies or strangers who will say this. Your nearest and dearest (those who haven't hanged themselves) will say it, too. When you say that Imogen Curwood bully-murdered your Grace, they will frown and say, 'Well ...' and 'Ahem, I'm not sure ...' and 'Ah, but you see, another child in your daughter's situation would have said "Fuck you" before moving cheerily on. And, well, didn't you and your wife recently have an acrimonious divorce? And ... not that anyone wants you to think* you're *to blame, but ...'*

*But, but, but ... your only child is still dead. Nothing is ever going to change that.*

*You could of course kill the devil who bully-murdered your child. It wouldn't bring your beloved daughter back to life, but it would make you feel a hell of a lot better. Justice would have been*

298

*done, at least. Except she's fled across an ocean and is now beyond your reach. And even if you did follow and killed her in Arizona instead of in Kent or London, you'd be put to death. Arizona is a death penalty state.*

*And so what do you do, when you can't do any of the quite reasonable things that might actually make you feel a little less dead inside? I wish I could report that you perform some brilliant maneuver to correct all these injustices, but I can't. You fantasize about traveling to America and hunting the monster down, but you know you never will. So you try to accept your fate: the endless misery and grief, the burning feeling of injustice that never goes away. You accept it all, and try to get on with the empty, agonizing life you have left, hoping that one day the pain will start to ease ever so slightly.*

*In the meantime, you have plenty to keep you busy: mainly hiding your true self, which is bloated with bitterness. Nobody would like what you have become if you were to let that beast loose, so you have to conceal it behind a theatrical facade.*

*And then one day everything changes. Suddenly, your inability to do what you yearn to do to Imogen Curwood the bully-murderer doesn't matter quite so much any more because a new girl enters your life—also a bully, also vicious; every bit as vile as Imogen. And even better: She's from America! Imogen has gone there and, in exchange, Fate has sent this girl to England. To you.*

*The new monster's name is Ruby Donovan ...*

\*\*\*

I run all the way along the main road out of Villiers's grounds. Once I'm past the gates, I wait until I've got my breath back, then pull my phone out of my bag. I have twenty-three new texts: one from Dan, one from Jess, and all the others from Elise, Bronnie, and Kendall.

*Where are you?*
*What's happening?*
*This is crazy!*

*We all need to meet and talk.*

*Carolyn, you can't just go AWOL like this.*

Can't I?

I send a message to Dan and Jess saying, *Don't worry, all fine. Back later tonight, will explain then.* Then I find Adam Racki's mobile number in my contacts and ring it for the first time. He gave it to me last year when he took a group of students, including Jess, to New York for a week of workshops with Broadway professionals.

'Adam Racki.'

It's a name I used to hear and think nothing about, that used to be part of my ordinary life. Now it sounds very different. I don't know what 'Adam Racki' means any more. To hear the man who owns that name speak it out loud, after everything I've just learned, makes me feel as if the ground beneath me has been pulled away.

Is it the name of a man who took an ordinary music box and worked for days or maybe weeks to turn it into the grotesque taunt that ended up in Jess's locker? Is it the name of a head teacher who should have been protecting his students, doing all he could to ensure their safety and well-being, while secretly . . .

What?

I try to put together the story in my head—the most likely one I can come up with. Racki's daughter Grace died after being bullied at Villiers by Imogen Curwood. Imogen was never punished. Instead, she went off to start a new life in America.

Then, years later, Ruby Donovan arrives *from* America, where she's been unable to get into a performing arts school because she's a nasty piece of work, too, and word has spread. But . . . how would Adam Racki know that? Did Kendall and Ruby lie to the rest of us, but tell him the truth about Vee's death and the suspicions around Ruby's role in it?

Wait. No, that didn't happen. I know it didn't, because I once eavesdropped on a conversation between Racki and Kendall that I shouldn't have heard. It was last year, after I'd made my second complaint about Ruby's disgusting treatment of Jess. I'd been called in by Racki for a meeting—one of the many pointless head-to-heads we had, where he spouted platitudes like 'I'm sure we can sort this out, since they're both lovely girls deep down,' and I screamed at him about how evil prospers when good men do nothing.

He was running late on this particular day, so I sat and waited outside his office. I heard, through the door, the cadence of an American accent, and I wondered . . . could it be Superbitch Ruby's mother? I walked over to the door and pressed my ear against it. Sure enough, it was Kendall. Racki was in full bullshitty flow, telling her he had no doubt that Ruby meant well, that she was such a lovely, talented girl, with such glowing references, sought after by every stage school in America. Pretty please, just for Adam, couldn't Kendall persuade Ruby to try to smooth things over with Jess?

Neither of them could have known I was pressed against the door, listening. Which means Adam didn't know about Kendall and Ruby's lies, and Ruby's fake references. He couldn't have known. And if he didn't know about Ruby's past, why would he have brought in 'Imogen Curwood' in order to torment her—to get some sort of symbolic revenge? In which case . . . what the hell is going on?

'Hello?' Adam says now. 'Is anyone there?'

'Adam, it's Carolyn Mordue.'

'Hello, Professor Mordue.'

'I need to talk to you urgently. Call me Carolyn, by the way.'

'Um . . . I'm afraid—'

'It's non-negotiable. I need two hours to get to you. Tell me where you are, or where I can meet you.'

'I'm still in my office.'

'At the Academy? Fine. Wait there. I'm on my way.'

'Can I ask—'

'Face-to-face, you can ask anything you want. Not over the phone. Just stay where you are.'

I end the call and ring the local taxi firm number I stored in my phone earlier. When a woman answers, I say, 'How much for a taxi from Villiers School all the way to central London?'

Adam Racki's office door is open when I arrive. He's standing by the window looking out at the spire of St. Paul's Cathedral in the distance.

I walk in and close the door behind me. Before he has a chance to ask me to sit, I march over to his desk and sit behind it, in his chair. His mouth drops open. His opposite-of-a-poker face tells me that he's shocked, but busy telling himself he shouldn't be. *This is Carolyn Mordue*, he is thinking. *She says and does outrageous things, remember? I've known some irritating parents in my time, but this woman is the most obnoxious by a mile. Still, to have the nerve to stride over and sit behind* my *desk, in* my *chair . . .*

'So,' I say, leaning my elbows on a pile of papers. 'Do you have something you want to tell me?'

'Do *I*?'

'That's what I asked.'

'You were the one who wanted to see me urgently.'

'I was. Why do you think that might be?'

'I have no idea.'

'I've been to Villiers. I know about Grace.'

He remains absolutely still, by the window. I try to read his expression but it's impossible.

'I know about her killer, too: the real Imogen Curwood.'

'Her killer? You seem to have been misinformed. My daughter took her own life.'

302

'After being bullied by Imogen Curwood. In my book, that's not suicide. It's murder by bullying.'

Adam turns violently away. I can't see his face. His whole frame starts to shake. It makes my heart feel heavy and sore to watch him. If Jess—Christ forbid—had killed herself after being bullied by Ruby, I would have made it my number one priority, my only goal, to end Ruby's life. I'd have made sure it hurt, too.

*Don't start feeling sorry for him. Not without knowing the whole story. Remember the music box . . .*

'So,' I say brightly. 'Doubtless you're going to say that I can't prove you were the one in league with Lisa Daisley, that it's all circumstantial.'

'No.' Adam turns to face me. His face is wet with tears. 'You're right. It was me. It was all me. Lisa was just the hired help. Irrelevant. I was the one.' He looks up at the ceiling. Laughs. 'Never did I dream that anything—any circumstance whatsoever—could ever induce me to admit it.' He smiles at me suddenly, as if he's only just noticed me there. 'Murder by bullying. If you hadn't said those words . . .'

This is so strange. He has the same face, but he looks nothing like the Adam Racki I'm used to seeing.

'Wait here a moment,' he says.

He leaves his office, closing the door behind him.

I can't sit still. I pace up and down, wondering what it was about those three words, *murder by bullying*, that made him want to tell me the truth. Whatever he intends to show me might explain it. What can it be?

Unless . . . I breathe in sharply. What if it's a trick? What if . . .

I run to the door, open it, and call his name. No response.

*Shit*. What do I do now? I don't want to go running off somewhere, in case he comes back.

He'll come back. I know he will.

*Yeah, right. This man who's hidden his true character and agenda from the second you met him. Forgive the pun, but you don't know him from Adam.*

What if I go back into his office and he comes back with some kind of weapon? Can I be sure he won't try to hurt me physically?

Yes, I can. That's a ridiculous idea. He's never actually killed anyone. He wouldn't.

Would he?

My eyes land on a part of the corridor outside Adam's office that looks different. What's that door, and why's it open? I've never noticed it before. Some kind of cupboard, maybe.

I walk toward it. 'Adam? Are you in there?' Maybe he's searching through some old files. 'Adam?'

Pulling open the door, I see stone steps. It's not a cupboard; it's a staircase with a door separating it from the corridor. Cold air hits me, as if someone's poured it over me. I look up and see, in the distance, a rectangle of sky. This staircase leads to outside. To the roof.

*He's on the roof.*

'Adam!' I yell, running up the steps as fast as I can.

Soon as I'm up and out, I see him. He's on the very edge, lurching forward, then back. 'Taking my time, I'm afraid,' he says apologetically. 'Goodbye, Carolyn. And thank you. I mean that sincerely.'

'No!' I scream. 'Adam, don't jump!' I lunge toward him and manage to grab his arm. That's when he starts to pull.

# IO

# The Final Act

*B.A. Paris, Clare Mackintosh, Holly Brown and Sophie Hannah*

# CAROLYN

There's nothing I can do. He's so much stronger than I am, and he's pulling me toward the edge, fast.

I scream. My thoughts blur to a sharp point of fear and all I can do is keep screaming as loud as I can. I stop and fall silent when my body tells me something has changed, something important. I open my eyes, only realizing as I do so that I'd screwed them tightly shut.

Adam's hand has let go of me. That's what I felt: him releasing me. He's standing a short distance away. Close enough to the edge to jump, easily.

'I'm sorry,' he says. 'I have no right to take you with me.'

*Think, Carolyn. What should you say?*

I push my hair behind my ears to stop the wind blowing it across my face. 'You owe me an explanation,' I tell him.

'Perhaps I do.' He nods. 'Yes, perhaps I do. As I say, you're the only person who's ever acknowledged that Imogen Curwood killed my Grace. That she murdered her.'

'Of *course* she did. Seriously, no one else has ever said that?'

'Not a single, solitary person. And when I used to say it— before I gave up—people argued with me, explained to me why I was wrong. I couldn't believe it.'

'I can.'

Adam's face screws up in puzzlement. 'Why? You've

never . . . I mean, perhaps you have. Have you ever lost someone who meant the world to you?'

'No. But . . .' Fuck. I'm so the wrong kind of person to talk a suicidal man down from a roof. I don't know how to sound sensitive and caring. Only angry and vengeful. 'You don't need personal experience of tragedy to know that people are shit, Adam. You just need eyes, a brain, and access to the internet.'

'I expect you're right. For a long time, I preferred to believe that people were basically good. Grace was good.' He makes a strange noise, almost animal-like, and crouches down, tries to cover his head with his arms. I move toward him but he's on his feet again, looking disoriented, as if he doesn't quite know what just happened, what his body just did.

'Some people are good,' I say. 'Lots aren't, though. Imogen Curwood isn't. Ruby Donovan isn't, either—though, last year, whenever I said that to you, you told me I should try to be more understanding of poor Ruby, who was probably missing her friends and family in America and feeling insecure.'

'I had to say that, didn't I? You were putting pressure on me to expel her. That was the last thing I wanted to do. I needed to keep her *here*, where I could teach her a lesson.' Adam sighs heavily. 'Teaching her a lesson she'd never forget: That was the plan. That was always my intention. For *her* sake. Otherwise what Lisa and I were doing would have been completely immoral.'

'Did you want to teach her a lesson or did you want to kill her? Or drive her to suicide the way Imogen Curwood drove your daughter to suicide?'

'I always thought a suicide attempt on Ruby's part would be the most pleasing outcome. Still. Made a total hash of it, didn't she? I often come up here, you know. Have ever since I came to the Academy. Not to the edge, normally. I'd sit

308

there, where you're standing, where no one could see me, and think things through. Think about Grace.'

'Sometimes you walked right up to the edge, though, didn't you?' I say.

'Yes. How clever of you.' He turns to smile at me with his new face, the one I've never seen on him until today. 'I did. To reassure myself that if the pain ever became too great . . . And one day, there she was: Ruby. Sitting there, all innocent. I must admit, I forgot my plan to teach her a lesson. In that moment, I wanted to crush her out of existence. If Lisa and Bronnie hadn't, between them, got Ruby out of the way just in time . . . To be fair to Lisa, I'd never sold the deal to her as any sort of murder plot. Just a few nasty tricks, I'd told her. Naughty old me. I saw Ruby down there in the courtyard and I couldn't resist . . . improvising a little. Ah, well. All things considered, it's good that Lisa and Bronnie scuppered my effort. Now we have a best-of-both-worlds scenario, I suppose. Ruby *has* learned her lesson, I think. Don't you?'

'I don't know,' I say truthfully.

'Oh, I'm sure she has. Having been on the receiving end of Lisa's and my little campaign, I doubt she'll be doing any more bullying any time soon. And I proved to myself that I'm willing to put my money where my mouth is when it comes to delivering justice: I *tried* to kill Ruby. I did it for Grace, and for the girl in America that Ruby killed. Vee, her name was. One life—a guilty, worthless one—for two innocent lives. That strikes me as an honorable equation.'

'You're aware of Ruby's past, before she came to England? Did Kendall tell you the truth, then?'

'No. She fed me a pack of lies. But I was cunning, you see. I'm a cunning chap, when I need to be.' His eyes have taken on a glassy, detached look.

'I agree,' I tell him. 'Cunning enough to invent students who don't exist to get more money.'

'Ah, so you know about that too? How well-informed you are. The arts are terribly underfunded, as are most worthwhile things these days. Sadly.'

'How did you find out that Kendall faked all of Ruby's brilliant references?' I ask him.

'Hm? Oh, that. I suppose it was thanks to you that I stumbled on the truth.'

'Me?'

'Yes. Last year, when you told me what Ruby was doing to Jess, it reminded me of Imogen Curwood, the way she tormented Grace. There were striking parallels. I thought, "A girl who has it in her to behave this way, and yet she gets such over-the-top, glowing references?" I smelled a rat. So I rang the school in question, the last one Ruby attended in LA, and soon found out the truth. I saw an opportunity: another teenage girl who'd got away with taking the life of one of her classmates. I honestly felt as if fate had given Ruby to me as a sort of . . . gift.'

'Why bring Lisa Daisley into it?' I ask. 'I mean, presumably you had to pay her?'

'Handsomely and happily. She was worth every penny.' He takes a step back from the edge and looks down at his feet. Deliberately, he kicks the ground—the roof—with his right foot.

'But why did you need her? As the head of OFA, if you'd wanted to make Ruby suffer—'

'Again, fate helped me out. Several things converged unexpectedly. Don't you find that often happens? You're wondering what to do, and then the perfect solution lands in your lap, and it feels like magic.'

'What do you mean?'

'Two years after Grace was bully-murdered, as I call it, I went to the Edinburgh Fringe and spotted a young woman whose face I recognized in a dreadful, low-budget show.'

'Lisa?'

Adam nods. He walks back to the edge of the roof and peers over it, as if to check that the courtyard is still there. 'I introduced myself to her. She offered her sympathies and said nice things about Grace. When I told her I was head teacher here, she nearly jumped on me. She was desperate for me to use my influence to get her some opportunity or other in London. Said she was flat broke, and looked it, I have to say. Very shabby package, she was. I tried to extricate myself tactfully from her clutches, but I couldn't deter her from giving me her contact details. I kept them, though I don't think I had any intention of seeking her out. Fate, you see? Then, years later—dish best served cold and all that!—once I'd started to make my Ruby plan . . . well, it's not exactly a starring role in *Guys and Dolls* at a Delfont Mackintosh theater, but I offered Lisa a fascinating and unique assignment and I paid her well for it. She was delighted by the whole package—the money, obviously, and the chance to do something for Grace's memory, and to help me. I think she was rather fonder of Grace than I'd realized. Quite attached to her, she seemed to be.'

'I still don't understand why you needed her,' I say.

'Symmetry. I wanted to give Ruby a taste of her own medicine, so she'd know how it feels when another girl, a girl you haven't harmed at all, suddenly launches a hate campaign against you. I wanted Ruby to feel the ache of loneliness that comes from knowing someone has chosen you and only you to victimize—someone who is a stranger to justice, who accuses you of things you haven't done, who does things to you and then denies them when you know it must be her.' Adam laughs. 'And then, when we escalated to the noose, and the notes . . . well, I wanted her to think she might die. Or, even better, to decide that was her only way out.'

'What was your planned endgame? If I and the others hadn't found out the truth about Lisa, and if she hadn't fled as a result, what would have happened?'

'Oh, once she'd reduced Ruby to a cowering wreck who would never be the same again, once Ruby had slit her wrists or whatever method she chose, "Imogen" . . .'—he makes air quotes with his fingers—'. . . would have moved to a different school.'

I don't suppose it matters, but there's one more question I have to ask. 'Is Lisa a really terrible actress, or did you tell her to act like a creepy psycho throughout? I mean . . . she wasn't subtle. Pretty much from the word go, she behaved like the worst cliché of a sociopath.'

'She did.' Adam nods. 'On my instructions. I told her to ham it up, to really go for it. I said, "Ruby and Kendall Donovan will never be able to prove it's you because you'll have alibis, and so the more obvious you are, the more it will torment them that you're getting away with it."'

'Why target Jess, with the music box?' I ask.

'Ruby was the target—I knew everyone would be sure it was her. And I didn't want to be *too* obvious. But, Carolyn, I would never harm Jess.' He sounds offended. For a moment, he looks like the old Adam again. Then his new face reappears. 'I like Jess. Really. I'm sorry I couldn't be more obviously on your side last year. I hope you can understand the extent to which I truly *was*, in my heart of hearts. I thought to myself so often, "How Carolyn disapproves of me! And how she would approve if she only knew the truth!" I was protecting Jess, you see—I wanted her to feel safe here.'

'So you were already making your . . . plan, last year?'

'Oh yes. Plans as complex as this take a good few months to put together.' Racki frowns. 'And still they can go wrong.'

'Your plan hasn't gone wrong,' I tell him. 'Like you say: You protected Jess, and Ruby's learned her lesson. You don't have to . . .' I point to the edge. He's so close to it now, and keeps looking at it. I feel sick. What if I can't do anything to stop him?

I have to. I want to, for the simple reason that he was always on Jess's side. He tried to save her from Ruby—went out of his way to do so, spent money on it.

He lurches forward suddenly, toward the edge.

'Adam, you don't have to go to prison,' I say quickly.

He stops. Stares at me as if I'm mad. 'What are you saying?'

'Perhaps we can . . . reach an agreement. Make a deal—one where I keep your secret and you get to keep your job.'

His eyes dart back and forth: to me, to the edge.

Am I really going to do this? Looks as if I am. 'It's not a joke,' I tell him. 'I can convince the others that Lisa Daisley acted alone. You can keep your job, your life, everything.' *Everything you haven't already lost.* 'At least come inside and let's talk about it.'

Slowly I walk toward him, holding out my hand.

# ELISE

On stage, one of Adam's more athletic students backflips down a 'marble' staircase made from blocked foam and cleverly painted card. She comes to a halt at the bottom of the stairs in a smooth center split before throwing her torso forward until she's lying flat on the stage, facedown and with her arms outstretched. Unmoving. I shake my head slowly, in a mix of incredulity and respect. Carolyn is ballsy, I'll give her that.

'You can fall out, you can fall fast, you can fall hard . . .' The chorus paces menacingly around their friend's prone body, their voices crossing over in rapid rounds that remind me of childhood nursery rhymes. 'But fall too deep and you'll fall apart.'

I seem to be the only member of the audience to have noticed that the end-of-year production is a thinly veiled dramatization of what happened last year. Adam introduced the play as 'the most exciting and original musical since *Hamilton*,' and Bronnie and Kendall have sat, rapt, since the opening notes. Surely they recognize themselves in the mild, rather dumpy deportment mistress and the once-glamorous etiquette queen who's gone rather to seed?

Set in a girls' finishing school in the 1940s, Carolyn's *Minding Manners* is a murder mystery musical clearly

314

designed to showcase Jess's talents above all other partici-
pants. Carolyn's tweaked the facts (she is a lawyer, after all—
no libel suits for her . . .) so there are three friends, not four;
two baddies, not one; a host of cameo parts and chorus roles
and some surprisingly catchy tunes. A song from the first act
runs through my head.

> *There's a bigger life to live outside of paying a bill,*
> *no one ever got rich from a corporate treadmill,*
> *I got money to burn but now I know I gotta earn*
> *your love.*

I smile wryly. No prizes for guessing that Carolyn based
that particular character on me. On the old me, that is. I still
work hard, but I close the laptop in the evening. Most
evenings. Well, some evenings. The point is, I'm trying. Sadie
and I spend more time together: She joins me for yoga from
time to time, and I go to see films with her and resist the
temptation to sneak a look at my emails. I've started running
every morning—replacing one addiction with another—and
when I get back I make a smoothie and take one up when I
wake Sadie. Almost like a proper mum . . .

In the aftermath of Imogen-gate, it was obvious Carolyn
was hiding something. Obvious to me, at any rate. Perhaps
not to Bronnie, whose ostrich approach to bad news is at
times irritating and at others enviable. I look at her now,
clasping Carl's hand, smiling broadly at the stage, where
Bel is singing a duet in a key a fraction higher than her
natural range, and I feel a twinge of envy. A lack of ambition must be very relaxing. She swears she's stopped any
shady dealings with ghost students, but I've discovered I
don't really care. In fact, I like her more for knowing that
she's capable of breaking the rules from time to time. Bel
sings:

*Whatever they say, I've got your back.*
*However much you hurt, however under attack,*
*I'll be there, by your side, with a ready comeback—I've got*
    *your back.*

Carolyn isn't sitting with the rest of us. She's in the wings, a spiral-bound score clutched to her chest. Every now and then, as a performer enters or exits the stage, the tabs will swing to one side and we'll catch a glimpse of her black-clad figure. Her lips move almost imperceptibly, following every line, every lyric. She's in her element.

And in a flash I understand what's been niggling at me ever since our showdown with Lisa Daisley, ever since Carolyn stormed off, saying she was determined to find out who Lisa had been working with, only to return with an air of casual indifference. *It's all sorted. No big deal. No mystery. Nothing to see here ...*

Adam Racki.

Whatever Carolyn found out was important enough to Adam for him to strike a deal with her: to allow her a platform as a debut musical theater writer.

*He bought her silence.*

Adam's changed too. He's lost weight, hair. Aged a decade in one academic year. Whereas once he strutted around school like he was Laurence Olivier himself, now he scuttles along the corridor and skulks in his office. The pretentious quotes from plays are a thing of the past. Despite his fine performance that day, I'm convinced that Adam Racki knew full well who Lisa Daisley was. Maybe he knew full well what she was doing in his school, what she was planning. After all, there's no record of Lisa—or Imogen—in the student files, and Bronnie swears blind she knows nothing about her arrival.

Could Adam have been helping Lisa? What else would make Adam nervous enough to hand over his famous end-of-year production to an unknown writer? After all, the reputation of the school depends on the quality of its students, its performances.

I don't care. Lisa's gone. Adam Racki's handing over the Academy reins. He'll be someone else's problem now. Sadie and the other girls are leaving OFA and going their separate ways. Jess has a job already, much to Carolyn's undisguised triumph. Only chorus, but it's *Les Mis*, and it's West End, and—well, maybe she has what it takes to make it in show business. We'll see. Ruby's auditioning for *42nd Street* on the West End, so according to Sadie she's been tap dancing like her feet are on fire for the last week. She doesn't stand a chance, but I have to admit the girl's got guts.

Bel spins across the stage, leaping into the arms of a boy who doesn't look old enough to leave school, before joining him in a reprise of their duet. I wonder if she's told her parents about her own audition plans.

'Bronnie will never allow that,' I said when Sadie told me.

'Bel's determined. Full board, a hundred quid a week, *and* you get to see the world.'

I can see the appeal, and a seasonal contract on a cruise ship is certainly more secure than touting audition pieces around the West End, but I don't fancy Bel's chances wriggling out of those apron strings of Bronnie's.

As for Sadie . . . My heart swells with a smugness that must surely rival Carolyn's. I was dreading the end of the year, building myself up to *that* conversation, where I sat Sadie down to tell her a few home truths about the future. *Ninety percent of actors are unemployed at any one time. Only a tiny number of those earn enough to support a family . . .*

In the end, I didn't need to say anything.

'I'm going to start a business,' Sadie announced. She handed Nick and me a sheaf of typewritten papers. We were sitting around the table, having dinner—another of the small changes we've made over the last few months—and I spread out the papers so I could see them better. It was a business plan. A brilliant one. SWOT analysis, financial projections, a list of potential clients and investors. A clear argument for need, and solid research into the competition.

Mediplay, Ltd. will provide role-play actors for healthcare training, giving trainee doctors the chance to break bad news to a 'real' relative, or to explain a diagnosis to a difficult patient. I've invested, of course—it's too good an opportunity to pass up. Nick, Sadie, and I have spent hours working through the fine print.

> *I'll be there, by your side,*
> *I've got your back (and I've got yours)*
> *I've got your back.*

Bel and her partner finish their duet and we all applaud. I sneak a glance down the row, to where Kendall is clapping feverishly next to Bronnie. Ruby still comes over from time to time, but she's quieter now, and Sadie says she wakes crying in the night sometimes, haunted by the feeling of a noose around her neck. Kendall has her in *therapy*, of course, for what that's worth. Eighty-five pounds an hour, Greg says.

*Greg.*

I soften. A sweet man. It almost went wrong—in the way it often goes wrong when men confuse great sex with something more complicated.

'You've got history with Kendall,' I pointed out, when he said he and I would be good together. *Were* good together. 'You've got a daughter.'

'But this . . .' We were lying in bed, and he ran a finger down between my breasts, leaving the rest unspoken.

I was firm. '*This* is good because it's new. If you have *this* every day, you'll get bored.' *So will I*, I added silently. No need to dent the man's ego.

'My relationship with Kendall is broken.'

'Mend it.'

'I don't know how.'

So I told him. Infidelity gets such negative press, but let's face it: You're happier with your run-of-the-mill home cooking when you know you can eat out a couple times a month, right? Greg tells me he and Kendall are much happier now, and I get to add some excitement to my San Fran business trips. Everyone's a winner. Kendall should thank me, really. Okay, so I'm breaking the rule about no return matches, but . . . rules were made to be broken, right?

I scrutinize her profile: the soft hair, the innocent eyes, the fragile bone structure. *You don't fool me, Kendall Donovan.* For all her self-help claptrap—her cancer 'journey,' her existential angst—Kendall is not a nice person.

Greg finally told me everything.

He told me about Ruby, and the bullying at school, and the night Vee died. About the call from Kendall, hysterical and incoherent, and the race to save a life already snatched away. He told me how traumatized Ruby was, and how desperately Kendall wanted to make things better, and how everyone leaped to conclusions that made it Ruby's fault.

And then he told me about the security system. 'Kendall worried a lot when she got sick. She got nervy. Paranoid. She bought drapes, in case someone might look in, even though the garden wall is ten feet high. She worried we'd be burglarized, or that someone would snatch Ruby on her way home from school.'

'So you got an alarm?' I remembered the flashing light I'd seen on the outside of Greg's and Kendall's gated home.

'And cameras.'

I raised one eyebrow.

'Kendall got me jittery, too. What if we *were* burglarized? What good's an alarm if the cops don't get there in time?'

Greg's alarm company installed cameras above each entrance to the house, and one in the hall, facing up the stairs. 'If anyone climbed through an upstairs window,' Greg said, 'the hall camera would get their face as they ran out.'

Despite the warmth of the restaurant we were in, an icy chill began to creep down my spine. I wanted to stop him talking—I didn't want to hear the rest—and yet, at the same time, I couldn't not know how it ended.

'You didn't tell Kendall about the cameras, did you?' My voice was barely a whisper.

Greg shook his head. 'I figured if she thought I was taking her concerns too seriously she'd get even more paranoid. To be honest, I didn't think about it myself much.'

Until the night Vee died.

The camera in the hall, facing up the stairs, didn't capture intruders, their pockets stuffed full of the family silver. It captured Ruby and Vee and Kendall.

It captured what really happened.

I picture Greg sitting in a darkened study, the light from his monitor flickering across his face as the ugly truth unfolded, frame by frame.

I think about sleeping with Greg. I think about ditching the pills, and cutting down on the booze, and helping my daughter go into business. I think about how much has changed in a year. No, I don't feel guilty at all.

I look at Kendall. *But you should.*

# BRONNIE

Sometimes I thought this moment would never come, I thought we might never get to the end-of-year musical that marks the beginning of the summer holidays. Considering how much I love my job, it's amazing how happy I am to be having a break from the Academy and everyone in it. It's been quite a year. Even though Imogen—I still can't call her Lisa—was no longer around at the beginning of the January term, the repercussions of her actions are still being felt. Something fundamental has changed within the school; the dynamics are no longer the same, and I'm not sure whether that's a good or bad thing.

The one thing I'm glad about is that my illegal work for Adam was brought to an abrupt end; at least I can sleep easy at night now. I feel very lucky to have got away with it, but that was largely due to support from the other mums, who told Adam he was wrong to have coerced me into creating ghost students, using the threat—even if only implied—of losing my job if I didn't comply. They made him put a stop to it at once, and although there might be payback at some point—pretending that twenty students had suddenly decided not to come back for the January term was a bit risky—the authorities concerned don't seem to have picked up on it so far. And, of course, my salary is back to what it was before, which means no more silk dresses for me. Not that I mind; every time I see mine hanging in the wardrobe, it's a reminder of what I did, and a reminder never to do anything illegal again. I'm glad that Carl doesn't know, and only hope that he never finds out. I hate having secrets from him, but when it comes down to it, I realize that we all have secrets.

I might have created accounts for ghost students, but I didn't know that Imogen wasn't registered at the Academy. It's why there were no background checks, which would have picked up that she was using a false identity. Adam said it was an oversight, and I still don't know whether to believe it. Maybe that's his secret. There's definitely something he's not telling us about Imogen's presence at the Academy, but when it comes down to it, I don't really care. All I care is that she's gone, and has taken her creepy ways with her.

To be honest, I almost felt sorry for her when she said, at the fake audition we put her through, that coming to the Academy was her last chance to make it as an actress. It must be terrible to feel obsolete at twenty-one. But the fact that she went all-out to eliminate the person she saw as her biggest rival quickly squashed any feelings of sympathy I might have had toward her. I'll never forget the look on Carolyn's face when it registered that Imogen saw Ruby as her rival, not Jess. It was just another of the many things that didn't add up in Imogen's story. Why did she think that Ruby was her biggest rival when anyone could have told her that the student-most-likely-to-succeed was Jess? And how did she know that Jess had been bullied by Ruby the year before, allowing her to use that knowledge to her advantage? It quickly became obvious that someone with inside knowledge of the Academy must have been in league with Imogen. But after we'd all finished accusing each other of being that person—I can't believe that Carolyn actually thought it was me!—we all seemed happy to accept that she acted alone, probably because we were fed up with the whole thing by then.

There were other things that got swept under the carpet in the wake of Imogen's disappearance, including the road-rage incident involving Carolyn and Elise. Carolyn, ever since seeing the CCTV image of the blond-haired driver in the other car, had been convinced Imogen was behind it, and so as far as she was concerned, once Imogen was no longer around, it was no longer important. And Elise hadn't seemed to care one way or another.

'You must be pleased to be here and not backstage for once,' Kendall whispers, as one of the songs comes to an end and we break into applause.

'Yes, I am,' I whisper back. 'And the parents seem to be enjoying it, which is a relief.'

I couldn't believe it when Carolyn told us that not only had she written a musical but also that Adam wanted to stage it for the end-of-year performance, rather than a tried-and-tested musical. It's always a risk when we perform a new piece of work, as one of the things the audience loves is joining in with the songs they know. But Adam was insistent that Carolyn should have the chance to showcase her talent and, I have to admit, it's very good. She's standing just off-stage, and I can see her clapping her hands vigorously, her applause directed solely at Jess rather than at all the students on the stage. I don't know what her secret is, but for the last few months she's been walking around like the cat with the cream. She and Adam have become very pally; she's in and out of his office almost as much as I was last year. That's what I mean about the dynamics changing at the Academy. Maybe her secret is that she's trying to muscle her way on to the staff, as musical director or something. I wouldn't put it past her, and everyone knows she's sick of her law work.

'Now for Ruby's scene,' I say to Kendall as we finish applauding and settle back into our seats. I give her hand a squeeze. 'She's going to be brilliant. It's such a shame that Greg couldn't make it.'

Kendall's face clouds over and I could kick myself for being so insensitive. She and Ruby had thought Greg was coming, he'd promised he would. But then he changed his mind, pleading too much work.

Ruby walks onto the stage and Kendall leans forward in anticipation. I turn my head to where Elise is sitting farther along the row and I know from the look on her face that she's a million miles away—or maybe just five thousand. I think I know her secret. She's been over to the States quite a few times in the past six months, and I have a horrible feeling that she and Greg are in a relationship. I only suspect this because, not long ago, I was standing next to her while she was sending an email and I caught the name *Greg Donovan* in the header. Why would she be emailing him if there wasn't something going on? Part of me wants to say something to Kendall, because if it were me, I'd want to know. But Kendall has enough on her plate at the moment. She looks worried to death half the time, as if she's carrying some other dreadful secret around inside her, which she's scared will come out one day. She watches Ruby constantly, as if she's afraid for her. Or of her. That's only to be expected, given Ruby's suicide attempt. Carolyn and Elise think it was just a cry for help, although I'm not so sure. Imogen's bullying tipped Ruby over the edge, but imagine having to live with the knowledge that you killed someone, even if it was in self-defense. No wonder Kendall didn't want to tell us the truth. It's awful to say, but all those things that Imogen did to Ruby have taught her a lesson. She's a completely different person now and it's lovely to see the four girls getting along so well. If only the same could be said for us mothers.

'She was wonderful,' I say as Ruby's song comes to an end. Kendall gives me a grateful smile; she and I are fine—she never stops going on about how I saved Ruby's life, which is very sweet of her as I only did what anyone else would have done. I still don't know how I managed to close the distance between us in time to push Ruby out of the way of the falling slate, but I guess fear brings strengths out in you that you don't know you have. That's another thing that doesn't add up, though. At first, Imogen was adamant that she saw someone on the roof just before the slate fell, implying that someone pushed it off on purpose. But then she changed her story, saying she must have been mistaken. And once again, everyone just seemed to go along with it.

Carolyn and Elise might have agreed about Ruby's suicide attempt, but they're no longer close. The last time the four of us were together, it was really uncomfortable. I'd invited them over for tea and scones, as a thank you for saving my skin in relation to the ghost students, and Elise couldn't stop watching Carolyn, as if she was trying to work out something about her. And she kept throwing Kendall these looks of absolute disgust, which I didn't understand at all, because what happened to Vee wasn't Kendall's fault. But maybe Elise's disgust came from the fact that Kendall had lied to us again by not telling us the whole truth. She's nicer to me now than she ever was. She's never spoken to me since about her drug and drink addiction, but that's fine, I didn't expect her to give me a running commentary on how she's doing. I just hope she's getting the help she needs. I asked Bel if she knew anything and she said Sadie had told her that Elise is 'working through it'—whatever that means. It's awful, though; she's got a bottle of water with her and every time she drinks from it, I'm wondering what's actually in it. As if she can hear what I'm thinking, she leans forward and raises the bottle in a 'cheers' gesture before taking a long drink. And then she winks and gives me a big smile and I can't help smiling back. But I just don't know.

Carolyn was the only one who reacted positively when I told her about Imogen's boyfriend. She actually used the word 'awesome' and looked at me admiringly when I told her that I'd followed Imogen, and confronted her boyfriend. Not only that, she agreed with me that he was probably using Imogen as a way of getting drugs into the Academy. We'll never know if that was the case, because before we could do anything, Imogen had done another of her disappearing tricks. Only this time she didn't come back.

It was Carolyn who came with me to the police. We heard from them later that Imogen's boyfriend was indeed a drug dealer. He's now behind bars, so that's something I can be proud of, getting a drug dealer convicted. It goes a little way to making up for the other thing I did. It's also taught me that I don't need recognition from anyone to be proud of myself, and certainly not from Carolyn, Elise, or Kendall. I'm no longer in awe of them—why would I be? When it comes down to it, Carolyn is a schemer and manipulator, Elise has no morals, and Kendall is a liar. Harsh, maybe, but I'm certainly not referencing them anymore, and my life is so much better for it.

'Bel's turn now,' I say to Carl as the stage clears for the next scene.

'She's going to be brilliant,' Kendall whispers as Carl takes my hand in his.

'I hope so.' I lean in toward her. 'By the way, thank you for all those things you donated to the wardrobe department, they're great.'

'It's just things I don't need anymore,' she says. 'Look, here's Bel!'

I settle back to watch. Kendall's right: I can't see her needing the long blond wig anymore—not now that her hair has grown back.

As I said, we all have secrets.

# KENDALL

It'll be over soon.

That's what I tell myself about so many things, large and small. It's not always easy to tell the difference, though I've been fighting to regain perspective. I'd kill for the effortless calm from when I learned the cancer was in remission; when I felt, down to my marrow, that life was too precious to be wasted; when I knew just what was important. I wish that Ruby's suicide attempt could have had the same impact. Instead, I'm routinely plagued by irritation and resentment.

Not toward Ruby, thankfully. We're closer than we've ever been, with the full awareness that no one will ever look out for us the way we look out for each other. We'll see what happens with *42nd Street*, and if that's not her big break, then we'll head to New York City and she'll get what she deserves on Broadway. I hope the other girls and their mums get what they deserve, too.

Will this show ever end?

Ruby's already had her big number, so I'm about ready to check out. Her part is insultingly brief, especially given how essential she was to the real plot, the one that Carolyn has cribbed to make this travesty. Ruby wasn't even cast to play the 1940s version of herself! But at least the Ruby character isn't the true villain; Imogen is. All's well that ends well, as Adam Racki—I mean William Shakespeare—would have said.

I just need to count my blessings and endure. Afterward, I'll congratulate Carolyn on a job well done, and that'll be that.

But it's all pretty tough to swallow. Was Carolyn's big secret really that she wants to write musicals? Acerbic Carolyn goes gaga for a catchy chorus?

I don't buy it.

I remember Carolyn saying Imogen/Lisa had an accomplice. I think that accomplice was hiding in plain sight, and it was Carolyn. Maybe she didn't want to hurt anyone (not physically, anyway); things just got out of control. Perhaps Imogen went rogue. The intention was to threaten the school's reputation and make Mr. Racki look inept. Then she could let him know the way to get her (and Imogen) to stop was to stage her musical. Face it, the show is so awful that its production reeks of extortion.

If she starts anything with Ruby or me, then I'll see what proof I can dig up. But these days, I barely see her, probably because she's been at every rehearsal, fretting about every detail. That leaves Elise and Bronnie as the focal points for my current ire. I never forget a betrayal.

Well, it won't be long before the curtain comes down and I can put this night behind me. Soon, OFA and all its players will be a distant memory, grist for Ruby's theatrical mill. Hopefully, she can channel all these experiences into a part someday. She'll be so versatile, able to play both the predator and the prey. All she has to do is keep her eye on the prize and continue to resist her impulses. She's in therapy twice a week and her self-esteem is improving by leaps and bounds. She knows her worth, so I no longer worry about her hurting herself. Now, other people . . .

It's not that she's made any threats. On the contrary, she's been a model student and friend. But I can't help fearing that one sudden act can derail her.

I get that all too well. We're very similar, Ruby and I, in that we have good hearts, yet when provoked, our worst instincts take over. I don't condone her behavior, and I don't condone mine either. I know I should never have rented that car with the tinted windows to give Carolyn and Elise a scare, though it felt good at the time (and it was fun to find a use for one of my old cancer wigs). Afterward, I felt remorseful, just like Ruby always does.

I've concluded that Elise didn't fuck Greg to get at me, that it wasn't even a show of hostility. Elise just took what she wanted because that's what she does. It's who she is. I've had some nights of true fury thinking about it, and I've been able to control myself, but someday I might not be able to, and a small part of me welcomes that.

I have my fantasies, and they extend beyond Elise. Carolyn features sometimes, with her absolutism and her condescension. She must have known about Greg and Elise; I bet she and Elise found it uproarious. And Bronnie's in there on occasion, because in her way, she hurt me most.

I'll go to tea whenever I'm invited because you keep your enemies close, right? Keep monitoring to see what they know; stay privy to the conversations and speculations; seem normal and sweet so that they'll never suspect my final lie.

The truth? Ruby hated Vee right away. She didn't like Vee's personality but she wasn't threatened; Vee wasn't talented at all, in Ruby's opinion. But the teachers disagreed, and Vee was getting cast in leading roles that should have gone to Ruby. I was right there with Ruby, a partner in outrage. It was just so unfair that Ruby should lose out to a nothing like Vee. At least Jess was deserving.

Then one day I was shocked to see Vee at our kitchen table, and the two girls were talking and laughing. Later, I asked Ruby what was going on and she said nothing, she was just making a new friend. For the next show, Vee bombed her audition, and Ruby got the best part. That's when I figured it out: Ruby wanted to keep Vee close in order to get under her skin, to plant seeds of self-doubt, to subtly neg her, and to spread rumors untraceably. It worked. Vee was unsettled, and had been unseated.

I had mixed feelings about it. On the one hand, it was really just fair play, since Ruby deserved those leads. Additionally, the more I got to know Vee, the more I disliked her. She was genuinely annoying: overly dramatic and self-aggrandizing, and she'd been venerated her whole life for a talent that I couldn't even detect.

It's not like I did nothing. I tried to convince Ruby to abort her plan. She's gotten what she wanted. Vee was no longer a threat, no longer a rival. She'd been neutralized. Yet Ruby continued, playing the role of Vee's best friend and confidante, almost like she was enjoying her front row seat to Vee's destruction. But that was just Ruby acting out from all the pain of watching me go through chemo. She didn't know how to handle her fear of losing me.

The day Vee died, I came home and heard the two of them arguing at the top of the stairs. It sounded like Vee had figured out that Ruby was the one who'd been undermining her over the past months, and she was furious. Vee said cruel things about Ruby's appearance and talent, and talked about how she'd ruin Ruby at school.

I'd heard enough. I charged up the stairs and found that Vee was the one gripping Ruby, not the other way around. Ruby seemed frozen, paralyzed, and Vee was the aggressor.

All I meant to do was separate them. I wanted to make sure that in her rage, Vee didn't throw Ruby down the stairs. So I broke Vee's hold, and I must have done it with too much force because somehow, Vee ended up at the bottom of the steps.

I planned to call the police and tell the truth. Vee had been the one attacking Ruby and I'd intervened. It had been an accident. Or was it self-defense?

Ruby said I couldn't do that. 'Mom,' she said, 'you pushed her.' Her eyes filled with tears. 'You can't tell them what really happened. You can't leave me.'

She'd been so scared of losing me to cancer; I couldn't put her in a position where she might lose me to prison.

She insisted we lie to the police, and she was very persuasive. We got our stories straight. Since we're both great actresses, it was ruled an accident. But somehow, word of Ruby's bullying Vee had gotten out, and in the court of public opinion, Vee became a victim and Ruby a suspected murderer.

There'd been no way to clear her name unless I sullied mine, and Ruby didn't want that. When she wasn't able to transfer schools, London had been her idea.

Even in her suicide note, she'd stuck to the story. On the one hand, that made me feel terribly guilty, but on the other, it affirmed that she loved me more than anything, just the same way I loved her. She'd been willing to sacrifice herself for me. Thank God it hadn't worked.

All this time, I'd thought only Ruby and I knew the truth, but it's turned out that not only has Greg known, he's had proof.

He told me about it tearfully in the very same conversation where he confessed that he'd slept with Elise. 'It only happened once, and it made me see how much I love you,' he said. He wasn't trying to blackmail me, but I still don't believe in coincidences. 'I want to save our family,' he told me. What could I say back? 'I want to save our family, too.' I mustered a few tears while inside, I roiled.

I said that since he had the footage, he must have known that it was Ruby's idea to cover up the crime. Unfortunately for me, there was no sound. But I'm pretty sure I convinced him that my motives had been pure.

The surprising twist is what all this has done for our sex life. Confirming that Greg had slept with Elise ignited my spirit of competition, and I've been upping my sexual game. Since we're working on our family, Greg's visited a few times. He and I have started playing out some elaborately designed fantasies. Skype sex is pretty hot, too. Mostly, I like the role play, but some of Greg's suggestions—he's a cop, I'm a suspect; he's a warden, I'm an inmate—remind me that he holds the trump card. Giving Greg the sex of his life has an ulterior motive: It saves mine.

Sometimes, afterward, I feel pretty degraded. Trapped, even. And I wonder how long it can go on, how long I can let it go on. Before her suicide attempt, Ruby had talked about being free. What would I do for freedom?

I see a movement in the corner of my eye and glance over. It's Ruby at the end of the row, in her costume and stage makeup, gesturing for me to come with her. Because of the dimmed lights in the auditorium, it's not until we're out in the hall that I see just how wild-eyed with rage she is.

'It's still going on,' she tells me. 'Elise and Dad. I overheard Sadie laughing about it.'

I didn't know Ruby or Sadie had known about the one-off, let alone . . .

'I could fucking kill them! Elise, Dad, Sadie! And Bel and Jess for laughing! I could kill them all.'

I should make efforts to soothe her. That's what a proper mother would do: rein in Ruby's worst instincts, try to instill perspective.

But the betrayal is sinking in. The colossal, monumental betrayal. I'm sure Bronnie sat next to me in that theater, knowing, and Carolyn must be smirking backstage, and Elise actually told her daughter, and her daughter repeated it to friends who found it equally hilarious, and my very own husband, Ruby's very own father . . .

In the end, it's Ruby and me on the outs once again. We've been trying so hard to be so good and for what? No one else is.

Maybe those aren't Ruby's worst instincts; maybe they're some of her best.

It might be time for some mother-daughter bonding.

# CAROLYN

'This is our whole problem, and you can't see it. You expect me to deal with it. Why?'

'Because all of this is your . . . doing.'

'"Creation," not "doing." "All of this is your creation,"' I hiss from my spot in the wings. 'For fuck's sake.' Is it too much to ask that they don't massacre my elegant, carefully written lines?

'I can't fight about this anymore. I have to go to work. Is there anything you need, before I go?'

'Oh, just go. Just leave.'

I watch as the boy (playing a man) on the receiving end of this instruction does as he's told and just leaves, without delivering the line that ought to accompany his exit upstage right.

I shake my head in frustration. I can't understand why Olly Nevins was given the lead male role. He's attractive, yes, and sings like an angel, but he's incapable of learning lines. He changes words and word orders whenever it suits him. No attention to detail, that's his problem. Jess says his main hobby is smoking weed, so it's hardly surprising. If he doesn't watch out, his beautiful voice won't last long.

I could have insisted he be replaced—Adam would have done my bidding without question—but I made a deal with myself that night on the roof with Adam, in addition to the one I made with him. I don't want to be a blackmailer. I don't want to be the kind of person who has something on someone and uses it again and again, who grows accustomed to daily acts of coercion and starts to think of them as normal.

I wanted only one thing from Adam, and I got it. As far as I'm concerned, he's now a free man. Free to cast whoever he wants as leads in the end-of-year production. He might even be right about Olly Nevins, who knows? Star quality and the 'wow' factor probably matter more than the odd wrong word here and there. The audience—which includes anyone who's anyone from the world of West End musical theater—certainly seems to love Olly. From where I'm sitting, I can see the side of Cameron Mackintosh's face, two rows from the front. It's clear he's impressed by Olly and by the show as a whole.

He also seems spellbound by Jess, which is gratifying. I don't think Adam only cast her in the main female role to placate me. She's got a magical quality about her, and he knows it. No other student at OFA can sing, act, and dance like Jess, and learn lines quickly, and get them all right. No wonder Ruby was so jealous of her. Though, actually, Ruby has been lovely to Jess ever since the problems. Even when Jess was cast as the female lead for the most important show of the year, the one every girl at OFA has been hoping to get from day one of the two-year course, Ruby congratulated her and told her she deserved it.

She's become a different person since trying and failing to kill herself. A whole new Ruby, one I don't dislike, let alone hate, though I'm almost ashamed to admit it. The change in Ruby's character is why I can't bring myself to think and feel all the things I ought to think and feel about Adam. Yes, what he did was wrong, but . . . he saw evil, and he took action in a way that hardly anyone ever does. It's not that I believe Ruby was fully evil, in her former incarnation. I understand now

335

that it's more complicated than that, but still . . . it's hard to ignore the fact that the outcome of Adam's appalling, murderous behavior is . . . good. Great, in fact. Ruby and Jess are properly close friends now. The gang of four are tighter than ever. Last weekend they all had a barbecue at Bel's house, and tomorrow night they're having a sleepover at Sadie's.

Do I care that, if Adam had aimed a little more carefully, Ruby would be dead, killed by a falling slate, and we wouldn't now have this much-improved situation? I probably should, but try as I might, I can't bring myself to feel negatively about Adam. He lost his daughter in the most tragic circumstances imaginable. And he was the only person in the world who took action—real action—in defense of *my* daughter.

Jess sings the last line of her song and the crowd spontaneously rises to its feet. First standing ovation of the night. Hopefully not the last. While the crowd claps, I tiptoe from the wings, push through the bodies, and slip back into my seat next to Dan.

He reaches for my hand, leans closer, and whispers, 'Wasn't Jess amazing?'

I nod, my eyes full of tears.

'The song was amazing, too. You were right not to let me read the script or hear any of the songs before tonight. I know I tried to persuade you, but I'm glad you stood firm and said no.'

I gesture to him to be quiet. Any minute now the set change will be done and the next scene will start. Having forbidden him from reading any part of the script beforehand, I don't want him to miss any of the musical now.

'You realize you're going to have to go up at the end and get your own standing ovation, as the writer?' Dan whispers.

My stomach tightens. I've spent so many years dreaming

about writing my own musical and having it staged, but somehow I failed to realize, idiot that I am, that if it ever happened, I'd be expected to stand on stage, bow, be in the limelight. All I want, all I've ever wanted, is the music that's been living inside me all these years to get out into the world, have a life, be seen and heard by as many people as possible. Still . . . a spotlight's always nice too, as long as you're in it for the right reason.

That's what I told Adam that night on the roof. That was my price for keeping the truth to myself: that he must agree to stage a musical, written by me, as the end-of-year show, the one all the producers and agents and theater stars would flock to see. Adam agreed, of course. What choice did he have? It's a small price to pay for hanging on to his career and his freedom.

I think Elise suspects the truth, or something resembling it. She knows there's something I didn't tell her, for certain. Being a control freak, this meant she lost all interest in being my friend, after she saw that I didn't necessarily go running to her with everything I knew. I honestly don't care. I have all I need: my family, safe and happy, and now my musical on a proper stage. It doesn't matter that it's not a professional show; that phase of its development will follow shortly, I have no doubt.

I'll never forget the astonishment in Adam's voice when he rang me, having finally read the script and listened to the songs. 'It's actually . . . brilliant?' he said, making it sound like a question. *How can a law professor with no background in music or theater have written something this good?* That was clearly the question in his mind. I don't know the answer any more than he does, nor do I know if I'll ever write another musical. All I know is: This is the best and most important work I've ever done, no matter what the Department of Law at the University of Cambridge might think.

337

And now I must sit here patiently and with no further expectations, and try to be grateful and happy that my show has got this far, without worrying about what Cameron Mackintosh, Nick Allott, and Sonia Friedman are all thinking about it. Will they be the ones to help me take it further than the Orla Flynn Academy? I have no way of knowing.

A door on one side of the auditorium opens and there's a slit of light, closing to dark a moment later. Was it someone arriving? Someone peeping in? I'm so on edge with the thrill of all this, I might even have imagined it, in my hypersensitive state.

I push it out of my mind and try to focus on the next scene.

# LISA

She crouches down next to the wall, near the door. There's nowhere for her to sit, anyway. Every seat in the auditorium is taken. They all seem to be enjoying it, and she can't understand why. She's never liked musicals, apart from *The Rocky Horror Picture Show*. Most of them take themselves way too seriously, and all it does is make you realize how stupid they are.

She used to think she wanted to be an actress, but now she's not so sure. More and more, she's thinking that it's not what she was put on this earth to do. She's never felt entirely comfortable up on stage—not that she's had much chance to try it out. Hardly any good parts have come her way over the years, and her agent has all but given up on her.

Sometimes you've just got to face facts. She's not good enough, not got what it takes. End of story. Looking at the people on stage now, brimming with talent, making the audience's eyes shine with admiration, she doesn't feel the envy she might once have felt. This is their vocation—what they were born to do. It's their thing, not hers. That's fine. She can live with that.

She has other talents, as she discovered last year. A different sort of acting—that's her sphere of genius—one that doesn't involve a stage or a paying audience. She works better with a different kind of audience: one that doesn't know it's watching a performance or that anybody's putting on an act.

Some might call it lying. Scamming, tricking. The thing is, it no longer matters to her how awful all those words sound, because they're the words that define where her true talent lies. Once you know you're brilliant at something, you can't help craving the chance to do that thing again. Everybody at the Orla Flynn Academy believed that she was dangerous, creepy, compulsive liar Imogen Curwood. No one could have played that part better than her.

She sees a figure move in the shadows, up ahead: someone else without a seat, hovering near the black curtains on one side of the stage.

*It's him. Adam.*

A spasm of anxiety passes through her. If he turns and sees her here . . .

No, he wouldn't make a fuss and throw her out. He won't want to risk drawing attention to her presence.

If he wants nothing more to do with her, she can live with that. All she needs is five minutes of his time—a brief conversation. He paid her well for her work, and no doubt believes that he now owes her nothing, but she disagrees. And even if she's wrong, she doesn't care. She saw him up on that roof when the tile fell, and he knows it. She could get him arrested and charged with attempted murder. Hopefully it won't come to that, but that's largely up to Adam.

It's his loss, if he sends her away—in more ways than one. She's not generally a bitter person, but she winds herself up sometimes, thinking about how he sees her: talentless, dispensable. That's why he chose her. Yes, there was the Villiers connection, her relationship with Grace, but it wasn't only that. In the world of actors and acting, he knew she had no status at all. He probably saw her as a desperate failure, and imagined she'd be pathetically grateful for any crumbs he threw her way.

The crowd rises to its feet and the sound of applause rings in her ears. Adam Racki disappears inside the black curtain and she follows him.

He stops. Turns. As if he sensed her there.

'Lisa.'

He has no right to look at her like this—as if she's some moldy, stinking piece of rubbish that's just fallen out of his wheelie-bin. She wants to scream at him, 'It was all your fucking idea! I only did what you asked me to do!' Instead, she smiles. She has learned, over the years, that to let anybody know when you're upset, or why, is to give away power you can't afford to lose.

'Hello, Adam. It's going well, isn't it? The audience seems to love it.'

'I told you never to come back here.' He looks scared, but doubtful. As if he's wondering if anger might be more appropriate.

'I know,' she tells him. 'I remember.'

'Then what are you —'

'Doing here? I was wondering if you might have any more work for me.'

'You know I haven't. Lisa, we had an agreement. I asked you not to contact me again, and you promised you wouldn't. You know that.'

'And you seem to have forgotten what *else* I know.'

He shifts uncomfortably from one foot to the other. There's nothing he can say to that. She's got him cornered.

'So you're here to threaten me, is that it? How much? How much will it take for you to never come back?'

'That's not what I want. I'm not after blackmail money, I'm after *work*. I want you to listen to me, that's all. Five minutes. And yes—then I'll go and I won't be back. Not if you're sure that's what you want.'

'Haven't I made it clear already that I'm sure?'

341

'You have, but . . . the thing is, Adam, it makes no sense. I *helped* you. You wanted to make Ruby Donovan suffer—'

'Keep your voice down.'

'—and I helped you to do that. She suffered. A *lot*. Then, when you lost your cool up on the roof and decided you wanted to *kill* her—something you never ran past me as part of the plan—I saved her. I stopped you from becoming a murderer. Aren't you glad? I mean, don't I deserve some thanks for that?'

'You haven't come here for gratitude, Lisa, so don't pretend you have.'

It's time for her to get to the point. 'I've been thinking, Adam . . . about the real Imogen Curwood. The one who drove Grace to suicide and got away with it.'

He recoils. 'What about her?'

'When you first told me about Ruby—everything she'd said and done, her bullying of Jess—it was clear that you wanted to punish her because Imogen was beyond your reach. Ruby was your substitute, the one you decided would have to do. I'm right, aren't I?'

'So?'

Lisa smiles. 'Wouldn't you like to know exactly where Imogen is? Her address, for example?'

He doesn't answer. His eyes dart left and right as he tries to work out how to answer.

'Please leave now, Lisa,' he says in a strangled voice. 'I'm asking you sincerely.'

'Maybe you wouldn't like to know,' she says. 'Maybe you're a coward at heart. It's easy to do what you did to Ruby. No one would have any reason to suspect you. If something happened to the real Imogen Curwood, on the other hand, especially while you were in America, it'd be hard to dodge the blame for that, wouldn't it? You'd need help to pull that off, I'd imagine.'

'Stop talking about her,' says Adam weakly.

'I will soon,' Lisa Daisley says. 'Once you've answered the question I came here to ask you.' She smiles. Anyone watching will think they're having a normal conversation. 'How much would you pay me to take care of this for you?' she says. 'To go to America and find the real Imogen Curwood?'

# ONE DAY THAT WILL CHANGE A FAMILY FOREVER . . .

SUNDAY TIMES BESTSELLER

# B A PARIS

# THE DILEMMA

How far would you go
to give someone you love
a last few hours of happiness?

Order the new novel from B. A. Paris

 @BAParisAuthor  @BAParisAuthor

# ANYTHING CAN HAPPEN AFTER THE END . . .

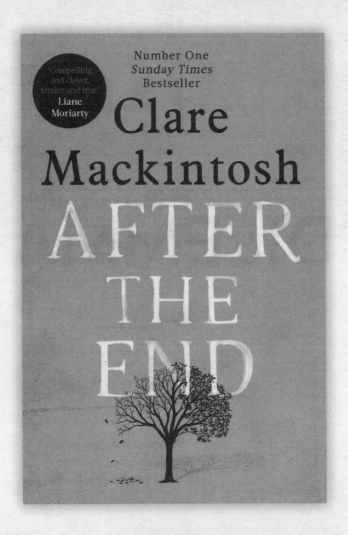

Twelve years ago, Thomas and Emily were five and three years old.

Today, they don't look a day older. Why haven't they grown?

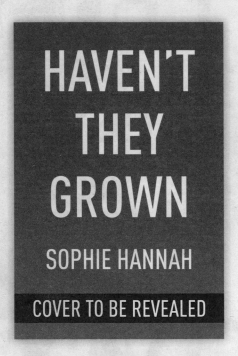

HAVEN'T THEY GROWN

SOPHIE HANNAH

COVER TO BE REVEALED

ORDER THE NEW NOVEL FROM SOPHIE HANNAH

COMING 23.01.2020

@sophiehannahCB1    @SophieHannahAuthor

www.sophiehannah.com